Discover the delights of the
Regency period—with these wonderful
romances by Dorothy Mack. . . .

The Blackmailed Bridegroom

and

The Luckless Elopement

Two stories of passion, seduction,
and scandal.
One unforgettable book.

The Blackmailed Bridegroom

and

The Luckless Elopement

Dorothy Mack

A SIGNET BOOK

SIGNET
Published by New American Library, a division of
Penguin Putnam Inc., 375 Hudson Street,
New York, New York 10014, U.S.A.
Penguin Books Ltd, 27 Wrights Lane,
London W8 5TZ, England
Penguin Books Australia Ltd,
Ringwood, Victoria, Australia
Penguin Books Canada Ltd, 10 Alcorn Avenue,
Toronto, Ontario, Canada M4V 3B2
Penguin Books (N.Z.) Ltd, 182–190 Wairau Road,
Auckland 10, New Zealand

Penguin Books Ltd, Registered Offices:
Harmondsworth, Middlesex, England

First published by Signet, an imprint of New American Library, a division of Penguin
Putnam Inc.
The Blackmailed Bridegroom was originally published in February 1984, copyright ©
Dorothy McKittrick, 1984
The Luckless Elopement was originally published in June 1984, copyright © Dorothy
McKittrick, 1984

First Signet Printing, May 2001
10 9 8 7 6 5 4 3 2 1

 REGISTERED TRADEMARK—MARCA REGISTRADA

Printed in the United States of America

PUBLISHER'S NOTE
This is a work of fiction. Names, characters, places, and incidents either are the product
of the author's imagination or are used fictitiously, and any resemblance to actual persons,
living or dead, business establishments, events, or locales is entirely coincidental.

BOOKS ARE AVAILABLE AT QUANTITY DISCOUNTS WHEN USED TO PRO-
MOTE PRODUCTS OR SERVICES. FOR INFORMATION PLEASE WRITE TO PRE-
MIUM MARKETING DIVISION, PENGUIN PUTNAM INC., 375 HUDSON STREET,
NEW YORK, NEW YORK 10014.

The Blackmailed
Bridegroom

Prologue

It was a glorious day proclaiming the annual renewal of the earth. Early-morning showers had washed the London streets and then given way to clearing skies and a warm spring sun. Most of the puddles were gone now, but the freshness clung to the shrubs and branches in the gardens in the square, whence voices of children drifted, calling excitedly to each other. A young housemaid tripped down the steps on one great stone house on the south side of the square and called to another leaving a doorway a hundred feet farther on. The one hailed waited for her friend, and the two proceeded on their errands in company. A stiffly starched nanny crossed the street toward the gardens holding the hand of a little boy who toted a huge red ball under his free arm. Halfway across, the ball squirted from its insecure position and bounced away. Boy and attendant gave laughing chase and succeeded in retrieving it near the gates to the gardens. They disappeared inside.

The only person in evidence who seemed not to share in the air of general bonhomie was a man who approached from the western boundary of the square with a purposeful but oddly reluctant stride. He was still a young man, probably two or three years under thirty, a tall, well-set-up figure with the easy grace of the born athlete. His countenance too would have been described as well favored by most, though its appeal was marred at the moment by a vivid half-healed slash across one cheekbone. He was neatly dressed in the blue coat, light-colored smalls, and

impeccable Hessians that constituted correct morning dress
for a gentleman paying calls, and a curly-brimmed beaver
reposed at an exact angle atop dark-brown locks brushed to
repress a tendency to curl.

The eyes of the two young maids swiveled involuntarily to
survey his person with shy approbation as he stood politely
aside for them to pass him. Their conversation ceased
abruptly, then resumed amid self-conscious giggling before
they were quite out of earshot.

The gentleman remained impervious to their interest as
he continued along the flagway absorbed in his own
thoughts. That these thoughts were of a serious nature was
attested to by a certain somberness of expression that was
evident when he glanced up occasionally as if checking the
numbers of the houses he was passing. At last he paused at a
red brick edifice whose entrance was hung with black crape.
For a few seconds his gaze was transfixed by this symbol of
mourning, then he squared his shoulders and climbed the
steps.

The door was opened by an expressionless individual whose
bearing and sober costume proclaimed his importance in the
household. The caller inquired for Lady Wendover and was
told by the butler that her ladyship was indisposed.

"Please!" exclaimed the young man. "It is extremely important that I see Lady Wendover. Would you take my card
up to her at least?"

A coin changed hands; the butler bowed and stepped
back to admit the gentleman into the hall to wait while he
carried the calling card up to his mistress. In the next few
minutes the young man stood motionless near the door,
staring with an unhappy intensity at the hat he was twisting
in his gloved hands. He glanced up eagerly as descending
footsteps announced the butler's return.

"I regret, Mr. Harding, that her ladyship cannot receive
you. She is seeing no one today."

At that moment a door toward the back of the hall
opened to admit a girl dressed from head to toe in
unrelieved black. As she came toward the entrance the man

thought he had never seen hair so fair; there was almost a look of silver to it, but perhaps that was due to the contrast with her black raiment. Becoming aware of people in her vicinity, the girl raised a pale face.

"What is it, Condon?"

"Nothing, Miss April," that worthy replied soothingly. "This gentleman was wishful to see her ladyship, but she is unable to receive him." He opened the door as he spoke.

The girl would have proceeded to the stairway without comment, but the caller demanded:

"Are you Miss Wendover? Perhaps you would convey to your mother my earnest desire to speak with her whenever she feels able to receive me?"

She turned an inquiring glance in his direction but made no reply.

"My name is Adam Harding. I—"

"*Adam Harding!*"

The girl's lifeless countenance was transformed with bitterness; her red-rimmed eyes flashed hatred as they dwelled on the wound on the man's cheek. "*Adam Harding!*" she repeated in tones that blended astonishment and loathing. "I wonder, sir, that you have the temerity to call at this house! Is there some further harm you have yet to deal us? Was it not enough that you drove my father to suicide? Did you have to kill my brother too?" She was shaking with emotion, her fists clenched at her sides, as she glared up at the man, whose face had lost all its color at the spate of invective.

He stepped back a pace and bowed slightly as he returned her look for a pregnant instant, his countenance rigid, his mouth a tight line of repression.

"I apologize for my presumption in coming here, Miss Wendover, and will bid you good day." The caller spun on his heel and walked quickly through the door being held open by the butler without even noting the reluctant sympathy in the latter's eyes. At the bottom of the steps he directed a final bleak look at the black-draped door before replacing his hat and striding away.

Chapter One

A loud crack stopped Mr. Jeremy Choate in his tracks, and the jerky movement caused the tankards on the tin tray he carried to spill a considerable portion of their liquid contents onto the tray and one grimy hand. This occurrence evoked no more than an absentminded oath from Mr. Choate, whose frowning attention was directed at the window whence the noise issued. He resumed his progress toward the only occupied table in the public room after locating a sleepy-eyed lad who was endeavoring to make himself inconspicuous by tending to the fire. The proprietor of the Cap and Bells, one of the lesser-used coaching inns on the Great North Road, indicated the window with a movement of his head.

"You there, Todd, get outside and fasten that shutter, and this time make sure it's tight."

As the boy thus addressed got to his feet with discernible reluctance, another spatter of wind-delivered rain hammered the window and the loose shutter set up a continuous banging.

"Look smart, you devil's whelp, before that there wind rips the shutter clear off." The lash in his tones changed to an ingratiating purr as he set the tray down on the table where three men sat in lounging attitudes.

"Here you be, gen'lemen, three pints o' the best ale within thirty miles o' London." He removed his wet hand from the tray and wiped it casually down the side of his catskin waistcoat, which, judging by the various stains thereon, already bore witness to similar treatment with regard to numerous items on the menu. While responding wholeheartedly to the jocularity of his guests, the landlord managed to keep one eye on the boy, who had donned a dirty cap unearthed from the vicinity of the hearth and was struggling to afford himself some increased protection from the elements by forcing as many of the remaining buttons on his ragged coat as possible into their holes, a procedure complicated by the undersized nature of the garment, which had never been meant to cover a gangly adolescent. Quailing under an impatient scowl directed at him by his employer, the lad abandoned the effort and departed hastily.

In the brief interval before the taproom door closed behind the boy a spate of rain and the noise of the storm entered the snug room along with another familiar sound, that of an approaching carriage. This last caused the innkeeper to leave his post by the occupied table to investigate.

"Sounds like more company," declared one of the members of the merry drinking party.

To this statement of the obvious Mr. Choate made no reply. He arrived at the door just in time to be forced to step smartly back to avoid a collision with a figure erupting into the room, a collision that would have had no very beneficial effect on Mr. Choate's person, for he was a small thin individual, roughly half the size of the man who entered.

The newcomer, intent on slapping the excess water from the once elegant beaver he had removed from his dripping locks, remained unaware of the near accident. "Filthy night," he said by way of a general greeting before beginning to struggle out of a sodden driving coat whose numerous shoulder capes must have marked it as all the crack when in its pristine condition.

"Lor, gov'nor, you ain't been driving in an open carriage in this weather?" expostulated the innkeeper, automatically coming to the assistance of this new arrival.

"Tried to beat the storm, the more fool I," explained the stranger with an economy of words that matched his manner as he handed over the coat and hat into his host's extended

arms. He gave a cursory glance around the dimly lighted
room, nodding slightly to the interested spectators at the far
table before heading straight for the warmth of the fireplace. "This is a welcome sight," he added, holding out his
hands to the blaze.

"You . . . you wouldn't be wanting a room for the night,
would you?" asked the landlord, whose sharp-featured face
had taken on a worried aspect.

The stranger stopped chafing his hands and favored the
speaker with a direct stare. "Naturally, I want a room and a
meal too — why else should I be here?"

The impatient query seemed to increase Mr. Choate's discomfort. "Well, you're welcome to the meal, though you'll
have to take what's left in the kitchen at this hour, and
you're welcome to stay here by the fire, but I'm afeared I
can't oblige your honor with a room, because the fact is,
there ain't an empty room in the place tonight." He recoiled
visibly from the thunderous scowl that descended on the
stranger's black-browed visage and quavered, "I'm right
sorry, your honor."

"Look, I'm not overparticular about the style of room —
any place I can lay my head will do. I've been driving for
fourteen hours, and I'll be damned if I go out in that again,"
with a hunch of his shoulders in the direction of the rain-
beaten window.

"I'm that sorry not to be able to oblige your honor, but all
my rooms are taken."

"Do some rearranging," ordered his unwelcome guest.
"I'll pay you double, triple the rate for your best chamber
for any room with a bed and a door that locks." Having expressed his wishes in the tone of one accustomed to being
obeyed, he turned away from the innkeeper and resumed
drying his person by the fire.

His host stood irresolute for a second or two, but his
shrewd little eyes had already assessed the value of his guest's
raiment, and he was not totally unaccustomed to the ways of
the quality. His inn, while perfectly respectable, did not
cater to the nobility in a general way, but there was no deny-

ing it would be a feather in his cap to accommodate one whose lofty manner clearly marked him as a member of this class. His quick greedy brain had been turning over possibilities, and he spoke now to the unconcerned back of the traveler in the manner of a man working out a problem.

"There are a couple of abigails in single rooms who appeared to strike up an acquaintance at dinner tonight. O' course it's late, after ten o'clock, but if the ladies was agreeable to sharing a room, I could make it worth their while, refund the price o' one room with no one the wiser, and your honor could have t' other."

"Fine," said the newcomer with patent indifference. "I'll want a meal for my groom when he gets in from the stables. He can bed down here for the night, if you've no objection."

"O' course, your honor, always happy to oblige a gentleman." His host's obsequious smile lasted until the door opened, admitting the now soaked adolescent, who had evidently succeeded in fastening the shutters. "I'll want you in the kitchen," he said, directing the boy toward the hall with a well-placed push and following in his wet footsteps after another ingratiating smile for the man who watched him with a sardonic expression on his stern-featured face.

It was almost eleven o'clock when the traveler was finally established in his room, seated in a chair that offered more comfort than its shabby appearance promised. He had changed his damp coat for a warm velvet dressing gown, and though the small room didn't boast a fireplace, the inn was solidly built and relatively free from drafts. There was a hot brick between the sheets of the single bed, promising additional comfort when it became too cold to read any longer. For the present, he was content to repose his limbs in the high wingback chair with its once garishly printed upholstery faded to a murky monochrome and lose himself in the company of his favorite poet. A branch of candles stood on the table at his elbow. From time to time he refreshed himself with sips of a surprisingly smooth brandy from his host's cellar. The storm still raged outside, but the only sounds in the cozy room were the faint rustling of pages and the occasional quiet click of a glass being returned to the table.

The soft tapping had barely penetrated his abstraction when it was succeeded by a somewhat breathless speech from the vicinity of the door behind him.

"Thank goodness you are still up, Mattie! I was reading and didn't realize how late it had grown. Diana's sound asleep and I cannot undo these pestilential buttons. Be a dear and help me, please!"

The man had replaced his glass and risen swiftly from the depths of the chair to confront the girl who followed her voice into the room, leaving the door open behind her. His initial impression was a regretful confirmation of the thought that had surged to his mind on hearing her first words — that no face could possibly match the beauty of that voice, low-pitched and melodious. It didn't.

The female who stared at him in openmouthed astonishment was past her first youth certainly, but he suspected it was a lack of interest in her appearance, not advancing years, that heightened the discrepancy between the vibrant voice and the rather drab impression created by the owner of the voice.

He bowed punctiliously. "I regret that I am not Mattie, but will respectfully offer my poor services in her stead if I may be of assistance?"

The presumption in this remark caused the woman's cheeks to flame and drove up her chin, but she ignored the suggestion and replied with creditable composure.

"I beg your pardon for the intrusion, sir, but I was under the impression that this room was occupied by my maid; in fact, I know it was! What have you done with her?" Voice and eyes conveyed accusation.

"I trust you don't suspect there is blood on my hands," he drawled, noting her tightened mouth with perverse satisfaction. "Your maid — er, Mattie, was it? — very kindly volunteered to move in with another abigail so the landlord might accommodate a weary traveler on this very wet night. I would deem it an honor to ascertain her exact whereabouts if you require her services tonight, but before we embark on what could be a time-consuming errand at this hour, may I, without the least intention of offending, reiterate my offer to deputize for her?"

Large eyes of a rare light gray surveyed him coolly. She permitted herself a slight supercilious curve to her mouth but declined his offer with well-bred civility. During the whole of their brief interview she had faced him with one hand behind her clutching the partially unbuttoned dress together at the waistline. Now she retreated a step with the evident intention of accomplishing the short trek to her own chamber by walking backward. The thought of this feat produced a widening of his lips, but at that moment an unctuous voice from the doorway wiped the smile from his face and caused the woman to spin around, her eyes dilating in alarm.

"I trust I don't intrude?"

A man already dressed for sleeping, wearing a black brocade dressing gown over his nightclothes, lounged against the doorjamb regarding the couple within the room with an expression of malicious enjoyment on his attractive but curiously lined face.

"Considering that you've perfected a natural talent for intruding down through the years, I presume you ask that question in a strictly rhetorical spirit," countered the owner of the room in accents that blended indifference and disdain.

The woman remained mute, but she edged back a pace in reaction to the malevolence that this offensive remark brought to the features of the man in the doorway. He was nearly as large as the occupant of the room, and for an instant gave the appearance of tensing for an attack on the latter, but he evidently thought better of this idea. The ugly look faded, he straightened his posture, and his voice retained its smoothness.

"How unfortunate for you that I just happened to be across the hall and opened my door in time to hear your familiar tones," he remarked to the room's occupant.

"Unfortunate? Unpleasant, I'll grant you, but in what way unfortunate?"

The cold blue eyes of the man in the doorway narrowed, and his too full lips bunched unattractively as his insulting glance swept from the unknown woman to the man he seemed to know all too well. *"Unfortunate* if the minister proves to be, shall we say, less broad-minded than you might hope about condoning intrigues among his subordinates, especially when these intrigues involve cits."

The woman opened her lips to protest angrily, but the man cut in first.

"Don't be a damned fool, Allerton. There is a perfectly innocent explanation for this scene, and—"

"Then you must hope the minister believes it!" sneered the other. "You will have your chance to lay your explanation before him as soon as you get to town. I'll bid you good night, Glenville . . . madam." He made the outraged woman a mocking bow and retreated across the corridor.

"Do your worst," invited his antagonist with perfect unconcern. This changed abruptly to alarm as his glance lighted on the woman for the first time since they had been interrupted. She was staring at him in outright horror, and her complexion was drained of any life or color. "Here, don't collapse on me!" he begged, reaching out instinctively to support her wilting frame. His concern gave way to a puzzled frown as she recoiled sharply from his outstretched hand, but he forbore to touch her, going instead to the big chair, which he seized by its wings and wrestled forward. "Sit down," he ordered, but when she had obeyed the brusque command, he subdued his irritation and infused a more gentle note into his voice.

"Don't allow that cretin's idle threats to distress you, ma'am. He doesn't know your identity; you'll never see him again. No one will ever learn of this incident." Something speculative yet disdainful in the quality of the stare she was directing at him caused him to break off his assurances in midstream.

The woman spoke for the first time since the recent

unpleasantness. Her voice was cold and very clear. "I'm afraid that is not quite true. He *will* discover my identity because I have discovered yours, Lord Glenville. I should have recognized you from the scar!"

"So, we have met before? It does not signify. Allerton doesn't know what room you are occupying. Just keep out of sight tomorrow until after he leaves. He'll have no way of identifying you."

"I am constrained to differ with you. He *will* know who I am."

The man's frown deepened. "How will he know?"

"If necessary, I shall tell him."

This bald statement uttered in perfectly composed tones brought a dangerous look to the man's already stern-featured countenance. There was a short, tension-packed silence during which dark-gray eyes warred with light.

"I begin to comprehend. Underneath that respectable exterior lurks the soul of an adventuress, after all," he sneered. "What is your game, blackmail? I should advise you not to try it, my girl. I'm an ill bird for plucking. You will suffer more than I by any recounting of tonight's activities."

"I think not, Lord Glenville."

He had turned abruptly away from her to stalk across the room, feeling it was safer to put a distance between them, but at this he whirled around and snapped, "Why not?"

She rose from the chair and met his challenging regard squarely. "You haven't asked my name, Lord Glenville."

"I suppose that provocative statement is meant to convey something to me. You are too young to be one of the royal princesses," he said with an insulting little laugh. "Very well, I'll bite; who are you?"

"My name is April Wendover."

There was a definite quality of menace to the stillness that followed this disclosure. The man's hands were clenched at his sides, and a spasm of some strong emotion contorted his features momentarily. He inhaled deeply.

"I see."

She continued with cold calm. "You have managed to climb steadily in the ranks of government despite what happened nine years ago, but I seriously doubt whether your career would withstand the notoriety attendant on charges of seducing the daughter and sister of the men you killed. You'd be an embarrassment to your party."

"You know that isn't true, any part of it!"

"Not the seduction part, no, but you cannot deny you are responsible for my father's and brother's deaths."

"I could deny it and do, but it is a waste of breath. You refused to believe me nine years ago, and you obviously have not softened your position in the interim. What is it you want of me, money or revenge?"

For a moment the woman squirmed under his hard stare and her eyes refused to meet his. Before he could press the momentary advantage, however, she had herself in hand again. Her slightly pointed chin tilted upward, and she spoke without any feeling at all.

"I don't know whether you ever bothered to discover what became of the family of the men you killed. My father was ruined, of course. He had gambled away all his private fortune. The estate was entailed, and when my brother died it went to a distant cousin who had long been estranged from our branch of the family. My mother's constitution was always delicate. She never recovered from the double shock, although she clung to life until I came of age to be legally responsible for my young sister. Then she just . . . faded away. I was seventeen and betrothed when my father and brother died, but I soon discovered my fiancé was quite willing to release me from the engagement when he learned my marriage portion had gone with all the rest. Mother had a tiny income and we lived frugally in a rented cottage in the country, but with her long illness we were forced to use some of the capital. It is nearly gone now. I could manage if I had only myself to consider, but my sister is now seventeen and very lovely. She *must* have her chance to marry, but how can I give it to her? We are here tonight because I decided to swallow my pride and approach my cousin to plead with him to do something for Diana. We were on our way to London to see him."

During this recitation Glenville's stare never wavered from the woman's wooden countenance. Now he said with a sardonic inflection, "But, having met me in, shall we say, unusual circumstances, you now feel that I might take your cousin's place as benefactor to your sister. Do I take your meaning correctly, Miss Wendover?"

Icy clear gray eyes bored into his darker ones. "Having met you in *sordid* circumstances, I now feel that as my *husband* you can give Diana all the advantages of a court presentation and sponsorship into the polite world to which she belongs by right of birth and which you took away from her when you killed her brother."

He had been prepared for a demand for money. It took a few seconds for the meaning of her words to strike home, then he reacted with leashed violence.

"*Marry* you? I'm more likely to *murder* you! What's to stop me from strangling you this very minute?" He flexed long fingers as he flung the angry words at her and noted the signs of fear she could not control. Her answer, however, came straightly back.

"The assurance that the crime would be brought home to you. That man across the hall would see to that!"

Reluctant admiration for the courage that enabled her to stand her ground warred with fury over the weakness of his own position. She had him in a cleft stick, damn her! The patronage of the minister disarmed his enemies at present, but he was well aware that there were those who would make discrediting him their first priority if they could see their way to accomplishing the feat. He eyed her consideringly for a long moment, but it never occurred to him to call her bluff. He paid Miss Wendover the tacit compliment of believing she meant exactly what she had threatened. There was determination and more than a little desperation beneath that carefully preserved calm of hers. Like her father before her, she was staking all on a desperate gamble. He was almost light-headed from rancor and frustration. She continued to stand a pace or two away from him, a quiet, expressionless, almost characterless female who held his future career in her hands.

He wrenched out of the paralyzing tension holding the two of them in place and walked stiffly over to the table near where the chair had stood such a short time before, though it seemed an eon had passed since he had been happily absorbed in the book reposing on its scratched surface. The brandy glass still held half an inch of liquid, and he reached for it, downing the contents under the girl's eye. He did not apologize for the rudeness, nor did she acknowledge the slight by so much as the flicker of an eyelid. With great deliberation he replaced the empty glass and remarked softly, almost casually:

"A matter of coercion, in fact. Allow me to congratulate you on your original methods of husband hunting, Miss Wendover. Are they the ones you employed in extracting your first proposal?"

He thought she winced slightly, but her reply was couched in the terms of sweet reason. "There is nothing to be gained by prolonging this discussion, my lord. We will both be more rational after a night's repose. I'll leave you now." She turned away from him, but her steps were arrested by his voice before she reached the door.

"You've forgotten something, have you not, Miss Wendover?"

"Forgotten something?" Her voice was carefully unaccented, but a certain wariness leaped into the smoky eyes.

"Your gown is still partially fastened," he pointed out without emphasis. "Unless you propose to sleep in it you had best let me undo those buttons."

She presented her back to him without comment, and he accomplished the task in a like silence. He did not offer to see her to her door.

"Thank you, Lord Glenville. Goodnight."

The door closed quietly behind his affianced bride.

Chapter Two

Adam Harding, eighth Earl of Glenville, watched the door to an inn bedchamber swing slowly into place with a wild sense of disbelief mixed with fury. The soft snick of the catch released him from the paralysis that seemed to grip his limbs and brain alike. He surged forward. This farce could not be allowed to continue a minute longer! He must have been mad to agree to a marriage with that female icicle. Not that it would be a marriage, of course, but the very fact of her existence — and there was a sister too, he recalled — would irretrievably alter his comfortable way of life for the worse. His hand was on the latch, the door was open, permitting an unobstructed view of the closed door across the corridor, the door behind which his long-despised opponent, Allerton, lay, most probably dreaming of the damage he would do to Glenville's political career with the scandal he felt he had unearthed.

A long moment of frustration and indecision elapsed with nothing to break the silence but a creaking shutter outside and the sound of his own harsh breathing in the room. At the end of it he shut the door quietly and walked over to the winged chair and dropped into its comfortable depths. He made no move to return it to its original place by the table where the candles still burned steadily. There would be no more reading tonight, and he did not require light to pursue his dark thoughts.

They were always present at some level of his awareness, ready to prey on him in moments of weakness or depression.

These had grown fewer with the passage of time as he had reconstructed his life, but he had never quite succeeded in putting the events of that bleak period permanently aside.

He had been a young care-for-naught in those days after the death of his father, leading the aimless existence of young men of his class, his interests bounded by sporting pursuits in the daytime and gambling and dalliance in the evening. His father had been the second son of the fifth earl, and since his uncle had secured .the succession with the production of two strapping sons, Adam had been allowed to pursue his own interests, which had in the main been frivolous. His father's property was small but well run, and on his death when Adam was four and twenty, his heir found himself able to afford most of his expensive habits if he didn't draw the bustle too outrageously. His mother was living in London at the time, having returned after her husband's death from an extended sojourn on the Continent. She had very little influence in his life, having deserted husband and child before Adam was old enough for Eton. Now married to the wealthy peer with whom she had eloped, she had resumed her social career with as much success as money could buy. The *ton* had a long memory, though, and there remained houses whose thresholds she could not hope to cross. He kept his own contacts with her to a minimum, never failing in the public courtesy owed to a parent and never allowing her one scrap of the affection she had forfeited by her desertion. In this pleasant, purposeless style he had reached the age of eight and twenty without making any commitments to the future when the affair with the Wendovers, *père et fils*, had blown up in his face.

Sir Charles Wendover was a chronic gambler. For months there had been rumors circulating among the clubs that he was all to bits and would soon be forced to sell out of the Funds. Being much younger than Wendover, Adam had no more than a nodding acquaintance with him, though he knew his young cub of a son, Basil, for whom he cherished a mild dislike that was reciprocated tenfold on the part of one always bested at every turn by Harding's superior strength and skill at various sports.

Looking back, he could see it was no more than a quirk of malicious Fate that he should have come to the attention of Sir Charles at the lowest point in the latter's fortunes. On the night in question he had just arisen from a most successful session of piquet with a man noted for his play and had found it impossible to refuse to give Sir Charles a game. The man was in his cups before play got under way and continued to make indentures on the burgundy throughout the contest. He had overriden Adam's tentative attempts to keep the stakes low, forcing up the price of each game and recklessly signing chits as he lost heavily. Perhaps a contemporary of Sir Charles's could have extricated himself from such a mismatch, but Adam had not known how to accomplish it without mortally offending a man old enough to be his father. He had pleaded fatigue and finally illness before the grimly obsessed baronet released him in the small hours of the morning, and he had departed for his rooms with no desire and little expectation of collecting his winnings. However, the payment had arrived the next day and with it the unwelcome news that Wendover had blown his brains out.

There had been witnesses enough at White's to absolve him of any suspicion of lying in wait for a victim incapacitated by drink, but he had experienced all the natural regret of a man involved in the senseless tragedy of another. Sir Charles was scarcely in his grave when the situation took an unexpected turn. Basil Wendover, in the presence of witnesses, had accused Adam of cheating his father, and Basil was *not* foxed at the time. He had convinced himself that this was the true situation and was not to be persuaded otherwise. Adam, at the mercy of a man determined to force a quarrel, had been unable to refuse the challenge. He had chosen swords, confident that his superior skill would enable him to give the young hothead satisfaction without having to hurt him seriously. And so it had turned out. He had himself sustained a deep cut on his face and had pricked Basil in the shoulder. Who could have foreseen the tragic series of misadventures that culminated in young Wendover's eventual death from blood poisoning? The wound had been minor, but he had not received adequate medical care and within a week he was dead. Adam had been wracked by remorse at the double tragedy, though he could not accept guilt where it did not exist.

In the rapidly chilling inn chamber, Glenville raised his head from his hand and rested it against the high back of the chair. His eyes, staring at nothing, were full of grim memories. He recalled his only previous meeting with Miss Wendover and experienced again the weight of her vilification and bitterness. That had been the worst moment of all, staring into the suffering face of a young girl who' was uttering manifestly unfair accusations, and being powerless to change the situation. Suddenly he lunged out of the chair and started an aimless quartering of the room's limited floor space as he pictured the cold features of the woman who had just left him. He had thought he would never forget her face, but tonight he had failed to recognize her. Frowning, he went over her appearance in detail. The hair, that was it! He recalled the incredible blondness of the young April Wendover and realized that her hair had been almost entirely hidden by a cap tonight. The image in his mind, though fixed, was actually fuzzy about details after nine years. Then she had been pasty-faced and her eyes had been swollen from weeping. Now that he dwelled on it he did recall that they had been of an unusual light gray, which tallied with his observation tonight. This older version had been coldly controlled in contrast to the unbridled passion of the young girl, but it was the same person. He no longer felt surprise that a comparatively young woman should look so *quenched*. Nor did he find himself unmoved by the bald tale she had recounted of her life for the past nine years. Enough rain had fallen in Miss Wendover's life to quench anyone's fire. He merely resented having everything laid to *his* account.

But nine years had made no difference to her hatred. Evidently she had not been able to take a more reasonable view of events even after grief had long abated. Tonight she had been living in the past with an ever fresh desire to revenge herself on the man she held responsible for her relatives' deaths and all the unhappiness that had followed. The thought was appalling enough to send a chill feathering along his nerves. And this was the woman he was to wed? A woman whose loyalty would always be to the past? To invite an enemy into one's house would be to carry self-destructiveness to extremes! Surely they could come to some other arrangement which would enable her to accomplish both her purposes. If he paid her expenses she would be extracting her revenge and, with her cousin's sponsorship, should be able to launch her sister into society.

Mentally he passed the present baronet under review and was forced to the conclusion that Sir Neville Granby, saddled with a hatchet-faced wife and an antidote for a daughter, was hardly the man to lend his patronage to cousins he barely knew, especially if one of them was likely to cast his unwed daughter into the shade. He paused in his pacing as another, more primary objection presented itself. Allerton would be bound to recognize Miss Wendover if he met her in society, and then the fat would be in the fire. A reluctant smile drove the sternness from his expression as he imagined the effect on the *ton* of his alleged partner-in-sin's attempt to insinuate her sister into its ranks in the light of disclosures of this nature. The smile faded as quickly as it had appeared. It would have to be marriage. Still, if he *must* nourish a viper in his bosom, then, by God, he'd see to it that the viper's fangs were pulled! Miss Wendover would find this marriage a two-way street!

On this thought he surrendered to the creeping chill in the room and, after undressing in record time and extinguishing the remains of the candles, crawled into bed and pushed the now cold brick aside, wrapping the comforter tightly around him.

Lord Glenville would have been surprised to learn that

the scene in the next room was not so very different from his own experience during the past hour. Miss Wendover had beaten a strategic retreat from his room, her recent triumph slightly dimmed by the humiliating necessity of submitting to his ministrations with regard to her gown. She closed her door behind her with great care so as not to awaken her sister and sagged back against its reassuring firmness. Her fingers crept up to massage her temples. How had she *dared* try to coerce that terrible man into marrying her? He had accused her of blackmail, and she stood convicted of that heinous crime in her own eyes! From the moment she had become aware of his identity some other self she did not know had taken over her mind and body and led her to act in a manner she would never have considered in her saner moments. She pressed her fingers across her eyes. Yes, that was it, she must have been *mad* for those few moments, but the madness must cease!

She whirled about and seized the latch. The door was already open when a cold draft on her back brought her own state of disarray sharply before her mind's eye. What would he think if she should reappear at his door half undressed? A deep flush rose from her throat and suffused her cheeks, but she berated herself soundly for a fool. What did it signify what he thought if she released him from all obligation to wed her? He'd be too relieved to notice her appearance. As she lingered in the doorway a sound reached her from the big bed across the room. Diana had moaned softly and turned in her sleep.

Diana! Her eyes flew to the darkened corner even as her hand pushed the door gently shut. Diana's future was the impetus for what she had just done. It was on Diana's behalf that she had undertaken this quixotic journey to London in the first place. She had come to terms with their reduction in circumstances for her own sake, but Diana was too lovely and too ill equipped to endure poverty. Her sister was urging her to marry Mr. Lynley, a retired merchant who had been exceedingly kind to the small family during Lady Wendover's last years.

It was through Mr. Lynley's influence that she had been able to start a school for village children, which brought in a pittance, but there was no denying their existence would be precarious indeed when their remaining capital ran out. Unless Diana made a good marriage or she herself consented to become Mr. Lynley's wife, it was inevitable that the money would run out eventually. And if she did manage to subdue her own instinctive revulsion of the senses and marry a man who, though good-natured and kind, was twice her age and physically unappealing, then Diana would be permanently barred from forming an advantageous connection. Mr. Lynley's money would keep her in comfort, but Mr. Lynley's lack of breeding would close forever those doors which her own birth entitled her to enter. This circumstance her sister seemed unable to grasp in her urgent desire to have the wherewithal to buy pretty clothes and go to parties. The older Diana became, the more pressing Mr. Lynley's suit and the more acute the problem.

It was in reaction to the seemingly inevitable surrender of her freedom that she had evolved this plan to appeal to her cousin for assistance. It had been her devout hope that he could be persuaded to underwrite the expense of Diana's debut if Diana's sister made herself available to his wife as an unpaid governess to their numerous offspring. Failing this full support, Miss Wendover had one more option in reserve. If Sir Neville could at least be induced to sponsor Diana's comeout to the extent of allowing his wife to chaperon her for the season, she would ask Mr. Lynley for the necessary funds to provide her sister with a suitable wardrobe, pledging herself to marry him when Diana contracted an eligible alliance. She resolutely refused to dwell on the necessity of fading out of her sister's life in such an eventuality. This last-ditch plan she had divulged to no one as yet. Nor had she been able to bring herself to depress Diana's optimism by confiding her own fears that one look at her beautiful sister on the part of Lady Granby would set up the latter's back and cause her to refuse to allow her own plain daughter to be brought out in the company of one who was bound to eclipse her. Instead she had permitted Mr. Lynley to persuade her to accept the use of his coach and horses for the journey, and look where the move had landed them!

Miss Wendover, standing wearily near the door, shivered in the cold air and forced herself to begin preparation for sleep. Anything she might have to say to Lord Glenville would be better said in the morning. And what she was to say to him she couldn't hope to know, the state her confused intellect was in at present. Making herself consider all possibilities as she folded her clothing with automatic precision, she acknowledged that the best they could hope for would be complete support from their cousin, and the least attractive option would be marriage with the man responsible for the deaths of her father and brother. Or would that necessarily be worse than marriage with a man she liked but shrank from? Her busy hands ceased their efforts as she summoned up an image of Mr. Lynley before her eyes. His short stature and tendency toward corpulence didn't repel her, but his noisy and greedy enjoyment of food and drink and the uncared-for nature of his pudgy hands with their dirty nails did. And she always found herself looking away from his too wet mouth with its thick lips covering yellowed teeth.

The hated Lord Glenville, on the other hand, though of a rather harsh aspect, seemed to be of a fastidious nature, and she had noted the well-shaped hand and immaculate nails. He might be a Bluebeard for all she knew to the contrary, but one thing she had learned was that he had no interest in her as a female. His look had been an insult, but it was a relief too.

Miss Wendover had no very good opinion of the stronger sex. She had loved her father and brother, but love and loyalty had not blinded her to the defects in their characters. At seventeen she had been flattered by the attentions of her fiancé, who had caused her youthful heart to flutter with what she had assumed to be love, but his protestations of devotion had meant so little that he had jumped at her offer to release him from the engagement when it became obvious that she would be a penniless bride. On the two occasions on which she had observed her cousin Neville, he had struck her as being a conceited popinjay without the intellect or resolution to stand up to his harridan of a wife.

At this point in her summing up, Miss Wendover realized that she was too exhausted and too mistrustful of the future to make any rational decision. Her last thought on edging into bed beside her sleeping sister was that if it really came to a choice between a marriage in name only to a man of her own class whom she hated or a union in which she would be expected to undertake a wife's obligations with a man of lesser breeding whose touch caused her to shrivel inside, she would elect the former. And so, protesting to herself that she could not make a decision, Miss Wendover drifted into an uneasy sleep, having already made her decision.

Chapter Three

Miss Wendover, not surprisingly, was loath to rise the next morning. Her rest in a strange bed was never guaranteed under the best of circumstances, and after the shattering events of the previous evening she had endured a disturbed night, finally sinking into a deep sleep just before dawn. Miss Diana Wendover, eager to embark upon the last leg of the journey that she, with the unbounded optimism of the very young, confidently expected would result in setting the mechanics of her presentation in train, rose betimes and was nearly dressed when Miss Matilda Denby arrived to wait upon the surviving members of the family she had served for nearly forty years.

This redoubtable lady had joined the Wendover household as a kitchen maid at the age of thirteen and had advanced to second housemaid by the time the late Sir Charles brought his bride home to the Grange. The new Lady Wendover had taken a great fancy to the discreetly efficient young woman and, when anticipating her first Happy Event, had declared she would have no other to act as nurse to her children. In the guise of a benevolent despot who stood no nonsense from her charges, Mattie had ruled the nursery until the tragic events that led to the dissolution of the estate. There was never any question that she would go wherever her lady and her daughters established themselves. Being of an intensely practical nature, she had taken the reins of the reduced household into her capable hands and had seen to it that Lady Wendover was not troubled with domestic matters during her final unhappy years. It was she who trained Miss Wendover in the mundane details of domestic management, which had not formed part of the education imparted by a very expensive French governess. Miss Wendover, impelled by the promptings of necessity, had proved an apt pupil, learning among diverse skills how to dress a joint, plan the stocking of a still room, and choose the most efficacious mixture for cleaning and polishing every surface in a home that could ever be thought to need maintenance. Later, she herself had taught her sister those accomplishments such as ease with the French tongue, watercolor painting, and needlework which were indispensable to a lady's education, but neither Miss Wendover nor Mattie had so far succeeded in implanting much practical or domestic knowledge in Diana's lovely head.

This morning Diana opened the door to the maid, who entered with her customary brisk stride, glancing in some surprise from the still-occupied bed to the girl engaged in buttoning the sleeves of a most becoming carriage dress of dark-green wool.

"Well, Miss Diana, you are up bright and early." She accepted the slim wrist thrust at her for assistance, but once her capable fingers had fastened the buttons her eyes returned to the bed.

"What's wrong with Miss April?"

"Nothing—that is, I do not imagine there is anything wrong. She was reading when I fell asleep. I don't know what time she came to bed. You know her way when she gets absorbed in a book. Wake her, will you, Mattie? I am persuaded she meant to get an early start, and, Mattie, you'll have to finish packing for me. Look what a muddle I have made of my nightclothes. I don't have your knack of folding things neatly."

"If you took more time, Miss Diana, you wouldn't need help."

"Dear Mattie," wheedled the girl, "you know I am a hopeless case past praying for. Please do it for me and I shall rouse April. I vow I am famished for my breakfast."

"Don't play off your tricks on me, missy. You know I take no notice of such nonsense." Though the words were minatory, Miss Denby's austere features softened at sight of the pretty, mischievous face confronting her, and she proceeded to repack the cloak bag, clucking her tongue in disapproval at the state of its contents. Her head with its uncompromising knot of salt-and-pepper hair was bent to her task, but her alert black eyes strayed frequently to the scene taking place in the corner.

"April, wake up, it's nearly eight o'clock. Don't pretend you're asleep, I saw your eyelids twitch. Oh no, you don't!" Diana pulled the blanket down from her sister's ears and continued alternately abusing and cajoling her until her victim rolled over with a groan and opened her eyes.

"Diana, you wretch, what is the big rush? Good morning, Mattie. Am I really so very late?" Miss Wendover gave a huge yawn and swung her legs out of bed, accepting the wrapper her sister handed her. She glanced briefly at the maid, then avoided the searching look the other bent on her, concentrating her attention on the vital task of tying the girdle of her wrapper. Now that the moment had come to disclose the fundamental change that was about to occur in their lives, she found herself woefully inadequate to the task. Anything less than an absolutely truthful rendition of the events leading up to the decision taken last night would sound fantastic, but every instinct of discretion forbade such a revelation. Besides, it was not beyond the bounds of imagination that Lord Glenville might have had second thoughts about capitulating to what was no better than blackmail. He might have made his escape at dawn, gambling that a woman in her position would not have the resources to follow up her threat to expose him. And she did not even know whether to regard such a possibility as a calamity or a blessing. She began to wash and dress for the day, thankful for Diana's excited chatter that covered her own lack of conversation. Her mind was still totally blank by the time she had donned the same brown dress she had removed the night before and brushed her hair into some kind of order before confining it under the cap she had taken to wearing since beginning her career as a teacher.

"Miss April!"

"Yes, Mattie?"

"Is something wrong? Do you feel unwell this morning?"

"No, no, I am fine, thank you, Mattie, but I haven't much appetite at the moment. Why do not you and Diana go down to the coffee room. All I wish is coffee, if you'll send some up to me. I'll finish packing in the meantime."

She summoned up the nerve to return the maid's concerned regard, but knew herself for a craven coward. The thought of coming face-to-face with Lord Glenville or his enemy, the man he called Allerton, in the public dining room robbed her of any desire for food, and she was inclined to think they would be well out of a bad situation if she never met either again. Diana and Mattie were staring at her in bewilderment when a knock sounded at the door. Miss Wendover jumped and put out a hand in an instinctive gesture of repudiation, then dropped the hand to her side as Mattie crossed to the door.

The landlord wished the ladies a cheerful good day and presented Miss Denby with a screw of paper for Miss Wendover. He prevented Miss Denby from closing the door by the simple expedient of a foot in the opening. "I'm to wait for a reply," he declared, noting with interest that one of the ladies had turned pale as a ghost on seeing the missive. When this was put into her reluctant hands, the trembling of those hands was obvious to all three observers. There was complete silence in the sunny room while she smoothed the sheet of paper and read the message thereon. It might have been a long message or the handwriting might have been difficult, because the lady's eyes remained fixed on the paper for an appreciable length of time. Finally she raised her head, ignoring the younger lady's importunities to be told what was happening, and spoke directly to the innkeeper.

"Tell Lord Glenville we shall be pleased to accept his kind invitation in fifteen minutes."

"Who is Lord Glenville?" asked Diana before the door had even shut behind Mr. Choate. "Invitation for what?"

Miss Wendover looked from her sister's puzzled face to the knowledgeable one of Miss Denby and spoke to the latter. "Yes, it is he, and . . . and I am, in all likelihood, going to marry him," she finished in a rush of words, the tone of which was slightly defiant, like that of a child confessing to an act of disobedience.

Her audience was stunned for an instant, then found its collective tongue.

"*Marry* him? Marry *whom*, for the Lord's sake? Are you funning, April?"

"*No*, Miss April, you *can't!*" Miss Denby's harsh whisper drowned out Diana's query.

"Yes, I can, Mattie. Don't you see, it would be the answer to all our problems!"

"It would be a disaster, mark my words! Nothing but misery could come from such a move," Miss Denby stated in a prophetic tone.

The eyes of the older women had been locked in a battle of wills since Miss Wendover had made her annoucement. Hers were pleading but determined, and her former nurse projected fear and rejection as her lips clamped in a thin line. Diana, who had been ignored during the interchange, looked from face to face, unable to make any sense out of what was happening. She stamped her foot impatiently.

"Will someone please tell me what this is all about? Who is this Lord Glenville?"

"He is a man I knew a long time ago before Mother died." Miss Wendover spoke slowly, addressing her sister, but she continued to look at Miss Denby. Some unspoken agreement had been forged between them, for Miss Denby remained mute, her expression grave but resigned.

"And he wishes to marry you? How did he know we were here? Have you seen him?" Diana was determined to get to the bottom of the mystery she scented in the atmosphere of the room.

"It is a long story, and there is no time now for explanations. He has invited us to have breakfast with him in a private dining room. We must not keep him waiting." As she spoke, Miss Wendover had collected her reticule, and now she tucked a clean handkerchief into it. "Are you ready?" she inquired of Diana, who gave a last pat to the curls Mattie had arranged for her while her sister finished dressing.

"I suppose so. I do not understand any of this, but there's no denying it's exciting," Diana replied sunnily. "What kind of a lord is he?"

Miss Denby emitted what sounded suspiciously like a sniff of disdain.

"He is the eighth Earl of Glenville," said Miss Wendover, avoiding her handmaiden's eye. "He inherited the title about seven years ago from a cousin who drowned in a boating accident together with the brother who was his heir."

"Goodness, you'll be a *countess*, April!" cried Diana, much impressed. "But why did he not ask you to marry him when he came into the title?"

Diana's reasonable question was greeted by a brief silence as Miss Wendover paused at the open door to await the others' exit. "There were reasons," she said at last in a manner calculated to discourage further questioning. That this end was achieved was due more to the brisk pace she set and the presence of the landlord at the bottom of the stairway than to any inhibiting effect her firmness had on her curious sister.

Mr. Choate bowed and conducted the ladies to the private dining room Lord Glenville had hired, where he stood aside for them to enter. The tall man with his back to the fireplace approached after a swift look at Miss Wendover and bowed formally. Miss Wendover made the introductions with a cool grace that would have concealed her nervousness from a casual eye, but Lord Glenville's was no casual eye. His first quick appraisal had assured him of both her determination and her uneasiness. She had more color this morning, but any claim to more than average looks was totally nullified by the sparkling young girl beside her. So this was the jewel that must not be left to shine unnoticed in the country even if it meant her sister must sacrifice her own interest and act in a manner contrary to her upbringing to achieve the opportunity to display her before the *ton.* He concentrated a hard stare upon the girl, who met his look with the natural assurance of one confident of her appeal. The absence of any signs of shyness on the part of a seventeen-year-old girl who had spent most of her life away from society struck him as rather significant.

There was a faint family resemblance, he thought, bending politely over the small hand, but the younger Miss Wendover was a more vivid edition, her hair a mass of bright-gold curls, her eyes thickly lashed and deeply blue, her complexion of rose-leaf perfection. Like her sister, she was of moderate height and graceful carriage, but in her case a slim nicely curved figure was displayed to advantage by a beautifully cut dress that flattered her coloring and, to his discerning eye, had cost at least three times as much as the nondescript brown thing Miss Wendover was once again attired in. Pretty? Yes, decidedly so, but in a style often seen among the buds at Almack's each year, and owing more to the eager glow of youthful spirits than to any bone-deep loveliness that would escape the ravages of time.

"I am delighted to make your acquaintance, Lord Glenville," Miss Diana Wendover declared with apparent sincerity, "but I must tell you that Mattie and I are still reeling with surprise. April has never mentioned you to me until just now when your invitation was delivered, but she says you have known each other since before our mother died."

"That is correct, Miss Diana," he concurred smoothly at the same time one level eyebrow elevated slightly as he flicked a glance at her sister's rigid countenance and tightly clasped hands.

"Lord Glenville, this is our good friend Miss Matilda Denby, who has been with our family since before Diana and I were born," Miss Wendover said before her sister could pursue the topic of their past acquaintance.

Miss Denby dropped him the merest suggestion of a curtsy

and treated him to a stare every bit as measuring as his own and much less approving from a pair of snapping black eyes that enlivened a gaunt-featured face. He responded with a genuine smile that narrowed those eyes as he murmured his pleasure at the introduction. The younger Miss Wendover, not about to see the conversation taken out of her hands, intervened in a voice that lacked the musical quality of her sister's but was not deficient in carrying power.

"April says that you are probably going to marry. Pray, what does that mean precisely, sir?"

His smile, tinged with amusement now, turned toward the curious face of his prospective sister-in-law. "Why, it means that your sister has done me the honor to accept my offer." He could sense the momentary relaxation in the woman on his right at this reply and the subsequent stiffening as he continued, "And that we shall be married later today in London when I have procured a special license."

"*Today!* But I . . . you—"

"Yes, why wait, my dear?" he said to the stricken female beside him. "Wasn't it Shakespeare who said, 'If it were done when 'tis done, then 'twere well it were done quickly'? This way we shall avoid any awkwardness about your arrival in town."

Whatever the well-read Miss Wendover's indignation at having her marriage likened to an assassination might have prompted her to reply in retaliation was aborted by the appearance just then of a waiter bearing a huge tray. She had to be content with shooting her intended husband a glance of undistilled loathing as he seated her at the table with an ostentatious courtesy that was an affront under the circumstances.

The meal that followed was destined to remain in her memory as one of the most unpleasant of her life. Her appetite had deserted her long before the actual confrontation with the man she had coerced into marrying her, but now as it became apparent that the balance of power had swung sharply in his direction, she found it a test of her endurance just to remain seated at the well-appointed table while her intended husband calmly played host and announced plans that would radically alter all their lives with the same degree of emotion he might expend on a decision as to which slice of meat to take onto his plate. The very smell of the food induced a sensation of nausea within her, which wasn't aided by a rising panic as she felt the trap she had designed closing relentlessly around her. Nor did the suspicion that she had bitten off more than she could chew contribute to her peace of mind. Her instinctive attempts to assert herself and prevent Lord Glenville from having everything his own way were enfeebled at the start by her urgent desire to keep Diana ignorant of the true circumstances behind this sudden decision to marry. Thus as the breakfast ordeal progressed she found herself agreeing between clenched teeth to a private wedding that very day wearing the clothes she stood up in, to the dismissal of Mr. Lynley's coach in favor of a post chaise hired by Lord Glenville, and most alarming of all, to the installation of the three of them in his lordship's town house immediately following the marriage. He apologized suavely for the lack of preparation for their reception at his home, sliding over the precipitate nature of the marriage when Diana would have explored the topic more thoroughly. In his future bride's somewhat biased view he exerted a shameless charm of manner (undoubtedly assumed for the occasion) accompanied by liberal doses of flattery to achieve his ends with an inexperienced girl.

His maneuvers were highly successful. Diana was quite won over by the calm good sense of his arguments and showed herself sparklingly responsive to the masculine magnetism he projected seemingly effortlessly. Even Miss Denby unbent a trifle under the benign influence of good food and hot coffee presented to her by a courteous host who contrived to appear attentive to her needs, a rare experience in her work-filled life. She and Diana made a very good meal, but April could not physically swallow anything but coffee even to supplement an earnest desire to conceal her mental agitation from the others. It was a slight degree of consolation to realize as the meal dragged on that her future husband was not making very deep inroads on the platters of eggs and cold meats despite the impression he gave to the contrary. Though common sense insisted he simply might not be a big-breakfast eater, she chose to believe he was finding the meeting as nerve-racking as she was. The thought revived her flagging courage enough to allow her to maintain a fragile composure imposed over a panicky desire to rise from the table and literally flee anywhere that offered an escape from the situation she had created.

It was a profound relief when Lord Glenville took out his watch and announced that it was time they took their departure in view of the busy day that lay ahead of them once they arrived in London.

Miss Wendover was on her feet before he had finished speaking. "Yes, of course. I must just pay our reckoning at the desk. We will not keep you waiting above a minute or two."

"Don't be foolish." His impatient words caught her before she reached the door. "The bill is already taken care of. There is nothing to be done except board the chaise at your convenience. I will see to the loading of your baggage if it is ready."

Suddenly it was imperative that she get away from him — from everyone — for a moment of privacy before embarking on a journey that was to turn her life upside down. "I . . . I must just write a note to Mr. Lynley to explain the return of his coach," she said in desperation. "My writing things are upstairs. I beg you will excuse me, please." She fled on the words but found him beside her as she reached the staircase.

"Is anything wrong?" he inquired with polite formality while his eyes remained watchful.

"No, of course not. I—"

"Quickly, put on your gloves!"

April stared at the enigmatic dark face that had leaned toward her. "I beg your pardon?"

"I said put your gloves on. *Do it!*"

The urgency in his low tones caused her to obey him without further delay. As she struggled into the worn kid gloves she noted that his attention was no longer on her, and her glance followed his up the staircase. Her cheeks reddened as she recognized the tall man slowly descending, and her hands shook slightly as she buttoned her gloves. It seemed there was to be no avoiding another embarrassing confrontation with their tormentor of the night before. She would have to pass Allerton to get upstairs, and Lord Glenville was standing like a monument at her side blocking any return to the dining room. As the victim of a bad dream she watched the approach of the man who hoped to ruin her future husband. Her fingers itched to slap the leering expression from his face, and her teeth went tight. She could feel the man next to her grow rigid. Later, the recollection of her own uncivilized reaction enabled her to better understand what happened next.

"You must be reluctant indeed to leave the delights of this very mediocre inn, Glenville, to forgo your usual crack-of-dawn departure." Allerton's insolent gaze lingered on Miss Wendover, who felt besmirched.

"My wife was tired from her journey, so we delayed our departure," the man at her side replied in an offhand manner.

The words had an electric effect on his listeners. Miss Wendover gave an uncontrolled start, but a warning grip on her arm kept her silent. She stared, fascinated, as the leer on Allerton's face gave way to mingled fury and incredulity.

"Married! Since when?"

"Since yesterday, but I'd rather the world at large remain unenlightened until I have told my mother."

"Rather a sudden decision then?"

"Just so."

"Strange you did not think to present your *wife* to me last night." Allerton had recovered his self-possession, though his whole manner bespoke disbelief.

"My marital status is none of your business, but as I said, I would prefer that my mother hear the news from me." He turned to Miss Wendover, who was giving an excellent imitation of a statue, and said with gentle solicitude, "Do you still wish to retrieve your writing materials, darling?"

"Yes," she whispered, unable to contribute more positively to this talented performance but eager to seize the opportunity to efface herself.

"Wait!" Allerton's command halted her foot on the first step and sent a shiver of apprehension down her spine. Had he guessed the truth? She turned with reluctance.

"You must allow me to offer my felicitations on your marriage, Lady Glenville. You have *captured* . . . the heart of one of England's most eligible and resistant bachelors."

She allowed him to take her hand for an instant then, though every instinct bade her ignore his outstretched hand. Her upbringing demanded that she respond, but she could not bring herself to utter more than a brief thank-you before resuming her ascent up the stairs, which only the severest self-discipline kept from resembling the rout it was.

Chapter Four

Some six hours later, April was seated in a chair in the bed-chamber that was henceforth to be hers in the large town house in Hanover Square that had been inherited by the earl along with the title and estates. She had been sitting in the same limp attitude since dismissing Mattie a half hour ago to assist Diana in settling into her new quarters. For the past two hours she had been a married woman, April Harding, Countess of Glenville. She repeated the title now aloud, but that didn't seem to give any additional substance to the fantasy world she had been inhabiting for less than twenty-four hours. Incredible that one's existence could be changed forever in less than a single revolution of the earth on its axis! And not just her own existence either. That was the truly frightening part, that by her harsh, perhaps even criminal action, she had radically altered the course of at least three other lives. She shivered and rubbed her upper arms fiercely to shake off the sudden chill. The one sure thing was that sitting here nursing regrets would not mend matters. She had to go on from here.

For the first time her eyes roved around the room, whose furnishings had not yet impinged on her consciousness. The results of this survey were not particularly encouraging. This morning Lord Glenville had dispatched his groom to Hanover Square on horseback with instructions that rooms be made ready for his wife and sister-in-law. Certainly there was evidence of a hasty dusting and airing in here, but April's fastidious soul was affronted by the atmosphere of neglect that clung to the room. The satinwood furniture was good, if a trifle old-fashioned, but would have been improved by a thorough application of beeswax. The brass fireplace appointments wanted polishing, and only heaven and the housekeeper knew when the draperies and bed curtains had last been taken down and cleaned. Not that cleaning would improve the look of them, she thought sourly, eyeing the faded wine-red draperies with disfavor. Then she brought herself up sharply. Pretty well for a woman who had been living in a cottage and teaching in a village school for the last several years to be criticizing such luxurious surroundings! She ought to be on her knees thanking the Providence that had led her to this place.

Only it hadn't been Providence at all but her own unchristian and, yes, *immoral* act that had achieved this new status. All it took was a few solitary moments when she was off guard to bring the whole sordid episode before her again. How could she, April Wendover, who had always considered her principles to be of the highest and her conduct above criticism, sink to such depths of degradation? Every moment spent in the company of Lord Glenville was a stinging reproach. She recalled his stern features as he had stood by her side for the brief marriage ceremony in St. Clement Dane's earlier. She had not yet learned to discern his emotions behind that unreadable face he presented to the world, but something in the set of his finely molded lips at that moment smote her heart. Even though she had done it for Diana's sake, she must be held deeply accountable. Did Diana's need give her the right to coerce another's actions? Last night she had answered one way, but today when it was too late to undo the wrong, her heart gave her a different answer.

Too restless now to sit, she prowled about the large square apartment, opening drawers and staring blankly at their equally blank interiors. Lord Glenville had already made plans to send for those of their belongings they wished to bring to London. Mattie was to go tomorrow to supervise the packing and removal. Could anything be more final? She

sighed deeply, then straightened slim shoulders. What was
done was done — irrevocably.

A knock brought her attention sharply back to the
present. It didn't seem to come from the door through which
a maid had led her, nor the open door to the sitting room
beyond. Her eyes lighted on another door she hadn't noticed
until now in the fireplace wall. After a momentary hesitation she crossed to it and pulled it open to stare in surprise at
Lord Glenville — her husband, she reminded herself.

"I hope I am not disturbing you?" he inquired politely.
"Were you in the sitting room?" He waited for her to step
aside so he might enter, and with reluctance she did so.

"No, I was in this room. You did not interrupt anything of
importance, my lord." Her voice sounded strange in her own
ears, and he must have thought so too, for a small frown
appeared between his eyes.

"My name is Adam. You really cannot go about
addressing me as 'my lord,' you know, my dear April, or we
shall undo all our careful work."

She essayed a tentative smile. "You are quite right, of
course, Adam. It is a name I have always liked. Things . . .
seem a bit strange to me at present, but I shall try to . . . to
fit into your life with the least possible disruption." The eyes
she raised to his were eloquent of unspoken apology.

He stared deeply into them for a moment before acknowledging this overture with an unsmiling bow. He glanced
around the room, his expression gradually darkening. "You
don't fit into this room, I fear. I had not realized how
gloomy and old-fashioned it is. You must effect any changes
you wish to make it more comfortable. Throw everything
away and start from the beginning if you like."

"Thank you, my lord — I mean, Adam. You are most
generous."

"Not at all. I am planning a few changes also. I thought
to approach the subject tactfully, but that was rather pre-
sumptuous; it cannot be done other than directly."

"Wh . . . what changes?"

There was an evanescent gleam that might have been

amusement in the dark eyes staring down at her, but it was quickly submerged by determination.

"Changes in your appearance. As my wife you'll be greatly talked about, and I intend that the talk be flattering. The first step is to discard this." They had been standing in the middle of April's bedchamber, but now he took a step forward and snatched the muslin-and-lace cap from her head. "Permanently," he added, tossing the rejected cap onto the bed and watching unmoved as she inched backward from his vicinity, her eyes wide with shock. Fetching up against the dressing-table bench, she dropped onto it, putting up a protesting hand to her tousled head, whose smooth coil had been disarranged by his rough action. She entered an unsteady demur.

"At my age it is necessary to wear a cap."

"Why? To prove you are an ape leader? Well, you are no longer April Wendover, spinster, of this or any other parish. You are the Countess of Glenville and one of society's fashion setters. At least," he amended, "you will be when I have finished refurbishing you."

April's heart had started an irregular hammering action that forced part of her attention away from the disturbing man looking her over so coolly. It took her a moment to assure herself that this vital organ, though noisy, was still functioning properly. She must remain calm. Lord Glenville, this *stranger,* had no power over her. Even as the thought took shape, she recognized the futility of it. Her *husband* had a great deal of power over her life, validated by law and tradition stretching back in time, but, as anger began to rise, her *appearance* was not his province. Just let him try to dictate to her! Her chin acquired a belligerent tilt as she brought her eyes back to the man, who seemed to be making a thoughtful inventory of her attributes. Oddly enough, she wasn't suffering any pangs of embarrassment at all. Indignation had its uses, evidently.

Lord Glenville spoke then, confirming her impressions. "You are no classic beauty, but with those strange eyes and that hair you could be eye-catching at the very least. It's

simply a matter of emphasizing your assets." He continued
to survey her person with a cool impartiality that caused her
to show hackle despite a short-lived resolve to remain impervious. It was neither embarrassment nor offended
modesty that brought about a faint becoming rise of color in
her pale cheeks but a fierce resentment at this judgmental
air, and it cost her something to maintain her stolid calm as
she replied with entirely spurious mildness:

"I have no slightest wish to be eye-catching and am quite
reconciled to my physical limitations."

"Well, I am not, and now is as good a time as any to
inform you that your wishes on this and other matters ceased
to be of paramount importance the moment you coerced my
acceptance of marriage between us." He ignored the sudden
indrawn breath of the figure seated rigidly on the dressing-
table bench as he leaned over her shoulder and tapped the
gold band on the slim finger of one clenched hand. "To you
that ring may represent the security of social position you
require to ensure your sister's success, but it grants me a
whole set of rights too that you'd do well to keep in mind."

Up to this point she had maintained a steely composure,
but now the clear gray eyes widened, then dropped before
the threat in his. Recognizing the flicker of fear, he nodded,
satisfied that his message had been received, before he resumed his original assessment. "Your figure is good even in
that outmoded gown and will appear to advantage in the
styles I intend to select for you."

This brought her startled glance back to his face. "*You*
intend to select my gowns?"

An abrupt turn to finger the mother-of-pearl-backed
brushes on the dressing table behind her concealed his
amusement at the expression of disbelief and outrage that
momentarily animated her previously impassive features.
The drawl became more pronounced. "Why not? Surely my
taste could not help but be an improvement over that which
selected the gown you are wearing. It's several years out of
date and all the wrong color for you." In the mirror he

watched her straight back grow even straighter, but there was no heat in the quiet reply.

"This gown was not considered dowdy when I purchased it five years ago. It has not been within my means to replace it."

He abandoned the mirror and faced her once more, a pace or two from where she sat on the bench. "Yet your sister is wearing a most attractive dress and pelisse, not expensive, I grant you, but certainly in the current mode."

"My sister is very young and very lovely. Clothes mean a lot to girls at this stage in their lives. She has missed out on so much because of the life we have been compelled to lead since the deaths of our father and brother."

He could almost hear the struggle within her to keep all defensiveness out of her explanation but chose to ignore it as he summed up the situation dispassionately. "By trapping me into marriage you have achieved your main objective." A pause produced no reaction save a slight firming of the soft mouth. Those unusual eyes looked unwaveringly back. "Your sister will make her bow to society rigged out in all the trappings girls set such store by. She will undoubtedly create something of a sensation, initially at least, and quite possibly might make an advantageous marriage if I settle enough money on her. I hope it will afford you great satisfaction to witness this triumph, because *you* will be paying for it with the loss of your freedom. I shall leave the dressing of your sister in your hands. I take no interest in members of the infantry, but you are my wife and your appearance and your deportment will reflect on me. *No one* is to guess that this marriage is anything other than an impetuous love match. I don't choose to set up as a laughingstock among any acquaintance!" Again he paused, but there was not the least reaction in the woman watching him with grave attention.

"I intend to orchestrate every detail of your debut as Lady Glenville. I may not have wished for a wife, but, by God, now that I have one she'll do me credit or I'll know the reason why!"

Again the implied threat, but this time curiosity was stronger than intimidation. "What precisely do you have in mind, my lord?"

"As I said before, it is my intention that you be decidedly eye-catching. I shan't stint you on what you expend on your sister's raiment, but I do not intend that you shall ever be cast into the shade by a brainless chit with yellow curls and a provocative smile!"

Her eyes flashed as she assimilated the insult to her sister, but the temper was concealed immediately by lowered lids. Her voice was merely curious. "And how will you prevent this, my lord, in the light of the fact that Diana is younger, prettier, and livelier than I and, if I may accept your words at face value, will herself be dressed in the height of fashion?"

His smile was neither warming nor reassuring, because it was not directed toward the woman seated a few feet away but at some inner vision he did not propose to share with her. "You may safely entrust that task to my, shall we say, more experienced judgment. I may not have any great liking for your sex, but I am generally accorded something of a connoisseur when it is a question of beauty."

"But as you have already pointed out, I am not a beauty."

"You haven't a classically beautiful face," he corrected. "Often the unconventional has a more potent appeal. Your sister is like a hundred other pretty girls and will appeal to ordinary men. When I am finished with you, you will attract those who reject the commonplace." He rather enjoyed her expression of doubt mingled with reluctant expectation as he proceeded to the heart of the matter.

"We'll start with your hair. Does it curl naturally?"

"No."

The hint of satisfaction in her denial was not lost upon him. She had no intention of cooperating wholeheartedly, and, perversely, this attitude lent an additional measure of enjoyment to the exercise.

"Good. Everyone must notice the unusual color at once, and I intend that their eyes return to it frequently. You will never under any circumstances wear any ornament, jewel, feather, or ribbon in your hair. We are going to draw attention by the silken smoothness of the style I shall devise so that every movement of your head will cause the light to catch and accentuate the silvery tone. The first step is a good cut."

Her hand went up to the prim coil in an instinctive gesture of protection. "You . . . you do not propose to do the cutting yourself?"

"No, but it will be done under my direction. I think we shall turn you into a feminine version of a medieval page. Your forehead is too broad, but with a long fringe almost to your eyebrows we can disguise that and at the same time call attention to your pointed chin. With those eyes the effect will be slightly feline, but I have no objection to cats."

"But I don't wish to look like a cat!" she protested, aghast at the picture of herself forming in her confused mind. "And no one appears with straight hair. Do you desire to turn me into a figure of ridicule? Is this your revenge for having married me against your will?"

"Must I remind you again that your wishes are of absolutely no interest to me?" he replied in bored accents. "You may rid your mind of any fear that I would ever allow my wife to make a figure of herself among my friends and enemies. You will be occupying a more elevated position than you ever dreamed of, and I intend that you make a decided impression. If people talk about the unconventional aspect, well and good; that is infinitely preferable to fading into the background. There is no denying your quality, and I presume you have sufficient understanding to converse on a social level with those of my colleagues whom I shall be entertaining. You will not find it all that taxing," he added somewhat dryly.

When she made no reply, he returned to his inventory of her features. "Fortunately your lashes are thick and sufficiently dark to enhance those eyes, but your brows must be darkened." He paid no attention to her gasp of indignation. "They are beautifully arched, but too fair to be effective. Don't worry about censure from the high sticklers. It can be

done with subtlety. It would not be to my advantage to have
people speculating whether I'd picked my wife from the
corps de ballet at the Opera. You haven't much natural
color; however, I'm not sure that cannot be regarded as an
asset. Your skin is as fine-grained as alabaster, and a slight
hint of fragility won't come amiss." He was ticking things off
on his fingers like a shopping list. "Hairstyles, eyebrows,
coloring, I think that's the lot, except to inform you that
when we have attended to these alterations, this afternoon if
possible, I shall make myself available to accompany you to
a modiste that I can trust not to load you up with ruffles and
furbelows. I shan't be able to spare more than one day, so
it's best to instruct you about my wishes in the matter of
dress now. It will save the annoyance of having to return unsatisfactory purchases at a later date." The light-gray eyes
had widened with a reluctant fascination. He sensed her
resentment and was amused by it.

"You are a trifle too slender, but I won't quibble about
that. Statuesque females tend to run to fat in middle age,
and that I cannot abide. The image I shall create demands
simplicity in style at all times, *costly* simplicity, emphasizing
perfect fit and made up in the choicest fabrics. Never succumb to an impulse to adorn yourself in strong colors.
They're not for you, the crimsons and deep blues that your
sister will undoubtedly choose. They will overpower your
delicate coloring and render you insignificant, as does that
brown thing you are wearing. Confine your choices to pearly
grays, pale rose, muted shades of blue and green and the
various mauve tints. Avoid deep yellow and never try to wear
dead white, though an oyster or champagne shade might be
flattering. You'll see what I mean when we call at
Mélisande's tomorrow."

Lord Glenville had come to the end of his assessment of
his wife's potentialities, for he fell silent and raised one dark
eyebrow, apparently inviting comment on one or all aspects
of his discourse. After an expectant pause when nothing
ensued from the expressionless figure on the bench, he
bowed mockingly and strolled to the door that led to his own

rooms, pausing only to mention in passing that he had sent for a coiffeur and had left word that he was to be notified on the arrival of this personage.

She was on her feet before the door quite closed, racing across the room to lock it behind him in a childish gesture of defiance that was foiled by the absence of any key for the purpose. How dare he treat her like some little lightskirt he had picked up on Bond Street! He was going to turn her into a lady of fashion, was he? She'd see about that! She turned from the door with an angry flounce and marched back to the dressing table to stare into its mirror. *A cat!* He thought she looked like a cat and he actually wished to emphasize the likeness! The man was mad, *utterly mad!*

It had been a very long time since April had taken the least interest in her looks. She had had no reason to bother about how she looked for longer than she cared to remember. Now she peered with impartial concentration at her own features. There was no denying her chin was a trifle pointed, and her eyes, now that she really studied them, were set at a slightly oblique angle, but they certainly weren't yellow like a cat's eyes. In fact, they didn't seem to possess any distinct color at all. She had always dismissed them as an uninteresting gray, but they did tend to acquire a blue or violet or green tinge if she wore those colors. Perhaps they weren't so uninteresting after all. She leaned closer to the glass to examine her lashes with new appreciation. She had never paid them any particular attention in the long-ago days of her comeout, but Lord Glenville's casual observation of their length and thickness was strangely comforting many years later. Recalling the outspoken strictures of her governess and Mattie against the sin of vanity when, prior to her presentation, she had demanded their opinion of her chances of being one of the successes of her season, and their insistence on concentrating her efforts on appearing modest and well mannered, she laughed aloud at the picture she would present to the long-departed Mademoiselle Fautier and the ever present Mattie if they could see her now, staring (at her advanced age) into a mirror, assessing her looks with all the anxiety of a seventeen-year-old. Feeling herself back in Diana's stage, although it must be admitted her sister never suffered from any qualms of insecurity with regard to her appearance, she abandoned the search for hidden beauty after a brief frowning inspection of her forehead. He was right, this annoyingly perceptive husband of hers, it was much too broad. Her hand went to her hair in a tentative gesture. She was unaware of the wistful expression in her eyes as they lingered on the shining silvery mass. At least he thought her hair an asset, she reminded herself with a touch of shamefaced defiance before eschewing the ridiculous, unprofitable exercise in which she had been engaging for a wasted half hour.

Several hours later, April allowed a surprisingly approving Mattie to slip her least-dated dinner dress over her shining head in preparation for the first meal in her new home in the company of her husband and sister, the two people whose interests she must advance and protect. She offered a silent prayer that these interests should never collide and turned her back obligingly at Mattie's command.

"Stand still, Miss April, do. How am I to do up these pesky buttons with you wriggling about like a fish on a hook?" The maid's eyes followed those of her mistress to the dressing-table mirror, and the lines of her face softened. "Though mind you, I don't blame you for wanting to look in the glass tonight. That's a right becoming haircut that Monsoor Maurice gave you. I disremember when I've seen you look so pretty with your hair all silky and shinin' in the candlelight."

"Thank you, Mattie. You . . . you don't think perhaps it's a bit young for me?"

The abigail's firm disclaimer was aimed at the suggestion of anxiety underlying this hesitant question.

"Young is it? And why shouldn't you look young, that's what I say. You *are* young, though small chance you've had to act it these last years." She cast an appraising eye over the sleek, below-chin-length hair that curved gently into April's graceful neck. "It's a mite unusual, of course. That straight fringe in front comin' down almost to your eyebrows and curving past the top of your ears is not what I've ever seen even in old pictures, but there's no gainsaying it suits you down to the ground. Makes you look entirely different from anyone else."

"Lord Glenville says he wishes me to be a leader of fashion," April offered doubtfully.

"And why not? He won't be the first man to want to show off a good-looking young wife."

This was almost heresy! April gazed in astonishment at her old nurse, unable to credit the transformation that her marriage to a peer of the realm had apparently wrought in one whose stern moral precepts had included vanity and worldliness among the seven deadly sins. "Handsome is as handsome does" had pretty well summed up Miss Denby's attitude in raising her charges. She was about to question the source of this turnabout when a knock sounded at the hall door and her sister entered.

The excitement of the journey and their sudden change in circumstances had caught up with Diana, and, once settled in her new apartment, she had fallen victim to the lure of a comfortable bed to indulge in a restorative nap. Now she bounced into the room eager to impart the odd snippets of information concerning the inhabitants of the household dropped by Alice, the maid detailed to wait upon her. She had just launched into a secondhand account of the head housemaid's lumbago when her sister's changed appearance registered. Her pretty mouth fell open, then snapped shut while she drew breath.

"April! What have you done to yourself? Where is your hair?"

"Most of it is in the fireplace," confessed her sister with a smile. "Do you like this style?"

Diana looked rather taken aback. "I'm not sure. Your hair seems very pale and smooth, but it makes you look different, much younger," she finished almost accusingly.

"You don't look like yourself, and you've darkened your eyebrows!"

"Well, yes, a little. Adam insisted, but he said no one would notice."

"Well, I noticed!" stated Diana primly, then added a trifle grudgingly, "I don't suppose anyone who didn't know you well would guess. You won't be in the current fashion with that hairstyle, though," she pointed out, "and how can you ever wear ornaments or feathers if there isn't length enough to put up?"

"Adam doesn't wish me to wear any ornaments in my hair at all."

"*Adam* doesn't wish it? Poor April! All I can say is that *I* shall never allow a man to dictate to *me* in matters of fashion!" She tossed her bright-gold curls to emphasize her independence from masculine domination.

At which point, April, feeling thoroughly dominated, thanked Mattie for her assistance, complimented her sister on her appearance, and proceeded to lead the way to the main saloon, where they found Lord Glenville awaiting them. The soft gray cotton gown with its low-cut neckline edged with lace and long tight-fitting sleeves was quite her most becoming, April thought, and in combination with the distinctive new hairstyle produced an almost forgotten sensation of mild satisfaction with her appearance. Having been subjected earlier to a gratuitous and unflattering assessment of the picture she presented in her dowager's cap and brown traveling dress, her tattered self-esteem would have benefited greatly by any comment from her husband on the dramatic improvement. This satisfaction was denied her, however, as Lord Glenville merely wished her a good evening in a bored voice before turning his attention to his young sister-in-law. For Diana there was no lack of smoothly expressed compliments, and April was astounded and disturbed at the depth of her own disappointment. She brought herself roundly to task. Surely the insincere and practiced compliments of a man of the town had no value for her, and besides, did she not already know his opinion of herself? An adventuress, he had called her, and had all but spelled out his doubts that her youthful betrothal had been in any way a tribute to her person. He had weighed her few assets as if she were a horse he was contemplating buying.

There had been a moment this afternoon, however, when Monsieur Maurice had nearly finished cutting her hair, when she had surprised an expression in her husband's eyes very unlike the impersonal appraisal she had resented earlier. It had been a dark, brooding look full of a significance that eluded her, and in any case it had been almost instantly supplanted by a measured judgment as he had indicated to the coiffeur that he wished the tips of her ears to remain exposed to show off earrings. At that moment, recalling her Ovid, the image of Pygmalion came into her mind. With just the same intentness must the legendary sculptor have fashioned his ideal woman. In the next instant she dismissed the comparison as inapt. Pygmalion had fallen in love with his Galatea, and one had to be human to fall in love. She had already noted and been repelled by an odd inhuman detachment about the man she had married. To the Frenchman's enthusiastic praises of the results of his handiwork, Lord Glenville had merely allowed that the artist had achieved the look he sought for his wife before taking an abrupt leave of them in the manner of a man who had already wasted too much time on trivialities.

He was talking charming trivialities with Diana now as April's considering gaze assessed him with some of his own detachment. Not precisely handsome, she concluded. His features were a bit too strong and his aspect too stern for that epithet, though each individual item of his physiognomy was good taken by itself. His brow was wide and not overly high, with fine lines crossing it when he looked thoughtful. Nose and mouth were perfectly carved, but she found his jaw too square and attributed the impression of harshness largely to this and to the deep vertical lines that creased his lean cheeks from nose to mouth. She liked his eyes least. Though full of intelligence and well opened with clear dark irises and long curving lashes wasted on a man, the hardness of his habitual expression negated nature's softer design. In the few seconds that had elapsed between seeing him for the first time nine years ago and discovering his identity, she had formed a swift impression of virile good looks, but that impression had been swamped by her emotional response to his name. Studying him now, she conceded the virility, but the quality that had made it a pleasure to look at him in his youth had not endured. Except for his mouth when it wasn't clamped in a straight line, nothing of youth remained in his face. There were even a few gray hairs among the brown over his temples.

She was roused from her covert study of her husband by his voice asking a question; in fact, repeating a question, one eyebrow slightly elevated as he waited for her reply. Fortunately Diana came to her rescue with a laughing rejoinder which gave April time to recover her poise and take an interest in the conversation.

It was an uncomfortable meal for the new bride despite her sister's animated chatter. Diana kept the wheel of conversation in her determined hands, steering her course through all the prospective delights of the season that would soon be upon them, plying her new brother-in-law with eager questions about Almack's, the Opera, and the possibilities of full-dress balls and rout parties. Lord Glenville was kept busy responding to this barrage, and April found she had nothing to do but supply an occasional word of agreement. The better part of her mind was free to contemplate the ramifications of the decision she had made less than twenty-four hours before, but there was no comfort to be derived from this line of thought. She was throbbingly aware of the brooding presence of the man sitting opposite her, an enigmatic personality beneath the surface charm. As dinner progressed she pushed most of the food around on her plate, making only a pretense of eating. This was only the second meal with the man who was now her husband, but if she continued to feel his presence like a blight on her appetite she would soon expire from malnutrition.

At some point she became aware that there were

empirical grounds for avoiding the food at Glenville House. The quality of the offerings from her husband's kitchen was, to set it at the most charitable, uneven. Granted there had been only a few hours' warning that the household was to receive a new mistress, that news should not have thrown a competent chef into a flat spin. She could only guess at the kitchen disasters that could have produced at one meal rubbery chicken in an overthickened, cold Madeira sauce, burned peas, fish that had definitely gone off, and inedible pastry covering an unidentifiable filling masquerading as a tart. The earl placed a modest amount of various foods in his mouth with no discernible reaction of pleasure or disgust, mechanically chewing and swallowing indiscriminately. Once April saw Diana's quick frown at her plate as she tasted some of the chicken, but in essence her sister was too intent on her conversation to notice what she ate. April's thoughtful glance dwelled with increasing frequency on Morton, the dour butler who served the meal with the aid of a young footman.

Nearer fifty than forty, the ascetic-looking gray-haired butler was above the average in height, but he walked with a round-shouldered stoop that, combined with shadow thinness, reduced his stature a bit. Except for this characteristic, which may have been the result of some illness, his appearance in his neat livery was impeccable. There was nothing to object to in his pale, smooth-skinned face with its thinly chiseled nose and mouth and light-blue eyes except perhaps an expression in those eyes that April had discovered once or twice in their brief encounters. For the most part they were almost expressionless, but when Morton had greeted his master on their arrival this afternoon, she had noted a glitter of something that came and went so quickly that she hesitated to put a name to it. Being all but excluded from the lively interrogation of her husband that Diana had conducted throughout the meal, April had been at leisure to observe the movements of the servants. Jacob, the pleasant-faced footman, was young and a bit awkward. He looked to the quiet-footed butler for guidance in the carrying out of

his duties. Morton directed him unobtrusively, his eyes never
losing the chilling ice-blue impersonality that she found a
bit daunting when leveled on her. Once when she looked up
swiftly at hearing her husband's rare laugh, she caught a
repetition of the disturbing glitter as Morton stood motionless regarding Lord Glenville for a moment before heavy lids
descended and he deftly retrieved a dish of vegetables from
the table. The next instant the impersonal mask of the well-
trained servant was back in place, but it was April's uncomfortable impression that the butler never fully removed
his attention (his *hostile* attention?) from the earl. All in all
she found her nerves at the stretch when the final serving
platter was at last cleared and a bottle of port was set before
Lord Glenville. As she prepared to rise, Morton's colorless
voice inquired:

"Do you wish the tea tray brought to the main saloon or
some other location, my lady?"

Since no help was forthcoming from her husband, April
indicated that the saloon would be fine, and turned as the
butler pulled out her chair to confront her sister wearing a
look of almost comical dismay.

"Oh, Lord, until Morton called you 'my lady' I had forgotten this was your wedding dinner!" Diana burst out in
consternation. "You two must be wishing me at Jericho! I
won't come to the saloon tonight."

"Don't be nonsensical!" April returned sharply, her cheeks
aflame. At a warning look from the earl, she achieved a
light laugh and softened her response. "I doubt you would
find Jericho at all to your liking, my dear, and you cannot
retire at such an early hour after napping all afternoon.
Besides, I am persuaded Adam would like to hear you play
and sing."

"I should indeed," her husband replied cordially. "I'll join
you both presently." He escorted the ladies to the door the
footman had opened and bowed them out with a charming
smile for each.

Diana made another feeble protest as April headed for
the main saloon but allowed herself to be persuaded by her

determined sister. Once she had glimpsed the beautiful black-and-gold-lacquered pianoforte she was eager to try it and complied good-naturedly with her brother-in-law's requests. Although her voice was not particularly strong, it was true and had been well trained by her sister. Neither was there any necessity to apologize for her performance on the pianoforte. She knew herself to be a competent musician and suffered no qualms of shyness when invited to perform. Her audience tonight, at least the feminine half, seemed loath to release her, but after one quick cup of tea she bade her sister and the earl a determined goodnight at ten o'clock.

April, who had formed the intention of retiring with Diana, was thwarted in this resolve by the earl, who had informed her in an aside during the performance that he desired to have private speech with her before she went upstairs. As the door closed behind Diana he broke the strained silence that had existed between husband and wife the whole evening.

"I won't keep you from your bed above a moment or two." He observed the yawn she was attempting to conceal, or pretending to conceal, and smiled a trifle sardonically. "Please try to relax. You remind me of a bird ready for immediate flight. It has occurred to me that I might reduce this wariness in my presence if I were to assure you that I have no designs on your virtue."

Her eyes flew to his as to a magnet, but she appeared incapable of speech, and he went on, "You may have noticed that there is no key to the door between our rooms. I am sorry not to give it into your keeping, but I do not wish the servants to speculate about our relationship. Will you accept my word that I will not enter without an invitation?"

Smoky eyes full of relief tinged with curiosity searched his. "Yes, of course. Are you, that is . . . do you—*no*, never mind—" She broke off, flushing hotly, and jumped to her feet to wish him an abrupt goodnight, but he raised a hand to detain her. His expression was wry.

"If all that stammering means that you are wondering

whether I prefer young boys, the answer is no; nor am I a monk, but I have never found it necessary to force myself upon unwilling females, and it is especially unlikely in your case. Do I make myself clear?"

"Very clear. Goodnight, my lord." Her voice was almost strangled by embarrassment and she sought release, but he arrested her flight once more.

"Whoa! There is one more item on the agenda before we adjourn this delightful meeting. I wish to present you to my mother tomorrow morning, but we must call at Mélisande's first. This afternoon I sent your measurements to her workroom so they might begin making up a dress and pelisse for you immediately. Please be ready to leave by nine so Mélisande can fit you and they can finish the outfit while you set about choosing fabrics and designs for the most pressing items of your new wardrobe. We shall not send out any 'at home' cards until these initial requirements have been met."

April was staring at him in disbelief. "My measurements!" she echoed, going right to the heart of the matter. "How could you know my measurements?"

"I asked Mattie, of course," he replied coolly. "What is there in that to upset you?"

Her voice outdid his in coolness. "You must pardon my missishness, my lord—I mean, *Adam*—but I am as yet unused to the intimacies of marriage. I shall study to do better in future."

"Thank you," he said gravely, and this time she did flee before he could subject her to any additional shocking revelations.

The earl remained where he was seated, staring at the closed door, his face unreadable, until Morton came in to remove the tea tray.

"Will there by anything else, my lord?"

"No, thank you, Morton. Send the servants to bed, and go yourself after you lock up the house."

"Very good, my lord. I'll bid you goodnight."

The earl continued to sit unmoving for some little while

longer, his gaze fixed in space, a slight frown furrowing his brow. Eventually he emerged from his reverie and, after checking the condition of the fire and extinguishing the candles, left the room. He took up the lamp in the hall and entered his bedchamber, only to reappear five minutes later wearing a greatcoat and carrying a black beaver. In the entrance hall he took a large key from the drawer in a console table and proceeded to unlock the front door.

Once out on the street, he pocketed the key and hauled on his gloves before setting off at a brisk pace for Oxford Street, where he hailed a passing hackney cab. A few minutes drive brought him to Tavistock Street. After paying off the jarvey, he mounted the steps to the entrance door of a slim house and let himself in, using another key he produced from a pocket in his coat.

Chapter Five

Upstairs in a surprisingly luxurious boudoir for what was from its exterior a modest house, sat a woman, comfortably established on a pink satin daybed, a mass of rose-colored wool in her lap. Evidently she had been reading earlier, for a book resposed on a table beside her that also held a good working lamp. From time to time her attention wandered from the slipper she was knitting and her eyes would roam aimlessly about the good-sized apartment, coming to rest with a wistful expression on a door in the wall opposite. They did so now, and her hands stilled in her lap for a moment before she sighed deeply, soundlessly, and resumed her task.

To a disinterested observer the woman thus occupied matched the elegant, slightly overdone furnishings of the room, which featured quantities of the same bright-pink fabric at the windows, as a skirt for the dressing table, and for elaborate bed draperies and covering. She was not by any means in the first blush of youth but was an exceedingly handsome creature in the full flower of her beauty. Thick black hair crowned her head, caught in a knot on top and allowed to frame her face in carefully careless ringlets. Her eyes, which she again focused on the door, were large and a deep velvety brown, enchanced by the thick black curling lashes and set in a complexion of pink-and-white smoothness. If a skillfull use of cosmetics had heightened the perfection of her complexion, this fact did nothing to negate nature's own benevolence in endowing the lady with abundant gifts. Her features were regular and, despite the high coloring, contrived to arrange themselves in a serene order, giving her face something of the look of a calm madonna. Her figure, on the other hand, was most voluptuously rounded and would never go unnoticed whatever the lady wore. In the rich red velvet dressing gown cascading over the pink upholstery of the day bed, she had achieved a spectacular background for her brunette beauty. Her hands and feet were small and plump, the former adorned with several sparkling rings that flashed as her fingers moved among the wool, the latter encased in red velvet slippers trimmed in brilliants and boasting absurdly high heels.

She teetered on those heels now as she rose with an abrupt movement that was alien to the image she presented of indolent sensuality. The unfinished slipper and rosy wool slid unnoticed to the floor. Her alert ears had caught a sound on the stairs, and she strained now to confirm her hopes, her hands clasped together in front of her ample bosom, her dark eyes fixed on a miniature of the Earl of Glenville which held pride of place on the bedside table. It had been almost a fortnight since he had last visited her, and, as always when he was away, the time had passed with a dreadful crawling slowness. An eager smile illuminated her lovely face as she recognized the tread, and she ran to the door (awkwardly on those heels) and flung it open.

"I did not think to see you back for another day or two, my lord. What a delightful surprise!" Her voice was something of a surprise, its quality slightly nasal and revealing remnants of a country accent which was out of character with its owner's elegant and costly appearance. Her face was alight with happy welcome as she raised it unself-consciously to the man, who halted near her to struggle out of one glove.

"Hallo, Molly." He smiled and took her chin in his ungloved fingers before kissing the upturned lips briefly. "How are you?"

As she responded to this greeting, he strolled over to the daybed and picked up the fallen evidence of her previous activity, tossing the yarn back onto the pink cushions. He glanced from the book on the table to the woman watching him and a look of amusement crept into his eyes. "Have you been reading Donne's poetry? How do you find it?"

"I'm afraid I find much of it beyond my comprehension, my lord," she confessed, then added with a desire to please, "But it does sound lovely read aloud, and I finished that last novel you brought me, *Sense and Sensibility*. I enjoyed that. Of course it wasn't very exciting, but it was a very good picture of the way respectable people live." Her earnest words, carefully enunciated to suppress a Suffolk accent, deepened the look of amusement on the earl's face.

"Respectability is a fetish with you, Molly, my sweet," he said with careless good humor. "At heart you are the most respectable creature I know. You should be married with a brood of children to keep you too busy to read, and much too busy to eat chocolates at all hours." He grinned, glancing at the open box on the table.

Molly looked a little guilty for an instant at the mention of chocolates, then returned his smile as she came forward to help him off with his coat. "It wasn't respectability I was headed for when you came into my life seven years ago, my lord," she replied quietly. "You saved my life and Charlotte's too, and I've no complaint to make about my lot. I'd lost my chance for a respectable marriage before she was born, but, thanks to you, Charlotte will have hers." She moved behind him to take his coat as he shrugged out of it.

"I've something to tell you, Molly. I was married myself this morning."

No sound escaped the lips of the woman behind him at this news, but she closed her eyes tightly and willed herself not to faint. Her hands clutched the collar of his coat with a deathgrip, but she was momentarily incapable of further movement. When the silence had continued for another second or two, the earl turned with one arm still in his coat and looked at her questioningly.

"Did you hear what I said, Molly?"

She tried twice before she could produce a voice. "I . . . yes, my lord."

"Well?"

She looked at him fleetingly, then dropped her eyes and remained silent as she accepted the coat and folded it carefully over her arm, all of her attention concentrated on the performance of this simple task.

"Have you nothing to say, no comment to offer?" he persisted.

"I . . . this is a great . . . surprise. I was not aware that you thought of marriage." Her voice was curiously lifeless, but he replied to the words only.

"I hadn't until yesterday."

Molly in turn seemed unaware of the emotion behind the words as she asked hesitantly, "Are you . . . very much in love?"

"*Lord, no!*" He read the puzzlement in her eyes and softened his response. "I'd scarcely be here tonight if I were in love with my wife, would I? There were sufficient reasons for the marriage, but love wasn't among them."

"Is she very young and beautiful?" The question was put with some timidity.

"No, she's not much younger than you. How old are you, Molly?"

"Almost one and thirty."

"April is twenty-six or seven, I believe."

"That is her name, April?"

"Yes."

"It's unusual but pretty." She avoided his glance as she aimlessly smoothed the collar of the greatcoat enfolded in her arms. "Is she as pretty as her name?" The question seemed forced out of her against her will, but silence was something to be avoided at all costs while she wondered if she dared voice her real concern.

He considered the question. "Pretty? Not really, but she has a certain appeal that is more intriguing than mere prettiness."

Molly had turned away from him during this explanation while she laid the coat on the chaise with elaborate care. Now, with her back to him, she took a deep breath and plunged, "Does this mean that you won't be coming here anymore?"

"Of course not, Molly!" He seized her shoulders and turned her gently to face him. "Is that what's bothering you? You know that I shall always take care of you and Charlotte, don't you? Don't you?" he repeated as her head remained bent. "Look at me, Molly!"

She obeyed, searching his face for something but unsure of whether she had found it.

"You need never fear that I'll fail to provide for you and Charlotte, Molly, no matter what happens," he promised in a gentle tone. "Do you believe me?"

She nodded, her eyes clinging to his.

"That's better." He released her shoulders after giving them a mock shake and stepped back to sit on the bed. "How is Charlotte? Have you heard from her lately?"

"I received a letter last week," she said with the first sign of animation on her lovely face since Lord Glenville had made his announcement. "She has a new dearest friend— this is the fourth since the term began—and she has taken the new dancing master in dislike, although she doesn't make it clear why this should be so."

The earl grinned. "That's to be preferred to having her take an unaccountable liking to him. Perhaps at twelve she's too young for that, though!" His coat was off and he was trying to remove the studs from his shirt as he spoke. After a short unavailing struggle he directed a plaintive plea to the woman watching him silently. "Molly, I need help."

Swiftly, wordlessly, she went to his assistance.

Hours later she heard him making preparations to leave as he dressed by the light of a single candle. Very rarely would he stay the night, and this time she experienced to an intolerably heightened degree the desolation that his leaving always brought sweeping over her in a tidal wave. She moved quietly in the bed, her hungry eyes following his every move, but she did not speak, having learned long since that he disliked conversation at this point. In a few minutes the door closed softly behind him and she fell back on the pillows, the scent of the candle he had just blown out filling her nostrils in the deepened darkness. Despair penetrated more deeply into her soul, spreading as the odor from the candle but not destined to be equally short-lived. There had been no joy in their lovemaking tonight, at least not for her. Despite the earl's reassurances that he would always take care of her, the existence of his wife meant the death knell to all her hopes, unadmitted even to herself until now. Thank heavens she had had the strength not to betray the agony that his announcement had dealt her! The earl had attributed her reaction to the fear, which would have been reasonable had she not known him so thoroughly, that his marriage would mean the withdrawal of his monetary support. Knowing full well what manner of man it was that she loved, this worry had not so much as crossed her mind.

She moved restlessly on the large, now cold bed, trying to force final acceptance of what she had always known. Members of the gentry didn't marry farmers' daughters, even farmers' daughters without illegitimate children. She had never expected, never really hoped for marriage, she insisted to herself. In the beginning when the earl offered her a *carte blanche* she had accepted out of a desire to see the end of the perilous existence she had led since the man who had seduced her and eloped with her had finally deserted her and their baby daughter. At three and twenty she had still been able to trade on her striking beauty to support herself and Charlotte, but the next step would have been the streets, and fear of this end enabled her to bear the shame of several short-lived liaisons with young men of good family who had provided generously while their passion for her charms endured. The earl had never pretended to love her —indeed, they had met just after his serious courtship of a well-known society beauty had ended with the clear-sighted lady marrying for a title and fortune just weeks before the earl had come into a title and fortune of his own. He proposed to keep Molly in comfort in return for exclusive rights to use her for his pleasure, and she had been relieved and happy to accept an arrangement that allowed her to provide an outwardly normal life for her daughter. When Charlotte became old enough for boarding school he made all the arrangements, achieving an acceptance at a prestigious institution whose directors would have shunned Charlotte had they known the truth about her background.

Looking back through the years, Molly could not discover when gratitude had become love. Most probably it had been a gradual evolution, but at this distance it seemed she had loved him with single-minded intensity ever since first clapping eyes on him. Her initial experience with a man had cured her of the error of self-deception, however, and she had never permitted herself the false comfort of believing the earl returned her feelings. True, she hoped continually, fool that she was, for signs of a deepening attachment on his part, searching for some new meaning behind each gift he made her and the ever present concern he displayed for her welfare. There was affection, certainly, and an ease born of familiarity, but never anything that could nourish her starving soul. In fact, on isolated occasions in the recent past she had wondered with a sinking heart if he actually found the weight of her undeclared but obvious emotion becoming something of a burden to him. She moved her head in torment on the pillow. It was not beyond her comprehension that love unsought and unreturned might tend to irritate a man of decent sensibilities, who would then feel guilty and resentful. She tried never to overstep the boundaries he had set for their relationship, instinctively responding to what she perceived as his attitude upon any specific occasion. Even tonight she had set aside her shock and misery to accommodate his mood, which had turned playful once he had reassured her of her future security.

Reassurance! What a bitter taste the word had on her lips! He might not love his wife—indeed, she believed him when he said this; he might never grow to love this April, but it was imperative that she accept the fact that he had had ample time and opportunity to fall in love with herself without doing so. The most she could hope for was a continuation of their liaison for some while longer. Truth was a bitter medicine and her reluctance to swallow it extreme. However, she had the rest of the long lonely night to begin the process. Certainly sleep was an unattainable goal this unhappy night.

After a most convincing reassurance of his lack of interest from her husband's own lips, April enjoyed an excellent night's sleep on the most comfortable bed she had encountered in many years. The next morning she was ready for their outing before the time set by the earl but was delayed by her sister, whose vocal disappointment at not being included in this first shopping expedition had to be tactfully dealt with. By the time Diana had been cajoled into a better humor by a promise to take her out shopping that very afternoon if the earl had no objection, so that she reconsidered her avowed intention of sending her breakfast tray back to the kitchen untouched, it was ten minutes past the hour. As April ran down the main stairs still tying the ribbons on her hat, the earl appeared at the foot of the staircase wearing an unmistakable air of impatience. The sight of his forbidding expression banished what little anticipation of pleasure in this rare treat had remained after the scene just enacted with Diana.

She greeted him soberly, offering an unadorned apology for her tardiness, which he accepted with a courtesy she knew was due solely to the presence in the hall at that moment of Jacob, the footman, who opened the door for them. He assisted his wife into the carriage in an unamiable silence that remained unbroken until they arrived at their destination. By this time April had overcome her lowness of spirits by allowing full rein to a silent but grim determination to show the man at her side just how little importance she attached to his boorish manners. Consequently it was a composed young woman whose proud carriage belied her *démodé* attire who entered the premises of the renowned modiste on the arm of her husband.

Fortunately for the picture of newly wedded bliss the earl

intended to present to this world, the events of the next two
hours were productive of enough satisfaction to improve the
tempers of both parties to this audacious deception. They
were received with an eagerness bordering on servility by
Mélisande herself, a buxom, florid blonde of uncertain age
and dubious French accent who soon won April's confidence
by her businesslike efficiency and undoubted good taste. It
was a decidedly modish young woman who finally emerged
wearing an elegant carriage dress of softest mauve wool,
covered by a matching pelisse sumptuously trimmed in
ermine. The dashing high-crowned hat of ermine now
setting off her silvery hair to perfection had been delivered
along with two others for her consideration from a well-
known shop whose canny proprietress had been only too
happy to accommodate the new Countess of Glenville as a
beginning of what she confidently expected to be a mutually
beneficial relationship. Clothilde herself had stripped the
sage-green satin ribbons and feathered trim from the most
becoming hat, substituting a single curled ostrich plume
dyed a deeper shade of mauve which caressed one cheek
from a position on the underside of the curving brim. This
innovation came about at the suggestion of the earl, who
had watched critically as each hat had been tried on by his
wife. The result had been greeted with instant rapture by
Clothilde, who envisioned the style becoming all the rage
once Lady Glenville had been seen abroad in it, and with
more moderately expressed approval by Mélisande, who
agreed the hat became her client and complemented the
pelisse, which was one of her own designs. The milliner then
returned to her own shop full of creative ideas guaranteed to
elicit the continued patronage of Lady Glenville.

The earl, with no more explanation than a promise to be
back shortly, had himself left the modiste's establishment for
almost three quarters of an hour while the final sewing of
the mauve costume was being accomplished in record time
by four of Mélisande's stitchers in her workroom at the back
of the premises. He had left his wife to look over styles and

fabrics being presented for her approval by the designer. Considering Adam's insistence only yesterday that he would guide her choice, April was surprised to see him absent himself at this point but delighted in exercising her own judgment without fear of contradiction. She spent an enjoyable half hour browsing through Mélisande's sketches and admiring fabric samples, only to find upon the earl's return that he had every intention of reviewing her decisions. To her chagrin he did reject several of her choices of fabrics, and she was not best pleased to witness the dressmaker's immediate about-face when the rejected samples had been largely accepted by April at her instigation in the first place. However, she swallowed her spleen and permitted herself to be overruled with a good grace, secretly rather gratified at the extent of the earl's involvement with the dressing of his wife. When he finally handed her up into the carriage after a cordial leave-taking from the designer, she tried to thank him for his generosity and assistance. Her shy expression of gratitude was brushed aside with a wounding brusqueness that deprived her of further speech.

She had entered the carriage more confident of her attractiveness than ever before in her life, but thanks to the earl's manifest disinterest now that there was no audience, her satisfaction was destined to be ephemeral. Her expanding spirit retreated to its former humility. How foolish she had been to allow herself to be taken in by Adam's performance as a devoted husband before the modiste and hatmaker. It had simply been an effective piece of acting. The knowledge of her new attractiveness in the stylish outfit had led her to credit him with an opinion he had already made it clear he did not hold of her desirability. Well, now she knew and would not again make the mistake of reading anything personal into his public performance of doting husband. Actually, life was much less complicated this way; the last thing she wanted was devotion from the man she had hated for nine years! It was a bit lowering to discover in herself a childish craving for admiration, a weakness she'd root out from this moment on. Lest he should think she was sulking over his lack of interest she roused herself to inquire pleasantly:

"What time is your mother expecting us to call, Adam? I trust we shall not keep her waiting."

The earl lifted one eyebrow. "She is not expecting us at all. What gave you to think that she might be?"

April gazed at him blankly. "Why I . . . naturally I assumed you had sent a message to her yesterday acquainting her with the fact of your marriage." Her voice tailed off as she continued to study her husband's unrevealing countenance.

"Why should you assume anything of this nature?"

"You would not wish your mother to learn of your marriage from another source, surely? You said as much to that awful man at the inn."

"Allerton is scarcely likely to call upon my mother to acquaint her with the news," he replied carelessly. "The latest crim. cons. are more in his style."

April assimilated this. "Then . . . then your mother will have no inkling of the truth when we arrive?"

"No. Why should she?"

"You . . . you plan to simply produce a daughter-in-law out of thin air, as it were?" Her voice held a rising note of panic and some of her color had faded.

"My mother's reaction need not concern you. You will not be much in her society. We meet but seldom. By the way, she is married again; she is Lady Ellsmere now, not Mrs. Harding."

April did not know what to make of the curious note in her husband's voice. She was shaken by the knowledge that he had not bothered to inform his parent of his marriage before confronting her with a daughter-in-law. She could sense his unwillingness to discuss his relationship with his mother, so she subsided, stifling her curiosity but unable to suppress her agitation at the thought of the awkward meeting to come.

After a moment's uneasy silence Adam said casually, "I

visited Rundell and Bridge while you were choosing gowns this morning. I'd like you to wear this."

April raised her eyes to his extended hand thrust in front of her nose. Held between thumb and index finger was a ring that featured a large diamond surrounded by a circle of smaller ones. Her breath caught in a gasp of admiration, but she made no move to take the glittering object as she stared into his impassive countenance. He tapped her mauve kid glove with the fingers holding the ring, and she began to pull it off slowly with a reluctance she barely understood. When her glove was removed he slipped the ring on her finger, noting with satisfaction that the jeweler had guessed correctly as to size. She kept her eyes fixed on the sparkling stones, but he didn't seem to expect any thanks from her; in fact, as she opened her lips he forestalled her by slipping a hand into an inner pocket of his coat.

"I also selected these to be worn with this outfit."

"These" turned out to be a pair of amethyst earrings in a delicate gold filigree setting. A half hour ago April would have been thrilled with something so exquisite to complement her lovely new costume, but her husband's coldness on entering the carriage had completely erased her pleasure in her appearance. "Thank you," she said politely. "They are lovely."

"Put them on," he ordered curtly.

She toyed with the idea of refusing so peremptory a request, but one covert glance at his firm jaw decided her against a course of action guaranteed further to increase the tension in the air. Wordlessly she untied the satin ribbons of the ermine hat, took it off, and placed it carefully on the matching muff reposing on her lap. She removed the gloves and accepted first one and then the other earring, which she inserted into the lobes of her ears under his steady gaze. She took the bonnet in both hands, but before she could complete the motion, Adam took her chin in his fingers. He tilted it upward, then from side to side to study the effect of the jewels. April kept her eyes lowered, unconsciously affording her husband an excellent view of the luxuriant thickness of her lashes. After a second she found herself released, and she proceeded to replace the hat and pull on her gloves. No words had been exchanged during this operation, and neither ventured any further remarks during the rest of the short ride.

Adam, sitting relaxed in his corner, was congratulating himself on his accurate analysis of his bride's potentialities. She had no power to attract him, but it was quite intellectually satisfying to see how really lovely she was when her assets were emphasized. At this moment she appeared scarcely older than her sister in his eyes. He found he was looking forward to presenting this glowing girl to his mother. He was going to enjoy the coming interview.

In her corner, April was a far cry from sharing her husband's complaisance. She had been horrified by the discovery that her existence was not yet known to Lady Ellsmere, and, though unconfirmed in words, there persisted a niggling little suspicion that Adam was seriously estranged from his remaining parent. Instinctively she knew that her sartorial transformation was meant for Lady Ellsmere's benefit and could only hope that Adam felt she did him credit. Nothing in his manner or words told her whether the results were satisfactory, however, so her anxiety over the imminent meeting increased as they drew nearer the Ellsmere residence. When the carriage halted she barely glanced at the impressive facade as her husband hustled her up the shallow steps to evade the drizzle that had begun to permeate the atmosphere.

The somewhat intimidating aspect of the silver-haired individual who appeared at the entrance altered substantially when he recognized the man on the doorstep, and he hastened to assure Lord Glenville that although Lady Ellsmere was not receiving this morning this prohibition did not of course include her son. The earl acknowledged this favor with a tiny smile. "Thank you, Foulting."

He did not attempt to gratify the butler's curiosity as to the identity of his companion, a curiosity that could only be guessed at, since Foulting permitted himself merely one lambent flick at April from under heavy-lidded dark eyes before leading the way up a singularly beautiful carpeted, curved, and carved staircase of some rich dark wood, polished and gleaming. At any other time she would have been eager to inspect the paintings in massive gold frames that lined the wall along their ascent, but in her present state of anxious anticipation she did no more than dimly record their existence in passing.

They were ushered into an unoccupied saloon and left with a promise that her ladyship would join them presently. The earl waited until his wife had tentatively seated herself on the edge of the nearest chair before taking a chair a few feet away. Slanting a glance at him from under her lashes, April was vaguely annoyed at his seeming lack of any emotion or tension when she was uncomfortably aware of an increased heart rate and a clamminess in her palms beneath their thin covering of kid. She could not recall ever before anticipating an introduction with such dread, but then, never before had she been called upon to sustain an introduction to the mother of a man she had forced to marry her! Adam was determined to conceal the truth from everyone, but how could a mother fail to guess after one look at her son's face?

In an effort to distract her mind from this unprofitable line of thought, she forced herself to take stock of their surroundings. They had been shown into a large well-proportioned apartment expensively furnished by someone with lavish tastes, judging by the sumptuous fabrics at the windows and on the upholstered pieces and the quantity of valuable ornaments disposed about the room. Even to April's inexpert eye the candelabra illuminating the glorious Venetian mirror over the fireplace were of gold and beautifully scrolled. On either side of the double entrance doors stood matching glass-fronted cabinets of rosewood containing a collection of china and porcelain figurines that might have come from Germany. She found most of them excessively convoluted and ornate, but though not to her personal taste, there was no denying their value. The outsize carpet beneath her feet was reminiscent of a small one from China that had been her mother's pride. Pale blue, pink, green, and gold formed an intriguing design against a cream-colored background. It was difficult to tear her eyes away from its serene beauty, but everywhere in the room beautiful items called out for attention, from the French ornamental clock on the mantel to a choice gold filigree pomander ball on the table beside her which her fingers itched to examine more closely. Strangely enough, despite the lovely decor and the number of choice objects, the atmosphere of the room was a trifle oppressive. It screamed of wealth carefully spent and cried out for admiration of its creator's artistic taste, but April would have exchanged a bit of the artistic perfection for some sensation of warmth. If anything could be considered too perfect, this room achieved the distinction. She glanced again at her husband, but any comments she might have ventured were frozen on her tongue by the frigidity of his aspect.

Just then the doors opened, though for an instant April was so confounded by the animation that leaped into Adam's face that she almost missed the entrance of her mother-in-law. Dragging fascinated eyes from her husband's countenance, she focused somewhat reluctantly on the woman poised between the two doors, a hand on each, while she smiled at them, fully aware, April was instantly persuaded, of the graceful picture she presented in her blue silk morning dress.

Two thoughts made immediate impact on April's mind while she rose to her feet—that here was the embodiment and creator of the beautiful room and, more prosaically, that Lady Ellsmere did not appear nearly old enough to be Adam's mother. She didn't know his age, but he looked to be deep in his thirties. Perforce, this slim woman of erect and graceful carriage with no trace of gray in her rich brown hair was well over fifty. It was scarcely to be credited visually, but her laughing voice somewhat distorted the illusion of youth. It was deep and assured and contained a hint of sly malice.

"My dear Adam, how do you do? Foulting informed me my son awaited *with a female companion*. I nearly accused him of imbibing the burgundy behind my back, but I see that he spoke no less than the truth." A gleaming white-toothed smile was produced to indicate her words were mere funning.

April's bemused attention was fixed on the woman who addressed herself to her son at the same time she assessed his companion with a lightning-quick female inventory that missed nothing from the curling ostrich plume on her hat to the tips of her mauve kid half boots. She realized with sudden unaccountable relief that her hand was being held in a comforting clasp as Adam drew her closer to his side. He met his mother's smile with one of his own and said gently:

"Mother, I'd like to present my companion to you. This is my wife, April."

Lady Ellsmere's smile solidified for an instant before disappearing completely. "*Wife!* You've married and I not there? When? How?" The assured tones threatened to escalate into stridency.

It seemed to April's hectic imagination that the others were unaware of her presence for the moment, that a duel was being waged between two pairs of dark-gray eyes, and then her husband spoke even more gently than before.

"Don't upset yourself, ma'am. We were married very quietly, but except for one other, you are the first to wish us happy."

Lady Ellsmere strove with herself to regain control of the situation, though she still could not bring herself to look at her daughter-in-law. She gestured toward the settee and chairs grouped behind them. "Shall we sit?"

When April and Adam were seated on the blue settee facing their hostess across a mahogany tea table, she disposed herself gracefully in a giltwood chair covered in straw-colored satin. After a deliberate survey of her son's wife, she conceded coolly, "At least she is exquisitely dressed and looks a lady, though not quite in your style, I would have judged."

"And just what, in your informed opinion, is my style?" inquired Adam with interest, not at all put out at the tone of his wife's reception by his mother.

"Ripe and luscious, I'd have said," his parent countered quickly, and turned to find a pair of light eyes, slightly violet-tinged, fixed on her face with unwavering intensity. "Perhaps after all she is not so young and unfledged as she appears at first sight," Lady Ellsmere remarked after sustaining that regard for a further few seconds. "Who is she?"

Deciding she had sat mumchance long enough while these two antagonists waged war over her corpse, April spoke up clearly. "Both my parents have been dead for some years, Lady Ellsmere. My father was Sir Charles Wendover, and my mother's family—"

"Wendover!" Lady Ellsmere interrupted her daughter-in-law and rounded on her son. "Adam, have you taken leave of your senses? Haven't you suffered enough at the hands of that feckless family? And not a penny to bless herself with, I'll wager! When I recollect some of the lovely and eligible girls I have introduced to your notice in the last half-dozen years I vow and declare you must be the most perverse creature in nature!" Her angry words trailed off as she caught her son's sardonic regard, and red coins stained her cheeks. She avoided the younger woman's eyes.

"May I suggest, ma'am, that you essay to take comfort in the knowledge that no other girl in the kingdom, no matter how eligible or beautiful, could have prompted me to marriage save April."

April caught her breath and lowered her glance to hide the anger that surged up in her heart. Oddly enough, she was less upset by the insulting comments bordering on the vulgar made by Lady Ellsmere than by the truthful words so softly spoken and so misleading from the lips of her husband. Feeling her hand seized, she raised her eyes to her mother-in-law's now smiling face.

"Please believe, my dear April, that there was nothing personal in my earlier remarks. They were entirely prompted by concern for my son's future. Naturally I am prepared to welcome Adam's wife into the family." The sound of the opening door spared April from the necessity of formulating any civil lies as her hostess's attention was drawn to the stolid figure of the butler approaching with a silver tray upon which rested a bottle and several glasses. "Ah, here is Foulting with some Madeira. Shall I ask him to bring champagne instead? Yes, of course we must drink to your happiness in champagne."

Adam demurred that Madeira was as acceptable as champagne for pledging their happiness, but Lady Ellsmere, evidently determined to atone for her previous lack of enthusiasm, insisted that nothing but champagne would do, and they had perforce to await the arrival of this token. In the hiatus she subjected her daughter-in-law to a barrage of questions concerning her background and her plans for the upcoming season. For the most part Adam answered before his bride could speak, but April upheld her end of the conversation with grave courtesy when she could edge in a word. When the champagne arrived she accepted her glass and went through the motions of sipping it but put the glass on the mahogany tea table immediately afterward, and there it remained for the duration of their call. She owed it to her breeding to be polite, but nowhere was it written that one must drink with enemies, and however harsh the term, she felt it was the *mot juste* to describe her companions at that moment. As for Lady Ellsmere's earlier complaint, she did not take it as meant for her personally, although it had been made painfully obvious that his mother had wished and actively worked for a more brilliant match for Adam. April had no way of learning the root and reason for the antagonism that simmered between mother and son, but she was shocked, chilled, and oppressed by its existence.

It was a palpable relief to be able to quit the beautiful soulless room when Adam at last stood up to make their adieux. It did not escape April's notice that her husband had been strangely ambiguous about any future social plans in conjunction with Lady Ellsmere, politely brushing aside a tentative suggestion on his mother's part that she host a dinner party to welcome April to London. Since her own reaction to her slightly overpowering mother-in-law had not been without a reciprocal touch of the hostility that seemed to simmer just below the surface cordiality, she was glad to follow Adam's lead, and they took their leave without committing themselves to any definite engagement.

The earl was just handing his thoughtful-looking wife up into the carriage when a jovial masculine voice hailed him.

"I say, Adam, I did not look to see you in town again so soon. Seems to me I recall Freddy's saying you weren't due back for another day or two yet, but he was more than half foxed at the time. How are you?"

"Good morning, Damien."

A tug at her elbow caused April to pause in her ascent, and she turned to inspect the man smiling up at Adam.

He was well worth inspecting. A few years younger than the earl, he was almost as tall but less broadly built, and appeared slim and straight in a drab overcoat featuring nearly as many shoulder capes as a coachman's. Waved and pomaded golden locks gleamed beneath his hat, and when he turned to include April in his regard she was almost stunned by the perfection of his chiseled features. In the instant before her husband's voice interrupted her assessment it flashed through her mind that he could be a Greek statue come to life.

"April, this Jack O'Dandy is my cousin, Damien Harding. Damien, may I present my wife?"

"Your *wife!*" Mr. Harding was facing April with his hat raised. For a split second he froze in incredulity and a look flashed into his eyes that nearly caused her to step backward instinctively, but before she could withdraw the hand she had extended, Mr. Harding was smiling again as he saluted her fingers with consummate charm.

"This is indeed a great pleasure, Lady Glenville, but how like Adam to spring a wife on the *ton* with no warning! You will have to suffer all the indignity of being a nine days' wonder before you will be allowed to take your rightful place as one of society's loveliest ornaments. Heartiest congratulation, coz," he added, turning to shake Adam's hand for the second time, his grin wide and knowing. "You have proved once again that you still have the best eye for beauty of any of 'em. Your April is the loveliest creature to appear on the London scene in years."

April accorded this extravagant compliment a cool little smile that matched the coolness of her rainwater eyes. She had no illusions about her nonexistent pretensions to beauty despite the recent transformation Adam had wrought in her appearance. This man was deliberately flattering her—trying perhaps to erase from her memory the thunderstruck fury that he had been unable to mask in the instant of learning her identity? Beneath an unrevealing exterior her mind was a whirling mass of confused impressions and·unanswered questions. Dimly, as on the edge of her awareness, she heard Adam acknowledge his cousin's felicitations and inquire into his presence at this particular spot.

Mr. Harding laughed and gestured with a book he had shoved under his arm. "I happened to meet Lady Ellsmere at Devonshire House last night. I don't quite recall how it came up, but we were trying to remember who wrote those old lines about proving all the pleasures."

" 'Come live with me and be my love, and we will all the pleasures prove,' " Adam quoted softly.

"That's the one! Oh, the advantages of a classical education!" grinned Mr. Harding. "Lady Ellsmere would have it that it was one of Jonson's poems, but I found it in this book this morning. It was John Donne!"

"But surely—Marlowe!" April's involuntary exclamation brought the eyes of the two men to her flushed cheeks. "I do beg your pardon," she hastened to apologize. "You are quite correct, sir, that Donne uses a similar beginning to one of his poems."

"Yes, but I've never been able to make up my mind whether he was more interested in the joys of seduction or the trials of fishing!" Adam laughed at his cousin's crestfallen expression. "Try again, Damien. It's beginning to rain, my dear. We'd best be going. Tell Freddy we'll be sending out 'at home' cards shortly."

Once again the earl assisted his bride into the carriage, and followed her after a casual wave to the man who stood watching the carriage out of sight with no vestige remaining of the charming smile he had preserved during the accidental encounter. It was several minutes later that Mr. Harding roused himself from a grim contemplation of the empty street and resumed a pleasant expression as he approached Lady Ellsmere's residence a second time.

Chapter Six

Inside the carriage, April sat pressed into her corner, her gloved hands clasped tightly together in her lap. Her features were frozen in blankness, a slight pucker between her brows the only indication that her mind was not equally blank. At this moment in time she could only wish passionately that that suddenly desirable state of nullity could be achieved. In the scant twenty-four hours of her marriage she had suffered an avalanche of impressions and emotions which left her confused, faintly belligerent, and more than a little disturbed by an inexplicable sense of foreboding. No, foreboding was too strong a word, but she was uneasy in her mind in a way not entirely explained by the natural consequences of a rash act. Setting aside her own initial reactions to a new position in life, a new dwelling, and a number of strangers who would become part of her new life, even setting aside the more vital question of her as yet undifferentiated but predictably difficult relationship with the man who was her husband, she was experiencing a tickling, teasing kind of unease, a general miasma of ill will. Slanting a glance at Adam from the corner of her eye, she could only marvel at his imperturbability.

He appeared in fact to be rather pleased with the results of their morning activities. Although it had been a brief encounter just now, she sensed that he bore his cousin a careless affection and enjoyed his company. She had received the exact opposite impression from the longer interview with Adam's mother. The disturbing factor was not so

much the lack of natural feeling between them — she was not
so naive as to believe that all families were bound as tightly
by the ties of affection as her own had been — but the unaccountable presence of a perverse pleasure she glimpsed in
Adam and to a lesser degree in his mother at causing discomfort to the other. Adam had enjoyed every moment of
the uncomfortable confrontation with Lady Ellsmere. For
some reason it had given him satisfaction to produce a bride
who would not be to her liking.

Disturbing though this conclusion was and prophetic of
unpleasurable future relations with her mother-in-law, it
was not the most destructive element to her peace of mind.
April closed her eyes, the better to bring two faces before her
mind's eye, two faces innocuous in themselves under
ordinary circumstances but remarkable for the similarity of
their fleeting expressions of acute dislike, if not actual
hatred. In her first two days in London she had discovered
that her husband's butler disliked his master intensely and
that her husband's cousin had conceived of an instantaneous
and equally strong disaffection for herself. What was more,
both of these individuals wished to conceal their feelings.
The unreasonable quality of the situation struck her
forcibly. She had not been in a position to observe Lord
Glenville as master of his establishment for long, but she
would have said that he was not much interested in the inner
workings of his household and was inclined to be too lenient
rather than the other extreme in his dealings with his staff.
Surely a difficult master would not have calmly accepted the
poor meal set before them the previous evening. Of course,
there could exist a more personal reason for Morton's
animosity, but why should a well-trained servant continue to
work for an employer for whom he cherished a personal
animus? It made no sense, nor did the existence of Mr.
Damien Harding's instant dislike of herself, but it had
spewed from his eyes when Adam had presented her as his
wife.

April sat very still, aware all at once of the importance of
a thought as yet unarticulated while she groped for it. *Not*

myself; it isn't April Wendover he hates but the *wife* of his cousin! She turned abruptly to her husband to find his considering gaze on her face.

"How . . . how nearly related are you and Mr. Damien Harding, Adam?"

A look of faint surprise crossed his face. "Damien's father was my father's youngest brother. He is my first cousin."

"I see. Is he next in line for the title?"

"No, his brother Freddy is my heir. Why do you ask?"

"No particular reason. It is simply that I know so little of the family. Have you other relatives that I shall be meeting?" April scarcely listened to Adam's description of various female cousins who resided in London; she was more intent on her own heartbeat, which slowed and settled down from the hammering that had begun at a ridiculous suspicion that had flashed into her mind. She relaxed perceptibly. Two people stood between Mr. Harding and the title! And yet she knew beyond doubt that the fact of her existence had come as an earthshaking shock to her husband's cousin, and she was strangely grateful that she had not missed his unguarded reaction, so quickly dissimulated and smothered in obvious gallantry.

Adam was speaking to her. He slewed his powerful body around better to enable him to study her countenance when he had to repeat his question.

"What did you think of my mother?"

"I . . . I found it nearly impossible to credit that Lady Ellsmere is indeed your mother. She seems far too young, and except for the eyes there is little resemblance between you. She must have been spectacularly beautiful as a girl." It was not a particularly clever evasion or alluring red herring — he had caught her unprepared — but April hoped it would be accepted.

She should have known better. There had been no lack of plain speaking between them in the course of their short and stormy acquaintance, and now Adam said impatiently, "Don't, I beg of you, think to fob me off with platitudes. Please answer my question."

April obliged with icy distinctness. "Very well, since you prefer the word without the bark on it, I found Lady Ellsmere frank to the point of incivility, nor did I particularly relish her propensity for indulging vulgar curiosity by asking impertinent questions."

Instantly she was ashamed of the waspish reply and was on the brink of tendering an apology when her husband said with a mildness that brought her eyes to his in quick suspicion, "Well, if we are to speak of frankness approaching incivility . . . " He allowed his voice to trail off suggestively.

"Yes, I know, but you did insist," she offered in a feeble attempt at self-exculpation and noted with surprise not untinged with relief that she had been correct. There was an incipient quiver of the firm lips, though he obviously had no intention of giving way to the amusement aroused by her harsh opinion of his remaining parent.

"You need not trouble yourself about getting along with my mother. We meet but seldom. She will, of course, be invited to the dance we'll give for Diana, but there is no necessity to include her when we entertain my colleagues."

"You did not tell me you were planning to hold a dance for Diana," April said, fastening on to the one vital point in his remarks. She was wondering how to express her gratitude without chancing another rebuff when he rendered any thanks impossible by returning an offhand rejoinder.

"There has scarcely been time to acquaint you with my plans, you will agree, but naturally I am prepared to launch my sister-in-law into society in the style to which you aspire. Can your brief tenure as a respectable matron have caused you to forget the reason for this farcical marriage, my dear April?"

His wife remained silent, struggling to retain her composure in the wake of this wave of sarcasm. Perhaps he sensed her chagrin, for after shooting a glance at her downcast eyes and compressed lips he looked away and moderated his tones.

"I have been used to entertain my various colleagues and

friends at an hotel, but now that I have a hostess I should like to repay past hospitality when you have become more settled in my house. However, that can wait upon launching Diana. No doubt the announcement of our marriage which I inserted in tomorrow's *Morning Post* and *Gazette* will provoke a spate of bride visits as soon as our 'at home' cards go out. She will have the opportunity to meet a number of people in an informal setting before being presented. Not that Diana would seem to suffer from any afflictive shyness, but it can be an ordeal for a young girl to be pitchforked into the *ton* with no prior acquaintance. I hope some of our callers will bring their daughters so she may meet as many young people as possible before her dance." He paused, apparently considering those of his acquaintances who might answer this need, and April studied him from under thick lashes.

She longed to express her gratitude for such wholehearted cooperation in the matter of Diana's presentation but feared to evoke the harsh side of his nature. She was groping for a better understanding of this strange individual to whom she was now bound in the closest of all human ties. In his dealings with herself and with his mother there was a repelling coldness that indicated an absence of any heart, but here he was planning for Diana's smooth entry into the polite world with the care one might lavish on a daughter—and after referring to her as a brainless chit! It was quite incomprehensible.

Adam turned and caught her puzzled regard. Instantly his face lost all expression. "We are nearly home. I shall have to go out this afternoon and shall be fully occupied with government business in the upcoming weeks. You will have to manage the outfitting of your sister and any charges in the house with minimal assistance from me. I shall make banking arrangements for you immediately. Buy anything you wish, but do not bother me with details."

"How do you know I won't bankrupt you with my extravagance or decorate the whole house in puce?" demanded April, nettled at his retreat.

If she hoped to wring an admission that he trusted her taste from her husband she was doomed to disappointment. "You may try to bankrupt me," he said with a glint of amusement in those hard gray eyes. "If you look like succeeding, never doubt that I'll take preventive measures, and if the decor is too outrageous I'll make a bonfire of it and hire someone to do it again. But I really suffer no qualms on that head, my dear April. These last few years must have taught you to hold household if Mattie has not. It will do you good to indulge in a spree of shopping and to know you have the means to indulge your slightest whim."

Utterly incomprehensible! April could only stare into those opaque eyes as she pondered this unlooked-for generosity.

"By the way"—Adam broke the silence that threatened to become permanent as the carriage drew up to the entrance—"I should like you to reserve the gown that is being made up in the tissue silk with the silver threads for our own ball." The keen glance that accompanied this request left her in no doubt that it was, in fact, an order. He jumped down from the carriage and assisted April to descend but left her outside the door.

"I'll have John drop me off at the Ministry, then the carriage will be at your disposal. Don't expect me for dinner." He gave an order to the coachman and reentered the vehicle without any recourse to polite formulas of leave-taking. Before the porter had even opened the door the carriage was halfway down the street.

April headed upstairs to put off her hat and gloves, but she had barely attained the first-floor landing when Diana appeared in the corridor.

"There you are at last! I feared I should have to eat luncheon all by myself in that great gloomy dining room." As the young girl took in her sister's changed appearance, her eyes grew wider. "April, that is a stunning outfit! The color is perfect for you, and what magnificent fur! Is it ermine?" Her tone had grown reverent, and she stretched out a hand to smooth the white fur.

April laughed. "Yes, it is ermine. Come into my room while I remove the pelisse and wash my hands. I won't keep you above a minute if lunch is ready." She had pulled off the gloves and was untying the ribbons of the fur hat as she spoke. She laughed again as Diana seized the hat almost before she had it off and pranced over to the mirror to try it on her golden head the instant April opened the door to her bedchamber. The young girl preened herself and postured with the muff in front of the mirror under the indulgent eye of her sister, who was drying her hands on a linen towel. It was with a decided reluctance that she abandoned the fur hat on the bed to follow April back into the hall.

"Did you not think the ermine excessively becoming to me, April?" she invited, almost running to catch up with that lady's determined pace. "May I have one like it, please? I have always dreamed of owning a fur hat and muff."

April smiled into the eager young face whose brilliant blue eyes had deepened with earnestness. "Certainly you may have fur, dearest, although that particular style is perhaps too old for you." Then as Diana's brightness dimmed and her mouth took on an incipient pout she added in a rallying tone, "Besides, think what figures of fun we should make of ourselves dressing alike as though we were twins."

"Of course, I never meant that we should wear everything alike," Diana muttered with a touch of pique. "I am well aware that I must present a demure appearance in my first season and dress in muslins and crapes when I should really like satins and velvet, but the ermine hat is just perfect on me. Mayn't I have it, April, please? You could get another hat. *Please*, April?"

They were approaching the bottom of the staircase, and April averted her gaze from her sister's beseeching countenance as she laid her hand on the newel post. There was a hint of constraint in her quiet reply.

"Adam chose the hat for me himself, Diana. I could not wound him by giving it away, but I promise we shall find something equally distinctive for you."

Fortunately the proximity of the dining room and the

appearance just then of Morton put an end to the discussion, though Diana's lips had a slightly mulish set. During the course of the meal her good spirits were restored by a lively description of the fabrics and designs April had seen that morning at Mélisande's. She was so eager to begin the pleasant chore of acquiring a wardrobe for her comeout that she scarcely noticed what she was putting in her mouth. In contrast, the new Lady Glenville, conscious of her position as mistress of a good-sized establishment, was judiciously sampling each of the chef's offerings. With the memory of last night's dismal dinner still fresh, she was wary of anything she could not immediately identify but determined to give the man a fair chance before taking some action. Today's mutton pie was edible, though no one could çall its creator a dab hand at pastry making. The vegetables were again overcooked, but, in justice, some people preferred all their food cooked until the original color and texture were totally lost. Lord Glenville, for all she knew of him, might belong to this school of thought. The meal ended with an assortment of jellies, probably presented as a concession to the presence of ladies in the house, but since they were universally rubbery, no feeling of appreciation for the condescension was aroused in April's breast. Diana flatly declined trying them. Any delay in the start of her first shopping spree was unwelcome, and she twitched impatiently as her sister lingered over lunch as though she had all the time in the world. As before, the service was perfect, with Morton guiding the most appetizing offerings onto their plates and unobtrusively removing those dishes that failed to appeal.

When at last April signaled that they were finished, Diana heaved a sigh of relief and bounced to her feet before the butler could assist her. After another seemingly interminable delay while the carriage was called for and they got into their outer garments, the two ladies finally set forth on their quest.

When they returned several hours later, April could only be grateful that she had managed to eat a good portion of her lunch before embarking on the ordeal. She'd had need of all the strength she could muster to match the pace set by her young sister in her aggressive pursuit of the latest modes to be found in London. Nine years of living on a tiny income that never quite stretched to cover essentials, let alone luxuries, had left April with a legacy of caution and an ingrained disinclination to accept less than real value for any expenditure. Diana, protected from childhood from knowledge of the true state of the family's finances and indulged to the extent permitted by those finances, first by her mother and then by her sister, was completely unburdened by any such inhibiting check on her ability to spend. Indeed, it had fallen to April's lot to control her volatile sister's orgy of purchasing in a diplomatic manner that would not diminish the child's pleasure in her first real shopping expedition. By the exercise of consummate tact and the liberal use of stalling tactics, she accomplished the feat and at length had the privilege of seeing Diana's bubbling excitement gradually simmer down into an informed satisfaction with the way her wardrobe was taking shape.

There was not time in one short afternoon to do more than initiate the process, of course. As her sister had had to do, Diana was obliged to order her basic requirements to be made up from the designs and fabrics paraded for her selection while her measurements were taken and a list of necessities was compiled. She did enjoy the good fortune to be the exact size and the right coloring to enhance a completed dress in a delicious soft apricot cotton that the original purchaser had decided did not become her after all. Since April agreed with Mélisande that the demurely cut neckline and tiny puffed sleeves with their matching velvet bows were exactly suited to her sister's youthful good looks, and since the designer, with an avid eye to the dimension of the order being amassed by Lord Glenville's ladies, had the shrewdness to offer a substantial reduction in price on an item that represented a total loss to her in any case, Diana had the happiness of carrying it away with her then and there. Clutching her new gown and armed with swatches of several fabrics, she eventually sallied forth from the modiste's establishment to begin the pleasant chore of selecting hats to go with various outfits.

The harmony of their concerted effort had been briefly threatened when it was revealed that Diana's taste in headgear was inclined to be rather too dashing for a girl of seventeen, but thanks to Clothilde's instant reading of the situation and the persuasive and flattering manner with which she guided the girl to more suitable styles, April was saved from seeming to deny her sister her own choices. She knew her earlier refusal to surrender the ermine bonnet still rankled with one who was unused to being denied any request within April's power to grant. It was with sincere pleasure not unmixed with relief that she allowed the purchase of a scandalously overpriced but wickedly becoming sable bonnet and outsized matching muff that Diana fell in love with at sight. For no reason that she could really explain, the idea of turning over to her sister the hat Adam had chosen for his wife had been peculiarly repugnant without even considering his justifiable annoyance at such a glaring circumvention of his intent.

They had emerged from the milliner's considerably lighter in the purse but happy in the possession of no less than five new hats. April would have retired for the day content with the assurance of a task well done, but in the face of her sister's confident assumption that they would continue while breath remained in their bodies and the shopes remained open, she sighed inwardly and meekly trudged onward, trying not to notice that her shoes were displaying an alarming tendency to shrink. Once Jacob had relieved them of the accumulated purchases, which he deposited in the waiting carriage, Diana continued her strolling progress, determined not to miss any of the myriad delights offered by the attractive shops in the area.

A beaded reticule had captured her fancy in one shop, and nothing would do but that she must sample each and every item in a *parfumerie* even though her sister sensibly pointed out that after smelling a half-dozen one was unable to distinguish among them anyway. Diana gaily brushed aside this prosaic reflection and proceeded to select the scent in the prettiest bottle after a lengthy deliberation that April suspected was prolonged by the shop assistant, a thin pallid youth with a receding chin, who was reduced to a state of stammering eagerness by Diana's big blue eyes and the charming air of helplessness she had recently perfected. During the interlude the young man contrived to remain oblivious of the claims on his attention being advanced by a sharp-featured matron in a green velvet bonnet whose available stock of patience and good humor was rapidly exhausted as she eyed the engrossed duo with a censorious eye. When clearing her throat loudly and planting herself in the assistant's line of vision as he turned back from the shelf from which he had selected yet another bottle for Diana's approval had wholly failed to deflect his rapt concentration from his lovely customer, the woman departed in a huff after first delivering herself of an unflattering opinion of the manners exhibited by the current crop of assistants who abandoned their clear duty to wait upon the public in favor of fawning over every pretty face that happened along. If she hoped by this forthright speech to bring him to some sense of his unworthiness, she failed utterly in her object, April noted with a mixture of amusement and sympathy, for the young man did not even become conscious of her voice until she had almost closed the door behind her. He did indeed look a trifle startled at the force with which the door closed, but he then returned to Diana the negligible portion of his attention the irate woman had succeeded in diverting. His engrossed client, still intent on comparing the perfumes in front of her, remained unaware of the incident, but her sister thought it time to put an end to the scene before any additional customer had been turned away from the shop. In a brisk voice, she recommended Diana to make a decision or return another day as she withdrew some money from her purse and looked suggestively at the assistant. His training came to his aid in persuading his client to make a selection. April was unsurprised that the chosen item was almost the costliest in the shop, but she paid without a murmur, feeling that they had cost the owner more in goodwill today than the purchase represented.

Back out on the flagway, an enthusiastic Diana would have continued her perambulations had her sister not decided she had abused her tired feet long enough. She stated firmly that it was time to rejoin the carriage. If Diana was inclined to protest the curtailing of her shopping, she took comfort in the reflection that she would soon have the pleasure of trying on all the new bonnets and the apricot gown for the approval of the maid, Alice, and the temporary cloud was banished from her face.

As they headed for the location of the carriage, however, she arrested their progress at sight of a tobacconist's, declaring that she wouldn't be a minute but there was one more errand she simply must accomplish. Utterly bewildered, April looked again at the swinging sign to see if she had misread it before following the golden head disappearing into the shop. She caught up with her sister as another assistant looked up and came toward them with an ingratiating smile.

April gave a small tug at Diana's sleeve and whispered, "What possible business could you have in here?"

"Adam mentioned last night that he liked to . . . I believe the expression is 'blow a cloud' . . . occasionally, and since he sent me ten guineas this morning for pin money, I thought I'd buy him some cigars." The young girl turned to the salesman who had now reached them and requested his assistance, leaving a silent April with much to occupy her thoughts.

She was struck once again by Adam's consideration with regard to his newly acquired sister-in-law—he had not even mentioned the matter to her during the hours they had spent together this morning—and she experienced a rush of gratitude to Diana for her thoughtfulness. There were occasions when April wondered uneasily if she and her mother had not perhaps spoiled Diana a trifle in their anxiety to make up to her for the loss of her father and the secure life she had so briefly led. And then the girl would make some sweet impulsive gesture that repaid her relatives for all their sacrifices. She was very young yet and intermittently careless of others' feelings, but April was persuaded her sister nourished a fierce affection for those few persons close to her. It could not fail to please that Diana was apparently ready to extend this affection to her new brother-in-law. As she watched the sparkling girl charm another salesman she was glad that Diana was doing something for Adam. She herself was prevented by the awkward nature of their relationship from making any spontaneous gestures toward her husband lest these be misconstrued by him as representing a bid for his attentions. Her face flooded with color at the mere thought of such a situation, and her eyes grew somber. It seemed not all the ramifications of this strange marriage had yet manifested themselves.

Diana's voice jerked her out of a melancholy reverie that suddenly shadowed their happy afternoon. "I said we can go now, April. You seemed a thousand miles away." The girl bestowed her most brilliant smile upon the assistant who was solicitously holding the door for the ladies' departure, then bent a curious gaze on her sister.

"I was merely thinking of my aching feet," April improvised quickly, "and longing for a dish of tea."

Diana's fleeting curiosity was appeased, and for the short ride home the carriage rang with her delighted comments on their accomplishments that afternoon, to which April made suitable replies when called upon to reinforce her sister's opinions.

Both ladies found themselves completely restored by tea and a rest before dinner. They came together in the saloon, where the first disappointment awaited one of them. There had been no opportunity for April to inform her sister that Adam would not be joining them, and Diana, clutching the box of cigars, was crushed that her surprise must be postponed.

"I hate waiting for things," she confessed with perfect truth, a small pout hovering around her lips. This was soon dispelled by her sister's sincerely expressed admiration for the effect of the new gown. She pirouetted gaily and expanded under April's praise of the hairstyle contrived by the clever Alice, which featured a perky bow of the same velvet as the trimming on the dress. April's own smooth hair remained unadorned, and she was again wearing the gray gown. Their exertions had given them a sharp appetite, and they were not sorry to have Morton announce dinner almost immediately.

The meal that awaited them did little to appease their hunger and much to increase the small worry that had lodged inself in the new Lady Glenville's brain on the previous evening. She had been encouraged by the mediocre luncheon to hope the chef was increasing his efforts on their behalf, but tonight's dinner was every bit as unappetizing as that of the previous evening.

"What is this?" Diana asked, eyeing with some doubt the dish being set before her by Morton.

"Salmon poached in white wine and served in a butter sauce with mushrooms, Miss Wendover," replied the butler smoothly as he deposited a similar dish before his mistress.

Diana took a tentative mouthful and grimaced as she swallowed. "It's not cooked!" she declared indignantly as she reached for her water glass.

April studied her own portion and discovered a section of spine with her fork. "Take it away, Morton," she said quietly.

The butler complied in silence, giving the plates to Jacob to remove, while Diana cast her eyes hopefully on the covered dishes residing on the sideboard. Morton served them with veal cutlets that had been coated in a batter and fried. They looked to be a rather dark shade, but both ladies accepted some without comment. Diana set her knife and fork in hers and sawed away for an unconscionable time before she managed to slice off a bit. She chewed it thoroughly for a full minute then had recourse to her water glass again to aid in swallowing. She remarked with deliberation:

"Well, there's no denying these are cooked. The question is, when was the deed done?"

"Possibly yesterday," April replied, putting aside her fork after one bite. "Don't try to eat them, love, you'll break a tooth. There are several vegetables here, and I see a dish of stewed pears, which you like. Also, is that a platter of ham, Morton?"

"Yes, my lady." Morton's thin lips were pinched even thinner, and he kept his eyes cast down as he served them with slices of cold ham and offered a dish of spinach and croutons.

The ladies managed to make a fair meal by concentrating on the items that had not received the benefit of the chef's attention. From their accumulated experience they summarily rejected anything in a sauce. Both were loath to sample the handsome fruitcake that appeared at the end of the meal until Morton confided in an expressionless tone that the housekeeper had made it from an old family recipe. This was discovered to be excellent, and April desired the butler to relay their appreciation to Mrs. Donaldson.

She had been rather quiet during the dinner, puzzling in her mind what it were best to do about the continuing situation of unsatisfactory meals, and at length had resolved to postpone action no longer. She might not be able to buy her husband presents without her motives being misconstrued, but she could rid his house of a cook who failed to provide his master with even a minimal standard of nourishment. Consequently, as Morton pulled out her chair she met his glance squarely and requested an interview with the chef as soon as he should be finished in the kitchen.

A shade of uneasiness crossed the butler's controlled countenance and he appeared to hesitate fractionally before replying. "I regret that Gregory is a trifle indisposed this evening, my lady. Will tomorrow do?"

April considered his pale composed features for a second longer. "Is Gregory ill, Morton?"

Again the hesitation, and now Morton's gaze was fixed on a point beyond Lady Glenville's shoulder. "Not to say ill precisely, my lady, but he isn't quite himself."

An unkind suspicion flashed through April's mind. She devoutly wished Mattie were here to counsel her or at least shed some light on the inner workings of the household, but Mattie would not be back for several days. She must handle the matter herself. She straightened her shoulders and forced the butler to meet her eyes.

"Do you mean me to comprehend that the chef is incapacitated by drink, Morton?"

Something that might have been relief flickered in the butler's ice-blue eyes. "I fear that is indeed the case, my lady."

"Is this a chronic problem with Gregory?"

"Not to say chronic, my lady, but more often than not of late he is under the influence of spiritous liquors."

"I see. And why have you not informed Lord Glenville of this circumstance before now?"

His reply was quick in coming, although she thought she detected a hint of discomfort in his impassive mien. "Gregory did not use to be as bad before, and his lordship has never complained about the food. I did not feel it was up to me to get a man sacked."

"Or to see that he kept away from drink? Well, never mind that now, but he'll have to go, Morton, and you will be obliged to visit the registry office tomorrow to engage another chef. His lordship has the right to expect decent, well-prepared food in his home."

Heavy lids concealed the butler's reaction to this speech. He was the well-trained servant in his reply. "Certainly, my lady. Will that be all?"

April nodded and signed to the engrossed Diana that she should precede her through the door Jacob hastened to open. For the first time ever she felt she was indeed mistress of Lord Glenville's establishment.

Chapter Seven

Over the next few weeks, April settled more comfortably into her role as Lady Glenville, wife of a prominent member of the government. She was too much occupied with the demands her new position made on her time and energy to have any leisure for reflection on the state of her own emotions. If she did not know whether she was happy or not, at least she knew that life had suddenly become more interesting than she could ever remember. Her own comeout so many years before had been moderately enjoyable while it lasted, and her brief tenure as a young lady quickly betrothed in her first season had given her a certain status among her contemporaries. In the dark years that followed her father's death and the breaking of her engagement, this short period of gaiety and irresponsibility had grown fuzzy and receded into the dim corners of her memory. Her position today was infinitely preferable to that of nine years ago. Unmarried girls were hedged about by numerous rules and strictures and were under all eyes at all times. As a married woman she had dispensed with these restrictions, and she frankly reveled in her newfound freedom. There were new responsibilities, of course, but nothing could weigh on her as heavily as had the task of keeping her family together under increasingly difficult financial stresses. From this too she was liberated by her marriage to a wealthy peer of the realm.

The first priority, on a par with the acquisition of a wardrobe for herself and her sister, was to refurbish the large and woefully neglected house she now shared with the last man on earth her youthful imaginings could have conjured up. The successful conclusion of her initial decision to replace the undependable chef gave her the impetus to proceed with confidence toward decisions with regard to changes in the furnishings. She had not quite believed that Adam meant to give her a completely free hand in the household, and, despite a resolution to remain calm, her nerves were on the stretch the first time he dined at home after the installation of André, the Gallic chef Morton had obtained from the registry.

It was almost impossible to credit that anyone could remain oblivious to the improvement in the quality of food that appeared on the table. André had the happy knack of cooking each item just to the point that enhanced its inherent goodness, and when he used sauces they were creations to be savored. The earl, however, let most of the dinner hour slide by before pausing with his fork halfway to his mouth, an expression of surprise giving animation to his stern features. "This veal dish is delicious!" His look invited comment.

April swallowed carefully, trying to decide what to say, but Diana solved the problem for her.

"If you'd been home for dinner the past three nights, dear Adam, you'd have discovered that everything André cooks is delicious."

Lord Glenville eyed the teasing face of his sister-in-law with amused tolerance. "I must confess the name of my chef escapes my memory at the moment, but I'd venture a small wager that it isn't André."

"Then you'd lose," giggled Diana. "The *old* chef was Gregory, and the *new* one André."

"Oh, my lamentable memory," sighed the earl. "No doubt I was informed of the change in cooks, but it has quite slipped my mind."

April squirmed mentally under a bland look directed at her. "No, I . . . there has been no opportunity to bring it to your attention. I beg your pardon."

"That's because you spend so little time at home, dear

Adam," inserted Diana in cooing accents. "Otherwise you'd have noticed long since that the meals Gregory served up weren't fit to be eaten — at least the dinners weren't. Breakfast was tolerable and one could swallow lunch, but by evening nothing that appeared on the table was edible."

He heard this in frowning concentration. "I fear I pay very little attention to what I eat, but is there some inference I'm to draw from this tale?"

"It seems that Gregory was a chronic drinker," said his countess, thinking it high time she entered the discussion.

In the pause that greeted this statement she observed that Morton's attention remained fixed on the tray he was carrying to the sideboard, so he missed the rapier look directed at him by his master.

"It seems I am the one who should apologize," Lord Glenville said to surprise his wife. "It was a very poor welcome indeed, my dear, to present you with a problem of this nature on the instant of your arrival."

April, concentrating on his face and voice, could detect no hint of sarcasm, and she relaxed visibly, but Diana saved her from the necessity of a reply.

"What is a wife for if not to run your house?" the girl inquired with mock innocence, her bright-blue eyes opened to their widest.

"If you think I am going to rise to that one, young woman, your optimism exceeds your wit."

Diana giggled again and allowed the earl to change the subject. The rest of the meal passed in pleasant inconsequential conversation, and April's composure was restored. She had been correct in assuming Glenville was almost totally indifferent to the quality of food served in his house. Perhaps he did intend to leave the decorating entirely in her hands. Perhaps nothing about the running of his house was of much interest to him.

The earl alluded to the change of chefs later that evening. Husband and wife were sitting in the main saloon, he engrossed in an issue of the *Edinburgh Review* and April occupied with a piece of stitchery. Diana had been entertaining them at the piano but had retired early with a slight headache. When April would have accompanied her sister upstairs, Adam had signed that he wished her to stay. After bidding Diana an affectionate goodnight she sank back in her chair and looked questioningly at him over her embroidery.

He apologized once more for not having prevented the unfortunate situation with the chef. "How did you become aware that it was a case of drinking with Gregory?"

"I requested an interview with him one evening to discover the reason for the poor meals. Morton tried to fob me off till morning, and it . . . came out on further questioning that he drank to excess. I hope you do not feel I was too hasty in dismissing him?" she ventured.

He denied this with an impatient wave of one hand. "There was nothing else to do at that point. However, I am at a loss to understand why it had not been brought to my attention before matters came to such a pass."

"Morton said you never complained about the food and he did not consider it his duty to get a man dismissed," April replied somewhat dryly.

Adam's black brows lowered at this. "It was his duty to see the situation did not arise in the first place," he snapped. "I'll have an explanation from him before he's a day older."

April resumed pushing her needle in and out of the cloth in her hands for a moment before putting a casual question.

"How long has Morton been with you?"

"Four or five years. He was a fixture in my uncle's home, but my Uncle Harry was as inveterate a gambler as your father." She winced at this, but he seemed unaware of her reaction. "When he died, Freddy could not afford to keep the estate going. It's rented now to a retired factory owner. He and Damien asked me if I'd take Morton on, since they both keep bachelor lodgings here in town with only a manservant." He shrugged. "Morton's a queer cold chap, but he and Mrs. Donaldson have run the house between them without bothering me, and I've been content to have it so."

Again there was a short pause, which April was constrained to break. "Our coming has meant a great deal of disruption in your life," she said with a note of apology in her lovely voice.

"The government is my life," he asserted brusquely, "and you won't disrupt that. I've told you before, you may have a free hand in this house."

A tingling silence descended on the pair, but this time April refused to run away. She continued to ply her needle, and eventually the repetitive motion exercised a soothing effect on her nerves. In another moment she would rise and bid him goodnight.

"April, how did we meet?" Adam asked in a musing tone that brought her eyes swiftly to his. A little frown knitted itself between her brows.

"Have you forgotten?" The noncommittal question revealed none of the thoughts churning in her head.

"I wish I could forget!" he clipped out before moderating his tone with a palpable effort. "I meant, what story shall we concoct for the delectation of our public? Ever since the announcement appeared in the papers I've been besieged by well-wishers, and I imagine cards have been left here as well."

She confirmed this, then ventured an objection. "Need we concoct any story at all? Even your mother did not ask how we met."

His smile barely qualified as such and was gone on the instant. "She was too stunned to have all her wits about her that day, but she'll be asking that question at a second meeting. I feel we should agree on the essentials of a story. Obviously I swept you off your feet, our marriage was so un-expected."

"I told Diana we met when Mother was still alive," April said slowly.

"Then why did we not wed at the time?"

Completely expressionless, she stared at him and answered levelly, "My mother would not countenance my marrying the man responsible for my father's and brother's deaths."

Nothing about Adam moved, and his stillness held April

mesmerized until at last he spoke softly to the original question. "If memory serves, your mother died when you were one and twenty. Why did we not marry long since?"

"I . . . I don't know." Although Adam had chosen to ignore her spiteful remark about his past, his wife was too overcome by shame and resentment that she should be experiencing such an emotion to be capable of creative thinking just then.

"Well, use your imagination, woman! Since I've shown myself so impulsive about rushing you into marriage with no hints even to my closest friends, why was I not equally rash several years ago when we were both younger and presumably more ardent?"

"Possibly because you'd forgotten my very existence!" April snapped, disliking the embarrassing subject more each minute.

A gleam of real amusement lightened those still dark eyes. "Perhaps we would be advised to stick as near the truth as we may. Shall we agree that we met long ago under circumstances that rendered any closer attachment impossible at the time, but having met again recently and having made the discovery that the years had not dimmed your attraction for me, I proceeded to pursue the acquaintance with a fervor that swept away your reservations, swept you off your feet and into marriage?"

He took her tight-lipped silence for acquiescence. "Then it only remains to decide when we met this second time. Through mutual friends, I feel sure. Don't you agree, my dear?"

April ground her even white teeth. "Of course. Perhaps you have friends among the parents of my scholars in the village school. Or, better yet, no doubt your father and Mr. Lynley were at Oxford together, and he dandled you on his knees when you were a babe."

The earl's mood had improved measurably in proportion to the decline in his wife's spirits. Now he said, cheerfully ignoring this latest contribution, "It was a house party I think — yes, where better to foster the growth of a whirlwind courtship than a country visit? It was known in town that I went north on business, so if we were to set our mutual friends in Warwickshire around Birmingham that should answer very well."

"No one would be so indelicate as to inquire into the identity of these matchmaking friends, of course?"

"Naturally not, but in any event, their name is Smith, Mr. and Mrs. Martin Smith. Possibly you and Mrs. Smith were at school together. Your dear friend Hepzibah with the dark ringlets married my old classmate, Martin Smith, who had ever an eye for a dark beauty."

"I didn't go to school, I had a governess," April declared dampingly.

"Oh? A pity. I was becoming quite enamored by the thought of a tender reunion with the friend of your girlhood, the sweet Hepzibah."

A reluctant little smile appeared on April's lips as she rose. "You talk a deal of nonsense, my lord, but if this is the Banbury story you intend to foist onto your unsuspecting — or should I say, rather, your *all too suspecting* — friends, I shall try to play my part. And now I'll wish you goodnight." She swept her sewing up in an untidy heap and departed with swift grace.

Adam bowed and remained standing, watching his wife's retreating back through half-closed lids. It was nearly five minutes later that he withdrew his gaze from the closed door and reseated himself. Even then he allowed another few moments to elapse before picking up the periodical he had been reading earlier. He held it unopened, mentally reviewing the recent conversation with April. As in every previous conversation with the woman who had become, so unbelievably, his wife, there had been an elusive element of barely repressed hostility in the atmosphere. Like two fencers they were constantly on guard, ready to repel an anticipated verbal thrust. Understandable, of course, under the circumstances, but unless and until they could manage to conceal this from those with whom they would be associating, their portrayal of newly wedded bliss would be revealed for the charade it was.

His fingernails were drumming an absentminded rhythm on the unopened periodical under his hand as he acknowledged to himself that the fault was mainly his own. It seemed he could not banish his resentment at the whole situation from his thoughts when discussing even the most innocuous of household matters with April. It was apparent that unless goaded to retaliation she tried to avoid crossing swords with him by adopting a propitiating attitude, and strangely enough, he resented this abasement on her part too. In fact, while he was assessing his reactions with ruthless honesty, he might as well admit that everything about his unwanted bride irritated him. He even resented the added attractiveness that was the result of the deliberate changes he had insisted on making in her appearance. Much as he wanted the whole of society to believe he had selected a particularly desirable bride, he did not intend to find her desirable himself. When he caught his gaze lingering on the silken swath of silvery fair hair gleaming under the lamplight as she sewed, and began checking the effect of various colors on those incredibly clear, almost colorless eyes of hers he experienced a tremendous surge of annoyance at his own stupidity. If he didn't wish to defeat his purpose it would behoove him to conquer this incipient weakness. The last thing he intended was to develop a *tendresse* for the woman who had married him to foster her sister's social ambitions, a woman moreover who still considered him little better than a murderer. He would do well to keep this fact clearly in mind when looking at his wife's lovely face or listening to the music in her voice.

The earl pulled out his watch and opened it. Not too late to visit Molly tonight after he had tackled Morton. He could be thankful that at least some things in life remained the same. He tossed the *Edinburgh Review* aside and went out of the room whistling softly to himself.

The following morning, April was alone in the small morning room waiting for Diana to finish arraying herself in preparation for yet another shopping trip when Morton ushered in a caller in defiance of the earl's expressed wish that the ladies remain incommunicado until the matter of their wardrobes had been fully attended to. She had been reading a letter from Mr. Lynley wishing her happiness in his genial though inelegantly expressed fashion when the butler entered. His bearing and voice when announcing "Mr. Frederick Harding, my lady," were so eloquent of proprietorial affection and pride in one whom she had considered totally devoid of all human instincts that amazement held her motionless at first and she was slow in transferring her attention to the man coming toward her with outstretched hand.

Mr. Harding had had ample opportunity to appraise the new countess before large clear eyes turned in his direction. He beheld a delicately fashioned woman of moderate height with extraordinary fair hair and pale coloring. He received the odd impression that she drew herself up as though gathering strength to face a trial, and the eyes that met his were guarded.

For her part April found herself responding to the friendly smile of her husband's cousin as her tentatively extended hand was engulfed in a warm clasp.

"Lady Glenville, this is indeed a great pleasure. I have been out of town for several days or I'd have called earlier to welcome you into the family and wish you joy in your marriage. Morton tells me Adam has already gone out this morning, so I shan't be able to offer him my felicitations just yet."

"Thank you very much, Mr. Harding. You are most kind." April withdrew her hand gently and waved her unexpected visitor to a chair. "May I offer you some refreshment — a glass of Madeira, perhaps?" She permitted herself to relax. The memory of her meeting with this man's brother had sent apprehension coursing through her body when

Morton had announced the caller, but one long look at Mr. Frederick Harding had relieved her mind of the initial fear that here was another enemy.

He declined refreshment with a smile, saying that he could stay but a moment. "I arrived at my lodgings last night to find a stack of mail waiting me. When I read Damien's note detailing his meeting with you I could not wait upon ceremony to make the acquaintance of Adam's wife. And how is my fortunate cousin bearing up under the flood of congratulations your marriage must have occasioned?"

As April returned a light answer, she studied her husband's heir with interest, marveling at the difference in two individuals who might pass for twins in a dim light. She had thought Mr. Damien Harding the handsomest man she had ever encountered until the enmity in his eyes had chilled her blood and altered her opinion. His brother was only a year or two older, but lines of dissipation had carved themselves deeply into his countenance and there were dark shadows under his eyes. There was a suggestion almost of sagging or softening in the bone structure of Mr. Frederick Harding's face, and he was thin to the point of attenuation, where his brother radiated vibrant health and vitality. This Mr. Harding was dressed as though he never gave his appearance a second, or perhaps even a first, thought, in contrast to the dandified image presented by the younger brother. Among all the comparisons that favored the younger, however, April had no difficulty in recognizing one element in the elder that attracted her strongly. Mr. Frederick Harding possessed too much genuine human kindness to resent the fact of his cousin's marriage. It stared out from his rather melancholy blue eyes and allowed her to accept the sincerity of his gentle smile. Nor could she accuse him of easy flattery when he remarked:

"Damien wrote that Adam had secured himself a real diamond for a bride, and I can see this is so, but he neglected to mention that our cousin had acquired an even rarer jewel, a woman with an understanding heart. For this blessing all who are close to Adam must be eternally grateful. That he would marry at all was considered doubtful. His early experience had made him intolerant and distrustful of your sex, my dear Lady Glenville, as you may have observed on first meeting him, but it is obvious that he recognized the compassionate heart beneath the lovely exterior."

If it had been possible to die of embarrassment April would have expired on the spot. He could scarcely have hit upon anything further from the truth! She blurted in protest:

"Mr. Harding, indeed you do me too much honor! It is quite undeserved. I beg you will say no more on this subject but rather tell me something about yourself. Are you and Adam close friends as well as relations?"

A shadow darkened Mr. Harding's brow, and he replied soberly, "Adam and I were good friends in our youth, but to my regret have grown apart of late. My strong-minded cousin rather despises me for my weakness. I must acknowledge the justness of this, of course. Unfortunately, we do not all possess Glenville's strength of purpose or single-mindedness."

Bewilderment was added to the squirming embarrassment overwhelming April. Mr. Harding seemed to take for granted that she was intimately acquainted with all the circumstances of her husband's life. "He . . . he is certainly dedicated to his work," she offered lamely in hopes of steering a safe course through conversational quicksands.

"As I noted, single-minded," agreed Mr. Harding, then his attractive smile reappeared. "You will add a new dimension to his life. For years Adam has devoted himself entirely to his career. He is long overdue for some satisfaction in his personal life. He will not have told you how badly hurt he was by his mother's desertion of husband and son. No doubt he makes light of it today, but I was at school with him and I know how deeply affected he was. Even to me he could confide none of his feelings, but I witnessed the change in him. Ah well." Mr. Harding banished his somberness and beamed at the bemused woman staring intently at him. "You must forgive me for harking back to ancient history. I hope I haven't reached the stage of the thrice-told tale."

April murmured a gentle negative and said earnestly, "Thank you for telling me this, Mr. Harding. I'm grateful to you for helping me to understand Adam better." She put out her hand with an impulsive gesture, and her husband's cousin took it in both of his as he got to his feet.

"I'd be honored if you could bring yourself to call me Freddy," he requested smilingly. "After all, we are now quite nearly related."

April returned his smile with interest. "Of course, if you wish it, and my name is April."

"The beginning of spring. The name suits you, my dear April. I—"

"I trust I don't intrude?"

Two heads turned to the doorway, where the Earl of Glenville stood, an expression on his dark-featured face that was less than welcoming.

"Adam, what luck to find you here after all!" cried Mr. Harding. He released April's hand to hurry across the room and grasp his cousin's. "Morton said you'd gone for the day," he added, beaming at the unsmiling earl as he wrung one hand and patted his arm with his free hand. He seemed not to notice the lack of response in the other man.

"I came back for some papers," said the earl, glancing from his cousin's eager face to the carefully blank one of the woman who remained standing in the middle of the room. "Inopportunely, perhaps?"

"Just the opposite," declared Mr. Harding with a laugh. "I was just taking my leave of April and had visions of chasing all over London to find you to offer my felicitations, deplorably late though they are. I've been out of town the last few days, didn't learn the happy news until I read a note scrawled by my brother which awaited me in my chambers."

"How gratifying that you should rush right over to wish us happy," drawled the earl, whose eyes had narrowed slightly at hearing his wife's name on his cousin's lips. "Since you seem to be on Christian-name terms with my wife already, I take it an introduction would be superfluous?"

"We introduced ourselves," returned Mr. Harding with a smiling nod in the direction of the silent countess, "and I sought immediate permission to abandon formality with one who is now so nearly related, which permission was kindly granted. My warmest wishes for your happiness, old fellow. You have won a most lovely and charming bride."

"Come over here, darling, and thank my cousin for his fulsome compliments," ordered the earl in a silky voice April had never heard from him. Obediently, she approached the men, who were still standing just inside the door. Both were smiling, but she didn't trust the gleam in her husband's eyes. To her great surprise he extended his arm and gathered her to his side so they were both facing Mr. Harding.

That gentleman was protesting that he took exception to his cousin's use of the word fulsome, that no compliment to such a lovely lady could be considered in any other light than inadequate to do her justice.

Adam laughed. "I cry quits, Freddy! Your eloquence overwhelms me. She is lovely, isn't she?" April had not yet recovered from the shock of finding herself clamped to her husband's side when another greeted her. Reluctance to verify the sardonic gleam she thought she had detected in Adam's eye when he summoned her to his side kept her standing stiffly in the circle of his arm, her unseeing gaze on Mr. Harding's face while her other senses registered her husband's disturbing nearness. She was therefore unprepared for his sudden swoop as he pressed a quick kiss on her cheek. For an instant as she stiffened involuntarily, his grip on her arm tightened to near painful intensity, then he released her and walked toward the bell pull, saying over his shoulder, "It's a trifle early in the day for liquid refreshment, but you won't let that prevent you from drinking our healths, I know, Freddy." He turned to confront the others again. "You should have offered our guest some refreshment, my dear," he remarked, gently chiding.

"Oh, April nobly upheld the hospitality of the house, but

thinking you absent, I planned only to stay a moment. Naturally I welcome the opportunity to drink to your future happiness."

Morton's entrance just then put an end to Mr. Harding's enthusing, and Diana, looking enchantingly pretty in a modish yellow gown with a triple flounce at the hem, danced into the room as the butler left to carry out his master's request.

"April, look, the most annoying thing!" she declared impetuously, holding out a box. Then, catching sight of her brother-in-law, her aspect became sunny again. "*Adam!* I thought you'd gone long since. I bought these cigars for you days ago and then you didn't come home for dinner so I could not give them to you, and when you did come home last night I forgot all about them. Here, for my favorite brother-in-law," she finished gaily, going up to the earl and placing the box in his hands. "I hope they're the sort you like?"

The earl smiled into the bright face looking anxiously up at him. "They are indeed, my child. I cannot recall an occasion for gifts, but I thank you most earnestly. Morton will put them in my study so I may enjoy one when I'm working." He grasped one shoulder lightly and turned her toward the other man. "Diana, may I present my cousin, Mr. Frederick Harding? Freddy, this is April's sister, Miss Wendover."

"You are the first member of Adam's family that I've met," Diana said with a friendly smile and a flirtatious flick of her lashes when Mr. Harding had bowed over her hand with a graceful gesture and expressed his delight in the meeting. "April has met your brother and Adam's mother, but we have been so busy shopping that I have not yet had the pleasure. In fact," she confided with a quaint little air of importance, "you are the very first person, except for shopkeepers, that I've met in London, so we must be friends."

"It will be my great pleasure, Miss Wendover."

"Oh, call me Diana, do." She wrinkled her perfect nose adorably. "After all, we are cousins of a sort, or at least connections, so why be formal?"

"I shall be delighted to be your cousin, Diana, as well as your friend," returned Mr. Harding gallantly. "This must be my lucky day. I have acquired two lovely cousins."

Morton returned with a tray, and the health and longevity of the bridal pair was proposed by Mr. Harding in a simple and, to April's grateful ears, sincere toast. Almost immediately the earl declared his regret that the pressure of work must take him away as soon as he collected the forgotten papers. His cousin accepted his invitation to accompany him part of the way and took a polite leave of the ladies.

"That reminds me," said the earl, sticking his head back around the doorway briefly, "we have an invitation for Friday that I should like to accept. Have your wardrobes reached a state to include evening dress?"

On being assured by a radiant Diana that they would put forth their best efforts to do him credit, he laughed, promised details that evening, and departed.

"My first party!" breathed Diana, showing her sister an ecstatic face and clasping her hands to her breast. "What shall we wear, April? Will the new blue silk trimmed with blond be suitable?"

Not receiving an immediate answer, she paused in the little dance step she was executing and glanced back to see her sister still facing the empty doorway. "April? Won't it do?"

Large gray eyes focused on the young girl's eager face. "Won't what do, dearest?"

"The blue silk," Diana repeated, and then, as her sister still looked blank, explained patiently, "for this party on Friday."

"Oh!" The older girl seemed to return from some distant place. Her voice became brisk. "The blue silk will do nicely, and I shall wear my rose-colored brocade." She glanced at the tiny watch pinned to her dress and became brisker still. "Goodness, look at the time! Hurry and get into your outdoor things, Diana, or we won't accomplish half of what we planned for today. The Pantheon Bazaar will already be crowded on such a pleasant morning."

Despite her request for haste, April fell back into a reverie as soon as Diana turned to obey her command, and it was several moments after the young girl had departed before she roused and cast a vague eye around for the pelisse and hat she had brought into the morning room earlier. Her thoughts had winged back to the scene just completed, and she replayed it in her mind. On the surface nothing had occurred but a friendly visit from her husband's cousin and heir, but she couldn't dismiss a feeling that it had had a deeper significance. She had been greatly cheered by the discovery that the earl's heir did not share his brother's dislike of the marriage that would in all eyes end his hopes for a possible inheritance. And then in the course of their conversation he had unknowingly imparted a vital piece of information. Now there was an explanation for Adam's cold, almost inimical attitude toward his mother. She had been more than a little disturbed by this flouting of the most basic of human relationships and was glad of a reason to think less poorly of him. She accepted his contemptuous opinion of herself as her proper payment for coercing his acceptance of the marriage but had been rendered acutely uncomfortable by the general dislike and distrust of the female of the species she had sensed in him. Small wonder his opinion of her sex was so low!

But what had he meant by that little performance of devoted husband just now? Obviously it had been staged for his cousin's benefit, but it had struck her as a bit excessive to the occasion at the time and even more so in retrospect. Her imagination was inadequate to the task of conjuring up a picture of the very reserved earl making public demonstrations of affection toward his bride. He certainly had not treated her with any marked degree of warmth in front of his mother or younger cousin. There was a cold-blooded reason inspired by that secretive intellect for this morning's charade, of course.

As she buttoned her new black wool pelisse with its caped shoulders she knew with intuitive certainty that questioning the reason would avail her nothing. Her intuition further told her that her husband had taken a malicious satisfaction in the confusion and malaise his action had produced in her. She bit her lip and concentrated on recalling the incident accurately. Adam had been abrupt and provocative, to put it mildly, in his demeanor toward his cousin, but he had not succeeded in arousing any similar reaction from the mild-mannered Freddy. There was some disaffection between the men — Freddy had alluded to it and Adam had confirmed it by his faintly hostile, or perhaps contemptuous, attitude toward the cousin closest to him in age. April sighed as she crossed to the oval mirror on the far wall to arrange a wickedly becoming hat of shirred blue velvet on her head with unseeing mechanical precision. It was disappointing to find her husband apparently harboring some ill feeling toward the one person she had met in his family who had struck a responsive chord in her.

Diana appeared at the door as April was pulling on her gloves and put an end to her sister's fruitless conjecturing.

"Mmmm, I do like that blue hat. The narrow brim set at an angle shows off your hairstyle better than most. I have a swatch of the blue silk with me. Do you think we shall be able to buy ribbon to match it?"

"We can try, certainly. I hope Morton thought to order the carriage. It is growing very late." The two ladies swept out of the room with an air of purpose about them.

Chapter Eight

Friday morning found the Countess of Glenville taking special pains with her toilette. The earl had agreed with his wife that it would be unseemly for her to begin moving in society without the courtesy of a formal call at the home of Sir Neville Granby, who was now the head of her father's family. Lady Granby had left her card in Hanover Square shortly after the notice had appeared in the papers, and it was essential that the call be returned today, since the earl was to escort his bride and sister-in-law to a musical *soirée* at the home of a colleague that evening.

April stood frowning at the results of her efforts in the long glass, and Mattie paused in her search for fresh gloves to inquire:

"What's amiss? We decided the mauve outfit was still the most elegant for the purpose, and your hair looks fine. By the look on your face a body would think you was off to the dentist's instead of a simple morning call that needn't last above half an hour."

April made a wry little face at the woman regarding her sternly. "I'm not sure I wouldn't liefer visit the dentist than spend a half hour in the company of my cousin's wife. We've met only once when she paid a visit of condolence after Basil's death. She was all sympathy and condescension, but she couldn't refrain from taking a mental inventory and affixing a price tag on every object in the room. It was perfectly obvious to me, though Mother was in no condition to notice, thank goodness."

"Well, if a mere baronet's wife can condescend to a countess, it's more than I ever heard tell of, and you're in no need of sympathy now," Mattie reminded her former charge in a practical spirit. "You'll both behave with civil propriety and that'll be the end of it. You needn't become bosom bows, after all."

"Yes, Mattie," April replied with a suspicious meekness that her tirewoman quite properly ignored. At least the frown had gone. She continued to follow her mistress's movements from the corner of her eye as she rearranged some items in the drawer. The tiny frown reappeared as April put her hand to her throat.

"Oh, I forgot Mother's little pearl brooch." She lifted the top of a silver jewel casket and stared at its meager contents, the frown deepening. "Not here! Now where — oh, I remember, I took it off my gown yesterday after it scratched my finger while I was sewing. I must have left it on the table."

Mattie closed the drawer. "In the morning room? Which table?"

"Never mind, Mattie, you're busy. I'll get it myself; I know precisely where it is." April pulled the door behind her, shutting off Mattie's protests, and ran lightly down the main stairway, her soft house shoes making no sound on the wooden treads. As she came around the corner she paused involuntarily and resumed at a more sedate pace. Morton was talking to someone at the front door, and as April reached the hall she caught a quick view of burnished gold locks beneath a brown beaver before the door closed.

"Someone looking for his lordship, Morton?"

The butler started violently at the sound of her voice and turned swiftly. "Excuse me, my lady, you startled me. It was just an individual inquiring at the wrong house. Did you wish something, my lady?"

April eyed Morton's cavernous figure thoughtfully. His voice was as smooth as ever, his manner as deferential, but she would take her oath he had been more than displeased at her sudden appearance, and he had not turned completely to face her. One arm was concealed from her view.

"No, thank you, Morton. I just came to get something from my morning room."

"Very good, my lady." Morton allowed her to precede him down the hall leading to the back of the house. April was acutely conscious of his presence behind her, and her nerves were tingling for some reason. She stepped swiftly into the morning room, leaving the door open as she found it, and noted the butler's nearly silent passage an instant later. His walk was as unhurried as befitted his station and there was nothing in the hand she could see, but she was unalterably convinced he was concealing something he had received from the person she had glimpsed at the door. Without stopping to consider her actions, she slipped out of the room just in time to see his back disappear into Lord Glenville's study. Silently she followed, but the closed door stymied her for a moment. What excuse could she give for barging in on him? She bit her lower lip and lifted her head proudly. She could say she was looking for a certain volume on her husband's shelves. In any case, why should she have to explain herself in her own home? Yet she stood there undecided a further second, one hand going tentatively to the paneled door. It moved a silent inch at her touch, and her heart shot up into her throat. Morton hadn't shut the door! Her suspicious mind suggested that he hadn't wanted her to hear the sound of the door closing from her position close by in the morning room. Cautiously she widened the gap a trifle until a slice of the interior was revealed.

Adam's desk was in front of the wall to her left, and there was Morton engaged in unwrapping a small parcel resting on the desk. She could hear the paper crackle slightly as he removed it and folded it with care, though she couldn't identify the contents, since the butler's back was essentially presented to her view. He put the folded paper in his pocket and proceeded to open a box on Lord Glenville's desk and remove the contents to his pockets. What on earth — *Adam's cigars!* Morton was removing the cigars from the box Diana had presented to her brother-in-law and substituting those he had brought into the room. April stared in puzzlement until concern for her own position spying on the man caused her to pull the door gently to and nip back down the hall into the morning room.

The pearl brooch was where she had left it, and she went over to the oval mirror to pin it at the neck of her gown. Her eyes were fixed on her fumbling fingers, but her ears were straining for a sound that would indicate that Morton had left the study and her brain was busily advancing explanations for the butler's conduct. Why would he substitute different cigars for those Diana had bought Adam? Her frown smoothed out as an obvious explanation occurred to her. Most likely the cigars were not, after all, the sort Adam enjoyed and he did not wish to hurt Diana's feelings by refusing to smoke them. Her fingers stilled at their task momentarily. Then why deny the delivery at the door just now? It took only a second to arrive at the conclusion that both master and servant probably thought it more expedient to keep the whole affair dark. Amusement gleamed in the cool gray eyes that met hers in the mirror. Those cigars must have been really obnoxious to have Adam go to such lengths to get rid of them. Still, it was sweet of him to avoid spoiling his young relative's pleasure in her gift. She gave a last look at the pin at her throat, realigned her ruffles slightly, and headed upstairs again, no longer concerned to discover Morton's subsequent movements.

An hour later two fair ladies dressed in the height of fashion sought admission to Sir Neville Granby's residence. The individual who opened the door to them had been trained to recognize quality at a glance, though his perception was not so great as to discern that the sparkling face of the younger concealed a naive satisfaction and curiosity at being once again in the house she could barely recall, and the cool correct manner of the elder was hastily assumed to disguise the churning sensation in the region of her stomach that had resulted from an avalanche of old memories and feelings jarred loose on entering her former home. He permitted himself a minimal relaxation of the muscles of his face, which resembled nothing so much as that of an elderly

pug dog, and indicated the visitors should follow him upstairs to the drawing room, where Lady Granby was receiving.

April's senses were reacting to the changes the Granbys
had made inside the house, but as they entered the drawing
room she was aware at the same time of a pause in the atmosphere as the butler announced them, and the slight
hanging back of her sister—and small wonder! The room
seemed at first to be overflowing with humanity, all of whom
were strangers. April was adjusting to the necessity of plunging rather than wading into the waters of society when their
hostess detached herself from the group in front of the fireplace and surged forward to greet the newcomers.

"Dearest April, at long last! Being a female, I well understand the need to attend to one's wardrobe before going into
society, but we had begun to suspect Lord Glenville meant
to keep you all to himself." She emitted a titter that rang
falsely from someone of such imposing proportions. A
whinny would have been more in character, April reflected
waspishly, smarting under the thinly disguised suggestion
that the earl was ashamed of his country bride. She
managed a civil murmur in acknowledgment and presented
her sister to Lady Granby.

"So this is little Diana! My, she is growing into quite a
young lady," their hostess said archly, eyeing Diana's curtsy
and shy smile with a cold blue stare that belied her honeyed
words.

The years had not been kind to her cousin's wife, April
decided as that lady led them over to meet her other guests.
What might have been called a statuesque figure nine years
ago by those predisposed to make kindly judgments was now
frankly past that description, despite rigid corseting that
pushed up a bosom of majestic proportions and whose
tight lacing increased her already high color at the least
exertion. The blond hair that had been her one claim to
beauty in her youth had been prevented from fading by
some means that could only be deemed partially successful,

judging from the brassy hue of the crimped locks showing beneath a real quiz of a cap. The passing years had also served to heighten the equine characteristics of her long bony face and the nasality of her piercing voice.

The latter characteristic was very much in evidence as she presented her husband's relatives to the expectant group watching their approach with varying degrees of enthusiasm and curiosity. Fortunately, three of the five people present were members of one family, thus reducing the feat of memory to be expected of Lady Glenville and Miss Wendover. Lady Eddington had called with her son and daughter and, as it turned out in the course of the conversation, had been accompanied by the other gentleman, a Mr. Navenby, who was a friend of Mr. Eddington's. The remaining member of the party was Miss Phoebe Granby, the eldest daughter of the house. One look at the latter had served to confirm April's past apprehensions that Lady Granby would never have consented to bring Diana out in company with her woefully plain daughter.

The best that could be said for Miss Granby at the end of a half hour's acquaintance was that she appeared to be a good-natured girl eager to be accepted by one and all. Unfortunately, this led her at times into the error of agreeing with every opinion offered even when consecutive opinions were diametrically opposed. April took pity on her embarrassment after one such exchange and engaged her in quiet conversation until the mottled flush faded somewhat from her lean cheeks. She had inherited her mother's bony facial structure and large frame, but there was no excess weight on Phoebe, the reverse indeed! April wondered that her mother would permit her to be seen in an ill-fitting dress that drew attention to the deficiencies of her figure. She had been aware of Lady Granby's swift appraisal of her own and Diana's attire, guessing that her shopkeeper's mentality had been busy estimating the cost of each item. That these estimates would be wide of the mark was a forgone conclusion, for everything about the furnishings of the room and her own and her daughter's appearance screamed of money spent for the sole purpose of display with little regard for value or aesthetics.

The mantelpiece was crowded with a motley collection of costly ornaments placed without regard to decorative effect, and both ladies were expensively but badly dressed, their choices seemingly unrelated to the coloring or figure type of the wearer. The coquelicot ribbons adorning Lady Granby's gown might be all the rage, but poppy red would ever war with its wearer's highly colored complexion.

April allowed her attention to dwell on the others in the group, pleased to note that Diana, unaccustomedly shy in company, was making a favorable impression on Lady Eddington. The fact that Miss Sarah Eddington was a lively, pretty brunette with, apparently, a devoted swain in attendance may have made possible her mother's disinterested judgment, but April was grateful for this evidence of good-will on the part of one who was likely to become Diana's hostess on occasion if the initial rapport between the girls was permitted to develop naturally.

Lady Granby was also quick to note the ease with which Diana had insinuated herself into the group of young people, but she viewed this with little evidence of pleasure. Her own efforts to prevent such an occurrence had begun when she directed Diana to a chair between the elder ladies, but after Mr. Eddington had several times leaned across his mama to include Diana in his conversation, that lady had laughingly demanded that Diana change seats with her so she might hear what Lady Granby was saying.

April was well aware that her hostess was eagerly awaiting a chance to quiz her on her unlikely marriage. She had determined beforehand to thwart this intention as far as possible, but now that the young people were enjoying themselves as they described to a rapt Diana some of the delights to be experienced during the season, she took a sudden decision to abandon her resolve and oblige her hostess. After all, what better way to ensure that a sizable portion of the *ton* heard the story as she wished it told than by allowing her relative to carry the tale forward? Accordingly, she gently eased the eager Phoebe back into the chattering group and exposed her lines for an attack.

"You must permit me to apologize for not calling somewhat sooner, ma'am, but as you so rightly surmised, Diana and I have been prodigiously involved with updating our wardrobes as well as making a start at redecorating the house. It has been sadly neglected for a period of years."

Lady Granby ignored the tempting red herring. "You had been living in the country until your marriage, had you not?"

"Yes." Lest this simple answer strike the others as too abrupt, April amended, "Naturally our sartorial requirements were a good deal less there."

Having no intention of detouring into a discussion of fashion, Lady Granby headed down another road. "The announcement of your marriage came as a great surprise to us, my dear April. I would have expected you to have consulted your cousin about so important a decision."

"And so I should have had I still been a green girl in the habit of turning to my father's cousin for counsel and assistance," April replied gently, permitting herself a slight stress on the final word. If her hostess chose to interpret this as a subtle reminder that no assistance of any kind had ever been forthcoming from this quarter, then she was perfectly at liberty to do so.

In fact, Lady Granby bridled slightly. "Well, as head of the family, I am sure your cousin always stands ready to render any assistance in his power to one so closely connected."

An incredibly sweet smile spread slowly across the countenance of the Countess of Glenville. "Such a generous expression of family feeling does you great credit, ma'am. I am more grateful than mere words can express. And your kind assurance gives me the audacity to beg a small service of you if you will be so good."

The gratified smirk animating Lady Granby's features at the beginning of this speech was succeeded by a rather wary expression.

"Indeed? And what might that be?"

April laughed merrily. "Only what I am persuaded you would have offered unprompted had you been aware that I meant to present Diana this season. I refer, of course, to procuring vouchers for Almack's for us."

"Of course. Naturally I shall be delighted to be of use." Outmaneuvered on all fronts, Lady Granby surrendered after a glance at the expectant face of Lady Eddington.

April thanked her sweetly, then sat back, highly pleased, and allowed Lady Eddington's expressions of delight at having such a charming addition to the ranks of debutantes to wash over her and assail the ears of her kinswoman. Lady Granby struggled to present a complaisant exterior while her good-natured friend assured her that Phoebe and Diana were bound to become devoted to one another, but at the first opportunity she turned the conversation back to the subject of her cousin's noteworthy marriage.

"I should be failing in my duty, my dear April, if I neglected to drop you a hint that your marriage has been a source of great speculation about town."

Clear light eyes with a hint of violet were directed at her, politely attentive, but their owner made no reply, and, after a tiny pause, Lady Granby rushed on: "Glenville is known to be a misogynist; it was settled among the town's matchmaking mamas years ago that his was a hopeless case. Not even that odious Lady Laleham with six daughters to establish, each one plainer than the next, bothered to send him invitations any longer. Even the cleverest of the designing widows had abandoned the chase with respect to Glenville."

"Really?" April experimented with a tiny smile that she hoped might convey amused understanding, *secretive* feminine understanding.

Lady Eddington's comely face looked almost the same vintage as her daughter's when she laughed, despite the faint lines fanning out from her eyes. "Do not allow your cousin's natural and laudable concern for your welfare to alarm you, Lady Glenville, as to your probable reception in society. You cannot avoid being the object of great interest and not a little envy just at first, but if you do not permit yourself to be alienated by the whispers of the disappointed or the insincerity of the toadeaters, you will soon find the vast majority of people eager to welcome you on your own obvious merit."

This time April's smile held real warmth, but before she could express the sense of her obligation to Lady Eddington for her kind words their hostess abandoned her attempts at diplomatic interrogation in favor of the direct approach.

"Naturally, with your own family connections and those of your husband you need have no fears of your acceptance, but people will wonder how you two met with you having lived in retirement for a number of years and Glenville so impervious to the usual run of feminine charms, not to mention other considerations, *past* considerations," she finished with a meaningful look at the new countess.

"Oh, my acquaintance with Lord Glenville is not of recent date, Cousin Louisa," April replied with seeming candor after a swift glance had assured her Diana was too engrossed to hear her. "Dear me, no, we have been known to each other this age or more. However, I must confess that the *ripening* of our friendship has occurred only lately. It was through the kind offices of mutual friends that the opportunity to renew our acquaintance arose." She gave a reminiscent little chuckle. "As Adam always says, there is nothing that provides a more encouraging atmosphere for the development of those tender sentiments between the sexes than a congenial house party."

Both senior ladies were listening avidly to this cloying performance, but April was spared the ordeal of inventing further details by the eruption just then of the vivacious Miss Eddington from the circle of young people.

"Mama," she entreated, then blushed and stammered, "Oh, I do beg your pardon, ma'am!" when she realized Lady Glenville had been speaking.

"What is it, my dear?" Lady Eddington turned to her daughter with an indulgent air.

"Mama, may Miss Wendover join us this afternoon when we go to Somerset House? Just imagine, she has never been there! If you do not object, Lady Glenville?"

April's quick look at Diana took in her eagerness but noted also the downcast eyes of her cousin, who was sitting beside her. When Lady Eddington stated her entire willingness to extend her chaperonage to Miss Wendover and urged her sister to permit the outing, the latter found herself asking quietly, "Does Miss Granby go too?"

"By all means," agreed Lady Eddington quickly. "Phoebe must come too. You girls will all be able to enlighten each other's ignorance."

The three girls giggled at this sally, and April was rewarded by seeing the pleasure that gave Miss Granby's plain face a momentary glow that rendered her almost attractive. Lady Granby shot her a look of mingled surprise and reluctant gratitude as she gave her permission for her daughter's inclusion in the party bent on inspecting the latest works by members of the Royal Academy.

The details of the excursion were arranged in short order, and the visit was terminated just in the nick of time as far as April was concerned to secure her release from Lady Granby's inquisition before she was forced onto the uncertain and untested resources of her imagination to supply further details of Adam's supposed courtship. She apologized to him mentally for her lack of cooperation on the occasion when he had raised the subject and took care to coach Diana in the bare essentials of the story on their return to Hanover Square. Beyond an expression of surprise that it should be thought necessary to improvise a tale to explain her marriage, Diana did not pursue the topic. April had no difficulty in attributing this welcome indifference to her sister's preoccupation with her own first venture into society and thankfully refrained from fuller explanations. That these would be necessary sooner or later she accepted with a fatalistic calm. Diana was curious about her sister's marraige, and April had put her off with deliberately vague answers up to now.

She could not quite account for her extreme reluctance to relate the whole truth to her sister. It wasn't that she feared to destroy the romantic illusions of a young girl regarding love matches. The fact that Diana had, not so very long ago, been urging her to marry Mr. Lynley, well knowing the lack of anything warmer than friendship in her sister's regard for the man, was sufficient proof of that young lady's practical turn of mind. She would not be shocked to learn that April did not love Adam, but she would be shocked to learn that the sister who had preached Christian ethics and guided her behavior from childhood was herself capable of seizing an opportunity in such a contemptible fashion and forcing a man to marry her. Also, for some inexplicable reason, she was loath to reveal the part Adam had played in their lives in the past, though she wouldn't give much for the chance that someone else would not spill the tale into Diana's ears on some occasion. Diana liked Adam unreservedly, and April hated to see this ease and liking diminished for both their sakes. One of the unexpected benefits of the marriage had been the natural shifting of some of her authority to a man's broad shoulders. The strong-willed Diana meekly accepted Adam's pronouncements on various subjects where she might have rebelled against the same decisions made by her sister. Well, it would not do any good to worry herself into a frazzled state over circumstances that did not rest with her. She must play it by ear and try not to concern herself overmuch with possible evil consequences in the future.

With an effort she switched her thoughts to the quite satisfactory results of their morning call. She had been a trifle nervous about that first meeting with her cousin's wife, and her nerve had nearly failed at the sight of strangers in her drawing room, but everything had turned out for the best. The presence of others had put some curb on Lady Granby's quest for minute details of the marriage, and Diana had been exposed most advantageously to an attractive group of youngsters who had made definite overtures of friendship. No doubt Louisa Granby would prefer to keep social contacts between the families to a minimum in order to spare Phoebe unfavorable comparisons with Diana, but it would not be possible to isolate Phoebe from all such comparisons in any case. Unless she was vastly mistaken, the girl had conceived a spontaneous admiration for her pretty cousin which would not suit her mother's book at all.

It was unfortunate the child was so plain, but she seemed to be of a sweet disposition and could be rendered more presentable if someone possessing better taste than her mother took her in hand. Her soft hair of an attractive shade between blond and brown could be dressed to better advantage, and her lean form could be disguised with a more suitable selection of designs and more attention to the fit of the garments. A few minutes of speculation, however, served to convince her that it would be no easy task, situated as she was, to contrive for Phoebe's benefit. The biggest hurdle would be to overcome her mother's inherent and understandable mistrust of the unwanted relatives who had succeeded in escaping the obscurity to which they had been relegated for the past nine years. The more she thought about it the more she allowed that she had been divinely inspired to secure the promise of vouchers for Almack's under circumstances that compelled Lady Granby to conceal her feelings and act as everyone would expect.

Diana, noticing the little smile that curved her sister's lips, paused in rhapsodic recounting of the conversation that had obtained among the young people, gratified to find that April endorsed her opinion of Mr. Eddington as a gentleman of superior address and pleasing appearance. In due course the carriage arrived in Hanover Square and discharged two ladies equally well pleased with their morning activities.

Chapter Nine

The Earl of Glenville, large and impressive in black-and-white evening dress, stood with his back to the green marble fireplace and surveyed his ladies with the eye of a connoisseur as they entered the small saloon. Diana was a bit ahead of her sister, but his glance passed over her to absorb his wife's appearance in a lightning assessment before returning to study the young girl with flattering interest. His all too rare smile shone out, untinged for once by mockery.

Diana blossomed like a spring flower under the warmth of her brother-in-law's fluent compliments, pirouetting slowly with innocent coquetry to present him with a more detailed view of the glory of her first evening dress. April watched the performance in silence, a prey to mixed emotions. The nagging anxiety that she and Diana might not come up to the earl's expectation had vanished with his first words, and she was grateful for the pleasure his praise gave her sister, but she found it necesssary before greeting him with quiet civility to suppress an unreasoning disappointment at the minimal share of the compliments that fell to her lot. His flattering words might be addressed to both; his attention remained on Diana. If April had not been so greatly heartened earlier in the evening by Mattie's gruff declaration that she hadn't realized just how good-looking her mistress was, her courage would have faltered at her husband's apparent indifference. Fortunately there was just enough feminine pique generated by his cavalier attitude to stiffen her spine and enable her to maintain an air of cool unconcern during the drive to Mount Street, where the Jeffrieses' hired town house was situated.

Adam had not been generous with information about their host. April knew only that Jason Jeffries was an opposition member of Parliament from somewhere in the Midlands and that Adam had known him since their days at Eton. The fact that they were the only guests dining with the family before the musical entertainment scheduled by Mrs. Jeffries rather pointed to a close friendship between the men, but April had been made too conscious of the negligible position she occupied in her husband's thoughts to wish to demonstrate her very real curiosity about his associations lest she invite a snub.

The warm welcome accorded them on their arrival confirmed her speculations in the carriage and marked the pleasantest encounter so far in her brief London sojourn. Mr. Jeffries greeted Adam with the casual ease of long acquaintance, and his wife, a plump and smiling brunette, put her hands on the earl's shoulders and kissed him unselfconsciously before turning a magnificent pair of hazel eyes to April with an expression that radiated goodwill. When introductions had been made she confided merrily that she had been dying to meet Lady Glenville and that her *odious* husband, and here she flung a saucy look at the amused Mr. Jeffries, had refused to satisfy her very natural curiosity about his friend's new bride.

"All the provoking creature would reply every time I inquired was that Adam said you were 'difficult to describe.' Is that not just like a man?" she pouted engagingly.

April produced the required social laugh and was relieved when Mr. Jeffries took over from his garrulous wife by declaring gallantly that he would now on his own authority be able to describe Lady Glenville as a prize far beyond the desserts of her inarticulate husband. He led her to a chair and seated her with a flourish, repeating the action for Diana, who dimpled adorably.

Their host then indicated a tray holding glasses and a bottle of champagne. "I wish I might have had the honor of offering this toast at your wedding," he said, looking at April with simple friendliness as he poured the bubbling liquid into the waiting glasses, which his wife distributed, "but at least you will permit me now to wish you the same felicity in marriage that Jane and I have found. To Adam and April."

April concentrated on the contents of her glass, unhappily aware of the obstruction in her throat and the man at her side, so close his shoulder touched hers but still as alien in spirit as on the night they had met. Though thankful for the sincerity of the good wishes being tendered them, she was made more miserably conscious than ever of the falsity of the situation. Strange, but she had never before considered the effect of the marriage on others, people like these kind friends of Adam's who genuinely wished him, and therefore her, well. Troubled gray eyes sought his involuntarily and blinked at the look they encountered. The moment stretched unendurably. She felt the heat rise in her cheeks but was incapable alike of preventing this betrayal or wrenching her glance from the incomprehensible intensity of her husband's regard.

Rescue came in the form of two small children who entered the room at that moment in the company of a middle-aged nurse. They were beautiful children, but the accompanying illusion of docility disintegrated instantaneously when they spied the earl.

"Uncle Adam! Uncle Adam!" shrieked the elder, a boy of about six with his mother's hazel eyes and his father's thin, regular features in miniature. He outdistanced his sister easily and launched himself upon Lord Glenville, who broke into laughter and tossed him high in the air. The unexpectedness of this action elicited a gasp of alarm from April and Diana, but the victim merely squealed with delight and demanded, "Again, Uncle Adam, do it again!"

"Do me, Uncle Adam, do me!"

April's eyes were drawn to the owner of the insistent little voice, a golden-haired cherub clinging to the earl's knees and imploring his attention with piping treble and huge blue eyes. As the man put down his protesting passenger to gather the small girl into his arms, his face came into his wife's line of vision, its hard planes softened by an expression of such tenderness as she had never thought possible from her knowledge of him. Her fascinated gaze was riveted to him as he raised the little girl slowly over his head for an instant before drawing her into a close embrace. The child squirmed in an agony of pleasurable fear. "Do it again, Uncle Adam, please!"

He pretended to consider. "Well, that depends. Who does Missy love?"

"Mummy!" replied the little girl promptly, casting him a sly look from under gold-tipped lashes.

"Anyone else?"

"Papa!"

A gentle shake was administered to the tiny temptress. "Anyone else?"

"And Uncle Adam!" she crowed with a squeaky giggle.

"That's better." As the earl again raised the enchanting little bit of femininity overhead, it was clear from the indulgent looks on her parents' faces and the dancing impatience of the small boy that this was a familiar ritual enjoyed by all.

"It's my turn now, Uncle Adam!"

"In a minute, Jonathan," said the mother. "We mustn't forget our manners. Come make your bow to Lady Glenville and Miss Wendover."

Despite his disappointment at the postponement of his treat, the boy performed a creditable bow and said a polite how-do-you-do to the ladies before returning his attention to the earl, who stood with the little girl in his arms watching the introductions.

"Missy's afraid to be tossed," pronounced her brother with more than a trace of satisfaction.

"I'm not afraid!"

"Then let Uncle Adam toss you."

Adam intervened quickly as two little hands clutched his lapels in a tightened grip. "Missy, I'd like you to meet Lady Glenville and Miss Wendover." He brought the child to the two women, but when Diana would have taken the small hand, Missy pulled it back and ducked her head against Adam's shoulder. April was careful to make no overtures to the little girl as Adam sat down beside her on the sofa with the child on his lap.

"Missy's almost four, but she's afraid of everyone," Jonathan informed the assembled company. "Nurse says she's shy." After this brief detour he went back to his primary objective. "You promised to throw me again, Uncle Adam."

"I will before you go to bed."

Mrs. Jeffries was telling the ladies (quite unnecessarily) how the children adored Adam, and had begun relating an amusing incident concerning him when April felt a tiny movement at her hair. She turned her head slowly to see a chubby hand withdraw. One blue eye stared daringly back from the safety of the earl's arms.

"You may touch my hair if you wish," she whispered with a smile, bending her head invitingly. After an instant she felt another little movement as Missy satisfied her curiosity by stroking the silken length with feather-light pressure.

April smiled again and this time was rewarded by an answering smile that revealed tiny white teeth. Seeing the earl's attention on this interchange, Missy explained solemnly, "Pretty hair," then, more comprehensively, "Pretty lady."

"Out of the mouths of babes." Mr. Jeffries sent a companionable grin in the direction of the bride and groom. Adam's eyes were still fixed on his wife's countenance, but he made no reply. She could only hope the color in her cheeks would be attributed to Mr. Jeffries's gallantry. It was a relief to be able to focus on Missy, whose exploring hand was reaching for the pearl pin fixed at the bodice of her gown. Unthinkingly, she extended her arms and the child went into them, all shyness forgotten in her eagerness to examine the pin.

Thanks in part to the numerous possibilities offered by the existence of the Jeffrieses' attractive children, an easy

conversation ensued for a further few moments, all of which
saw Missy comfortably settled in April's lap. Each time the
latter glanced up she was conscious of her husband's
enigmatic regard, however, so she was not too reluctant to
have the interlude brought to an end with the announcement of dinner. Jonathan was allotted the promised tossing,
then Nurse swept her reluctant charges off to their beds
after affectionate goodnights were taken of their parents
and Uncle Adam. April was honored to be the recipient of a
shy hug from Missy, and the little one even summoned up a
valedictory smile for Diana.

Dinner was a most relaxed and enjoyable meal. Conversation ranged over many topics, with subjects of general
interest interspersed with periods when the ladies left the
gentlemen to discuss political points while Mrs. Jeffries
eagerly sought details of the ongoing renovation of the earl's
house, which she recalled as being excessively gloomy on the
one occasion when she had visited it. When the talk swung
around to the latest fashions, April found her attention at
first wandering and then caught up in the men's discussion
of the chances of getting the latest of Sir Samuel Romilly's
reform measures through the House of Lords. Mr. Jeffries
was more optimistic than Adam that the peers might finally
relent and repeal the death penalty for the theft of five
shillings from a shop.

"Never!" Adam stated positively. "They've defeated it
before and will assuredly do so again even if Lansdowne,
Grey, and others speak for the bill. Each new report of a
workers' rally, a meeting of radicals, or even a window
broken by a street urchin sends them scurrying back to their
holes."

"At the moment perhaps, but reform of the criminal code
is inevitable. Romilly managed to get the penalty for pick-
pocketing reduced a few years ago, and sentiment around
the country is strongly for reform."

"One cannot argue that transportation is not preferable
to hanging," April said at this point, "but it is still dreadfully severe. A lad from the village where I lived was con-

victed last year in London. His parents know they will never see him again. He is their only remaining child, and their hearts are broken. It is pitiful to see them suffer so, and all for the theft of a few shillings."

Adam responded in all seriousness. "The system of penalties itself is a crime against justice and encourages witnesses to lie and juries to disregard their oaths and refuse to convict in the face of indisputable evidence. Many judges, too, arrest the course of justice by refusing to impose the sentence prescribed in the statutes. Jason is undoubtedly correct in reading the sentiment for reform around the country, but he is mistaken if he thinks those jumped-up merchants in the Lords will relent during this session *or* the next. The bishops are even more reactionary. I have great difficulty in comprehending their particular brand of Christianity."

"Romilly will keep hammering away at them, and he gains support daily," Mr. Jeffries repeated before abandoning the topic in favor of questioning Adam on the recent happenings in the Ministry.

April, marveling at the intellectual compatibility existing between a member of the government and a staunch Whig MP, couldn't help the silent reflection that the state of the country couldn't be expected to improve materially until the number of such reasonable men increased considerably in and around the government.

In due course the ladies filed out of the dining room, leaving the gentlemen to the peaceful imbibing of their port, although Mrs. Jeffries, with a beguiling wrinkling of her small, nearly *retroussé* nose, declared that the word "port" was merely a euphemism to cloak their transparent intention of filling her dining room with the noxious fumes of the vile cigars they professed, quite incomprehensibly, to enjoy.

"We shall open wide both windows, my love, despite the imminent danger to our lungs from the damp night air," her husband promised soothingly, thereby convicting himself out of his own mouth on his wife's charge.

She directed a look of mingled resignation and affection toward him before leading her guests to a small anteroom off the combined drawing rooms, explaining as they settled comfortably around the fireplace, "We shall be more at ease here while awaiting the arrival of the rest of the company. I think there can be nothing so destructive to a conversation as a room full of empty chairs."

The interval while the men remained absent was pleasantly taken up by speculating on the forthcoming wedding of the heir to the throne. Mrs. Jeffries assured her guests that the visit of Princess Charlotte to Brighton the previous month had gone famously, although her father's gout was still troubling him. She had it on the authority of one of the other guests that the Prince and his daughter had met with every evidence of filial affection on her part and paternal benevolence on his, and the result had been his freely given consent to her marriage to Prince Leopold. "It really is a love match, you know. After that other unfortunate affair and her subsequent confinement to Cranbourne Lodge she'd no doubt have accepted any suitor to achieve the status and freedom of a married woman, but by all reports she simply dotes on Prince Leopold. I must say I find his person rather severe, though attractive enough. I should be surprised indeed to find he possessed much in the way of a sense of humor. The Germans are so dreadfully dull on the whole, do you not agree?"

The other ladies, being newly arrived in town, were unable to voice an opinion on this important subject, but they displayed a flattering eagerness to learn as many details of the royal romance as Mrs. Jeffries could supply. Diana, just a couple of years younger than Princess Charlotte, was particularly keen to hear even secondhand reports on one who was destined to become her sovereign one day.

When the men ultimately joined them, the three women looked up in some surprise, so absorbed had they become in palace gossip. There was just time for a lingering cup of coffee before the guests were due to arrive. The earl, looking more relaxed and human than April had ever seen him, inquired as to the entertainment they were to expect. Mrs. Jeffries named the cellist and violinist whom she had engaged to play, and added with a smile, "And you will give us the pleasure of a song or two, will you not, dear Adam? I vow you are the main reason my musical evenings are so well attended. No other hostess can boast of producing such a fine voice from among her friends."

"After that highly exaggerated but most acceptable tribute I am desolated to have to refuse you, Jane, but my throat has been a trifle scratchy all afternoon and I fear it is worsening. I would not be an asset to your program tonight, I fear—very much the opposite, indeed."

April scarcely heard Mrs. Jeffries's polite murmurs of sympathy and disappointment. She was storing up in her mind yet another unexpected discovery about the man she had married. This had been an evening of surprises. She had barely assimilated the startling but unmistakable evidence that the man she had considered quite cold and inhuman had a definite soft spot for children, at least for two specific children, when she was confronted with another unsuspected aspect of his personality. That he enjoyed music was no surprise—his attentiveness when Diana played and sang had been repeated too often to be counterfeit—but she would not have guessed in a thousand years that his natural reserve could dissolve to the extent that it would permit him to perform before an audience. Mrs. Jeffries's disappointment was as nothing compared to that which swept through April as she searched her husband's countenance in an unsuccessful effort to discover whether or not his easy excuse had been genuine.

The sound of the door knocker below brought the company to its feet as the first guests arrived. As they passed into the larger rooms, Jason Jeffries mentioned to his wife that he had run into Damien Harding that afternoon and had invited him to drop in. Damien had planned to attend a boxing exhibition with a friend but said he'd come by if his friend were agreeable to a change of plans.

"Very good," said his spouse. "Freddy is coming, you

know." She turned to April. "Have you and Miss Wendover made the acquaintance of Adam's cousins yet, Lady Glenville?"

April had time for only the sketchiest reply before the main doors were opened and the earliest of the guests announced. The next half hour was spent in responding to numerous introductions to people she despaired of remembering at a later date. Among the hordes was only one familiar face, that of a girl she recalled from the days of her own comeout, once remarkable for her extreme silliness, and now to all appearances a sober young matron. In the press of new arrivals she was allowed time neither to reanimate the acquaintance nor dwell on the change in her erstwhile friend. Adam remained at her side giving a totally believable performance as a devoted husband. She felt there must be a permanent flush on her cheeks at the many ingratiating comments from the people presented to her. She glanced at her sister to see how that young lady was bearing up under the ordeal.

Diana was deliciously flustered by all the flattering attention being showered upon her and had need of all her innate self-possession to maintain a demure facade. April squeezed her hand and smiled encouragingly at the girl and thus missed the arrival of the two men she most hoped to avoid in London. It was Adam's casual-looking but insistent hand nipping her waist that alerted her, and she directed an inquiring stare toward him. At sight of Mr. Damien Harding's handsome face a foot away, the smile on her lips stiffened, but it was the man beside him who caused it to fade slowly away. Only the comforting pressure of her husband's hand at her waist enabled her to conquer an instinctive physical shrinking.

"You remember Lord Allerton, my dear," he was saying in a voice devoid of all emotion after having greeted his cousin warmly.

"Yes indeed. How do you do, sir, and you, Mr. Harding? May I present my sister, Miss Wendover. Diana, this is

Adam's other cousin, Mr. Damien Harding, and Lord Allerton."

If April hoped in the crush of arrivals to be able to slide by with no further contact, she was doomed to disappointment. Mr. Harding was greeting Diana with the same effusiveness he had displayed on being introduced to herself, and Diana's wholehearted response left her sister face-to-face with the detestable Allerton for some seconds while someone engaged Adam's attention on his other side. Allerton's initial astonishment upon seeing her, which she had no hesitation in ascribing to the marked improvement in her appearance, gave way to a narrow-eyed scrutiny which April found no less offensive. By exercising a stern self-command she was able to meet his glance with the cool composure of an actress when it returned from the thorough survey of her slim person attractively clad in glistening folds of pale-rose brocade.

"I nearly failed to recognize you, Lady Glenville," he offered with more haste than wisdom.

"Indeed."

With the single word uttered in freezing accents, the conversation languished and died. Lord Allerton seized the hand Diana had extended to him like a drowning man grasping for a raft and held it longer than was strictly acceptable.

"This is a great pleasure, Miss Wendover. Glenville is a fortunate man indeed to have surrounded himself with feminine loveliness. If I had only been permitted to make your acquaintance the day after your sister's marriage when I met her in the inn I might now claim the privilege of a friend to request the pleasure of your company for the entertainment this evening."

"Oh, did you meet April at the inn?" the girl asked, a trifle puzzled. "She and Adam weren't—"

"Diana, I require your assistance in pinning up this torn flounce before the music begins," April cut in quickly, conscious of the sudden alertness of both Mr. Harding and Lord

Allerton but unable on the spur of the moment to invent a
more convincing excuse.

"How did you tear your flounce?"

"Someone trod on it," was the curt reply as April placed a
firm hand under her sister's elbow and led her away, saying
over her shoulder, "I beg you will excuse us for a moment,
gentlemen?"

When the two women reached the ladies' retiring room,
April waved away the offer of assistance from the maid and
spoke to her sister in a quiet intense voice.

"There is no time to explain fully, Diana, but it is imperative that no one should learn the exact date or place of my
marriage. If Lord Allerton or Mr. Harding or anyone else
should refer to the subject again, be vague but allow them to
think we married before arriving in town. Do you understand?"

"Of course, but why should you wish to deceive people?"

"I cannot explain at the moment; we must be seated
before the entertainment can begin. Here, allow me to
straighten this bow on your sleeve a trifle before we return.
There, that's better. You have conducted yourself very
prettily tonight in the face of so many introductions,
dearest. Are you enjoying yourself?"

"Oh yes," Diana replied sunnily as they made their way
back to Adam's side. "Everyone is most kind." She twinkled
at her sister. "Why did you not tell me Mr. Damien Harding
was so handsome? Such an air of distinction, such address,
and his manners so exquisitely polished! I really believe I
prefer older men after all."

They reached Adam at this point, so April was spared the
necessity of commenting on this ingenuous and unwelcome
disclosure. The presence of Mr. Frederick Harding in
company with his cousin and the situation of his brother and
Allerton at a distance that precluded conversation went a
long way toward restoring April's serenity. Seated between
her husband and his heir, she was able in time to relax her
taut nerves and enjoy the musical program. It had been a
close-run thing, though, and she would have no hesitation in

wagering her entire wardrobe against the chance that either of those men would allow the subject of her marriage to drop without making an attempt to discover all the particulars. The earl had looked at her searchingly upon her return with Diana but had refrained from comment. It wasn't until a break in the music while Mrs. Jeffries introduced a friend who had agreed to play a selection on the harp that he leaned closer and whispered:

"What happened? Why did you disappear so suddenly?"

She lowered her voice to a thread of sound behind her ivory fan. "Did you not hear? Diana nearly revealed that we were not married at the time we met Allerton at the inn. I was obliged to remove her and warn her against any future disclosures."

Before Adam could respond, her attention was claimed by Freddy, and shortly the music recommenced, severing any opportunity for further communication. She had seen the tightening of her husband's finely chiseled mouth, however, and knew a selfish comfort in having enlisted a fellow sufferer in her anxiety. Thanks in part to a fundamental conviction that Adam was more than a match for Allerton, she was able to put the awkward incident clear out of her mind for the remainder of the evening except during the short interval when she discovered Diana in private conversation with the two men. How right she had been to heed her instincts in delivering a prompt warning to the girl! They had not let any grass grow beneath their feet in seeking her out. It was impossible to tell the nature of the conversation from the expressions on their faces, and in any case Diana's instant popularity among the younger guests served to curtail the tête-à-tête. She had the pleasure of seeing the men bow and remove themselves fairly soon, and neither approached her sister during the remainder of the evening.

With his quiet charm, Freddy set about making her feel at home in society later when refreshments were served. He seemed to know everybody and guided her into conversation with an ease born of genuine interest in others. While in the supper room with its lavish buffet, April was approached by

her former friend, whose idea of bridging the gap of years
was to bring her up to date on the number and ages of her
own progeny and those of mutual friends from that long-ago
season. During the enforced catalogue, Freddy melted away
with the acquired ability of the male to avoid boredom, and
when, her head stuffed with birth statistics, April at length
negotiated her release after a promise to call and meet the
children, it was to find him wending a slightly unsteady
course toward her again. His quiet manner was unchanged
and his speech unimpaired, but she noticed a trembling in
the fingers that held a wine cup and a hint of rigidity in his
bearing that caused her to suspect he had been dipping
rather deeply in the interim. A look of disgust on Adam's
face when he sought her out a few moments later gave rise to
some conjecture on April's part as to the frequency of such
behavior, but she dismissed the notion in the pleasures of
their first social engagement. Later when she bade Diana
goodnight at her door they agreed that it had been an altogether happy baptism in the waters of society.

Chapter Ten

It was close to five o'clock when the Earl of Glenville entered his house, heartened by an unusual sense of homecoming. The day had seemed endless, packed with irritating problems and petty skirmishes that took on additional weight because he was feeling well below normal. With heartfelt relief he stripped off his gloves and allowed Morton to divest him of greatcoat, hat, and cane.

"Ladies in, Morton?"

"Not yet, my lord, but Lady Glenville ordered tea for five-fifteen. They have gone driving with Mr. Frederick in the Park."

"Thank you. I'll be in my study until then."

Morton had been making a discreet survey of his master's person during this exchange, and now he asked, "Are you feeling quite yourself, my lord?"

"Frankly, Morton, I feel like something left for dead on a battlefield. Must have a cold coming on."

"Can I get you anything, sir? Shall I ask Mrs. Donaldson to brew you a posset?"

"No. I refuse to quack myself. Nature brought it and in due course Nature will take it away."

Following this clipped pronouncement, the earl disappeared into his study, where he remained until he had finished writting a letter begun the previous day. A mild commotion in the hall a few minutes before had proclaimed the return of his wife and sister-in-law with attendant guests. He frowned as he sealed the letter and franked it. Rarely had he felt less disposed to do the pretty to the assortment of tame cats April and Diana had collected about themselves in their brief exposure to society, but the promise of a hot cup of tea lured him upstairs. Or so he told himself as he headed for the main saloon, from which drifted animated snatches of conversation and trills of feminine laughter interspersed with the odd masculine guffaw. He was not prepared to admit that he missed the occasional peaceful hour spent drinking tea with his wife that had become almost routine before she and Diana had achieved their current popularity, but he didn't mind acknowledging a certain impatience at having his house constantly overrun with humanity, especially since the examples of such tended to run heavily in favor of the idle young sprigs of fashion whom he found mildly intolerable at best and totally irrelevant at all times.

For a moment his presence in the doorway went undetected by the merry group scattered about the tea table. He was relieved to discover the only guests were his two cousins, but the initial relief was quickly succeeded by a twinge of irritation as he noted Freddy's golden head bent attentively toward April. As usual his gaze lingered on the silvery fall of satin-smooth hair caressing his wife's cheek as she reached for her cup.

It was April who first became aware of the blue-coated figure that had entered the room so quietly.

"Adam! I did not hear you come in. Would you like some tea?"

Whether more influenced by his wife's spontaneous smile of welcome or the unwelcome presence of his cousin sitting close beside her on the green settee Adam did not attempt to assess as he set a course for the empty chair near the settee and deliberately leaned over to salute her cheek with his lips before responding to the bright greetings of the others.

"Let me prepare your tea, Adam," said Diana, jumping up immediately. "You look to be in urgent need of it."

"Too right, old man. You look like the end of a wet

week," was the unfeeling comment of his younger cousin.

April had reached the same basic conclusion after a covert study of her husband from under her lashes while she pretended to be absorbed in the contents of her cup. Now she rested a concerned glance on his face.

"It's my belief that you would benefit by a spell in your bed, Adam. You have been battling that cold for days." She watched his mouth tighten as he nodded thanks to Diana and accepted his cup.

"Nonsense. I am perfectly capable of functioning normally and refuse to be rendered bedfast. I'm probably over the worst of it by now in any case." He changed the subject determinedly.

April preserved an unconvinced silence while the conversation flowed around her. To her eye, Adam looked worse each day. His throat continued to be scratchy, as evidenced by the hacking cough that overtook him at intervals. His eyes were red-rimmed, and she was persuaded that he was a frequent victim of the headache. In fact, he presented all the appearance of a person with a feverish cold, except that until the present at least he had not run a temperature. She noted that he avoided the tempting scones and iced cakes on the tray but rapidly drank two cups of tea. His appetite at dinner, the only meal they partook of together, had diminished alarmingly of late, and this too was worrying.

Aware of her silent scrutiny, the earl turned and addressed her with determined lightness. "How go the riding lessons and dancing lessons? Will she be likely to put us to the blush at our ball?"

April laughed out suddenly, and a rare twinkle came into the cool gray eyes as they surveyed her sister's indignant face. "There is much less likelihood that she will disgrace us on the dance floor than on horseback, thank heavens. I have gleaned from among a plethora of complaints that Diana would be more inclined to profit by her instruction in horsemanship if only the noble beast might be persuaded to refrain from habits of twitching, sidling, dancing, snorting or sudden lifts of the head, and most vital of all, could be bred to a much smaller stature!"

Diana tossed her golden curls and pouted at the general amusement. "Well, they *are* too tall, and it cannot be denied that the stupid creatures are disastrously prone to sudden movements that are unnerving to the rider."

"Do not be discouraged, Diana," soothed Freddy. "You are experiencing the difficulties that beset most novice riders, but you'll find you will soon accustom yourself to the animal's peculiarities and will grow much more confident in the saddle."

"Lord, yes, you'll be leading the hunting field in a year," predicted Mr. Damien Harding, with what Diana could only consider a gross overestimation of the probable rate of her progress in the equestrian arts. "In fact," he added breezily, "I'll invite you here and now to hunt with me this fall."

"And I'll decline on her behalf here and now." The earl turned to his sister-in-law and said with mock seriousness, "Diana, you are never under any circumstances to put your life in jeopardy by joining Damien on the hunting field or in any shooting sport whatever. In a hunt he is sure to part company at the first fence, and the cawker doesn't even know how to carry a gun safely. He nearly killed me when we went out pheasant shooting last fall, but the pheasants had never been so safe."

April's eyes had flown to her husband's younger cousin, so she caught the flash of real anger that distorted his handsome face for a bare instant before he got it under control and produced a protesting laugh.

"Hey, now, that's libel or slander or something. I haven't fallen at a fence in years, and anyone could have tripped over that root and discharged his piece. It was an accident that could have happened to anyone."

"And I wouldn't be sitting here at this moment had I been two inches taller," retorted the earl, "as the hole in my hat can testify. Do I exaggerate, Freddy?"

That gentleman grinned at his discomfited brother. "Not a bit of it. Damien is a menace even with a harmless fishing rod, but judging from that exquisitely tied cravat, he's putting to good use the time he saves by keeping off the field of sport. A real pink of the *ton*, my little brother."

His little brother's rude rejoinder drawing attention to the crumpled state of his senior's own neckcloth and the haphazard style of his attire developed into a lively exchange that provoked laughter from Diana and the earl. April kept a smile pinned on her lips, but she heard none of it. The artless disclosure by the earl of a near miss at the hands of his cousin had rocked her more than was warranted by the facts of the matter. Her initial unfavorable impression of Mr. Damien Harding had undergone a slow revision in the wake of his persistent efforts to be pleasantly attentive and accommodating toward his cousin's bride, but in a flash all her instictive wariness had returned stronger than ever. She was hard pressed to hold up her end of the conversation during the remainder of the tea party.

The earl grew less animated presently, and he indulged in one or two bouts of coughing that left him looking drained and exhausted. His heir regarded him with sympathy on making his adieux and advised him to take things easy for a time until he had shaken off his cold. "The Ministry can run without you for a few days."

Damien added his advice. "Stay home and enjoy the benefits of your gorgeous wife's nursing skills. It's an ill wind, after all."

Adam dismissed them both summarily and cut short the earnest representations of his wife and sister-in-law on the wisdom of retiring early to bed with a tray for dinner. He joined them in the dining room at the appointed hour and exerted the utmost effort to conceal the fact that he could scarcely face any food with equanimity. With all parties constrained to avoid the topic of the earl's health, conversation was necessarily of a rather artificial nature, and the end of dinner was greeted with relief by everyone. April and Diana were scheduled to attend a small card party at the Eddingtons',

and as they took their leave of Adam, April mustered the
courage to express the polite hope that he would have an early
night and feel more the thing in the morning.

It was soon evident that her hopes were not to be realized.
Adam was no better the next day or on the days that followed.
The scratchy throat and coughing continued unabated, and
his eyes remained irritated — these symptoms were impossible of
concealment. Likewise it became obvious that he had lost
weight, which was not surprising, since he was eating poorly.
April suspected that the sight of food nauseated him, but he
denied this, as he denied any problem with headaches. He
persisted in reporting to the Ministry each day and flatly
refused to consult a doctor, though April had it from Freddy
that one of the Regent's own physicians, Sir Everad Howe, was
highly thought of around town. Her ears ringing from Adam's
pithy description of this physician's skills, she still found the
nerve to venture another name, but her husband was adamant.
Miserable though it admittedly was, he was only suffering from
a cold and had no slightest intention of involving any of the
charlatans of the medical profession in his affairs.

Perforce, April subsided, but the truth was that as the first
week of Adam's illness gave way to the second she began to
question that what he was suffering from was indeed a head
cold. For one thing, he never developed a fever, and for
another, his symptoms did not seem to worsen rapidly and then
gradually ameliorate as in the natural progression of a feverish
cold, nor did his nose stream. When she noticed a distinct
tremor in his facial muscles her mind started to query what else
might produce a similar effect on the human constitution, and
although it chilled her blood to consider it, she could not rule
our poison with complete confidence. Her instincts had been
too active about the enmity she was convinced Morton bore the
earl for her to dismiss the possibility out of hand. Suspicions,
however, were not evidence, and she could not see how such an
end could be achieved when she and Diana ate the same food
and were served the same dishes at dinner. Adam always
breakfasted early and alone, however, so one morning she
joined him unexpectedly, answering his surprise with a tale of

rising early to finish writing out the invitations to Diana's ball. She watched Morton closely but could discover no concern for her presence on the butler's part, and he served her the same food his master was doing scant justice to.

Adam never lunched at home, so April thought she was safe in ruling out that possibility as the source of any poisoning. Doubtless he ate with freinds, and Morton would not have access to his food supply during the day. She was reluctantly being forced to the conclusion that her suspicions arose from an intellect disordered by fears based solely on prejudice when the idea struck her like a *coup de foudre*.

The cigars! She found she was trembling physically as her mind raced back over the details of the scene when she had witnessed Morton receive the package of cigars from an unidentified caller with blond hair. The exchange had looked strange at the time until a reasonable explanation had presented itself to her. Fool that she was, she had never checked the truth of that explanation!

April had been changing for dinner when the idea hit her, and her subsequent actions caused Mattie to question her mistress's sanity. She halted her dresser in the process of brushing her hair, cast down the amber beads she had been about to clasp around her neck with such force the string broke, scattering beads all over dressing table and floor, rose from the bench in one precipitate motion, and rushed from the room without a word to the astonished woman, whose scolding was interrupted in midstream by the slamming of the door.

After pelting down the stairs as though all the fiends in hell were at her heels it was a decided anticlimax to find the saloon deserted. April's agitation of spirits was so great she could not stand still, and Adam found her pacing the floor when he entered a few moments later. She searched his surprised face for signs that the symptoms had worsened, but to her infinite relief he appeared a trifle brighter tonight. Without stopping to consider a tactful approach, she blurted out:

"Adam, did you ask Morton to order other cigars to switch with the ones Diana bought you?"

For a moment the earl eyed in astonished silence the tense

figure facing him with fingers laced tightly together against her amber gown. When no explanation for this extraordinary question was forthcoming, he said quietly, "No, Diana bought my favorite type of cigar. Why do you ask?"

It was here that April made the mistake that was to have such disastrous consequences. She continued to stare at her husband's curious, watchful face, her own blank with shock as the implications of his reply reverberated in her brain. Her legs felt incapable of taking her weight of a sudden, and she dropped into a chair. When she had assumed Adam had ordered a switch in cigars, Morton's lie with regard to the person at the front door had seemed unimportant, but now she berated herself for not challenging him on it. Why had she not realized that even if Adam had ordered a switch in cigars they would not have been delivered to the front door?

The mental picture of crisp blond locks beneath a rakishly tipped hat brim crowded out the question Adam had asked her. She recalled now Freddy's recent admission when she had idly wondered why she had not seen him driving his phaeton in the park that he had sold his fine chestnut pair to bail Damien out of a scrape. Subsequent delicate probing on her part had elicited the information that Damien was never more than one step ahead of the tipstaffs. He was an inveterate gambler, with the addict's irrational faith in his star. Adam, who had made good his cousin's losses periodically for years, had finally lost all patience with his worthless promises of reform and had warned him last summer that he had towed him out of the River Tick for the final time. Since then, according to his tolerant brother, Damien had made a real effort to reform his way of life, but he had been forced to apply to Freddy for assistance on one or two occasions when he fell into dun territory again. With stomach-turning conviction, April could imagine Damien's increasing desperation since Adam's ultimatum. Within his power, Freddy would always come to his brother's rescue, but Freddy's financial position was none too healthy either. If Adam were to die without issue, however, Freddy would inherit his consequence and his fortune, and Freddy would never deny his brother. She knew in her bones that it had been Damien Harding at that door passing over poisoned cigars to his former servant for the purpose of murdering his cousin! He had failed to kill him with a faked hunting accident but had been forced to hurry into a new attempt by the unexpected acquisition of a bride, who could not be allowed to produce an heir who would cut him out of the succession. Put into words, it was absolutely appalling, but all the facts fitted.

"April, are you feeling faint?"

Adam's voice, seeming to come from far away, brought April's dazed glance up from her twisting fingers. How could she possibly tell him his favorite cousin wanted him dead badly enough to do the deed himself when she hadn't a shred of actual proof? The enormity of the accusation and the impossibility of making it rendered her speechless. When Diana came into the room a second later, April was still gazing helplessly into her husband's puzzled eyes.

"You two look like statues in a tableau," declared the young girl with a giggle. "How are you feeling tonight, Adam? I do think you look a little better."

"Thank you, I am feeling stronger today. And you are blooming with health and spirits as usual, I see."

Perhaps it's all a ghastly mistake, April thought, staring intently at her husband. Adam does look somewhat recovered. Perhaps it never was poison at all. Diana turned to include her in the dialogue, and her sister gathered her scattered wits together and made a conscious effort to take part. During dinner she was not put to too much strain, thanks to Diana's bubbling spirits, which, as frequently happened, prompted her to assume control of the conversation.

It wasn't until the women rose to leave the table that April's surface attention was jerked back to the subject occupying her deeper thoughts to the exclusion of all others. In an unusual move the earl got up and walked to the door with them, explaining that tonight was the first night in several that he had felt well enough to enjoy an after-dinner smoke. "Bring some brandy to the study, Morton," he directed as they exited the dining room.

"*No!*"

April clutched Adam's arm. "Do not try to smoke a cigar tonight," she begged, moderating her tones. "I am persuaded they are bad for you while your throat is so irritated. Wait until you are quite recovered."

"I am touched by your solicitude, my dear," replied her husband in a smooth voice that gave away none of his thoughts. "Your wish must be my command. Since I am to be denied my smoke, may I request that you play for me tonight, if I am correct in assuming you and Diana have no engagement this evening?"

April was slightly taken aback. The earl had never asked her to play for him before. "Yes, of course, Adam, if you wish it, but would you not prefer to have Diana play and sing as usual?" He repeated his request, subjecting her to an intent study from unreadable dark eyes. She took her place at the pianoforte in some confusion.

Diana expressed herself as pleased to have an opportunity to finish sewing beads on the matching band she intended to wear in her hair when she wore her new yellow ball dress. She settled down contentedly to enjoy the delightful sounds April could coax out of any piano. The only luxury they had been able to bring to the cottage from the sale of their father's property had been the pianoforte, because it belonged to April and their mother had flatly refused to allow her to sell it to pay Sir Charles's debts. During those dreary years in the village, music had been Lady Wendover's only pleasure, and it would not be extravagant to say it had been her daughter's salvation when troubles pressed heavily upon her. Since they had been residing in Hanover Square their days had been filled to overflowing with activity; time to devote to music had been severely curtailed. Despite her general malaise and worry about Adam tonight, April felt a sense of peace and well-being steal over her as she began to play softly. In a few minutes she had forgotten the presence of others in the room as she gave herself over to the wholly satisfying pursuit of beauty. She never bethought herself to ask the others' preferences, and Diana and the earl were content to listen to the works she selected. There was almost no interaction among them until the tea tray was brought in. When April rose to join her husband and sister, Adam thanked her quietly for bringing him great pleasure. The implied compliment was more welcome than paragraphs of hyperbole, and she retired shortly thereafter in a glow of contentment that lasted until the door of her bedchamber closed behind her.

The fear and horror that music had set at a distance for a short time crowded in on her again as she made her preparations for bed in a mechanical fashion. It was almost impossible to credit that the very civilized Damien Harding might actually be capable of attempting to do away with his cousin, and if she, who disliked him, had difficulty accepting such a depth of depravity, how could she hope to convince Adam of such an evil intention on the part of one bound so closely to him by ties of blood and long association? The plain answer was that she could not, not without proof, and there was no way to obtain proof. The only truly convincing evidence, she thought bitterly, would be her husband's lifeless corpse. Morton would deny everything, of course. The best she could hope for was to have the cigars analyzed, but she could not persuade herself that Adam would accept her word against Morton's even then. He already thought her an adventuress; there was little reason for him to accept her word of honor. The problem seemed insoluble.

After a night of tossing in her bed with no more than fitful periods of sleep, April arose heavy-eyed and unhappy but determined on her course. The one essential action was to exchange those suspect cigars and have them analyzed. Her duty was clear. If Adam refused to believe her, at least she would have done her best. She refused to dwell on the likelihood of Damien's trying another method when this one failed. Whether her husband believed her or not he would be on his guard. But would she ever know another moment entirely free from fear? That question didn't bear examination.

Purchasing the cigars presented no difficulty. April left Diana browsing in Hookham's Library in the company of the Eddington ladies whom they chanced to meet there while she hastened out and made the purchase. This was accomplished in a matter of minutes, but making the substitution proved to be another matter entirely. Adam was in his study when she and Diana returned from shopping. Though he joined them briefly for tea, he intended returning to do more work before changing. The ladies were dining with Jane Jeffries, since Jason Jeffries and the earl had made plans to go to Cribbs's to see the latest bruiser to capture the public's fancy. April hoped to be able to slip down to the study before the carriage was due to arrive, but Mattie took so long over her dressing that Diana was ready first and came into her sister's room to peacock around for her old nurse's approval. This effectively canceled any early-evening attempt at effecting an exchange.

There was nothing to be done about it — she must possess her soul in patience, April told herself as she accepted her blue velvet cloak from Mattie's hands. But it was imperative that she make the switch tonight. Adam's cough was a trifle better these past two days; he might take it into his head to enjoy a smoke at the boxing match. She would be unable to prevent him from taking some cigars with him on his way out should he desire to do so, but she was resolved these would be the last.

The evening would have been most enjoyable had April been capable of keeping her mind directed at the affairs of the moment. Jane Jeffries was an easy-mannered, companionable woman with few ambitions to cut a dash in society. Being endowed with a sunny nature, she enjoyed herself everywhere she went, but her husband and children filled her world completely. Jonathan and Melissa again came to bid their parent goodnight and deigned to remember "Uncle Adam's ladies." To be sure, Jonathan was unable wholly to conceal his disappointment at not finding the earl among those present, but Missy, free from the shyness that had previously afflicted her, more than made up for her brother's forced politeness by running over to April and demanding to see the pretty pin again. Fortunately April was able to gratify this desire, and there followed a rather one-sided conversation as Missy explained that Nurse said Lady Glenville was Uncle Adam's wife like Mummy was Papa's wife and that Miss Wendover was Uncle Adam's sister like Auntie Rose was Papa's sister.

"Do you have any little girls like me?" she inquired after this informative discourse had been delivered.

It required a prodigious amount of effort on April's part to produce the necessary negative and accept Missy's sincere commiserations on the lack without betraying herself. Looking at the eager little face raised to hers, April had known with sudden painful intensity that she wanted desperately to have a little girl like Missy—or a little boy—it didn't matter which as long as the child was hers.

And Adam's!

The incredible thought took sudden and complete possession of her mind. She sat perfectly still, so stunned by what had just transpired that she could not fully take it in, didn't wish to take it in.

"April," Diana was saying, "Missy wishes to know if you would like to have a little girl."

The smooth silvery head nodded to the curly golden one. "Yes, Missy, I think it would be lovely to have a little girl just like you or a big boy like Jonathan."

Mrs. Jeffries laughed. "And now while my awkward infant is preening herself on her importance in the scheme of things, I think we shall dispatch her to her bed and go on in to dinner."

April and Diana were home by eleven-thirty, but the day would not be over for April until she had accomplished her self-imposed task. There was no call to arouse Mattie's suspicions by seeming desirous of curtailing her evening routine. Morton, whose pantry was near the study, never went to bed until Adam came home. Since she could not chance discovery by the butler, it was going to be necessary to wait until the whole household was asleep, which could

mean hours of tedium and anxiety. There was no question
that her resolution might fail, but she must guard against
falling asleep, especially after a nearly sleepless night
yesterday.

To this end, once Mattie had retired, she searched
through a small pile of books in a drawer and finally
emerged with a tattered copy of *The Castle of Otranto*,
which she had read when she was Diana's age. Comfortably
settled in the new velvet *bergère*, she was away in the land of
Otranto with the fair, doomed Matilda when she was alerted
by muted sounds from the adjoining room. Her eyes flicked
to the French ormulu mantel clock. One o'clock and Adam
was preparing for bed. She would give him an hour to fall
soundly asleep, even though there was little danger that a
quick careful trip downstairs would disturb him. She
resumed her reading, but now the story failed to grip her
completely, and her eyes kept wandering to the hands of the
clock, which had slowed to a crawl. All sounds from the next
room had long since ceased and she was growing a bit
chilled even with her legs securely wrapped in a woolen
shawl.

Throwing off this covering, April jumped to her feet and
headed purposefully for the drawer in the bedside table
where she had placed the cigars bought earlier today. Only
today! Weeks seemed to have passed since she had embarked
on this undertaking. Gripping the box in her left hand, she
opened the hall door with infinite care and went back for
the lamp burning on the rosewood table beside the velvet
chair. As she picked it up and headed again for the door,
the box containing the cigars caught the edge of the book on
the table, knocking it off. Had the book simply landed on
the rug, the noise would have been minimal, but it glanced
sharply off the pedestal foot of the table with a crack that
froze April in her tracks. She stood there immobile for
countless seconds while the lamp flickered in her shaking
hand and her heartbeats magnified alarmingly. There had
been one creaking sound from the other room, followed by a
reassuring silence, and eventually life and the ability to

move flowed back into her limbs. Swiftly now she went through the door and along the corridor toward the main stairs.

The light from the lamp was adequate to illuminate her path, but she was unprepared for the unfamiliarity of her surroundings under this condition, and after one nervous glance around at the shadowy shapes that were not immediately recognizable, she returned her eyes to the path ahead of her and kept them so directed. Her bare feet padded steadily down the wooden stair treads but faltered at first when they struck the cold tiles in the main hall. She increased her speed, anxious to attain the comfort of the thick turkey carpet that covered the floor of the study.

Unfortunately the door to this room was firmly closed, necessitating a careful repositioning of the cigar box under her right arm to free her left hand for the task of opening it. This was accomplished with scarcely any sound, and she slipped into the room, leaving the door slightly ajar behind her. It was a matter of a few seconds to deposit the lamp on the desk and remove the cigars remaining in the box. No doubt it was an excessive precaution, but she counted these carefully before taking an equal number from her own box. As she arranged them in the empty container she was vaguely conscious of the flickering light glancing off the gold inkwell reposing on the desk top and picking out the gold lettering on the spines of books on the shelves behind the desk. In a compulsive gesture she counted the cigars once more before replacing the top to the container.

Suddenly there was a prickling sensation in her spine that radiated rapidly to all parts of her body, arresting the hand that was reaching for the lamp. A dreadful coldness made her shudder, and it was agony to turn her head, but turn her head she must. Reluctantly, her heart pounding frantically in her throat, she peered into the deeper shadows and thought she discerned a figure standing silent and motionless just inside the door.

For a painful eternity neither figure moved a muscle. The silence was so complete April had the queer notion that she could detect their two separate breathing rhythms, hers shallow and irregular, his harsh and deeper. When she could stand it no longer she opened her lips and managed to produce a faltering whisper.

"Adam?"

The figure at the door, as though released from a spell, removed his hands from the pockets of a dressing gown and moved forward.

"So it was you," said her husband.

Chapter Eleven

The earl continued to walk slowly toward the woman whose hand retreated from the lamp and fell at her side as she watched his approach with strained concentration.

"So it was you who tried to poison me," he repeated, sounding as if each syllable were jerked out of him.

"You *knew* about the cigars?" whispered April in agonized unbelief. "Then how could you allow—"

"No, I didn't know until yesterday, though I had begun to suspect it was a case of poison. What happened—did your nerve fail you at the last moment, or did you suffer a belated attack of conscience?"

The bitter sarcasm of his words and the icy sternness of his expression, made malevolent by the wavering shadows, struck fear into the marrow of his wife's bones, but still she could not credit her ears. "You cannot believe that I did this terrible thing!" she protested strongly.

"Who else then? Wasn't it enough of a revenge to force me into marriage? Did you feel you could not sufficiently avenge your father's and brother's deaths except by achieving mine? Why did you not go through with it, or are these cigars even more lethal than the others? Perhaps they are intended to finish the job?"

Her head came up proudly. "I bought these cigars today. I meant to have the others analyzed—I knew you wouldn't believe me if I told you I suspected that you were being poisoned, so I meant to get at least that much proof before confronting you with my suspicions."

These words produced a vibrating silence that lasted so long April thought her nerves would snap.

"And whom did you intend to accuse?"

It had come, the moment she had dreaded, and under circumstances more horrible than she had ever imagined. She must convince him that she spoke the truth! Summoning up all her dignity, she forced herself to speak in reasoned tones. "The morning of the Jeffrieses' musicale I saw Morton speaking with someone at the front door. He was disconcerted at my discovering him and said it was a case of someone coming to the wrong house. I suspected that he was concealing something behind his back, and when he passed on down the hall after I had gone into the morning room, I followed him in here. He had left the door pulled to but not shut. By pushing it open a trifle I could see that he was exchanging the cigars Diana had bought you for others. It seemed strange behavior, but I assumed you hadn't liked the cigars and did not want to hurt Diana's feelings. I didn't assign much importance to Morton's lie about the person at the door until much later, after I had begun to suspect it must be the cigars that were making you ill. Last night when you confirmed that you hadn't ordered a switch, I knew I was right." Here she paused fearfully and swallowed dryly. Adam's unbelieving expression had not altered during her recital, and it was supremely difficult to say what must alienate him further, but it had to be done. Her voice shook slightly as she continued, "I had caught a quick glimpse of the man at the door that morning, just his hat and the back of his head, but he had blond hair. It was Damien!"

She rushed on, aware of his sharply indrawn breath, aware of his mounting fury but committed now. "It *was*, I tell you! I hadn't been in this house twenty-four hours before I realized that Morton hates you. Sometimes he gets such a look on his face when watching you that it frightens me, and I saw the same look of utter rage on Damien Harding's face when you announced that I was your wife. How could it be personal? He didn't know me—it was the fact of my existence he hated, because I might produce an heir. You said he is always in debt, forever outrunning the constable. If Freddy were to inherit your wealth, no doubt he would take care of his brother's debts." At his impatient movement of one hand she let out a sobbing breath but still persisted, "I can see you do not believe me — I was afraid of this — but it is true! He tried it once before and failed in that shooting accident, and he has just tried again! Can't you see — "

"Enough!" thundered the earl. Though he had not closed the distance between them physically, April felt menaced by his barely controlled anger, and she shrank back against the desk.

"I have never heard such a farrago of lies in all my life! It wasn't bad enough that you should use the medium of an innocent girl's gift to achieve your evil design, but to choose one who has been like a brother to me all my life upon whom to foist your guilt is beyond anything! Damien knew nothing about those cigars! No one knew about them but you — *and Freddy!*"

"And *Morton!*" flashed April defiantly. "Do not forget Morton. He saw them and told Damien about them. Why should *I* wish you dead? I achieved my object when you married me!"

"Perhaps you'd prefer to be a rich widow instead of a nominal wife to a man you've hated these nine years. Do you think I've been blind to the attachment growing between you and Freddy? With one husband conveniently disposed of you could marry his heir and never even have to change the name on your calling cards or bother about decorating another house!"

"You're mad! Completely mad!"

April regretted the words the second they left her lips, and she wrenched away from the desk which had been taking her sagging weight in a blind attempt to escape from the threat of violence that had been swelling like a balloon in the atmosphere surrounding them. She had taken only one step when strong fingers biting into her arm arrested her flight. Adam's other hand seized her free arm, and he dragged her shrinking form so close she could feel his breath in her hair.

"Mad, am I? The real madness would be to believe this faradiddle you've concocted. Why light on Damien if you must have a scapegoat? Why not Freddy? As my heir, he stands to profit much more substantially than Damien by my death. And his hair is also blond. Why must this mythical man at the door be Damien if all you saw was the back of his head? Why could it not just as well have been Freddy?"

She was silent for a split second of paralyzing doubt, then the rough shake he administered loosened her tongue.

"Freddy is incapable of such an act," she said with quiet conviction.

The sneer in Adam's voice was cruelly evident. "Freddy is incapable of *any* act. He's even incapable of getting on with his life. Ever since his fiancée died of pneumonia six years ago he's been trying to drink himself into the grave, and one of these days he'll succeed. But you would know all about the tragic story, would you not, the two of you are so close. Have you promised to make it up to him after you are his wife?"

"Adam," she pleaded desperately, "don't say any more in this vein. You know it isn't true. This has all been a great shock to you, but you will see things more clearly in the morning. Let it rest until then."

Her propitiating words served no other purpose than to increase the heat of his simmering anger to a full boil. "Let *what* rest? The trifling question of who is trying to kill me, the cousin I have known all my life or the wife who isn't a wife, the woman who has assured me on more than one occasion that I am guilty of the deaths of her relatives, the woman who sought my name and fortune as her due but expected to give nothing in return? Am I to let this rest while you try again? You may succeed yet if you are clever enough and persistent enough, but you will never go to Freddy unsullied. If I'm to be saddled with a murdering bitch for a wife, at least let her *be* my wife!"

As he spoke, Adam released one of her arms to enable himself to take up the lamp, but as he started to drag her bodily toward the door, the meaning of his words belatedly penetrated April's brain, and she was galvanized by a more intense terror than any that she had yet experienced.

"No!" she screamed, and tried to break away. She wrenched her arm free from his grasp and sprang instinctively toward the door, her soft draperies floating in the breeze thus created. Her action in its unexpected vigor nearly succeeded. The earl managed to regain possession of one wrist before she reached the entrance, but he was compelled to replace the lamp on the table. Her nails were digging into his fingers in a furious attempt to loosen his grip; one hand was not going to be adequate to the task of preventing her escape.

The ensuing struggle took place in semidarkness in an atmosphere of menacing silence on the man's part that was later to form the most frightening aspect of the recurring nightmares that haunted April's sleep for weeks. He was deaf to all her pleading, unmoved by her cries, and finally, untouched by her pain. His actions were never those of a thwarted lover; not once did he try to woo her with kisses or seduce her ultimate acquiescence with caresses. Inexperienced though she was of a man's passions, there was never any doubt in April's fear-maddened intellect that his intention was purely and aggressively punitive. Once he had succeeded in getting both her hands imprisoned behind her in one of his, and not before suffering several deep scratches on his own wrists, he twisted her down onto the rug, more or less on her back, with her arms beneath her. He paid no attention to her writhing attempts to free her arms or the harmless and ineffectual thrashing of her legs as he efficiently swept aside an excess of fabric in her bridal-night regalia. April's panic was augmented to near frenzy by the fact that he never glanced at her face and never responded with so much as one syllable to any of the pleas she gasped out. He proceeded in the same grim silence to force his eventual way between her tightly gripped legs while controlling her arms with bone-crushing pressure. It was not until days later when her shocked brain could bear to

examine the events leading up to the final act of violation
that April realized that she had contributed immeasurably
to her own pain and suffering by the strength of her instinctive resistance. She had fought him fiercely and mindlessly
until the very end, even sinking her teeth into his shoulder
when his weight descended on her, giving no quarter and
thereby securing no amelioration of the inevitable tearing
agony of such a violent possession.

When he finally withdrew and removed his smothering
weight from her quivering body, she was in no state to
appreciate her release. The intolerable weight was gone, but
the pain remained, and her wild sobbing continued
unabated. She was unaware that he had pulled down her
nightclothes to cover her limbs as he got first to his knees
and then to his feet. Nor did she hear the clink of glass as he
found a bottle and glass and poured himself a generous
measure of brandy.

His back remained to her as he drank the brandy down in
two gulps, but, though he might not be forced to look upon
his victim, he could not prevent the keening of her low,
continuous sobbing from assailing his ears. After a moment
or two he said over his shoulder, "Would you like some
brandy?"

There was absolutely no diminution in the rhythm or
volume of the weeping, and he turned reluctantly. Except
that she had drawn her legs up at the knees and curled her
body slightly into itself with her hands over her face, she was
as he had left her. He approached with the glass and
repeated the offer with the same lack of result. Growing
anxious, he knelt beside her and proffered the glass more
insistently. The only reaction was an accentuation of that
protective posture.

"Come, you cannot remain here all night." He set the
glass down on the desk and returned to the huddled figure,
intent on helping her to rise. At this tentative touch on her
shoulder she shied violently away, and the sobbing
intensified.

"April, this has to stop! You'll make yourself ill if you continue."

At this point he scarcely expected his words to have any effect, nor did they. Leaping to his feet, he seized one of the candelabra on a side table and lighted the candles at the lamp's flame. He walked rapidly out of the room, shielding the flames, and headed for the stairs, where he deposited the candelabrum on the landing. He moved back to the study, feeling his way along the wall. Another light was going to be needed if he was to accomplish his end without chancing an accident in the dark that would bring the whole household down upon them. Consequently he lighted another candelabrum and placed it on the floor midway down the hall.

When he returned for April, he noted that the tempo of the abandoned weeping had subsided, at least he hoped it had. He picked her up from the floor, not knowing whether to be grateful or alarmed at her lack of resistance, and proceeded to carry her up the stairs to her room. Her hair streamed across her wet face, from which every vestige of color had drained. Her eyes were closed and her dark lashes rested on her cheeks in wet clumps. Her breathing shook her body periodically. She was slightly built, but in his debilitated physical condition even her light weight proved to be an enormous strain by the time he reached her bedchamber door, and his task was not aided by the stygian darkness that prevailed beyond the top of the stairs. By the time he reached the door, which was, thankfully, not latched, his breath was coming in gasps and his arms felt as though they were being pulled out of their sockets. He lowered her onto the bed and sagged down onto it himself for a few minutes until he could recover his breathing and control the spastic twitching in his limbs.

April lay quietly now, seemingly insensible of his presence, and Adam admitted a very real concern. He felt like death himself, but this girl—his wife, he reminded himself bitterly—was near to complete collapse, and he feared to leave her alone. Dismissing personal considerations, he rolled off the inviting surface of the wide bed with a groan and gazed down at the still form sprawled diagonally across the bed. There was not enough moonlight coming in through the blinds to make out any details of her appearance, but pushed by an instinct of urgency, he looked around for candles and flint and succeeded in kindling a light.

April still hadn't moved from her former position, but when he brought the light closer he saw with relief that her eyes were open. She closed them at sight of him and flung a hand across her face for good measure. He abandoned the idea of taking her pulse, knowing his touch would agitate her.

"April, are you all right? Shall I bring Mattie to you?"

Her eyes remained covered, but she answered him in a low voice that he strained nearer to hear. "Don't bring Mattie— just go away."

"Are you sure?"

"Yes!" Just go *away!"*

This time her voice was stronger, and, after one last assessing look at the crumpled, swollen-faced, and disheveled figure of his generally exquisite wife, he blew out the candle and went into the hall with no further words.

He retrieved both candelabra on his way back to the study and replaced them on their table, drank the brandy April had spurned, poured himself another glass, and drank that off too. As his eyes fell on the box of cigars his wife claimed to have bought that day, his mouth tightened unpleasantly, but he gathered it and the lamp up and, abandoning the empty glass where he had set it down, removed himself from the room and made his way back to his own bedchamber.

A glance over at the open door leading to his wife's room told him that she hadn't moved since he had left her. Never would she have allowed it to remain open had she been aware of the circumstance. There was still a vague worry that she might become ill during the night after the hysterical collapse he had witnessed, and he had no intention of closing the door. He listened intently for a moment, and then, reassured by the silence, dragged over to his bed and eased his weary body onto its welcoming surface. There wasn't much point in getting right into it; his chances for achieving a restful oblivion for what was left of the night had vanished with his first look at April after he had raped her. He examined the word gingerly and found, whether attributable to the numbing effects of the brandy he had drunk or a deplorable lack of conscience, that he had as yet no real feeling about committing an act he would have had no hesitation in condemning in anyone else. Had anyone ever told him he would be as capable as the next man of such disgusting behavior he would have demanded an apology. In the last hour he had learned something about himself that gave him no cause for satisfaction. Before tonight he would have denied on the rack that any woman could arouse him to a degree of anger that could produce such bestial retaliation. What was there about the Wendover family that they should all have such power to destroy his life? He had never wished to feel anything for or against April Wendover. He had been determined to keep his emotions inviolate when she had invaded his life, and look where he had come in less than a month!

His fingers traced and retraced the carving on the bedpost behind him. He knew more about the shapes and designs on this post even in the dark than he had learned about April since she had been living in his house. How could a cool civilized woman who looked so delicate and innocuous plot a murder? And how could this same delicate creature fight him with the single-minded intensity, if not the strength, of a jungle cat as she had done tonight?

He groaned and rolled over on his side, but the thought could not be suppressed. Would-be murderess or not, how could he, Adam Harding, alleged gentleman, with all deliberation have inflicted such humiliating and painful punishment on this same delicate creature? An hour later he still couldn't answer his own questions.

A small rustle from the next room brought his thoughts

forward. It was really too chilly at this hour near dawn to remain on top of the covers, especially for someone clad as lightly as April. He slid off the bed and crossed to the doorway. He recalled promising in all good faith that he would not cross the threshold unbidden, and a wry grimace twisted his mouth at the unlikelihood of ever receiving an invitation to enter this room, but she should not be allowed to grow chilled in her present state. Slowly, almost against his will, he approached the bed. She was still lying on the diagonal on top of the coverlet, but she had curled up again in that oddly protective posture, and she looked so small and so young that the whole situation struck him suddenly as impossible. He shook his head unbelievingly. None of it could have happened!

He bent closer and stiffened for a second at sight of the dark stains on her frothy, light-colored dressing gown. A muscle twitched in his cheek, and he averted his eyes as he gently lifted her to pull the bedclothes out from under her and replaced them, tucking them closely around the softly breathing girl. Before straightening his back he yielded to one last impulse and lightly brushed strands of soft hair back from her face. After another long look at the sleeping girl he went back to his own room, and this time he closed the door behind him with deliberation.

Chapter Twelve

The next few days were the worst of April's life. She had grieved for her father and Basil and the loss of her own future; her mother's death had revived all this feeling plus an added dimension of loneliness; but the period following the rape was characterized by a nightmarish quality of undifferentiated anguish.

She awoke slowly to bright sunshine accompanied almost instantaneously by a sense of hovering calamity. The sun streamed in the large window, causing tiny dust motes to dance in its path. As April lay watching them, small busy sounds impinged on her consciousness — Mattie selecting her clothes for the day. She changed positions in the bed and drew in a gasping breath as her wounded body protested. With the pain came memory rolling over her with relentless pressure. Her head fell back onto the pillow, and sweat broke out all over her body. She gripped her lower lip with her teeth to suppress a groan.

"So, you're awake at last? Will you be wanting the ivory wool carriage dress for the morning? It's easy enough to get in and out of for fittings."

The eyes of the woman on the bed flew open and focused for an instant on the uncompromisingly honest face of her oldest friend before long lashes swept down in defense against the shrewdness encountered in Mattie's snapping black eyes.

First things first. She swallowed hard and produced a weak voice. "Don't bother getting anything ready, Mattie. I

. . . I don't feel quite up to shopping this morning. I think I'll sleep awhile longer. Please convey my regrets to Diana."

"Are you sickening for something?"

April averted her eyes from the concern on Mattie's face as she bustled over to examine her former nursling more thoroughly. She spoke quick words of reassurance. "No, no, but I didn't sleep well last night. I shall be quite myself presently." The untruthfulness of this intended reassurance struck her completely dumb.

"Why are you wearing a dressing gown in bed?"

Blankly April stared down at one shoulder encased in light-blue silk. "I . . . I must have been cold. Mattie, you take Diana shopping this morning," she urged, anxious to fix the woman's attention elsewhere. Mindful of the concerned appraisal being accorded her, she yawned ostentatiously, snuggled deeper under the covers, and determinedly closed her eyes.

Mattie's hesitation was palpable. Her instinct told her she should remain with her mistress, but Miss April was not a child and she clearly wished to be relieved of her maid's presence. After a long moment while the figure on the bed listened with all her senses, Mattie rustled over to the hall door and said shortly, "I'll have a tray sent up in an hour."

April's faint expression of gratitude was more for the promise of privacy than for a breakfast tray, which held no appeal at all.

At last the closing of the door released her from the necessity of pretending she was suffering from nothing more than a lack of sleep. For a bit longer she lay still, postponing the time of assessment. The bed was comfortable and protective and quite warm. She had been so cold.

The dark lashes swept up. How had she come to be *in* the bed? A frown of concentration wrinkled her brow. Adam had carried her upstairs and put her on the bed, but then he had gone away. Then how—? She shook her head once, aware as she did so of an ache behind her eyes. What did it matter how she had gotten here? What did anything matter any longer?

Experimentally she moved her legs, sat up, and swung them over the side of the bed. A hiss of pain escaped her as she took her first step, and she clenched her teeth against it. Her hand went out to the bedpost to steady herself, and her eyes winged to the blue marks on her wrist. Her mouth set grimly as she noted the matching bruises on her other wrist, but after one look, she dropped her arms to her side and headed for the mirror to assess the damages.

She could walk unaided, but she felt like a rag doll that had been torn in two by a child who had grabbed a leg in each hand and gleefully ripped away. There was a beading of perspiration on her upper lip by the time she reached the mirror. At first she was relieved to find she had changed so little outwardly; the same pale face stared back at her from under tangled lank hair. After the first assessment, however, she turned away from her image and tears sprang to her eyes. She was afraid to look further, afraid the degradation she had undergone might have left a visible mark for the world to see and judge.

April was trembling and sweating, standing with down-bent head, unable for the moment to command mind or body to decision or action. A tear ran down the side of her nose, and she flicked it away with an angry jabbing finger. Enough of that! She had wept a lifetime's allotment of useless tears last night. She wanted a bath; she must have a bath! Her head came up decisively, then her eagerness receded as quickly as it had arisen. It would be necessary to wait until Mattie had gone out with Diana. She couldn't face Mattie yet.

Suddenly the proximity of her bed seemed like heaven's gate to April. She stumbled toward it and burrowed into it, closing her eyes and willing her jangling nerves to quieten. In a while she slept.

The arrival of a maid with a breakfast tray woke April from her nap. Though she avoided the toast and eggs, the coffee was welcome and kept her from fretting over the necessary delay in securing the hot water for a bath. In the meantime she wrenched off the blue dressing gown and

matching night rail and changed to a heavy robe of lavender
velvet, which she tied tightly about her waist. After one dry-
eyed look at the evidence of her ravaged virginity she con-
signed the stained garments to the fireplace, watching with
bottom lip firmly gripped in her teeth until the loathsome
items had burned beyond any recognition. Thus the woman
who had squeezed every penny until it squeaked for nine
difficult years!

Still dry-eyed, she climbed into the tub when it was ready.
The hot water was marvelously soothing to her aching
muscles, and she lay back unmoving and almost unthinking
until the cooling temperature forced her into action. By the
time she had washed her hair and toweled it dry before the
fire, April was feeling much more herself, enough at any
rate to have overcome her first quavery desire to seek
comfort from Mattie or Diana by revealing the whole sorry
chapter of events. She knew as she dressed in the prettiest of
her new morning gowns, a long-sleeved, softly tucked cotton
in pale green that flattered her coloring, that she could
never oppress the two people in the world who loved her with
the burden of such knowledge.

As she brushed her drying hair in front of the mirror she
peered at her sober reflection with disinterested curiosity.
Who would have thought that a woman could undergo a
violent, life-changing experience accompanied by a
surcharge of all the vilest emotions and emerge looking substantially the same except for a lack of natural color? She
remedied this lack with a delicate application of the
contents of the rouge pot on lips and cheeks and studied the
results. She had been wrong in thinking her outward
appearance unchanged. Her eyes were smoky dark and dull-
looking, and the rouge only accented the shadows beneath
them. Annoyed, she wiped it off and flung down the hairbrush after a check of the mantel clock.

Almost noon. Diana and Mattie should be back shortly.
Lunch was generally served at twelve-thirty, and she found
herself listening for their arrival as she wandered around the
large room, her feet sinking into the silver-gray carpet. The

apartment had taken on a different character with the addition of carpet and light-blue hangings and bed covering. The ceiling too was painted blue, with the delicate plaster designs picked out in a fresh white. The walls were striped in silver and blue, and until today she had thought the effect light and charming. At the moment it resembled nothing so much as a prison. Perhaps she would go to the morning room and look over the early post — anything to postpone the moment when she must admit her husband into her thoughts.

Glad to have something positive to do, April tucked a lace-edge handkerchief into her pocket and set off for the morning room. She met the footman in the hall and returned his quiet greeting pleasantly but was unable to meet his eyes. It was all she could do not to break into a run and race for the privacy of her sanctuary. It was necessary to monitor her pace the entire distance, and she shut the door behind her in trembling relief. What was the matter with her? Jacob knew nothing; not another soul in the world would ever learn what had happened between the earl and herself last night. She must stop acting as if she had a communicable disease! She was guilty of no crime except the initial one of marrying Adam against his will.

After a few minutes of railing against her own cowardice, April had calmed down enough to seat herself at her charming painted desk, where she fixed her attention on the everyday chore of going through her mail. As usual, the major part of her post consisted of invitations and dressmakers' bills. She caught herself up short making a little moue of distaste. Why the sudden dissatisfaction? Was it not precisely for this reason that she had come to London? Firmly cutting off all tendency to indulge in tardy regrets, she embarked on the task of replying to the various hostesses seeking the pleasure of their company and was thus employed when Diana bounced into the room.

"Here you are, lazybones!" teased the girl, glowing with good looks and good spirits. "Can't you stand the pace at your advanced age?"

April was spared the necessity of concocting a suitable reply by Mattie, who appeared in the doorway behind Diana. "Your sister doesn't look a day older than you do, Miss Impudence, she just has more sense, that's all."

April smiled affectionately at her old nurse for her blind championship and made an easy response to Diana, who wrinkled her nose at Mattie before unwrapping a parcel she wished to show her sister.

Aware that she was being subjected to prolonged scrutiny by the person who knew her best in the world, the Countess of Glenville applied herself to the chore of giving a convincing performance as a carefree young society matron. She must have succeeded, for Mattie's brow cleared presently and she bustled off to check on the maids, reminding the sisters that lunch would soon be served.

One hurdle overcome, thought April as she headed upstairs with Diana and the results of the morning's buying spree. She walked a bit stiffly, conscious of various aches in her body but hopeful that Diana's overriding interest in her new life would blind her to any slight changes in her sister. Mattie was much more observant, however, and she was at a loss how to conceal the vivid bruises Adam's fingers had made, not only on her wrists but on the soft flesh of her upper arms also. The best she could come up with was to plan to be dressed before Mattie came to her room for the next few days and to continue to wear long-sleeved garments exclusively.

The rest of the day passed quietly. One of Diana's admirers took her driving in the Park at the fashionable hour, and April was grateful for the solitude this won for her. Her nerves had been tightening up as the hour for tea drew near, and she found herself straining to listen for sounds in the hall that might herald her husband's arrival, though she ventured to hope he would have the grace to absent himself today. When, during the late afternoon, Morton delivered a message that the earl would not be in to dinner, she relaxed perceptibly and was able to cast her mind forward to the necessity of dressing before Mattie arrived to assist her.

She accomplished it, just barely, ignoring Mattie's surprised glance at the clock as she came into the room in time to see her mistress struggling with buttons down the back of her gown.

"Why the rush?" inquired that lady with raised eyebrows.

"I . . . I was not sure if I would care for this gown and so decided to try it first," April improvised, pretending to look through her jewel box as Mattie took over the buttoning operation.

The dangerous moment passed, the long dinner hour wound to its conclusion, the uneventful evening with only her sister's undemanding company eventually ended, and April successfully diverted Mattie's attention to something in the wardrobe while she slipped out of her gown and into her nightclothes. The blackest day she had ever known had been lived through, and she climbed wearily into bed with a faint sense of satisfaction lightening the depression in which she was becalmed, only to awake hours later from the first of the nightmares. The content of the dream was too elusive to be grasped and explored; the details faded the instant she tried to fix them in her mind, leaving only the suffocating sense of dread to contend with and overcome before sleep was again possible.

The essentials of the pattern repeated themselves during the days that followed, though not again did April try to excuse herself from her social commitments. To the contrary, indeed. She plunged into activity in a feverish desire to tire herself so greatly that she could overcome the dread of falling asleep at night. In this quest she was successful as far as achieving the desired fatigue to enable her to drop off to sleep, but the dreamless oblivion she sought continued to elude her efforts. Each night she came tremblingly awake, full of half-remembered tears, sentenced to hours of desperate wakefulness before her restless mind permitted her tired body the necessary repose.

Sometimes she was able to recapture the calm necessary for sleep by lying very quietly and willing her tense limbs to a state of relaxation. Sometimes she gave up the effort and sat up reading till nearly dawn. The worst times were those nights when she could not settle to a book and indulged in a compulsive pacing of the floor until sheer exhaustion claimed her. On these nights she gave thanks for the warmth and comfort of the silvery carpet under her feet, and especially for its sound-deadening properties.

April was frequently aware of the hour of Adam's homecoming. He did not allow his valet to put him to bed, so any sounds issuing from the next room during the night were an indication that the earl had returned. The first time she heard his arrival was the night after the assault, and she froze in her tracks, terror flooding back over her in a cold tide while her eyes strained for any faint sounds that might indicate an approach to the door. Time lost all meaning as she remained standing, poised for instant flight but unsure whether her limbs would obey her brain's command. The idea of returning to her bed and feigning sleep occurred to her, but still she stood motionless while a chill that had nothing to do with the room's temperature crept over her body. It was an effort to remove her eyes from the door long enough to check the time. The light from her bedside candle was barely adequate to reach the mantelpiece, but she thought the clock read two-thirty. Her uncertainty and fear were mercifully brief. In a matter of five minutes all sound from the other room faded into the consuming silence.

On shaky legs April sped to her bed and achieved the security of its solid surface. She huddled under the covers with a sense of calamity averted and tried to compose herself for sleep.

The first meeting between husband and wife did not take place until the third day after the violent scene in the study. They had little to say to one another and that little confined to labored exchange of commonplaces, but Diana's presence served to dispel some of the natural constraint under which each could be judged to be functioning. Theirs was the manner of slight acquaintances striving to perform a mildly distasteful social duty with the grace expected of them. There was only one moment when either let slip the mask of well-bred formality. When dinner was announced, the earl extended his hand in an automatic gesture to escort his wife into the dining room, only to draw it back as she flinched away from him involuntarily. For an instant both hastily averted faces displayed the same rise in color before April placed none too steady fingers on her husband's rigid arm and allowed herself to be led into dinner. As he seated her the colorful Paisley shawl draped artistically across her arms slipped momentarily, revealing fading purple marks on her upper arm beneath the short puffed sleeve of her gown. April, who was studiously examining the table appointments, missed the twitching of a muscle in Adam's cheek as he moved away to his own place at the head of the table.

Diana, appearing to notice nothing amiss, took up the slack in the conversation. The ladies were being escorted to a private ball that evening by Freddy Harding, so the embarrassment was not prolonged beyond dinner. As the time passed, however, even the young girl's happy preoccupation with the excitements of the world opening up to her was pierced eventually by the continuing pall cast over the occasional meetings of husband and wife. Adam rarely acted as escort to the parties, routs, and dances that occupied the time of a new debutante, but April's presence was required except on the rare occasions when Diana attended an affair under the chaperonage of another matron.

About a week after the incident in the study, there was a ball given for the daughter of one of Adam's colleagues to which he did escort his ladies. It was a glittering affair lasting far into the night. By now Diana had acquired quite a train of admirers, and she enjoyed her customary popularity, taking her pick of the eligible dancing partners throughout the evening. At one point while partnering her brother-in-law she glanced over to a group of dowagers against the wall and pointed out that his wife wasn't dancing. Adam made no comment, but when the dance ended he delivered the girl to her sister, excusing himself immediately with no conversation expended on April. Diana stared after him in surprise, which was converted to indignation a moment later as the earl deftly cut a stunning redhead out of a crowd and proceeded to conduct an elegant flirtation with her on a settee directly opposite his wife's position.

"Well, of all the *uncivil—*"

"Shush, dearest!" begged April, smiling in sympathy with Diana's indignation but maneuvering around so she blocked her sister's view of this tableau. The smile widened but didn't reach her eyes. "Did you by any chance suggest to Adam that I might require a dancing partner?"

"Yes, I did!" sputtered Diana.

April chuckled and cut in calmly before Diana could elaborate on the insult, "Well, that should teach you a valuable lesson, my love. Gentlemen don't take kindly to feminine attempts at directing their conduct. Now smile— here comes your next partner, if I am not mistaken."

Diana whirled off on the arm of the gentleman in question, and April herself was solicited to dance at that moment. When in due course her partner waltzed her past the spot where Adam was still being entertained by the vivacious red-haired beauty, she was careful to be completely engrossed in her own amusing conversation.

The incident was not allowed to sink into oblivion, however. Diana was decidedly cool toward Adam on the drive home, despite April's attempts to smooth the situation with chatty observations on the party they had just left. She abandoned her unsuccessful efforts to pour oil on troubled waters after the earl bade them a formal goodnight at the foot of the stairs. It was obvious from her expression as they climbed the stairs that the young girl was more troubled than indignant by this time, and April decided it was imperative to air the grievance before relations between Diana and her brother-in-law deteriorated. In the ordinary way the child was no grudge bearer, but she was fiercely protective of her milder-mannered sister when the occasion demanded, and April would not put it beyond her to say something injudicious that would damage the rapport she shared with Adam. This cordial, almost affectionate relationship between her sister and her husband was the only good thing to come out of this marriage, and she dreaded to see it threatened.

As they approached Diana's bedchamber, she studied her sister's face with a discreet sideways glance and, reading the indecision there, made her own decision.

"What's troubling you, dearest?" she invited softly.

For a moment Diana remained still, her fingers tight on the door handle, then she faced her sister with resolution written on her lovely features.

"More to the point, what is troubling you and Adam? Have you quarreled or something?"

"Something of the sort," she admitted with drastic understatement, "but you must not allow any . . . differences between Adam and me to affect you. Believe me, Diana," she added earnestly, "it would distress us both to see you worrying about us, and it is totally unnecessary in any case."

Diana regarded her sister steadily. "Do you love Adam, April?"

"Why I . . . I feel for Adam all those sentiments that are most appropriate to the married state, respect—"

"Please answer one question truthfully, then I promise I'll not pry further," begged Diana, holding up a hand to stop this faltering speech. "Did you and Adam marry for love?"

On the point of delivering an untruthful affirmative for the sake of her sister's youthful illusions, April read the curiously pleading expression in those intensely blue eyes and paused. Was Diana pleading for reassurance or was she begging to be treated as an adult capable of dealing with the reality of the situation?

"No," she confessed quietly, "we did not marry for love."

The tenseness seemed to go out of her sister's shoulders. "Did you marry for my sake?"

April hesitated fractionally. "In a way, but you mustn't feel respon—"

"It's all right, I understand. It's just that I learned something tonight and I was afraid it might wound you, but since you and Adam married for convenience I don't suppose it matters after all."

Apprehension held April's faculties suspended for an instant. Could it be that the true story of the marriage had become one of the *on dits* of the season despite the care they had taken to conceal it? She cleared her throat of hoarseness. "What did you learn?"

"Do you recall the redhead Adam was flirting with for ages tonight?"

April smiled wryly at the likelihood that she might have forgotten the creature but confined her reply to an affirmative nod of her head.

"Her name is Lady Ellis. Sarah Eddington told me Adam wanted to marry her a long time ago, but it was before he inherited his uncle's title and she threw him over for Lord Ellis, who was already a baron. Sarah says people claim he never got over her, and it did look tonight as though he . . . he might still love her." Her voice trailed off, and it was with relief that she heard April's warning that Alice was coming toward them ready to put her mistress to bed.

The sisters bade each other a hasty goodnight, and April continued on down the hall to her own room. So there was another woman, apart from his mother, who had treated Adam badly in the past! There was no reason to question that the vivid Lady Ellis had once been the object of Adam's affections, but that she still retained her former position in those affections, his wife, not being an impressionable seventeen, took leave to doubt. It had been perfectly apparent to her that Adam had indulged in that public flirtation tonight for the sole purpose of punishing his erring wife. In fact, she seriously questioned whether he was capable of loving any woman. Small wonder, though, that he had reacted so strongly against herself on scant evidence! After all, she had already convicted herself of being an unprincipled opportunist in his eyes. With his history she was no longer surprised that it had been such a short jump to believe her also capable of murder. He was well and truly disposed to suspect all women of duplicity!

She sighed prodigiously as she removed her jewelry, having sent Mattie to bed early to nurse a cold. How the fates had conspired against this marriage! And to think that she had, just hours before his cruel attack, begun to wish, under the influence of a winsome child's attentions, that she were in fact his wife! The irony of having one's wishes granted in this world was not lost upon her as she slowly slipped out of her costly gown. She had wished for a husband who would provide her with expensive clothes. Well, she now had the clothes and the husband, and the dream had turned to dust and ashes at his touch. Perhaps the most disturbing element of all was that knowing what she now did about his past dealings with the women he had loved, she could not even hate him wholeheartedly for what he had done to her. If she had been what he thought her she would have merited the treatment he had meted out. Her heart ached for the pity and waste of it all.

Chapter Thirteen

If April was deeply unhappy in the period immediately following the rape, her husband didn't escape scot-free of emotional repercussions himself. Far from having a cleansing action, the release of his retaliative fury left him physically drained, depressed, and rather defiantly determined not to acknowledge any regret even in the privacy of his thoughts.

His first action on appearing in the breakfast room the next morning was to ask Morton outright whether he had substituted other cigars for those Diana had given him. Under his basilisk stare the butler preserved an apparently unthreatened composure. His thin colorless eyebrows rose fractionally.

"Naturally not, my lord, since such a request was not made of me." He cast a professionally assessing eye over the table and turned an expressionless countenance back to his employer. "Is there anything else you require, my lord?"

Adam continued to regard his butler under lowered brows for another moment, then dismissed him with a wave of his hand, staring in frustration at the stooped back disappearing from the room at an unhurried pace. Well, what had he expected, for heaven's sake? That the man would reveal his guilt, even supposing for the sake of argument that he *was* guilty? His clenched jaw grew even more rigid as he denied the existence of any faint hope that April had been telling the truth; after all, her innocence would mean Damien's guilt! He pushed the almost untouched plate away and concentrated on black coffee. *Damn her for a lying jade!* How dare she cast aspersions on one who had been an integral part of his life for as far back as memory reached! Not content with complicating his life in the present with her unwanted presence, she had contaminated his past with her accusations.

The coffee was too bitter for his taste, and he pushed it away too. Nothing tasted right anymore, thanks to those filthy cigars. Well, the one constructive action he could take would be to get them analyzed, not that he was particularly interested to learn what she was trying to kill him with. His face expressing thoughts more bitter than the rejected coffee, the earl took his bad temper and the remnants of his hacking cough off to the Ministry, where he put in an unprofitable day and offended at least two unsuspecting persons who had the temerity to question one of his decisions.

His mood was marginally improved by a brisk canter in the Park late in the afternoon. The imminence of nightfall made this a practical compromise between his desire to gallop off on an endless ride and the necessity to fulfill a dinner engagement with several members of Parliament in less than two hours.

The benefits of fresh air and exercise did not outlast the long dull dinner, however, and it was with minimal enthusiasm that he went on to the Cocoa Tree with his companions. Gambling held little allure for him at any time, and tonight the thought of concentrating on the turn of a card or the numbers that appeared on dice cubes was positively repellent. He bore the tedium in silent but growing restlessness until eleven o'clock, when, casting diplomacy and courtesy alike aside, he took abrupt leave of his party, but not without having to endure a few pointed and puerile comments on the tendency of newly married men to become spoilsports.

Once outside in the air, his restlessness increased as he debated his next move. His own house had no appeal, yet he hesitated to inflict his presence on any of his friends who might be happily engaged at another of the gambling hells in the area. After a few aimless steps he reversed his direction, setting a course for the one person who could always be relied on for uncritical acceptance of his moods.

Molly rose nobly to the occasion. Her lovely face glowed with pleasure when he entered her boudoir, and she exclaimed with relief at the improvement in his appearance as she helped him off with his coat. At her innocent mention of his alleged cold, a shadow darkened the earl's countenance. He shot her a quick questioning look, then dropped into an upholstered chair.

"Tell me what's been going on around here, Molly," he requested, breaking in on her eager flow of chatter about his improved health.

She looked faintly puzzled, but stopped hovering over him after he refused Madeira, brandy, and a cigar, settling herself on the pink chaise to begin a chronicle of the day-to-day events of her quiet life. Her puzzlement grew as she continued with a tale of some beautiful peacock satin that Mr. Norris, the draper, had set aside because he thought it perfect for her coloring. The earl never took his eyes from her face, but she had the oddest impression that nothing she said was reaching him. It was almost as though her words fell one at a time into an invisible chasm somewhere in the three feet of space separating his chair from the daybed. Disturbed, she paused and glanced uncertainly at him. The silence lengthened, then the earl's eyelids flickered.

"Go on," he invited.

"What is it, my lord? What is troubling you?"

"Nothing. Why do you ask?" he evaded, removing his eyes from her face at last. Her glance followed his to the lean-fingered hand that fiddled incessantly with a small china ornament on a nearby table.

"Because you are very unlike yourself tonight and because you have not heard a word I've said to you," she answered daringly.

The earl's laughter sounded forced to her ears, and she

watched him warily as he set down the ornament and rose from his chair to tower over her.

"Is this more like me?" he teased, bending to kiss the side of her neck, exposed by the low-cut bodice of her figured-lace gown. For an instant she was still under his familiar touch, then her body relaxed and her arms reached for him. His went around her, and she made room·for him on the chaise.

A few minutes later Molly slowly removed her mouth from under his to protest laughingly, "You are nearly suffocating me, my darling. May I suggest that the bed would be much more comfortable?"

To her surprise there was no immediate rejoinder from the earl. Nor did he resume kissing her. He shifted his weight to ease her beathing, but his own sounded uneven, and his next words, low though they were, rang harshly in her ears.

"It's no use, Molly, I . . . *can't!*"

The handsome brunette froze as the blood seemed to stop beating in her veins. The coals in the fireplace hissed loudly in the silence that succeeded his blunt admission. Then all her loving instincts prompted her to tighten her arms protectively around him. Her voice was calm and reassuring.

"Do not let it worry you, my lord. You have been very ill just lately. This will pass; it means nothing."

Very gently he disentangled himself from her embrace and stood up, raking his fingers through his dark locks. He didn't look at her.

"You don't understand, Molly. Something has happened. I wish I could explain, but—"

"You do not have to explain anything to me," said the steady voice at his back. "And you need not concern yourself about a temporary incapacity, either. Let me pour you some brandy."

He did not protest as she left the chaise and occupied herself at a table against the fireplace wall. Presently she glided over to him, glass in hand, and eased him back into the chair he had abandoned. "Here, you'll like his brandy, you selected it yourself," she said lightly, and resumed her position on the chaise.

The earl eyed her appraisingly over the rim of his glass. It was he who ended the silence a short time later. "You've been good for me, Molly, and I'm grateful, believe me."

"You have nothing to be grateful for," she insisted in low tones. "You've always treated me well, and your generosity is astounding." She closed her lips as he waved away her protests. There was a terrible tingling along her nerves like a warning of creeping death. She had dreaded this moment from the instant he had announced his marriage. She hid her clenched fists in the folds of the black lace gown and waited in quiet hopelessness for the blow to fall.

He looked at her fleetingly, then focused his attention on the liquid in the glass. After a moment when she had nothing further to add, he raised his head and said as though the words were pulled from him individually:

"Last night I raped my wife."

This admission, unlike the former, drew no immediate reaction from the woman on the chaise, and Adam glanced up from the brandy to encounter faint bewilderment in the soft brown eyes. Seeing that he expected a response, Molly said hesitantly, "There can be no question of rape between husband and wife, surely?"

"You do not understand, Molly. I was furious at discovering . . . at something I found out. I wanted to hurt her, I think I almost wanted to kill her. Well, I did hurt her — desperately." His voice, impatient at the beginning of this impetuous speech, lost its force, and his self-disgust was perfectly evident to the woman regarding him with compassion.

"If you forced yourself on her, no doubt in your anger you did cause her some pain, but she is your wife, after all. Perhaps you do owe her an apology, but surely it is unnecessary to castigate yourself to this extent."

"You still don't understand, and why should you," sighed the earl, "when you know nothing of the real situation between April and myself. The marriage had never been consummated." He saw her eyes widen at this but continued without pause. "I had assured her, in fact, that I had no intention of ever touching her, and then last night I lost my head and my self-control and deliberately raped her. She is smallish and slightly built, but she fought me like a tiger right to the end. So it *was* rape," he finished.

Both were silent. Molly had lowered her eyes to hide her reaction to an odd note in his voice that might almost have been pride when he had described his wife and her resistance. The earl took another sip of his brandy and then addressed the down-bent head. "Well, do you still think it wasn't rape? Do you believe a man would ever be justified in doing what I did?"

"I think perhaps it would depend on what *she* had done," she temporized, and added at once as he opened his lips, "I understand that you feel you cannot tell me that." Now she seemed to be searching for the right words to express herself. "It is clear that your wife hurt you very badly." Large brown eyes searched hard gray ones until the latter were veiled by lowered lids. "Are you quite certain she is guilty of . . . whatever it is you said you had learned?"

Again the words seemed to be dragged from the earl. "She denied it, of course, but she was lying."

"I see."

"Dammit, Molly!" he exploded. "She *must* have been lying! Nothing in the world makes any sense if she was telling the truth!"

"Except that if she was telling the truth she had not hurt you." Now it was Molly who had difficulty in enunciating the words that would sound like a defense of her rival. For it had become appallingly clear to her in the course of this extraordinary conversation that the earl had fallen in love with his wife. It was equally clear that he was unaware of his feelings as yet, and she was *not* going to seal her own doom by saying one more word that might reveal this state of affairs to him. Consequently, for the first time in their long association she was more than willing to see her lover leave her presence, though she stared at the door in flat despair when he departed full of brandy and confusion. The happiest period of her life was coming to an inevitable end. Nothing would ever be so satisfactory again, but for Charlotte's sake and for her own she had best start thinking about a future that would not contain her love. And with this sensible resolution taken, she threw herself on the big empty bed and gave way to a storm of weeping for the hopes that had never been fulfilled.

The earl made his way home on foot, whiling away the time in compiling a list of his wife's iniquities. In addition to impinging on his consciousness to a degree he deplored and trying to kill him so she might marry his cousin and enjoy his fortune at the same time, she had now managed to emasculate him. It hadn't been enough to fight him to the point of collapse rather than submit to his possession, she had even succeeded in preventing him from enjoying another woman. Molly's presence in his life these last years had served as a balance to his unwavering pursuit of his political career. He had always enjoyed his relationship with her, and what was even rarer when he considered the so-called "respectable" women he met in society, he *liked* her and admired her essential honesty and simplicity. And now April, with her deceptive softness and her damnable duplicity, had insinuated her image between himself and Molly and rendered him impotent. Lord, how she'd laugh if she knew this!

He reached his bedchamber and the conclusion that he was indulging in ridiculous fantasy at the same time. April had no interest whatever in him as a man. She'd been relieved early in the marriage when he'd intimated that he'd be content to find satisfaction elsewhere, and his behavior on the previous night would have rendered him forever repellent in her eyes.

The restlessness that had driven him earlier in the evening had seeped away, leaving him feeling the effects of a sleepless night and a totally frustrating day. It took no more than five minutes for him to seek the comfort of his bed.

The future looked no less dismal the next day, but at least

he was gradually regaining his normal good health. He made a firm resolution to table his personal problems, and, by determinedly refusing to allot any time to them, he managed to get through the next few days without attracting undue attention to his depressed spirits.

The first meeting with his wife brought the events of that night vividly before his mind's eye once again as he took in every detail of her appearance with an avidity he attempted to conceal behind a precariously maintained air of bland unconcern. His last sight of her, crumpled and disheveled, her slight form lost among incongruous wrinkles of what had seemed to be an acre of filmy material as she slept in an exhausted sprawl across the bed, had intruded into his memory at unoccupied moments ever since. He assured himself that there was nothing personal in his reaction; he would feel the same regret on seeing a beautiful painting slashed or a temple desecrated. One slanting glance reassured him that this particular artwork had been completely restored as April entered the room with her customary graceful glide, a figure of slender elegance in a floating creation of seafoam green. He would have said she was intrinsically untouched by the ugly experience could he have ignored the way her eyes shied away from any contact with his and the instinctive knowledge that her composure was a very fragile edifice supported solely by grim courage.

They circled around each other like boxers in the first round, but he resisted the urge to dwell anew on the incongruity of a murderous soul being contained in that exquisite exterior. It was only when she recoiled from his touch that he had difficulty in controlling an impulse to force her to submit to his possessive handling once again. The sight of the bruises he had inflicted marring her white skin sobered him instantly, however, and he realized how imperative it was that he confine his necessary contacts with April to the bare minimum. If society wished to question the success of the marriage, then society must be allowed its diversion. It was more vital that he retain his control over his own

conduct, and he couldn't guarantee this control if he was
forced into frequent contact with the woman who despised
him enough to connive at his death.

Two long weeks passed in this manner, with Adam spending very little time at home. He indulged in a spate of social
activities that served the sole purpose of wearying him sufficiently to allow him to fall asleep at night. For some reason
he didn't query, he kept away from Molly during this period
also.

Thanks to hours spent riding and driving in the fresh air,
he had regained his health and strength, not to mention his
appetite. The chemist to whom he sent the cigars reported
that they were laced with arsenic. He was furious at the
weakness that permitted final confirmation of his suspicions
to shake him at all, but at times he could barely keep his
hands off April's lovely throat. Merely looking at her caused
his temperature and his spleen to rise to an unhealthy
degree. Though he avoided looking at her whenever
possible, it had not escaped his attention that his wife was
not in her best looks of late. She was thinner, and there were
dark shadows like bruises under her eyes. The eyes themselves, those clear pools of luminous gray that he had once
found so mesmerizing, held an appealing hint of tragedy in
their depths. There was no question, the woman was an
accomplished actress! Had he not known how impossible was
her story he would have been taken in by that air of
wounded innocence she projected so convincingly.

He was becoming increasingly irritated by her persistence
in presenting what he could only call a haunted appearance,
and when Jason Jeffries asked him at a rout party one
evening if April had been ill, sending a concerned glance
after the slight figure, Adam determined to nip any such
rumors in the bud. He had told her that first day that he
intended her to cut a dashing figure in society, and he was
prepared to enfore his edict if he had to beat those die-away
airs out of her personally!

Chapter Fourteen

Spring was making tentative advances into the city when the Earl and Countess Glenville gave a ball in honor of their young sister. The affair was expected to be one of the highlights of the annual round of frenzied activity known as the season. Diana's excitement had been rising with each day that brought the dreamed-of event nearer. Shopping for the perfect gown for the occasion turned into a marathon ordeal, since the younger Miss Wendover's tastes ran to the kind of highly visible, dashing styles that no conscientious guardian could approve for a girl in her first season.

Battle was joined early and continued until April abandoned cajolery and tact in favor of exerting her authority. Deprived of the daring design of her dreams, Diana proved almost impossible to suit, and her sister nearly despaired of finding fabric special enough to awaken her admiration in time to have the gown finished before the date of the ball. They were cutting the margin perilously close when Diana admitted that a length of ivory silk discovered in a little shop off the Oxford Road and woven with a tiny pattern of flowers did not absolutely disgust her. She conceded that it might make up into a tolerably attractive gown if April meant to persist in taking up such a gothic attitude as to insist on her wearing pale uninteresting colors for her formal comeout. When Mélisande suggested that it be fashioned as an overdress to be worn with a slip of palest blush satin discreetly ornamented with embroidered roses at the hem, her reluctant interest was caught. After April

189

agreed to a neckline a whole inch lower than those approved so far and made no objection to the purchase of pearl rosettes to use as fastenings, a mild enthusiasm awoke in her breast and she was even able to participate in the more mundane details of preparing for the ball in a manner which, if it could not be described quite accurately as helpful, was at least amiable.

There was a ballroom on the ground floor at the back of the Hanover Square residence, which was certainly an advantage in planning an affair on a grand scale. That it would require extensive redecoration before appearing to advantage had been obvious from the start, but April, taking Adam at his word, had had no hesitation in setting matters in train almost immediately with scant regard to cost, and by the week of the ball nothing remained to be done but the washing of the countless lusters from the three chandeliers and numerous wall sconces and the final polishing of the handsome parquet floor. The designs on the pilasters and ceiling had been regilded, and the fresh paint smell had departed from the room in good time. The new curtains of seafoam green at the long windows hung perfectly, and dozens of spindly gold-painted chairs had been cushioned in matching fabric. The peeling panels of painted designs spaced around the walls between the pilasters had been replaced with mirrors that would reflect and multiply the shifting sea of colors in the ladies' gowns and jewels. Several banquettes done over in orange-pink velvet formed areas of eye-catching color at intervals. April had decided to use masses of flowers in the pink and orange color range as well as lacy greenery to bring the huge room to life. Though it was too early in the spring to stroll outside, gardeners had been hard at work bringing the neglected grounds into order, and strings of lanterns were to hang from the trees to illuminate the scene for those inside.

Mrs. Donaldson, with Mattie's able assistance, dealt with the caterers, but April, who preferred to have as little contact as possible with Morton, turned the problem of supplying the wines and other liquid refreshments over to her husband with the information that she did not plan to concern herself further in the matter. This represented almost the sum total of conversation between husband and wife for nearly a week, as Adam continued to be more often absent than present at dinner unless they were entertaining. It was, therefore, something of a surprise to find him in the saloon three days before their ball.

His critical eye was upon her as she entered the room and checked for an instant when he rose from a chair near the fireplace. She resumed her pace at once, trying to return his measuring stare with one of her own.

"You look terrible," he said by way of greeting.

"How kind of you to notice," she replied coolly, seating herself with careful attention to the fall of her skirts. "Hasn't today been unseasonably balmy? I do hope it will continue so for our ball."

"It is not my intention to discuss the weather with you. Cancel whatever engagements you have made for the next three days and take to your bed if necessary to repair the ravages of whatever is making you look like a ghost. And eat something for a change. You look as if a puff of wind would blow you away."

April had been unable to control her surprise at this attack, but by the time he had barked out his orders, she had the polite mask back in place.

"Whatever you say," she murmured obediently.

A sound that fell somewhere between a growl and a sigh of exasperation escaped the earl. "And don't be so damned meek—we both know that pose for the fiction it is. I said in the beginning that I had no objection to my wife's being the talk of the town for her style-setting. I have a rooted objection to the talk being caused by purple shadows under your eyes and a haggard air about you."

Diana's fortuitous appearance canceled any further criticisms the earl might have planned to level at his wife, and she was spared a reopening of the subject later by the arrival of the carriage immediately after dinner to take the ladies to Almack's subscription ball.

The earl had been quite correct in one accusation, at least. His wife was not meek. Although his verbal attack had come as a nasty surprise, it had not served to cow her spirits, nor was it allowed to influence her activities over the next few days. She and Diana went about their accustomed routine with no thought to their lord and master's possible disapproval. He would have been pleased to see that one command was being obeyed, however. April's appetite had improved of late, and she was sleeping better. The nightmares had not ceased entirely, but she was able to get back to sleep after a shorter interval of wakefulness these days. She was too occupied with the various details of their upcoming ball to spare much time for personal problems.

Diana's ball gown was completed and much admired by her sister and its creator, who predicted that all the young ladies would be envious of her appearance that night. Mélisande assured Lady Glenville that her own gown was nearing completion and would be ready the next day. April thanked her politely, having long since forgotten about the special design Adam had selected for her to wear at Diana's dance. She was unprepared, therefore, to handle the storm of protest that arose when her sister first cast her eyes on the gray silk creation with its elaborate overall pattern of silver threads. The gown was cut very plainly, relying for its effect on the beauty of the fabric with its shimmer of silver and sparkle of hundreds of crystal beads sewn into the pattern. April's gown, Diana hotly declared with what was no less than the truth, clearly outshone her own and would cast her into the shade at her own ball. She was deaf to her sister's protestations that nothing a matron past her first youth might wear could in any way detract from the combined appeal of youth and beauty. With tears of temper filling her eyes, she accused her sister of trying to spoil the most important night of her life by stealing the limelight. Perfectly appalled to be thought capable of such an act, April promised to wear a less spectacular dress, smothering any concern over Adam's reaction in the deeper concern that Diana's party should be perfect for the girl. It was no personal sacrifice at all events; she had dozens of gowns now, any one of which would do. In fact, if she were to confess the shaming truth, she was not best pleased to find the shadows under her eyes fading after a couple of restful nights. It would have been soothing to her bruised pride to have been able to deny her heartless husband this small satisfaction. Far from being flattered that he was still determined to have his "murdering bitch" of a wife do him credit in public, she felt reduced to the status of a snuffbox or some such object selected to complement a costume.

Fortunately there was little time to spare for unprofitable musings of like nature. The day of the ball was upon them, and there were the usual last-minute crises to threaten the success of the affair. The florist's helpers dripped water all over the polished floor, thus incurring Morton's wrath, and the caterers delivered the wrong kind of rout cakes, which he summarily returned with a blistering message. The staffs of the caterer and florist clashed head on with the resident servants on several occasions, setting tempers to fray. April's diplomatic skills were worn thin by five o'clock, when Mattie ordered her to her room to rest until it was time to dress. She dropped onto her bed and fell fast asleep until Mattie's hand on her shoulder roused her.

"I'd have let you sleep a bit longer," her tirewoman said with gruff affection, "but I expect you wish to see Diana finish dressing tonight."

"Thank you, Mattie, you're a dear. I do want to make sure Alice doesn't pull her hair back too severely. A *dégagée* style suits her best."

April's own toilette was achieved in record time, barring five minutes spent arguing with Mattie about the silver dress. Her simple hairstyle never wanted arranging as such, and as a peace offering she allowed Mattie to select a gown for her. Her mother's pearls, the one item aside from the little brooch that had not been sold, gleamed around her throat as she gave a quick glance in the mirror to approve Mattie's choice of dress, a pretty lavender satin that tended to imbue her eyes with a hint of that shade. Together they hurried down the hall to bestow their loving approval on the girl they had raised together.

The two women could be pardoned their partiality as they gazed with pride on a radiant Diana, for she was the epitome of youthful appeal and eagerness, her golden prettiness enhanced by the ivory and pink of her gown. Its sleek lines produced the illusion of added height, and the pearl Adam and April had presented to commemorate the occasion added the perfect finishing touch.

Not quite the finishing touch, evidently. When they entered Diana's bedchamber she was attempting to decide which of five posies sent to her would best complement her appearance while poor Alice tried to effect a becoming hairstyle on a head that wouldn't stay still. They had decided against a wreath of flowers in favor of a simple ribbon in the same blush pink threaded artfully through an abundance of golden curls falling from a Grecian knot. Mattie took over the final arrangement of the curls from a rattled Alice, who was almost as excited as her mistress, and under her nononsense approach Diana obediently sat still for this operation, only begging her sister to tell her which of the flowers to choose. April obliged in the full knowledge that Diana would overrule her, and was proved correct. It seemed the posy she had selected had been sent by a gentleman with rabbity teeth and an importunate air, two characteristics that rendered his gift quite ineligible in Diana's eyes. The final choice devolved on a very pretty bouquet of pink rosebuds in an ivory holder. The pink ribbons complimented the gown, and its presenter, Mr. Lawrence Eddington, was one of Diana's favorite beaux. April was secretly relieved that the honor had not gone to an all-white posy containing Mr. Damien Harding's card. The fact that the latter was one of her sister's most persistent gallants contributed not a little to Lady Glenville's general worries. That his motives were totally corrupt was not open to question—impecunious men of four or five and thirty did not dangle after new buds of seventeen, even ravishingly pretty girls like Diana, unless they were notable heiresses. Knowing he had not made a hit with his cousin's bride and unsure of her influence on Adam, he pursued Diana as a means of harassing herself while keeping close to the situation in Hanover Square. She gathered up her sister's netted reticule and the charming ivory silk fan with its painted pink roses that had been a lucky find in the Pantheon Bazaar, and urged the girl into the hall. After a hasty hug and a knowing grin for Mattie, who was determinedly holding back sentimental tears at the picture her nursling made tonight, Diana joined April in the hall and proceeded gaily down the stairs, having long since lost any vestige of nervousness in society.

At the door to the small saloon, Diana gave her sister a playful push, whispering, "You go in first, April, then I'll make an entrance for Adam."

Perforce, April entered the saloon alone, her eyes automatically seeking her husband's, her spine suddenly stiff as though braced for a blow. She did not have to wait long for Adam's reaction. Those dark brows flew together and his lips became a straight line before parting, but his words were deceptively mild.

"Where is the gray silk gown?"

"We . . . I decided it was a bit too spectacular for anything less grand than an event at Carlton House."

"Well, you may now *un*decide. Go and put on the gray."

She faced him squarely, her head high, aware that Diana had come into the room behind her. Her sister's big entrance was spoiled anyway, so she might as well be hanged for a sheep as a lamb. The angle of her chin elevated a trifle. "I prefer this gown. It is more comfortable for dancing."

"Do not try me too far, April. Either you go upstairs and put on the gown I ordered or I'll put you in it myself."

By this time Diana had assimilated the situation.

"But Adam!" she wailed, and her sister quaked for her temerity. Adam held up a restraining hand, not even glancing at the guest of honor.

"Later, Diana. Well, madam, do you desire me to act as your abigail?"

April swung around on one foot and flounced out the

room without another word. Fury drove her up the stairs at
twice her normal pace, but it was anxiety for Diana that
caused her to call loudly for Mattie, who came out of
Diana's room almost on her heels.

"What's the matter?"

"Get out the gray silk, Mattie," she ordered shortly, already ripping open the buttons she could reach before she
entered her boudoir. "And take that look of satisfaction off
your face," she added with the remnants of temper. "I'll
need the silver sandals too."

In less than five minutes she was hurrying back down the
stairs arrayed in the most beautiful gown she had ever seen
and unaware of how it became her, since she had not spared
the time for a glance in the mirror. She was impelled by a
fear that Diana might have thrown a tantrum over the dress,
exposing herself to the rough edge of Adam's tongue in the
process. If he *dared* to ruin that girl's big evening he would
have more to deal with than he bargained for, she vowed! By
the time she burst through the saloon door, sweeping past an
astounded footman, she was in a fine rage.

"Excellent! Every bit as lovely as I hoped," Adam said
smoothly to take the wind out of her sails. "I had intended to
recommend a touch of rouge, but I see something, exertion
perhaps, has given you a fine healthy color. May I pour you
a glass of sherry?"

April's eyes had gone immediately to Diana, who though
a trifle subdued, was smiling easily. She barely heard her
husband's comments as she searched her sister's face for
signs of a recent storm or one to come, and was reassured.
For a moment she stood there feeling remarkably foolish.
Obviously Adam had acquired the knack of turning Diana
up sweet if he had averted a scene tonight. His patient
repetition of the offer of a glass of sherry rescued her, and
she clutched at it, glad to have something to occupy her
hands for the moment. She flicked an uncertain look at the
earl, but his reaction to her change of costume had passed,
leaving her strangely dissatisfied. Now he was being the
suave host as they waited for Morton to announce dinner.

She sipped her sherry in mute discomfort, wishing her paralyzed brain would dredge up even one acceptable topic of conversation.

Dinner passed off very smoothly, with Diana and Adam shouldering the burden of conversation while April concentrated on achieving a state of relaxation. By the time Morton had cleared the table she felt able to greet their guests with a semblance of ease. As they rose from their chairs, Adam said casually:

"One moment, my dear. Before we head for the ballroom, I have a little something for you to wear tonight." He was taking a jeweler's box out of an inner pocket as he spoke, and now he strolled toward April, who stood still, blinking in surprise.

"Oh, how absolutely *gorgeous!*"

The exclamation was Diana's. April was too dumbfounded to speak as her husband drew a delicate necklace out of the case and motioned for her to remove her pearls. Huge gray eyes questioned him, but there was nothing to be read in his face. He laid the necklace against her throat and fastened it. Womanlike, April headed for the nearest mirror and stood staring in awestruck admiration at the exquisite thin chain of diamonds supporting a center pendant consisting of a teardrop-shaped diamond that must have been worth a king's ransom. It was the most perfect thing she had ever seen, and she struggled to find the words to express her pleasure in the gift.

"Adam, I don't know how to thank you — I—"

"I'll show you," he said lightly. Before she knew what he was about, he had taken her chin in one hand and was pressing his mouth to hers. Shock kept her perfectly still under his touch at first. Memories and fears, along with strange new sensations, sent the blood pounding through her veins, but before she could react in any way it was over. Adam had released her and stepped back. April's eyes were glazed, but she noted the dark color under his skin before the sound of Diana applauding the event brought her attention to her surroundings.

"Bravo! Perhaps someone will kiss me tonight. I do hope so!" declared the irrepressible girl.

"Diana, you *wouldn't!*"

"That's quite enough out of you on that subject, minx!" Adam's laugh sounded forced, but he continued in a nearly normal tone to describe in detail the unpleasant fate in store for any young gallant who attempted to take such a liberty with his sister-in-law. "For tonight, all your kisses belong to me," he finished, saluting her briefly on the cheek.

"Pooh! Tame stuff—kisses from an old married man!" scoffed Diana, voicing an opinion that was definitely not shared by her silent sister.

But the girl's nonsense had relieved the moment of embarrassment, and they went into the ballroom in unusual harmony, which was increased by the warmth of the earl's approval of the renovation and decoration of the beautifully proportioned room. The members of the orchestra were already bustling about on the dais arranging their music stands, and there was barely time to inspect the refreshments in the supper room before the first of the guests were upon them.

It was nearly two hours before April and Adam felt free to mingle with their guests, as they were constrained to keep visible to greet latecomers for whom this event might be the second or third stop of the evening. Diana had been released earlier to enjoy the dancing, and she was doing just that, April concluded as she drifted toward a group of young ladies without partners who were chattering vivaciously to demonstrate how little they regarded this circumstance. Glancing about for reinforcements, she noticed Adam disappearing into the card room with the Duke of York. A lifted brow brought Freddy to her side, however, and they reached the girls just as two gentlemen approached from the opposite direction. Three men and four girls meant one young lady would remain partnerless, and with a sigh April realized it would be Phoebe Granby who would suffer this indignity. Not only was her unhappy prediction confirmed, but one of the gentlemen stepped on Phoebe's gown, tearing a ruffle, as she bent to retrieve her dance card.

"I always said William Dixon was a clumsy lout," April pronounced mildly as the offender, all unknowing, led a giggling brunette off. "How fortunate you did not get landed with him for a partner, my dear child. Come, let us go upstairs. Mattie will see to that ruffle."

"Oh, please, you must not bother about me, Lady Glenville. I shall be able to pin it myself in the ladies' retiring room," Phoebe protested, quite distraught at the idea of inconveniencing her hostess.

April had noticed the girl's trembling lip, however, and was busy weaving her toils, seeing this accident as a heavensent opportunity to do something for the unfortunate Phoebe. Louisa was nowhere in view—probably she was settled in the card room trying to win back the cost of her daughter's dress—and her cousin was resolved to try her hand at improving Phoebe's appearance. Thus she slipped a hand under the girl's arm and piloted her toward the main wing.

She talked a spate of cheerful nonsense that finally succeeded in drawing a shaky laugh from the embarrassed girl by the time they reached April's bechamber, where she rang for Mattie. While awaiting the maid, April sought in her mind for a tactful approach to what she planned to do and decided there wasn't one.

"Phoebe, do you trust me?"

A startled look leaped into the girl's light-blue eyes. "N—naturally I trust you, Lady Glenville."

"Good. Then I am going to ask you to put yourself unconditionally in my hands for the next few minutes and we'll try to see what can be done about that gown to make it fit better. Will you let me try?"

Slow color mounted in Phoebe's cheeks, leaving her skin with a mottled effect, but she nodded silently.

"That's a good girl—ah, there you are, Mattie. Take a good look at this gown. There is a torn ruffle, but that is nothing. Do you think if we took a tuck here and here perhaps, it would fit better and show off her neat waist?"

Mattie made a lightning assessment and declared herself capable of fixing matters in twenty minutes. "Can't do anything about that color though."

April was unhooking the gown before she finished speaking. "No, but I can tone down her own coloring. Sit here, Phoebe." She placed the bemused girl on the bench at her dressing table and handed her bright-pink gown over to the maid, who had already possessed herself of the work box.

While Mattie set strong stitches, April dulled Phoebe's high color with a careful application of powder. After a critical appraisal of the results, she ordered Phoebe to close her eyes, telling her what she didn't see she couldn't confess to her mother. It took only a moment to darken and define the pale brows. "There, that brightens your features. Now for that hair. You have lovely hair, Phoebe, but it is crimped too tightly. If you do not object, I propose to brush some of the curl out and give you a fuller style." She was removing the pins as she spoke, so it was just as well that Miss Granby was too cowed to voice any objection. After a vigorous brushing, April started to form larger, softer curls, which she anchored securely, letting several fall free over the ears. Rummaging through a drawer, she emerged with a length of white ribbon. "With your permission, child, I am going to substitute this for the wreath of roses you were wearing." An almost imperceptible nod being accepted as permission, she carried out her intention, calling over her shoulder to Mattie that Miss Granby was now ready to be redressed.

The girl said nothing at all when her hostess had done up the last button and positioned her in front of the mirror with a flourish of triumph. April flashed a look of consternation at Mattie. Had her juggernaut tactics offended Phoebe? Her lips parted to offer a sincere apology, which was forestalled when two brimming blue eyes turned to her in mute gratitude.

"Very nice you look indeed, Miss Granby," said Mattie, easing the situation for both.

April hugged the girl, who shyly thanked Mattie for her assistance, then bustled her downstairs. The first young man they encountered on entering the ballroom was Mr. Eddington. In answer to the countess's speaking look, he grinned and politely requested the honor of standing up with Miss Granby. As the two walked off to enter a set forming near the center of the room, April was well rewarded by his casual remark that he'd never seen Phoebe looking better.

It was time to circulate. Her glance roved along the sides of the room where small groups of chaperons were conversing and lighted on a still-lovely woman wearing an elegant purple gown and a frankly bored expression beneath her feathered headdress. As she wended her way toward her mother-in-law, stopping to acknowledge the complimentary remarks of several people in her path, she schooled her own features to an expression of pleasure. The two had met at two or three large gatherings and achieved a moderately amiable *rapprochement* under the curious eye of the *ton*. Lady Ellsmere, with her air of world-weary skepticism, was never going to be a prime favorite with her daughter-in-law, but it was an act of Christian charity to rescue her from the garrulity of General Smythe-Thomas, who looked settled to recount the entire history of his military career.

She had cause to be grateful for her own rescue ten long minutes later as the earl came toward them with an old friend of his mother's in tow.

"Mrs. Anselworth was just saying, ma'am, that she has not set eyes on you for an age, so I brought her over to enjoy a comfortable coze, and since the orchestra is striking up for a waltz I propose to solicit my wife's hand for our first dance. Your servant, General. As you see, I have not depleted your court, merely added some new blood."

"Adam, what a thing to say!" April protested laughingly as he swept her onto the floor.

He held her off a trifle and stared down at her with a glint in his eye. "Did I mistake the piteous looks you were casting about the room? Shall I return you to the general?"

"Wretch!" She subsided, smiling at his absurdity.

"Was he recounting the details of his last military campaign?"

"I'd have preferred that! No, it was the inside story of his life—stomach, kidneys, liver, and the rest. It seems the general has always suffered from an excess of—"

"Enough! Fascinating though anything to do with the general must always be, right now I would rather have you tell me where you disappeared to for half an hour."

"It's a long story," replied his wife, "which I'll tell you some other time."

"Does it have anything to do with the fact that the maypole Granby girl's appearance is suddenly improved out of all reason?"

Astonished at his perception, April looked more closely at him than was her habit and saw a smile lurking in his dark eyes.

"My fingers have been itching to undo some of Louisa's work," she confessed with a self-congratulatory air. "Phoebe is a sweet girl and more could be made of her."

"If she needs a partner, I'll stand up with her for the next set."

"Thank you, Adam." She gave him an unclouded smile reflecting her satisfaction in her night's work and her pleasure in the dance.

An answering smile appeared on his face, then faded. "Moonbeams and stardust and mountain lakes," he said slowly to mystify her.

"I beg your pardon?"

"That is what you remind me of, looking as you do tonight."

There was a new and unfathomable element in the intense regard Adam bent on her that quickened April's pulses and drove down her lashes in an instinctive need to protect herself from some unidentified threat to her peace of mind. She did not even attempt to reply. Adam too fell silent, but he drew her pliant body closer and gave himself over to a sensual abandonment to the beauty and rhythm of the waltz music. April was content to follow his lead; in fact, at that point in time she would have been content to continue moving in this weightless floating fashion forever.

But no dance lasts forever, and inevitably the music wound to a close. April and Adam found themselves in the corner near the orchestra with the earl's back to the room. For a second after the music stopped he continued to hold her loosely, and she held her breath as he seemed to be pulling her nearer without actually moving. It flashed through her mind that he intended to kiss her again, and of course she could not permit such a breach of good taste, but still she stood there, waiting.

"Now, now, this is a respectable party. That sort of thing won't do outside of the Cyprians' Ball," admonished a jovial voice.

The earl and countess jerked toward the speaker as if pulled on strings. Mr. Damien Harding's face had assumed a teasing expression, but April had seen icy rage in his eyes before he had quite mastered it, and fear struck through her like a knife blade. She turned unconsciously pleading eyes to Adam, but the stiff formality of the past few weeks was back in full sway, all traces of recent softening gone.

"How are you, Damien?"

"How nice of you to ask, cousin. I've seen almost nothing of you lately, old chap."

"I've been busy. Jason Jeffries and I are going to drive to Exton to watch a mill tomorrow night. Come with us if you like."

"Unfortunately I am already engaged for tomorrow evening. And speaking of engagements, I have not yet had the pleasure of dancing with the beautiful bride, though the guest of honor favored me with a waltz. May I request the pleasure of the next dance, Cousin April?"

April excused herself on the grounds of neglected hostess duties, uncaring if her excuse sounded fabricated. If she was to conceal her feelings for Mr. Damien Harding it was necessary to put the greatest possible distance between them at all times.

The rest of the evening was devoted to conscientious

carrying out of her role of hostess. The magic that had hovered over the affair earlier had dissipated and she was unable to recapture the mood, but at least for Diana the party was a resounding success, and she went reluctantly to bed in the small hours of the morning basking in the glow of her triumph.

Chapter Fifteen

Neither of the ladies rose very early on the day after Diana's ball. Having had the foresight to order Morton to deny them to morning callers, they gave themselves over to the rare indulgence of a leisurely breakfast abovestairs at a deplorably late hour while they engaged in the enjoyable activity known as talking over the party. When Diana had finally related all the most original and eloquent of the compliments paid to her by her numerous partners and happily criticized the gowns of most of the females of her acquaintance, she bethought herself to mention the improvement in Phoebe Granby's looks and was regaled by the story of her cousin's transformation at the hands of her sister and Mattie. She was less confident than April that the improvement could be sustained in the face of Lady Granby's blatant poor taste but agreed to try to aid and encourage Phoebe whenever possible.

"Everyone mentioned how lovely you looked last night, April. I'm sorry I made such a fuss about the silver dress," she admitted, shamefaced. "I'm a selfish beast at times. I think perhaps you spoiled me a bit."

Her sister laughed and hugged her shoulders briefly. "Perhaps a bit," she agreed, "but I would not trade you for anyone else's sister."

"Adam thought you looked beautiful too," Diana added, slanting a glance at her sister's still face. "He scarcely spoke to Lady Ellis all evening and couldn't seem to take his eyes off you."

"Playing matchmaker, Diana? You'll catch cold at that ploy."

The bitterness in her sister's voice silenced the younger girl, who sought a quick change of topic.

During the afternoon they had the felicity of being complimented by numerous callers on a most successful ball. Adam was not in to tea or dinner, and the ladies were promised to the Eddingtons for a theater party that evening. April found it a trifle flat surrounded by youngsters, agreeable though they all were. The play was lively, however, and well worth seeing.

It was the following morning before April saw her husband. For no particular reason she decided to go down for an early breakfast, garbed in her most becoming morning gown of soft lavender muslin. On the threshold of the breakfast parlor she halted in consternation.

"*Adam!* What has happened to your arm?"

The earl leveled a somber glance at her concerned face. It seemed an inordinately long time to the expectant girl before he replied in a wooden voice, "Someone tried to kill me last night."

April swayed and reached out to grasp the back of a chair as her husband jumped up and came toward her.

"Don't worry," she said, holding him off with one hand and meeting his eyes squarely. "Murderesses never faint."

"Ah, please don't!" he begged, his mouth twisting in a grimace of pain. "I know you didn't do it."

"Not personally, of course," she agreed. "I have an alibi, but I might have hired someone to do the actual deed."

Husband and wife confronted one another across a gulf of misunderstanding, Adam's eyes reflecting the pain in April's heart.

"I know you had nothing to do with it or the other," he stated quietly. "I owe you an abject apology for suspecting you, and for . . . for—"

"*How* do you know?" she interrupted, pride keeping her stiff and emotionless.

"It was . . . Damien."

Her eyes never left his face, but some of the stiffness drained out of her body. "You have proof?"

He nodded grimly. "Damien's corpse."

This time April really did sag, and the earl pushed her onto the nearest chair with the arm that was not resting in a white sling. Her head came up after a second or two and their eyes met.

"Adam, I am so terribly sorry. What else can I say?"

"Nothing." He sighed as he settled wearily back into his own chair. "It is the best way. The scandal would have been impossible to avoid."

"How did it happen? How badly hurt is your arm?"

"You heard me invite Damien to go with us to a mill? He declined, you will recall, on the score of a previous engagement. After the fight, Jason wanted to get back to town, and there was a full moon, so we set out. About halfway across Hounslow Heath we were ambushed. The assailant, who was masked, got off one shot, which winged me. Before he could shoot again, Jason shot him, and he fell. The team bolted, and it took me a few minutes to get them back under control and return to the spot. Jason insisted on bandaging my arm with our handkerchiefs before we took a closer look at the highwayman, as my groom had already pronounced him dead. Perhaps you may imagine my feelings when we unmasked him and discovered his identity."

"Yes, I think I know how fond you were of Damien."

He gestured impatiently. "That was only part of it, as you *must* know! *You* were the rest of it, you and the way I treated you. April, can you—"

"How will you explain Damien's death to Freddy?"

He hunched a shoulder and fixed his gaze on his fingers toying with a spoon. "We took his purse and watch and a signet ring he always wore, got rid of the mask, and left him for someone else to find. It should look as though he had been set upon by highwaymen."

She winced, and he said harshly, "I know, it's damned

callous, but what choice did we have if Freddy and the world
are to remain in ignorance of the truth?" His eyes challenged
hers, and hers fell.

At that moment the door to the pantry opened and Jacob
entered, carrying a large tray. April and Adam watched
him in silence as he deposited the dishes on the table. The
earl waved him away when he had finished.

"Where is Morton?" April wondered as the door closed
behind the footman.

"Packing his gear. Did you think I'd keep in my employ a
man who tried to kill me?"

"You kept a wife who tried to kill you — or so you
thought," she returned steadily.

The color drained from beneath his dark skin, leaving
him as ghastly as she was. The scar on his cheek stood out
redly, and his eyes were two black holes with no life behind
them.

"April, I . . . you must know how greatly I regret what
happened in the study. Can you ever forgive me?"

"How *could* you believe I would do such a horrible thing
after all you had done for Diana and me?" she cried, tears
starting to her eyes.

"I didn't *want* to believe it!" he replied in desperate
earnest. "But there was Damien, whom I'd known all my
life, and of course I knew how you hated me and blamed me
for your father's and brother's deaths."

"You knew I *hated* you?" she echoed in disbelief. "Why I
. . . I —" Suddenly April tore her gaze from her husband's
tormented face, gave one nauseated glance at the food
spread on the table, and turned even paler. "I don't believe I
care for breakfast after all," she whispered, and bolted for
the door before Adam could intervene.

He rose halfway out of the chair, then sank back in
defeat. Nothing had changed at all. For a moment last night
when he had recognized the face under the mask, wild
intoxicating elation had surged through his veins at the
realization that April had not tried to kill him. The truth
had been horrible enough to sober him in the next instant,

of course. Jason's shock had to be dealt with without revealing all the circumstances surrounding the attempted poisoning. And the situation itself had demanded an instant decision as to the best way to avoid a scandal. Thank God, his own groom, Delsey, had been with him since he was a young stable boy and was completely loyal.

It had been a grim ride home, and thoughts of the blow ahead for Freddy had weighed upon him, but not so heavily as the weight that had been removed by the proof of his wife's innocence. At last he would be able to stop denying his love for the woman who had married him against his will and invaded his heart with the insidious stealth of a fog creeping in over the city. He had fought it, denied her attraction, refused to admit that he was lost from the moment she had faced him from a dressing-table bench in a quaking fear and still defied him to try to turn her into a fashion plate.

In the beginning, confident of his indifference toward women, he had relegated her to the negligible position in his life befitting a wife in name only, but she had refused to occupy that position and had climbed by insensible degrees to a permanent perch in his heart before he was aware of what was happening. And when he did become attuned to the possible benefits of such a situation it was to discover the woman who fascinated him was conniving at his death. How he had despised himself and railed against the weakness that made him desire her while knowing her for the unprincipled adventuress she was! All that was in the past now. He was free to love her, but after what had happened between them it was entirely possible that her original antipathy, based on misunderstanding of his role in her past, had become immutable loathing.

Ignoring the food on the table, he poured himself a cup of coffee and drank it scalding hot without noticing taste or temperature. He deserved to lose her if he gave way to despair. He had expected too much too fast this morning. She was shocked, naturally, by the events he had related, but he could not believe a woman who could cherish the burden

of a dependent sister and unself-consciously cuddle someone's else's child on her lap could remain forever unfor-
giving. There had been moments when their eyes had locked
in a long searching look void of animosity, moments when
an expectant electricity seemed to spark between them. He
thought, he *hoped,* the feeling had not been all on his side.
He must curb his impatience and try to insinuate himself
into her affections. She felt guilty about coercing him into
marriage — this had been evident in her eagerness to disturb
his life as little as possible under the circumstances, to fall in
with his plans and comply with his wishes. There was a solid
conviction in his mind that if he played on that sense of
guilty obligation she would submit to his possession out of a
feeling of duty, but, dammit, he didn't *want* a dutiful wife!
Better to wait forever while there was the slightest chance of
winning her love.

The earl was so busy over the next week or so that there
was relatively little strain placed on his good resolutions with
regard to his wife. There were all the details connected with
Damien's death to arrange. Freddy had accepted without
question the circumstances as they appeared to come to light
and had been grateful for his cousin's emotional support. As
Damien's debts began to surface after his death, he had
cause to be grateful also for Adam's willingness to discharge
his brother's financial obligations. Adam took care that
Freddy never knew the full extent to which his brother had
been under the hatches. Small wonder Damien had been so
desperate.

He saw relatively little of April for over a sennight. When
they did meet, he found her a trifle guarded but cordial.
With great thankfulness he observed that the haunted look
had vanished from her eyes. He took consolation in the hope
that it had been the result of distress at being wrongly
judged rather than fear of being physically abused by a
vengeful husband. She made no overtures toward establishing a warmer relationship, nor had he expected any, but it
did seem as if her eyes held a welcome when he came into a

room these days. With this he tried to be content for the present.

Several weeks had elapsed since he had last visited Molly, and something must be done in that quarter. The years of using Molly as an emotional crutch had ended with the realization that his wife's image filled his life. Even if she never came to love him, his own feelings for April were too strong to permit him to seek consolation elsewhere.

He dropped in on Molly one afternoon not long after Damien's funeral to tell her of the financial arrangements he had made for her and Charlotte. She received him with a pleasure that dimmed when the reason for the visit was explained, but Molly possessed an inherent dignity that stood her in good stead. She thanked him most sincerely and surprised him very much by acknowledging that she had known at their last meeting that he had fallen in love with his wife. The occasion was saved from the usual awkwardness attending such partings by Molly's revelation to her protector that Mr. Norris, the draper, having decided to retire to a modest establishment outside of York to become the nonparticipating partner in another business venture, had proposed to her and was patiently awaiting her answer. He knew the whole story of her past and was prepared to welcome Charlotte as a daughter. She successfully hid the pain that filled her at the earl's patent pleasure and relief on receiving this news. They parted with perfect amity on both sides, and the earl wasn't to know, as he ran down the stairs with a light step, that his discarded mistress, with silent tears coursing down her cheeks, was regarding her secure financial future and long-desired respectable marriage in the light of a lifetime banishment.

The period following Damien's death was viewed by April as a much-needed respite from the state of emotional turmoil that had evolved in the frightening manner of a snowball sent rolling downhill over the relatively short span of her marriage. She was released at last from the gnawing fear that Adam was targeted for death while she herself stood by powerless to avert the catastrophe. It was nearly as great a relief to know herself vindicated in her judgment and freed of the weight of unjust suspicion that had had a crushing effect on her spirit.

At times she had to force her features into a semblance of somberness befitting a family in mourning. This might have been more often necessary had not all her patience and sympathy been called upon to help ease the shock and sorrow that Damien's death had produced for Diana. The young girl had unreservedly admired the handsome cousin who flattered and amused her and occupied a prominent place in her court. She was disconsolate for a time and clung to her sister literally and figuratively. April knew that it was a reaction to additional loss in a young life already marked by loss rather than a lover's despair, but the girl needed a good deal of comfort and reassurance at first. Her own sunny nature reasserted itself after a time, aided by the pull of all the distractions offered to a popular young lady during the London season. Gradually she began to take a renewed interest in the activities of her friends, and her dependence on her sister lessened.

At last April had opportunity to consider her own emotions and long-suppressed, only partially acknowledged dreams. What she discovered was not entirely to her liking. It was amazing how quickly one could accustom oneself to passive blessings such as the absence of fear, and begin to seek greedily after more positive gratification. All she had requested of life for the last few years was the opportunity to give Diana a London season, and she had achieved this goal in a luxurious style inconceivable just three months ago. What was wrong with her that she could not convince herself of her perfect contentment with the privileged existence they were leading? What more did she wish from life?

For a considerable period April shied away from this question, refusing to admit unconscious longings into her conscious mind. This determined avoidance dated from the morning Adam had told her of Damien's last attempt on his life. When he had tried to defend his earlier suspicion of his wife he had mentioned as an accepted fact her hatred and blame of himself for causing the death of her relatives. Freddy had long ago told her Adam's side of that unhappy period, and she had not even thought of the earlier acquaintance after the first week or so of their marriage. In her utter shock at hearing him cite her hatred as fact she had almost blurted out — what? A simple denial of hatred? Or a declaration of love? Whether through cowardice or reticence, she had fled the scene before baring her soul, and for a time successfully managed to suppress the memory of that moment.

It refused to be buried for good, however, and as April and Adam began to resume the pattern their lives had begun to take before the poisoning episode, her thoughts returned with the regularity of homing pigeons to the scene in the breakfast parlor. What would have followed had she finished that sentence? It required very little cogitation to decide that anyone would be pleased and relieved to know himself not hated or held responsible for another's death. It required an increase in courage, however, to examine the other possibility. *Had* she been about to declare her love for her husband? *Did* she love him? Once she finally admitted the question to consideration the answer was abundantly clear as far as her feelings were concerned. Of course she loved her husband!

She didn't know when the process had begun, but if she'd used the intelligence she'd been born with she'd have long since recognized the cause of her terror over Adam's vulnerability with regard to his murderous cousin.

At first the mere acknowledgment of her love was sufficient to produce a quiet happiness. She went about in a private haze of contentment that fed on Adam's presence and attentions, wanting nothing save his continued good health and good humor for its nourishment. After a time, though, she couldn't prevent herself from seeking signs of increased interest on his part, and thus began the distressing period in which her spirits alternated from the dismals to soaring into the boughs, wholly depending on Adam's attitude. In her more rational moments she was wryly aware that her moods, if not her behavior, were on a level with those of her seventeen-year-old sister. Diana, however, delighted in achieving the complete subjugation of all the hopeful males in her train, while April would have been more than content to settle for the exclusive attentions of one specific man for the rest of her life.

Adam *was* attentive and seemed to seek out her company more than formerly, but always her burgeoning hopes were kept in check by the knowledge that except for the period of their estrangement, it had ever been his object to convince the *ton* that theirs was a love match. She found to her dismay that she had passed beyond the age of innocent coquetry without having gained the confidence (or wit) to throw out serious lures to the man she wanted. Not that she was unhappy, far from it, but there was and perhaps would always be an unfulfilled yearning to matter to her husband on the deepest level.

This was the state of affairs existing between the pair three weeks after Damien's death when Adam and April were bidden to an intimate dinner and conversable evening at the Jeffrieses'. It had not been deemed improper for Diana, who was after all not even related by marriage to Damien, to resume her social activities at this point. Tonight she was attending Almack's under the less than wholehearted chaperonage of Lady Granby, who had been prevailed upon by her daughter to invite her pretty cousin to spend the night so the girls might continue to enjoy the event by recapitulating the highlights into the wee hours of the morning.

The earl and countess arrived early in Mount Street, as was their custom, in order to enjoy a visit with the Jeffries children. To her brother's satisfaction, Melissa was content to go to April after one quick toss by Uncle Adam, leaving him a clear field for rougher play. After ten noisy minutes that sated even Jonathan's lust for action, the earl dropped onto the sofa occupied by his wife and Melissa. His breathing was a little rapid, and he complained, "I must be getting old—Jonathan wears me out."

Missy looked up briefly from examining April's pearls, which were adorning her small person at the moment.

"Nurse says Jonathan has rag manners," she announced coolly before returning her attention to her bedizened self.

"I do *not* have rag manners!"

The earl's eyes smiled into his wife's. "Someone sounds rather prissy," he remarked, *sotto voce*.

Jonathan heard this, and his indignation changed to teasing. "Prissy Missy, Prissy Missy!" he chanted at his sister, whose lip trembled warningly.

Mrs. Jeffries intervened, silencing her son with a stern look before all-out battle flared. April hugged the insulted Missy, who suddenly remembered something.

"Do you have a little girl like me at your house yet, Auntie April?"

"No, not yet, Missy," she replied hastily, keeping her head down to conceal the hot color that spread over her cheekbones and praying that Adam's attention was elsewhere.

"But you *said* you wished you had a little girl," the child pointed out in her clear, carrying treble.

"Yes, I know, darling, but—"

"It takes time to find a little girl as nice as you, Missy," finished the earl, coming to his wife's rescue. Their eyes met over the child's golden head. For a time the other occupants of the room receded to a far distance as husband and wife looked measuringly at each other, then the arrival of the first dinner guests shattered the intimacy of the moment.

They sat down ten to dinner, and as usual the conversation around the Jeffrieses' table was of the same high order as the delectable food that issued from the kitchen, whose control Jane never wholly relinquished to the resident chef. If the talk was weighted on the side of political issues and governmental happenings, that was only to be expected from guests involved in the daily process of governing the country.

When the men joined the ladies in the saloon later, the
atmosphere shifted to an emphasis on music. Their host and
hostess enjoyed listening and performing, and drew other
enthusiasts to their home. April applauded the Jeffrieses'
sprightly duets and was enthralled by the beautiful violin
rendition of a Bach cantata by an undistinguished-looking
king's councilor, but she realized as Jane begged Adam for a
song or two that this was the moment she had been waiting
for since first learning that her husband sang. She repressed
the little pang that racked her at the thought that she was
probably the only person present who had never been
privileged to hear him, and composed her features to a
listening attitude. He complied good-naturedly with Jane's
requests for a couple of rollicking old country songs. April
experienced the thrill that comes from hearing a superb
artist performing with the ease of total control. Adam's
speaking voice was rather low-pitched, so the range he displayed in singing was a revelation to her. Her shining eyes
followed his every movement as he directed the songs
smilingly and impartially to his eager audience. His wife led
the applause with unself-conscious pride when the last note
sounded. Only a stern recollection of propriety kept her
from leading the chorus of requests for another number,
and a delighted smile beamed when Adam leaned over and
whispered to Jane, who was accompanying him at the
pianoforte.

As the first notes of the introduction rippled softly, April
sat up straighter in her chair, and her eyes, which had been
fixed on the pianist's hands, sought her husband's in
astonished, half-fearful questioning. The intensity of
Adam's stare affected her so strongly that she missed the
opening bars of the beautiful *Per la gloria d'adoravi,* but
never could she be mistaken in this loveliest of all love songs.
Hadn't her father sung it to her mother on every musical
occasion that she could remember from earliest childhood?
It had been their special song and, consequently, one much
loved by their daughter as she grew up. Memories washed

over her and glazed her eyes with unshed tears as Adam sang the well-remembered lyrics in a voice as breathtakingly tender as a caress. *Amando penerò, ma sempre v'amerò*— in loving I shall suffer, but I shall always love you. How could he know, *did* he know what this song meant to her, or was it simply another number in his repertoire? Did he even know the meaning of the lyrics, or had he merely learned the Italian syllables by rote as children learned their ditties? Questions, doubts, hopes spun about in her brain, the internal activity at total variance with her appearance, which was that of a slender statue. Not a muscle moved in her face or body during Adam's rendition; she sat as one mesmerized by the power of his dark eyes which never left her face and the beauty of the rich voice rolling out the final tones of Bononcini's lovely melody.

Loud applause brought her back to her immediate surroundings with a start. Adam acknowledged it with a small smiling bow and prepared to resume his seat, firmly declining to sing anything else when pressed.

"I didn't understand a single word," declared Mrs. Elvin, the plump middle-aged wife of a Member of Parliament, "but I just know I'd love to have it sung to me, whatever it says." She waited for the general laugh this brazen confession elicited to die down, then pursued her line of thought. "What does that *luci care* mean, Lord Glenville?"

"It is difficult to translate exactly, ma'am," Adam replied, "but 'sweet eyes' is a fairly close rendering. When I saw my wife's eyes on our wedding day, the phrase came into my head. It seemed to fit."

"No need to look so conscious, my dear," Mrs. Elvin told the blushing Lady Glenville. "You should be pleased as punch to wring a public declaration from your husband. The most romantic thing Mr. Elvin ever said to me was that I had a good seat on a horse."

"Well, Adam's never seen me on a horse," replied April, rallying, "but I should consider such a compliment highly romantic indeed and shall endeavor to deserve it."

At this point another lady was reminded of a blatantly un-
romantic compliment that had been paid by a gentleman in
all sincerity, and this led to a spate of amusing recollections
which reduced the company to helpless laughter. April summoned an alert look to her face and laughed at the proper
places, but her laughter held a note of excitement unrelated
to the story being told at the moment. Adam *had* known the
meaning of the Italian lyrics of Bononcini's song! He
thought the part about the eyes was applicable to herself.
She stole a look at him as he threw his head back and roared
with laughter at an incident being recounted by Mr. Elvin.
Did the rest of the lyric apply to himself? Was it possible that
he loved her in secret and expected nothing but suffering to
come from such a love? At the moment he looked like a man
unacquainted with the meaning of the word "suffering."
Never had she seen him more completely relaxed and seemingly in spirits. Her own excitement mounted as the hour
grew later. Never had she been so eager to see a delightful
evening come to a close. Perhaps Adam would say something in the carriage, refer to the song he had sung to her.
How would she respond? Should she reveal her own knowledge of Italian?

In the event, April's hopes came crashing down upon her
during the drive home. They chatted quietly about the
evening they had just spent, and Adam replied with perfect
amiability, but his high spirits had evaporated, and he
appeared thoughtful, leaving the burden of conversation on
April's shoulders. Those slim shoulders seemed to sag
literally as the carriage drew ever nearer to Hanover Square.
At last she had to acknowledge that Adam was not going to
refer to his singing. Her fingers were gripping her fan so
tightly that she bent the sticks out of shape as she assessed
her courage and found it wanting. Surely she was not such a
sapskull that she could not even toss off a casual remark for
fear of being thought to tread where she was not wanted!
Where was her hard-earned worldliness? Every instant was
bringing them nearer to the point when they would part for

the night, for Adam never came upstairs with her. It was his invariable custom to detour to his study for a glass of brandy before retiring.

The door was open and the earl was assisting her down from the carriage when she said in desperation, "I have never heard you sing before, Adam. Yours is a magnificent voice. I enjoyed listening to you more than I can say."

Had his fingers tightened around hers for an instant, or had she imagined it? He inclined his head in acknowledgment but made no reply.

They were ascending the shallow entrance steps and April had admitted herself defeated when her husband said quietly, "I have always enjoyed singing."

"I . . . I hope you will permit me to accompany you at home sometimes. Diana will be enchanted with your voice," she added lamely, and mentally kicked herself for dragging her sister in as a shield.

Again he inclined his head politely. They were in the hall walking side by side, not looking at each other. The stairway was dead ahead. In less than thirty seconds the enchanted evening would be over.

"Would you care to drink a glass of brandy with me in the study?" Adam asked hesitantly. "It's not so very late."

"Thank you, I'd like that," said April, who loathed the taste of brandy. She thought she sensed a tension in his bearing as he stood back for her to precede him into the room. This was the first time she had entered it since that terrible night, but perhaps it was time to lay that particular ghost.

Neither spoke while the earl busied himself at the table holding bottle and glasses. Watching that strong back and bowed head and loving him fiercely, April was suddenly filled with resolution. What did her pride matter? If he wanted her, and she suspected he did, she was his, and somehow she'd find a way to tell him so.

As she accepted the glass from his hand, she met his eyes squarely. "That song by Bononcini is one of my favorites," she ventured. "My father used to sing it to my mother."

There was a flicker in the steel-gray eyes. "Do you know what the words mean . . . in English?"

Their eyes remained locked. A muscle twitched in Adam's lean scarred cheek as he awaited her answer. When it came it was scarcely more than a whisper.

"What do they mean, Adam . . . in English?"

"They mean that until I met you I had no idea of what love meant or what suffering meant."

"And now you do?" she prompted softly.

He gazed down into huge smoky eyes made even more luminous by a film of unshed tears, and his own softened, as did the straight line of his mouth.

"Oh, yes, although until this moment the emphasis has been on suffering. I never wished to put my heart into any woman's keeping. I thought I was in love once a long time ago, but when she turned me down I soon found consolation elsewhere. Loving you means there can be no consolation for me any longer." His mouth twisted wryly. "If you cannot bring yourself to love me, it will have to be more suffering. I won't rush you . . . I promise."

"Adam," April broke in with desperate earnestness, "please, *please* rush me!"

Through a mist she saw the light that entered those dark eyes as he closed the gap between them, then the impatient little frown as he registered the presence of two untouched brandy glasses in their hands. Time stood still as he disposed of them on the table and gathered her into his arms with deliberation. His eyes searched her face with a peculiar intensity that she knew, in a sudden flash of loving protectiveness, reflected a lingering concern that she might struggle in his embrace as she had on that other occasion. Her ardent response to his first kiss served to dispel any fears on that head, and his arms tightened convulsively about her as his mouth claimed hers in mounting passion.

"April! You *have* forgiven me!"

She heard his broken murmur over the accelerated clamor of her pulses as he released his lips for an instant, but she was beyond articulation by then. Adam had to accept the assurance conveyed by a warm slender body pressed urgently to his.

He had always sensed that her overactive conscience at having coerced the marriage would impel her to submit to him had he invoked his rights as her husband in the ordinary way. Now the wisdom of waiting and suffering was bearing abundant fruit. Tonight she clung to him with all the surprising strength with which she had resisted on that other occasion. He could scarcely credit that here was the silvery cool creature he had once assumed to be passionless. Lips, arms, body, all flamed into response at his touch. When he recalled his resolve to proceed slowly and woo her with gentle patience, he nearly laughed aloud with exultation. She was fire and ice, and the fire burned for him!

After a third consuming kiss, both were sorely in need of a respite to replenish their oxygen supply and take stock of their surroundings.

"Come on, darling," Adam said thickly. "The way I feel about you can best be expressed upstairs!"

Sudden mischief danced in April's eyes, and she lowered her lashes, then raised them in a provocative glance. "The last time, you carried me—*no*, Adam, *please!* I was only funning! Please put me down, I'm too heavy for you," she pleaded.

A quick hard kiss silenced her as he pushed open the door with his shoulder. "You asked for it, madam," he said on a note of reckless laughter. "You know you weigh a feather, and I'm in much better shape now."

His composure was sorely tested by the unexpected sight of Jacob in the hall as they emerged from the study. The footman was young but by no means lacking in wit. One swift glance from his mistress's crimson cheeks to the devilish gleam in his master's eye reassured him as to the state of health of the countess, and he wished them goodnight in the expressionless voice of the well-trained servant without even breaking his stride.

They were nearly at the top of the stairs before April mastered her embarrassment enough to meet her husband's gleaming eyes. "It will be all over the servants' hall by tomorrow, you know," she said with commendable command of her voice.

"Do you mind?"

"No."

His eyes were serious again as he paused outside her door and gazed hungrily down at the silver fair head resting confidingly against his shoulder.

"I promised once that I would not enter this room without an invitation. May I assume that I am welcome?"

April's face was irradiated with the love she bore this strong, sometimes difficult, and formerly lonely man.

"Now and forever," she replied with a throbbing note in her low, musical voice. "That is *my* promise."

The
Luckless Elopement

1

A percipient eye would need less than two seconds to unmask Lord Ellerby's studied calm for the pose it was. He looked relaxed in the black and white evening attire that so became his well-set-up figure, and he was holding up his end of a light conversation with the younger of his two companions, but his eyes betrayed him. Their anxious expression as they strayed repeatedly to the silent woman sitting opposite belied the pleasant smile he kept on his lips. One hand crept up to twitch the elegant arrangement of his neckcloth as he glanced involuntarily out of the carriage window. Still another two blocks to go to Berkeley Square.

"Does your silence indicate disagreement, Gregory? Can it be that you found something to admire after all in Amanda Westcott's vulgar display of the major part of the family jewels on her opulent person?"

Lord Ellerby's head swung back toward the speaker. "What? Amanda Westcott? Lord, no, Vicky! The woman glittered like an opera dancer. No taste at all."

His companion heaved an exaggerated sigh of relief. "Thank heavens! For a moment I feared I'd been guilty of disparaging a dear friend of yours. I'm relieved to find myself acquitted of such a breach of etiquette."

The light mockery in his *fiancée*'s voice was not lost upon Lord Ellerby, who sent her a beseeching look as a restrained snort issued from the other corner.

5

She ignored him and turned to the older woman, asking sweetly, "Did you say something, Aunt Honoria?" When a determined silence greeted this question: "No? You really should consult a doctor about this persistent throat trouble of yours," she continued in tones that dripped solicitude.

A strangled gasp from the man brought her inquiring gaze back to his face, but the horses had come clattering to a halt. It was with heart felt relief that Lord Ellerby assisted the ladies down from the carriage and escorted them to their front door. For the first time in their five-month acquaintance he was not reluctant to bid his betrothed good night; in fact, he was dangerously close to the unthinkable heresy of questioning the perfection of his goddess as he accepted the cool, slim hand she extended and raised it to his lips. Frank blue eyes searched hers but derived no comfort from the gleam of amusement that persisted in dwelling in the brown depths. If any criticism were possible of such a glorious creature as Vicky—and of course it wasn't, he reminded himself loyally—it would only be that she found so many situations in life fit subjects for amusement rather than concern. Lord Ellerby stifled a sigh as he bade a punctilious *adieu* to Lady Honoria, whose face was set in rigid lines of disapproval as she disappeared within the confines of the stone mansion.

Vicky treated him to a charming little grimace that revealed her awareness of the scene about to be enacted before following her aunt inside. Lord Ellerby remained on the step for a moment or two, his face reflecting an inner disturbance; then he settled the silk hat on crisp curls and headed slowly back the way they had come, dismissing the carriage with a wave of his hand. Perhaps the brisk night air would clear his head and enable him to sort out his muddled thoughts.

There was no doubt in his mind that he should be the happiest man in London at present; certainly he was the most fortunate. Hadn't his determined siege of the hitherto impregnable fortress resulted, against all the odds, in his betrothal to the most desirable girl in the world? His steps kept pace with his thoughts as he recalled his first glimpse of Victoria Seymour. It was at a full-dress ball and she had been resplendent in a gown of gold satin whose dull sheen had been eclipsed by the wealth of shining gold hair swept high on her head in an elaborate style that allowed two provocative curls to caress one smooth ivory shoulder. Her beauty and grace had reduced every other woman in the place to a nonentity. Naturally such a vision had been constantly surrounded by admiring swains. It had taken the better part of the evening to wangle an introduction to this golden goddess, but he had managed it and, though in danger of being rendered tongue-tied in her presence, retained enough address to secure permission to call on her before being edged aside by jealous members of her court.

That had been the beginning. He had adored her on sight, and longer acquaintance had only confirmed his instantaneous impression that here was a creature totally unlike the rest of her sex, as far removed from the ordinary run of females in personality and intelligence as she was in beauty. He had pursued her with a single-minded intensity of purpose that had made him a byword in the clubs, where the betting at first had run heavily against his chances. The sympathy and warnings of his friends had meant no more to him than the sly laughter of acquaintances, and in the end he had triumphed. The night Vicky had finally accepted his proposal (his fourth, actually) had been the happiest of his life. He knew she didn't return his love—she had always been perfectly open about the quality of her feeling for him—but he had been convinced that they would grow closer together as they came to know each other better and shared more of life's experiences. He thought his passionate eloquence on the subject had persuaded her of the inevitability of a true union of their hearts and minds.

Then what had gone wrong? How had he failed? What had happened or not happened in the two months of their engagement that forced him to the admission that he and Vicky were no closer today than on the evening of their betrothal? They had certainly shared a number of experiences, enjoyed each other's company, and respected each other's differences. This much he felt entitled to claim, but it would be self-deceiving to assert that he was any nearer to understanding Vicky's mind and her heart in their essentials than on the night he met her. She had consistently refused to set a date for their marriage, teasing him laughingly for his impatience. The closest she ever approached to earnestness was early in their engagement when she had reminded him soberly that since they would spend the rest of their lives together after marriage, it was essential to be certain the decision was the right one. In a twinkling she was laughing again, brushing aside his fervent assurances that heaven had ordained this decision. Since then he had discovered that beneath her seeming openness, her willingness to discuss any topic under the sun, there dwelt depths to his *fiancée* that were impenetrable to his insight. As an iceberg's tremendous mass was only hinted at by the part above water, so it was with Vicky, her surface smile not really indicative of what was underneath.

This would not have taken on the character of a problem had he not come to suspect with a sinking heart that this was the way she preferred to keep matters. She had shied away from any reference to her father's death two years before, yet it was well known that the two had been mutually devoted. Neither had the slightest reference to that earlier tragedy, the death of her *fiancé* in the Peninsular fighting, ever passed her lips, though he had related his entire past history to her. His footsteps lagged, then nearly stopped as with furrowed brow and compressed lips he pondered Vicky's steadfast avoidance of any serious mood in their infrequent private conversations.

Of course that was only one side of the coin; the other was that never in his life could he remember laughing so wholeheartedly with another person, not even during schooldays. His steps recovered their rhythmic pace, even approached jauntiness. Vicky was a grand companion: her golden laughter was a musical treat, and her lovely face alight with mirth and a hint of mischief was an unending delight to his eyes. Was it foolish and carping of him to wish on occasion that she might fail to discover a diverting side to everything? She even found the six weeks' difference in their ages a source of amusement, twitting him with seeking a mother figure, in the

8

Prince Regent's invariable style. He had been vastly relieved last month to attain his twenty-fifth birthday and parity with his beloved. The crease between his brows appeared again as honesty compelled him to admit that, too often to ignore, he detected something in Vicky's manner toward him that brought this parity into question. Her behavior was scarcely that of a girl about to entrust her life into her husband's keeping. What he had regarded as charming individuality at the beginning of their acquaintance was now taking on an aspect of determined independence.

This was not so surprising, really, when one considered that her father had left her sole mistress of a large fortune, unencumbered by any of the usual restrictions that bound feminine inheritors. However, he could not help wondering if she would act thus were he her senior by several years. His well-cut mouth twisted momentarily as he acknowledged the wry thought that he must be one of a tiny minority of persons who actually wished themselves older, but obviously he could not wish Vicky younger, since she would not then be the same shining creature who had so enchanted him.

What had Vicky been like as a young girl of seventeen or eighteen? Lovely, of course—that went without saying; less assured perhaps? The novelty of the idea so intrigued Lord Ellerby that he walked right past the entrance to his lodgings. The realisation didn't dawn until he came to the corner and took his bearings, at which point his lordship made a supreme effort to jettison all thoughts of his capricious *fiancée* as he retraced his steps. Tomorrow might just yield a new approach to solving the riddle that was Vicky.

Miss Victoria Seymour smiled a bright thank-you and good night to the elderly man who opened the door for the ladies. The smile slipped a notch as she turned away from him to ascend the curving staircase, and her slim shoulders beneath the attractive brown velvet evening cloak sagged perceptibly. As the older woman attained the first-floor landing, a whisper of taffeta charted her course and drew the reluctant gaze of the younger upward. Lord Ellerby would have been comforted to see that the perpetual amusement had fled the brown eyes, succeeded by a weary sombreness at great variance with her mood of moments before. Perhaps, she thought wistfully, Aunt Honoria would elect to bottle up her spleen until morning, when presumably she would have the additional benefits of a night's repose to restore and increase the energy at her disposal for dressing down her errant niece. Unconsciously her ears were following the rustling sounds. When these proceeded into the small drawing room at the front of the house, the forlorn hope that she would be permitted to retire temporarily unscathed died aborning. After an instant's hesitation she resumed her ascent, deliberately straightening her shoulders and erasing all signs of weariness from her features.

It was an elegant, composed young woman who entered the pleasant sitting room seconds later to confront her wrathful relative. She closed the door behind her gently and stood with her back to it, watching her aunt's efforts to divest herself of her outer garments. That these were impeded by her heightened emotional state was perfectly apparent to the younger woman. When the angry jabbing motions of the elder's fingers only succeeded in knotting the ties of the black cloak, Miss Seymour cast her gloves onto a table and hastened to her aunt's assistance.

Lady Honoria warded her off with an out-flung hand. "You may think me in my dotage, but I trust I am still capable of untying a knot," she snapped, proceeding to do just that. She drew herself up to her full height as she draped the garment over the back of the nearest chair and regarded her niece balefully.

The amusement that so disconcerted Lord Ellerby leaped into Miss Seymour's eyes as she riposted with reassuring promptness, "Don't be nonsensical, Aunt. Nobody I know is further from her dotage than yourself. However, I do think you are tired. You may read me a lecture in the morning just as well as now—and in greater comfort," she added coaxingly as her aunt shifted her weight from one leg to the other to ease her aching feet in tight satin pumps.

Lady Honoria, however, was not to be seduced into bow-ing to the demands of the body. Her already straight spine stiffened further.

"Don't try to evade the issue, miss. There isn't the remotest possibility that I shall be able to close my eyes until I have discovered whether your current behaviour arises from ignorance of the consequences or a perverse desire to ruin yourself once and for all."

"Now, Aunt, do you not think you are exaggerating the significance of what was no more than a minor incident after all? What did I do but refuse to dance with a man? And since Harcourt is known everywhere for his propensity for leering at and squeezing defenceless girls at every opportunity, my refusal was excusable surely?"

"Since when have you been a defenceless girl?"

Lady Honoria was unable to resist this irrelevant shaft, though she was not to be long diverted from her purpose. "If you had simply excused yourself from dancing, I would have nothing further to say. These matters can be handled delicately. But no, you must point up your refusal by immediately accepting another bid and flaunting yourself all over the dance floor in the most conspicuous fashion possible, with no concern for Lord Harcourt's sensibilities."

"If the man possessed any sensibility I wouldn't have done it. Can you deny that he's an offensive, ill-mannered, insensitive lout?"

"That's beside the point," declared Lady Honoria, refusing to be drawn into a discussion of Harcourt's virtues or lack of same. "His *mother* is *all* sensibility, and she was standing not ten feet away when you publicly spurned her son and whirled off with Tommy Granville. You are as aware as I that Lady Harcourt and Mrs. Granville detest each other. It was madness to compound your offense by allowing Tommy to bring you over to talk with his mother when the dance ended. Lady Harcourt never took her eyes off you, and she is not one to forgive such an affront to her pride. Mark my words, she'll initiate a whispering campaign that will harm your reputation."

"Just because I preferred another man as partner to her

odious son?'' Vicky asked sceptically. ''Then there are countless girls whom she must include in her reputation-blackening, for not even the most man-hungry creature amongst the debs cares to subject herself to Harcourt's sly advances. A girl would have to be at her last prayers indeed to submit to him. Believe me, Aunt, you are blowing the incident out of all proportion.'' She had discarded her cloak and was perched on the arm of a blue sofa, idly swinging one slim sandalled foot, her expression polite but unconcerned.

Lady Honoria, staring at the serene face of her niece, drew an exasperated breath. ''If it were only one incident, I would not be standing here at this moment remonstrating with you. I hope you do not imagine me incapable of squelching any rumours set about by Lavinia Harcourt,'' she said haughtily, an abrupt *volte*-face that made nonsense of the fears she had expressed earlier and brought a faint smile to the lips of the younger woman. Ignoring this, Lady Honoria continued without pause, ''It was less than a sennight ago that you were observed in conversation with Hector Greenbough on Bond Street in the afternoon without even your maid to lend you countenance.''

A gurgle of laughter escaped Vicky at this pronouncement. ''You are not going to tell me poor Hector is a danger to my reputation, are you? A more harmless creature never walked the earth, let alone the streets of London.''

''Walking the streets of London alone is what I am talking about,'' retorted her aunt. ''And I do not wish to hear again that your advanced age protects you from criticism on that score. *I* would not care to walk about the streets unattended myself at *my* advanced age.''

''I am not a green girl any longer, Aunt,'' Vicky said mildly. ''When I was first out, I bowed to all the conventions governing the behaviour of young girls, though even then I found it vastly tedious to conform to such nonsensical restrictions . . . but heavens, that was eight years ago! A woman of five-and-twenty is scarcely in the same category as a girl of seventeen, even if she is still unmarried.''

"She is if she looks like you," replied Lady Honoria with decided grimness.

"Why, Aunt! I declare you are making me blush," simpered Vicky, casting her eyes down in pretended confusion.

Lady Honoria was neither amused nor deterred. "You may spare your blushes," she said coldly. "You are perfectly well aware that you are getting yourself talked about by your . . . I can only call it *reckless* behaviour of late." Suddenly all the irritation disappeared from her manner and she directed a look of real concern at her niece. "What is it, Vicky? What is troubling you lately?"

The girl on the sofa had ceased swinging her leg. She sat in a graceful attitude, her hands lying motionless in her lap. "Why, nothing, Aunt. What could be troubling me? Am I not the girl who has everything? Am I not known widely as an Incomparable who also possesses the twin advantages of fortune and birth? Am I not betrothed—at long last—to a man admired by all the Ton for his good looks, breeding, and character?"

The words were lightly spoken, but an undercurrent of something disturbing reached Lady Honoria's ears. She pursed her lips and continued to study the bland countenance of her niece. "Nevertheless, I am considerably past seven and cut my wisdoms years ago," she went on slowly, "and I know that this reckless gaiety of yours just lately is assumed. Can you not trust me with the truth, my child? Who else if not me?"

In the face of an unwavering scrutiny from a pair of wise eyes regarding her with affectionate concern, Vicky averted her gaze at last and got to her feet. She wandered over to the fireplace and moved the portrait of her father that hung over the mantel a hair to the left. Without turning, she said in a voice devoid of all emotion, "I don't think I can go through with it, Aunt."

The ensuing silence lasted a full half-minute by the mantel clock ticking monotonously away six inches from Miss Seymour's ear. The next sound to reach that ear was a soft sigh from across the room and a rustle of taffeta as Lady Honoria sank onto the sofa.

"I was afraid that might be the case," the older woman admitted heavily.

"Then you do understand?" The golden head turned eagerly from a contemplation of the portrait. Beseeching brown eyes sought support that was not forthcoming.

"I do *not* understand," replied Lady Honoria acidly. "What I *do* understand is that you are five-and-twenty and still unwed because you are too particular in your requirements for a husband. No man could hope to live up to your expectations. It was all well and good to cherish romantic notions at eighteen, but at your age you should have learned better. If it were not for that face and your considerable fortune, you'd have been on the shelf years ago, and that is where you'll end up, my girl, if you whistle Ellerby down the wind! You cannot play fast and loose with men for years without acquiring the kind of reputation I should very much dislike to have associated with a relative of mine." She paused to draw breath and glare at her niece, who was smilingly shaking her head from side to side.

"Where *do* you find your expressions, ma'am? 'Fast and loose' indeed! You know very well that until Gregory came along I never encouraged any of the suitors who courted my fortune so assiduously, and I don't think I gave him much encouragement either, but he was so *persistent*." Her voice trailed off and the smile faded from her eyes, leaving them bleak.

"Vicky, Ellerby is head and shoulders above the rest. I believe him to be really worthy of you," her aunt said earnestly. "Oh, I don't mean dull and worthy. That type would set your teeth on edge within a month, but he has great charm of manner, thinks just as he ought on important subjects, *and* is quite the handsomest man I've seen in two score seasons. And he is sincerely in love with you! It wouldn't matter to him if you hadn't two pennies to rub together. That kind of devotion is not to be winked at."

"I know, I know." Vicky made a little *moue* of distress.

She raised a hand to her face and kneaded her forehead in a weary gesture. "I think that is the reason I feel I must break it off now. If he only regarded me as a decorative or suitable wife and didn't *need* so much from me, perhaps I would feel differently, but he deserves so much more than I can give him."

"Fustian!" asserted Lady Honoria. "If you would just stop living in the past and allow yourself to accept Ellerby's devotion, you'd find in time that you could return it."

"I'm sorry, Aunt. That is what Gregory said, and I allowed myself to be persuaded against my better judgment, but it isn't *true*! Believe me, I wish it were! Do you think I would not enjoy being married, that I would not love to hold my own child in my arms?"

"Well, then, stop yearning for a dead man and enjoy the benefits of a living man's devotion."

"It isn't that," Vicky explained patiently to her exasperated relative. "I assure you I'm not pining for Edward after all these years or measuring every other man I meet against him. In some ways Gregory is superior to him—no, hear me out, please," as Lady Honoria opened her lips to speak. "The thing is that I was *in love* with Edward, all I wanted out of life was to become his wife, so you see I recognise the difference now. I know what I should be cheating Gregory out of and what he deserves to find with another woman."

"Ellerby doesn't think he's being cheated, and he's the best judge, after all."

"He doesn't now perhaps, but he will. I have seen a change in him over the weeks of our engagement. I've noticed the hurt look in his eyes when I've been brisk or said wounding things with this serpent's tongue of mine. And what is infinitely worse, though I despise myself afterwards, I do it again! I can't seem to prevent myself from being clever at his expense, and I can't seem to lessen the distance between us or allow him to lessen it. He'll end up by hating me, and I couldn't bear that! The end seems hideously inevitable, as though I were digging myself deeper and deeper into a hole. Like Macbeth, I feel 'cabin'd, cribb'd, confin'd, bound by saucy doubts and fears.' "

During this speech Vicky's calm demeanour gradually disintegrated, and by the finish she was pacing back and forth in front of the fireplace in her agitation.

"Don't you think you are being overly melodramatic about this?" demanded Lady Honoria in an astringent voice. "And do stop that eternal pacing; you put me forcibly in mind of a lion I once saw at Exeter Exchange. What makes you think your situation is unique? Other women, and men too, I have no doubt, have experienced doubts and qualms before marriage. Yet they seem to muddle through somehow and make a fair success of wedlock eventually."

"I don't want a *muddled* marriage! If I cannot have a real one, I'll do much better to stay unwed. At least this way I shan't be responsible for ruining another's life as well."

"What about this child you say you'd like to hold in your arms? How do you plan to acquire it without a husband?"

Vicky merely hunched a shoulder at this dry interjection. "There are worse things in life than remaining childless," she said shortly.

"There are indeed," agreed her aunt in level tones, "but not many."

Contrition spread over the girl's features and she bounded forward to clasp strong young arms about her aunt in a brief hug. "Forgive me, darling Aunt!" she cried, sliding back onto her knees in front of the sofa, squeezing her relative's hands lightly. "I always think of myself as your child. You've been as good as a mother to me for these dozen years and more."

Lady Honoria absently patted the hands resting on her knee. "It doesn't signify," she said, "but, my dear child, consider the alternative. If you break your engagement, there will be the usual nine days' wonder. You have always provided the jealous tabbies of the town with plenty of ammunition for their gossiping tongues, but it was all nothing compared to the sensation this announcement will produce. Can you face the talk and the censure?"

"I could for myself. What I cannot face is to be meeting Gregory everywhere and seeing his unhappiness as a constant reproach. Even though I am persuaded he will shortly fall in love with a tractable young girl who will adore him, I know he's going to be miserable for a time, and I am wretchedly at fault for having accepted his offer. I'll have to go away. It's only fair."

"Where will you go, back to the Oaks?"

Vicky nodded and gave her aunt a twisted little smile. "Where else? I never should have left. I have outgrown the delights of London, I fear. I thought I should enjoy being part of society again, but it palls quickly, I find."

"Thank you for prevaricating," said her aunt with a wry smile of her own. "You returned to town solely because I was bored to extinction in the country, but I did it as much for your good as my own, my dear. It worried me to see you grieving for your father and wasting your youth in a locality nearly devoid of eligible males. Richard should have seen to it that you married years ago if he meant to die in that untimely fashion."

This time Vicky's smile was real and lighted up her face. "Papa was as bad as you for trying to get me safely riveted. I lost count of the sons of old friends who 'just happened to be in the neighbourhood' and were pressed into staying at the house to be paraded in front of my eyes. Obviously it isn't meant to be."

"Nonsense," said Lady Honoria briskly. "You'll change your tune after a few weeks' solitude in that great ark of a house. It will be too late for Ellerby, perhaps, but there are as good fish in the sea as ever came out of it."

"You won't come with me, then?" Vicky asked a trifle wistfully.

Lady Honoria was very decided. "Not this time, my child. The little season has scarce begun, and I have a mind to play the socialite yet awhile. Besides, you will have need of me here to line up the next candidates when the quiet and monotony of the country drive you back to London with, I trust, a more realistic attitude toward marriage."

Vicky laughed. "Very well, ma'am. I see I am to be banished as I deserve. But I beg of you to spare your efforts to matchmake on my behalf. It is quite apparent that I was born to lead apes in hell."

A ladylike snort greeted this pronouncement. "Fustian! You are no more intended for a life of single blessedness than Cleopatra! I always said nothing good ever came from reading Shakespeare. And now I am off to my bed for what is left of the night. I cannot forbid you or chain you up or physic you to eliminate this foolishness. You are a woman grown. All I am going to request, my dear, is that you consider all the consequences of this rash step you are proposing to take before you do something you are sure to regret."

Lady Honoria pressed a rare kiss on her niece's bowed head before rising with a groan. She went away muttering about the stiffness of her joints, leaving Vicky staring unseeingly at the portrait over the mantel. It wasn't until Barrows poked his head into the room to see why the lights had not been extinguished that she too rose to her feet and headed for her bedchamber.

2

For the past hour there had been a welcome silence in the chaise, but this had been achieved only after a persistent and determined pretence of sleep on the part of Miss Seymour. They had been on the road close to eight hours now and she had been regretting for almost as long the impulse that had caused her to take a young housemaid in her dresser's place so that Lady Honoria might continue to reap the benefits of Trotton's matchless skill at hair design. Certainly she herself would not be requiring the elaborate coiffures that were Trotton's specialty and delight in the wilds of Leicestershire, but she might have thought long and hard before electing to travel with Lily as her companion had she had the least notion of the little maid's penchant for mindless chatter.

A certain amount of nervous excitement was to be expected, of course, for the town-bred Lily had never been farther from London than Windsor, and Vicky had been prepared to be indulgent while the novelty of rolling over unfamiliar territory in a luxuriously appointed chaise held sway. Long before the first change of horses at Welwyn, however, indulgence had worn thin. As the monotony of travelling over an unending post road set in, it had the unsuspected effect of loosening the young maid's tongue. Unresponsiveness on her mistress' part had done nothing to stem the resultant tide of confidences. Vicky had been regaled with sundry details of Mam's sinking spells and Pa's inability to keep a job for more than a few months, which seemed to bear some direct relation to his periodic disappearances. He never failed to reappear after a sennight or so, chastened and somewhat the worse for drink, but by then it was generally necessary to find a new employer. Apparently Lily and her five brothers and sisters accepted this familial pattern as the norm and were none the less happy for the lack of stability. Two of her brothers had already embarked on promising careers, she confided. Joseph was working as a printer's devil in Fleet Street, and Tom, who had a passion for horses and an ambition to be a gentleman's groom, had been fortunate enough to secure employment in a livery stable, where he could hope that his diligence and skill would sooner or later catch the eye of some gentleman who shared his ideas on the care of prime horseflesh.

By the time the ladies had partaken of a light lunch and stretched their cramped legs in a short walk, Miss Seymour felt as familiar with all the individual members of Lily's family as if she had dwelt among them for years. It was her own fault, of course; a sufficiently brusque rejoinder at any moment would have crushed the timid maid and stemmed her cheerful garrulity, but Miss Seymour found herself incapable of administering such a rebuff. Her own spirits having been strangely in eclipse these past weeks, she could not be the instrument to depress those of a girl who contrived to remain optimistic in the face of difficult home conditions and the unenviable prospects of a life of servitude before her.

In desperation she had resorted to feigning sleep, which had served to dam the flow of chatter. Unfortunately, silence had proved a mixed blessing. Granted, the sound of Lily's breathy, slightly nasal, and more than slightly slurred tones had ceased, but only to be succeeded by a train of disturbing memories of the uncomfortable scenes she had enacted with Gregory during the past week. With her eyes closed there was no keeping them at bay by focusing on her young companion's comely and eager countenance. Gregory's face as she had seen it last, quietly set, an eloquent reproach in its unhappiness, though he had uttered no words of reproach, persisted in remaining stationed behind her eyelids, as vivid as though he were sharing the chaise with her. She had known it would be a difficult task to convince him her decision was necessary, and only a strong conviction that she was sparing him greater pain in the future had sustained her resolution to persist in the face of his persuasive arguments against ending their betrothal.

Aunt Honoria had proved correct also in predicting that the rupture would produce a sensation in society. In the two days that elapsed between the appearance of the announcement in the *Gazette* and her departure from London, she had been greeted with decided coolness by two matrons encountered by chance in the Pantheon Bazaar while doing some hurried shopping. That she had been the subject of their conversation, broken off abruptly as she came around a corner, had been made perfectly apparent by their conscious expressions. It would be a decided relief to sink once again into the welcoming atmosphere of the Oaks, where she could be herself without a care for anyone's opinion of her behaviour, but even the thought of her home and the horses was not sufficient to dissolve the pervasive fog of depression that had been creeping up on her these past weeks. Lately she seemed unable to summon up any resistance to this perpetual midnight of her spirits. The skies would lighten with the first sight of the lane of oaks leading to the house. *They must!* Most likely she was low in her mind because for the first time there would be no one to greet her return. Papa was gone forever and Aunt Honoria had held steadfast to her decision to remain in town for the little season.

Miss Seymour's eyes flew open as an obvious explanation for this sensation of emptiness occurred to her. Lunch had been a long time ago and had consisted of bread and butter and tea, for neither woman had been particularly hungry when they had stopped. She looked quickly at her companion and was relieved to note her blue-bonneted head angled against the padded backrest, straight brown lashes resting on pink cheeks while her breath came evenly and softly. A glance at the jewelled watch pinned to her dress confirmed the impression Vicky had gathered from peering outside. It was after four o'clock. A slight frown appeared on her smooth brow as she did some rapid thinking. The final change of horses was always at Stamford, where they left the post road. Normally they would proceed directly to the Oaks, which was located a few miles east of Melton Mowbray, arriving in good time for a late dinner. They had been delayed earlier today by unexpectedly violent showers, which had settled down to a steady light rain as they came farther north. Surely they must be nearing Stamford soon. She couldn't remember another such interminable trip home. Though the day couldn't be described as especially cold, the continuing damp had penetrated the comfortable carriage and taken possession of her extremities. Uncomfortably she flexed chilled fingers in their kid gloves and wriggled her toes inside their admittedly lovely but inadequate half-boots of softest leather. Suddenly the immediate advantages of a warm fire and a hot dinner far outweighed those of an earlier arrival at home. She let down the window on the driver's side, admitting a gust of the damp air, stuck her head out, and called to the coachman. "Amos, how far are we from Stamford?"

"I calculate we'll be there in about twenty minutes."

"Good. We'll stop there for dinner."

"Can't stop long if you want to get to the Oaks afore dark, Miss Vicky," cautioned the old driver in his restrained bellow.

"We won't, but if this rain worsens I'll wager you'll be glad of some hot rum punch inside of you before we go on," his mistress predicted, closing the window on the low rumble of laughter that signified Amos' agreement with this prescription for warding off chills.

Smiling in sympathy, Vicky turned back to the interior to find her maid, bonnet askew but bolt upright, rubbing her eyes.

"Are we almost there, Miss Seymour?" she asked, looking around in confusion.

"No such luck, I'm afraid. We are going to stop for dinner in Stamford. One more change will do it, but we have another couple of hours ahead of us after we leave the post road."

As Lily, prattling compulsively all the while, straightened

her hat, Vicky watched indulgently, her good humour restored by the promise of warmth and food. She had been confusing discomfort and hunger with lowness of spirits, she told herself firmly.

All was hustle and bustle at the Candle and Unicorn when the ladies entered the public dining room some twenty minutes later. Miss Seymour's request for a private parlour had been met by a regretful denial on the part of their host. All his dining rooms were already reserved, unless Madam cared to engage a bedchamber and order a repast to be sent there. Seeing a quick frown gather on her brow, he had assured the ladies that the patrons in the public room were a quiet, genteel crowd tonight, and had offered them a private table in a corner and a waiter to see to their needs. Miss Seymour hesitated fractionally, but the sight of Lily's dark eyes growing round as she gazed about with patent anticipation decided the issue. The landlord looked a respectable sort; he'd see they were not subjected to unwelcome attention. She nodded acquiescence and allowed herself to be led forward. After a half-dozen paces she paused and looked back to make sure Lily had come out of her trance and was following. She was, just barely, her head swivelling on her shoulders as she tried to take in the whole of the busy room at once. A tolerant smile tugged at Miss Seymour's lips as she resumed her walk.

The room was crowded with diners, many of whom were in the process of finishing their meals. She stepped aside to allow a clear path to a young couple with a recalcitrant child who was indicating in no uncertain terms his displeasure at having to quit the table. Her understanding smile for the mother's embarrassment deepened to a chuckle as the harassed father's patience deserted him. Swooping suddenly, he scooped up his reluctant son and carried him past the newcomers, who found it necessary to dodge the youngster's flailing arms. Amusement still sparkling in her eyes, Vicky turned once more toward the corner and was pinned like a butterfly by a bold black-eyed stare. The contact lasted no more than a second before she removed her gaze, but in that

23

brief span she was subjected to a comprehensive masculine survey that missed nothing, summed her up and dismissed her. Not a muscle moved in her face, but she continued toward the table being indicated by the patient landlord, palpitatingly aware that she had undergone a novel experience.

Vicky would have been stupid indeed not to know that her person was universally admired. Unhampered by any false modesty, she appreciated that her looks were more than passable, though her own taste ran to a more exotic style. In her opinion, yellow hair and pale skin could never compete with the attraction of lustrous black tresses, rich olive colouring, and dark brown eyes. The flattering attention excited by her own unusual combination of golden brown eyes with burnished hair, while gratifying, didn't alter her views, which were apparently shared by the rude man occupying the only other small table in the room. Before averting her gaze, she had noted that his own ravishingly pretty companion was just in this dark style, as was the man himself. Brother and sister perhaps? As the landlord seated her with a flourish and summoned a waiter to the table, she speculated idly on the couple's relationship, then dismissed the pair in favour of restoring the strength depleted by a day of travelling.

They dined more than adequately on the inn's ordinary bill of fare, choosing from roast mutton and a roasted veal leg, a perfectly browned game pie, and dishes piled with vegetables. Such additional niceties as butter sauce for the potatoes and little dishes of pickled onions and walnuts had Lily's round eyes opening even wider. In the days that followed, Vicky was to recall with longing the food left untouched on the Candle and Unicorn's groaning table. At the time, though, both ladies felt they were more than doing justice to their host's hospitality. Lily could not be said to have dined as fully as her mistress, however, because her attention was continually being diverted to something or other in the large dining room. More than once a morsel of food would be raised to her lips, only to sit there poised on the fork while her head rotated to study one of the patrons or exclaim over the deftness of the constantly moving waiters. If the food didn't fall harmlessly back onto the plate before her mouth came into range again, there was always the danger that she would poke herself in the eye with the sharp implement. At one point Miss Seymour gasped out a warning whose sole effect was to cause herself to choke on a French bean. Lily, narrowly averting contact between eye and fork, dropped the latter to ring against the pewter plate as she jumped up to thump her mistress on the back in an overly enthusiastic manner that went beyond being helpful and caused every eye in the place to turn their way. Miss Seymour, her cheeks aflame, opened her lips to scold the unconscious Lily, then closed them again with a sigh after a glimpse at the little maid's concerned face. Lily always meant well. Why spoil what was undoubtedly the most exciting adventure of her cloistered young life? She mumbled a brief thank-you for the first aid and resolutely returned her attention to her own dinner, refusing to permit her eyes to focus anew on that wavering fork.

Her eyes drifted instead to the handsome couple sitting alone at a small table against the wall not ten feet away. Part of her concentration had been on them since she had looked up while coughing and being pounded on the back to meet the amused mockery directed at her by that dark brute. And he *was* a brute, despite the fashionable garments and civilised exterior, she decided now as she covertly studied the pair from beneath lowered lashes—the personification of Byron's Corsair, with that laughing sneer of his.

"Doesn't he look like a pirate?" whispered Lily, unexpectedly proving herself on the same mental track as her mistress when she intercepted the latter's gaze.

"He does indeed." Vicky laughed.

Encouraged by this response, Lily expanded her interest. "Do you think the lady is his wife? She looks awful young to be married, but he doesn't treat her like a sister."

Vicky was silent for a second, trying to readjust her thoughts to include this new possibility. "How does a man treat a sister?" she inquired in some amusement.

"Well," responded Lily in all seriousness, tilting her head

25

like an inquisitive bird, "brothers mostly ignore their sisters, I think, or order them about."

Involuntarily Vicky's glance returned to the dark couple in a more assessing fashion. The man could not be said to be ignoring his companion, his attention was almost exclusively on her, but it did appear that he might be attempting to impose his will on her despite the element of importuning in his manner also. While she was thus occupied in speculation, the dark man seized his companion's hand and brought it to his lips in a lingering gesture. Definitely not a sister, then, but a wife, that pretty child? Lily was quite astute in assessing her age as rather young for marriage. Seventeen? Eighteen? No more, surely. From here it was impossible to tell whether or not the girl wore a wedding ring, but it was apparent that she was becoming somewhat agitated. She pulled her hand away and glanced down at the table, biting her bottom lip. To the man's earnest representations—from here it looked as if he were barely controlling a rising impatience—she made no response, even refusing to look up.

Glancing up herself, Vicky noticed an engraving on the wall over the young girl's head, depicting a rustic couple under a tree. The youth in the picture had one arm about the maiden's shoulder and was obviously pressing his suit for all he was worth, in the face of a coy denial. Surveying the downcast eyes and trembling lip of the pretty girl under the frame, it was obvious to Vicky that her suitor, if he was her suitor, would have more trouble persuading his lady than the youth in the engraving.

"I'll bet they are an eloping couple." At her side Lily once again demonstrated that she was in accord with her mistress' observations.

"You may be right," admitted Vicky, returning her attention to her plate while she polished off the last of the succulent game pie.

"Don't you think that's the most romantic thing ever?"

"No, I do not," retorted Vicky, eyeing her companion sternly. "That girl is a mere child, too young to be married at all, let alone to that big bully. He is well over thirty, and a man of the town, unless I miss my guess. I should be astonished to learn that she is as much as eighteen, and it is clear as crystal that she is afraid of him.''

''Ohhh!'' Lily looked quite abashed at this tirade, and her mistress added in propitiating tones, ''It is none of our affair, however, so let us enjoy this delicious cheese and fruit the waiter has just brought, unless you would care for a pudding or jelly?''

''Th-thank you.'' The subdued maid indicated that she would like some of the pudding being offered, and silence settled over the table while they proceeded to eat. In a few minutes Lily had recovered enough to resume her interested scanning of the rapidly emptying room, and Miss Seymour relaxed, glad she hadn't permanently squelched the girl. If the truth were known, her sharpness with Lily just now had concealed a concern that she did not wish to acknowledge for the frightened child at the other table. After all, even assuming their speculations were correct, what earthly help could she, a perfect stranger, be to the chit? And she could easily be grossly mistaken. Despite her air of innocence, the dark-haired girl might be more than capable of taking care of herself. Perhaps she loved the man to distraction. Glancing over to their table again, however, she saw nothing to confirm this supposition. The man was still speaking in low tones, but the girl's passive resistance seemed to have driven out the hint of pleading she had noticed earlier in his manner. Now he was clearly issuing commands, and at last the girl looked fully at him, nodding reluctantly when he paused, her dark eyes huge in an unusually pale face beneath a charming red velvet bonnet with a high poke. She looked away almost immediately, resigned but unreassured by the man's gleaming smile.

At the other table, Miss Seymour felt her fingers curling into fists at the blatant triumph in that smile. Unashamedly she watched it disappear as the man made a tentative motion toward his companion with a hand that hovered in the air between them for an instant before being withdrawn. He shrugged impatiently, murmured something to her, then thrust back his chair and headed for the door to speak with an ostler who had stuck his head in, obviously searching for someone. The girl stared after him uncertainly for a moment. She half-rose, looking around somewhat desperately, then sank back into her chair, eyes downcast once more.

Some half-understood impulse animated Miss Seymour at that moment. Gesturing to the surprised Lily to remain seated, she rose from her chair in one fluid motion and approached the solitary figure, saying in a low voice, "I beg your pardon, but you seem to be suffering some agitation of spirits. Is there any way I may assist you?"

The eyes raised to hers had the wary look of a woodland creature startled by the intrusion of man into its habitat. Sensing the girl's instinctive withdrawal, Vicky smiled at her encouragingly and was rewarded by a flickering response before she said through trembling lips, "You are very k-kind, ma'am, but no one can help me—that is to say, I am in need of no assistance."

"May I sit down?" asked Vicky, indicating the other chair.

After an instant's hesitation the brunette said, "Of course, ma'am." She looked down again, unable to sustain the steady regard of the other.

"My dear child," Vicky began in persuasive accents, "believe me, nothing is irrevocable at this point. You need not marry him at all if you fear you might not suit, and in any case there is no need to continue with an ill-advised elopement tonight."

"Oh, but I *must*! It is impossible to return to London before dark, and if I don't return tonight, I will lose my reputation, so I *must* go through with it!"

This dramatic statement of the case confirmed Miss Seymour's guess that here was a gently bred innocent about to take what could be a disastrous step. The fact that she showed no surprise to be thus addressed by a complete stranger proclaimed her youth and inexperience. Obviously she still saw all adults as omnipotent and was no more ready for marriage than a babe.

Miss Seymour's opinion of her would-be husband descended even lower.

"Fustian!" she declared cheerfully, smiling into the anxious dark eyes that were surely looking at her with a desperate hope in their depths. "There is no danger that you will lose your reputation, because I am a very dull respectable person"—this pronouncement was uttered without a blink—"and we shall put it about that you have come north to visit me. I suppose you left a letter for your parents detailing your intention?"

"Well, yes, I left a note for my aunt and uncle. My parents are dead. I live with my mother's sister and her husband, and I hate it! They are Methodists, you see, and they don't believe in dancing or going to parties or anything!"

"I see," said Miss Seymour, seeing very well indeed. "So you thought it would be more amusing to be married?"

"Yes, and also to get control of my fortune, which is in the hands of trustees until I wed. My uncle gives me only a beggarly allowance. Extravagance is another thing he doesn't believe in!"

Miss Seymour stepped in before her young friend could get fairly launched on what appeared to be an old grievance. "Well, if we are agreed that you are to pay me a visit for a while until you decide what you wish to do, we had best set about leaving, for we have almost twenty miles to go." A brilliant smile lighted golden-brown eyes. "Perhaps we should exchange identities so that you may tell your young man that I am an old family friend who has convinced you to pause before doing something so rash as eloping. My name is Victoria Seymour and my home is called the Oaks, a few miles ahead in Leicestershire."

At the beginning of this speech the young girl's ingenuous countenance was alive with eagerness, but the mere mention of her swain was tantamount to extinguishing a candle. Animation left her face, her cheeks blanched, and she actually recoiled. "I . . . I c-can't tell Drew that I won't marry him! He'll never let me go!" she wailed.

"Nonsense!" said her prospective hostess briskly. "He has

no control over you. If you decide not to go ahead with an elopement, he has nothing to do but accept your decision.''

The girl shuddered. "You do not know Drew. When I am with him I always finish by doing as he wishes.''

"The masterful type," sniffed Miss Seymour, who had an ill opinion of this species. "Are you afraid of him, for heaven's sake?''

"Not afraid, precisely," replied the girl with a touching attempt at dignity, "but I hate it when he gets angry . . . Oh, I cannot explain, but he gets all cold and grim and says cutting things that make me feel I am the stupidest creature alive.''

"How could you ever contemplate marriage with such a one?" demanded Miss Seymour in honest amazement.

"I am putting it very badly, I fear, because he can be wonderful also; he knows just how to act everywhere, and I feel so safe with him.'' Her voice tailed off and she stared helplessly at the older girl.

"Let me get this straight," pursued Miss Seymour, beginning to grasp that her rescue operation would not be the straightforward proposition she had outlined a moment before. "You would like to visit me while you think further about this prospective marriage, but you don't feel you can explain this to your . . . er, Drew?''

"That's it exactly!" Relief flashed across the girl's countenance and she relaxed her tense posture in the Windsor chair.

"Then what is to be done?''

Silence followed the gentle question while the reluctant bride wrestled with its implications. Obviously decision making on such a scale did not appeal, but at last she raised her chin and ventured timidly, "Could we not just . . . leave?''

"Without telling your . . . er, Drew? He'll think you've run away or been kidnapped. He'll be running to the nearest magistrate with your description, or even to Bow Street.''

"*Oh, no!*"

This new aspect of the situation threw the young girl into a quake of terror. She glanced nervously around the room like a hunted animal and jumped visibly at the sound of a dish striking a table rather loudly, then seemed to gird her forces for action. "Well, then," she said with more decision than she had yet demonstrated, "we must write him a note so that he will not cause a hue and cry in the neighbourhood. Only it must be done at once, before he returns from the stables." She searched in a capacious reticule reclining with a velvet muff on the carpet at her feet and emerged with a notebook from which she proceeded to tear out a leaf. Beckoning a waiter to the table with an imperious finger, she requested a pen and some ink and waited impatiently while he went to fetch the items.

Miss Seymour observed the changes in her *protégée* with some amusement. She took advantage of the interval to acquaint Lily with the bare outline of the situation and settle their reckoning with the landlord. Amos, she knew, would be waiting for them in the inn yard, anxious to begin the last stage of the journey. She kept an eye on the main door to the dining room, preparing herself half-expectantly for a scene with the thwarted lover—there were a few home truths she would enjoy delivering to him—but he did not appear during the moment or two that his erstwhile *fiancée* took to pen her note. When Miss Seymour next glanced over at the other small table, it was to see the girl donning her cherry-red pelisse with an economy of movement that spoke of her determination to escape. She twisted the paper into a screw and tossed it back onto the table as she joined the other two women without a backward glance. Miss Seymour raised an eyebrow at such coolness, but a penetrating look at the pale face under the dashing bonnet revealed that the girl's poise was a brittle facade hastily erected to cover extreme perturbation. It was well to depart quickly before she gave way to the hysterics that were threatening, her protectress decided, gathering her flock about her and shepherding them through the door being held open by an interested waiter. It would also be to their advantage to avoid another meeting with the landlord, she realised simultaneously, and she breathed a sigh of relief as they attained the inn yard without meeting anyone who might delay them.

Amos was waiting as expected. A heavy frown settled on his brow as his mistress blithely explained the existence of another passenger as a chance meeting with an old friend that had resulted in an impulsive invitation to visit the Oaks.

"What mischief be you up to, Miss Vicky?" he demanded with the freedom of an old retainer as Vicky ushered her guest into the travelling chaise. "Taking up with a young person without so much as a bandbox to her name! And don't trouble to spin any farradiddles to me about chance meetings and old friends, neither, for I'm not so green as to swallow 'em." His voice was a low growl and he planted his substantial person firmly in front of her, ready to block her ascension into the chaise until he received an answer that satisfied him.

Knowing him of old to be entirely capable of refusing to budge until the explanation was forthcoming, and strongly desirous now of avoiding a confrontation with the prospective bridegroom in case Amos threw his weight on the latter's side, Miss Seymour abandoned any idea of telling him a harmless Banbury story (assuming she could invent one on the spur of the moment). She clutched his arm in her earnestness.

"Listen, Amos, you can see the child is perfectly respectable, but she is completely friendless at the moment, and it is up to us to save her from making a mistake that will ruin her life."

The coachman remained unmoved, his shrewd old eyes uncomfortably penetrating. "What kind of mistake?"

"She had embarked on an impulsive elopement with a man she's really afraid of. Too old for her by far, and I wouldn't put it past him to be a fortune hunter, either. He's sold her some tale of having ruined herself if she doesn't go through with it, when anyone with half an eye can see she's too young and innocent for marriage at all. All I am doing is lending her countenance to protect her reputation. Now, let's go!" she finished, assuming an air of crisp determination she didn't entirely feel as she pulled open the door to the chaise.

To her immeasurable relief, Amos allowed her to enter the vehicle, merely muttering, "I don't like it, no good ever came from a body's meddling in what don't concern them."

32

THE LUCKLESS ELOPEMENT

The burly coachman climbed heavily up onto his perch behind the fresh team. He nodded somewhat grimly at the waiting ostler to release them, and drove out of the inn yard. The delay had cost them more ways than one, he reckoned. The rain had at last dwindled to a fine mist, but it was going to be full dark before they reached home, and unless he missed his guess, carrying a load of trouble into the bargain. Nothing about their circumstances caused a lightening of the coachman's lowering expression as he expertly guided the unfamiliar horses through the streets of Stamford.

Ten minutes after the Seymour coach rumbled out of the inn yard, a tall, dark-visaged gentleman walked back into it from the town street wearing an expression of such dangerous annoyance that it caused a stable boy who found himself in his path to do an abrupt about-face and scurry away. The man was totally unaware of the byplay. As he headed for the dining room, he seemed to make a conscious effort to relax his features, and he swept a smoothing hand over waving dark hair when he had removed his grey beaver. A swift survey of the half-empty room was enough to bring the frown back to his face, however, and he spun on one heel to go in search of the landlord.

"Where is the young lady who is with me?" he inquired upon locating that worthy on his way back from the kitchen.

To the landlord's reply that he supposed her to be still in the dining room, the gentleman retorted that he had just been there.

"Perhaps she has returned by now," replied his host soothingly, taking him by the arm and retracing his steps.

"I'm not blind, man!" The patron shook off the guiding hand but entered the room, gesturing toward the empty table, which was being cleared by the waiter. When questioned by his employer, the waiter denied seeing the young lady leave but handed over a screw of paper he had just spotted on top of the tablecloth.

With a professionally disinterested mien the landlord gave the paper to the customer, but he was quick to notice the

33

sudden flare of the latter's nostrils and the tightening of his chiselled mouth as he untwisted the note and rapidly mastered its contents. His eyes flashed around the room once more and the frown intensified. It was a moment before he could subdue his chagrin; then he said quietly, "She writes that she has met an old friend and has decided to pay her a visit for a few days."

"Ah? Then everything is fine, sir?" replied the landlord jovially.

The customer's expression did not alter and he was obviously doing some rapid thinking. "I am going after her. I shall be bringing her back here. We would have had to stay tonight in any case, as the center pole of my chaise was cracked. It was promised for tomorrow. We shall require two rooms."

"Very good, sir. And the name?"

"Andrew Massingham. The young lady is my sister. I am bringing her back to school against her wishes, hence the unheralded departure. Send someone to the smith's for our baggage, please."

He spoke easily, with a rueful grimace that was quite convincing. The landlord relaxed his facial muscles into an understanding smile which was briefly returned by Mr. Massingham.

When he reappeared in the inn yard a moment later, however, there was no evidence of a smile on the tall man's features as he began to question the ostlers about recent departures. On learning that a dark-haired young lady in a red pelisse and bonnet had been seen entering a private carriage with two other ladies, one of them a most attractive young woman with fair hair, the man snapped his teeth together, causing the ostler a nervous twinge, but he made no comment. The employee was unable to identify the unknown woman, but further questioning of the others elicited the information that the coachman was known at the inn. He was thought to be in the employ of a Mr. Richard Seymour from somewhere outside of Melton Mowbray. He had been in a pucker tonight, anxious to set out, since the drive was close on two hours.

THE LUCKLESS ELOPEMENT

With a commendable foresight and efficiency of action, Mr. Massingham had ordered a horse saddled before he talked to the ostlers, and it was led up now while he inquired more detailed directions to Mr. Seymour's estate. The intermittent drizzle had paused for the time being as he rode out in pursuit of the Seymour carriage scarcely twenty-five minutes after its departure from the yard of the Candle and Unicorn.

3

Miss Seymour settled herself comfortably against the padded corduroy backrest and examined her travelling companions with amused interest. Lily was quiet for the moment, her large brown eyes covertly surveying the newcomer, though she must be given credit for attempting to disguise her curiosity for the sake of good manners. Meanwhile the girl beside her was smoothing her gloves with short, compulsive motions and trying unsuccessfully to banish the anxiety from her expression as she smiled shyly at her benefactress. It would be helpful to know whether the anxiety represented uncertainty and regret for not continuing with the elopement, worry that what she had done by escaping might result in an even more unfortunate situation, or perhaps just a simple fear that the formidable Drew might yet have his way.

Suddenly Miss Seymour gave way to the mirth bubbling up inside her. "That was a close-run thing!" she remarked cheerfully.

Two pairs of dark eyes alike in their innocence sought enlightenment.

"I was petrified that Amos was going to demand the identity of his newest passenger before consenting to leave the inn. Then we should have been in the basket indeed."

Neither listener seemed to find this explanation particularly illuminating, judging by their puzzled expressions, and Miss Seymour chuckled outright as she addressed her new friend in tones of gentle admonition. "You never did tell me your name, my dear."

"Ohhh, how goosish of me! You must think me perfectly hen-witted, ma'am." A red stain crept up over the cheeks of the pretty brunette, alleviating the pallor that had persisted since her disastrous discussion with her former *fiancé*. "My name is Drucilla Hedgeley and I live in Russell Square in the home of my uncle, Mr. Bernard Mortimer."

"Well, I am most happy to make your acquaintance, Drucilla, but you really must call me Vicky, since we have already agreed that such an impromtu invitation could only arise between old friends."

A shy smile of acquiescence further melted the nervous stiffness of Miss Hedgeley's features and her red-clad figure eased itself somewhat into the other corner of the seat. She acknowledged the subsequent introduction to the maid with pleasant civility, not seeming in the least put out by the other's eager inspection of her fashionable attire.

Miss Seymour again warned her new friend that they had a journey of nearly two hours ahead of them and made polite inquiries as to her comfort, which were responded to with equally polite assurances that Miss Hedgeley had never travelled in such a well-sprung carriage and that she was warm as toast, thank you. The residual sensation of warmth arising from a good dinner in a comfortably heated inn enabled the three passengers to endure the next hour without much noticing the gradual increase in dampness and the rapidly fading light in the sky as the coach moved at a steady pace over the wet road.

Despite Miss Seymour's invitation to her guest to dispense with formality, Drucilla displayed a rather becoming diffidence at first, responding willingly to questions but not proffering any comments or inquiries of her own. She handled the problem of instant intimacy with one who was clearly her senior in age and experience by avoiding the use of titles at all, a difficult feat not unappreciated by her hostess, who found it necessary to hide a smile on occasion when the younger girl stumbled verbally, then plunged ahead to make an observation. Vicky's acquired social sense and genuine interest in her companion eventually succeeded in putting the latter at ease, however, and she was prattling away about her dull existence in her uncle's household before they had gone many miles.

It was abundantly clear that a certain moral severity and concomitant heaviness of spirit in the life-style of her relatives, arising quite probably from their religious beliefs, had caused the young girl, who had been reared in a very different atmosphere in her extreme youth, to chafe under the restrictions imposed upon her by a set of well-meaning but dull persons for whom she cherished no lifelong affection which might have mitigated the situation. From her eager questions about Vicky's activities during her residence in the city, that lady deduced that Drucilla avidly followed the doings of Society as reported in the daily press and most probably read widely of the nonimproving sort of literature that would have been censored by her relatives had they been aware of her leanings in this direction. Before an hour had passed, her hostess felt entirely confirmed in her first judgment that the impetuous elopement had been entered into solely from a desperate desire to escape an uncongenial mode of living. Drucilla's feelings for her former *fiancé*, Mr. Andrew Massingham, were ambivalent, to say the least, a blend of admiration, fear, and excitement. What the blend did not seem to contain was any smidgen of the deep affection conducive to success in marriage. Vicky was able to set the girl's mind at rest concerning her "lost reputation" by promising to inform her family of her whereabouts by the earliest possible post. She expressed regret that their flight had made it necessary to leave Drucilla's baggage behind, but ventured to suggest that by the time Mr. Massingham arrived at the Oaks with it, the girl would be able to meet him with a more composed mind to discuss their possible future together.

Surprisingly, this suggestion caused the colour to rush into Miss Hedgeley's cheeks once again, and she hung her head in a guilty fashion.

"Why, whatever is the matter? What did I say to upset you?" asked Vicky in quick concern.

"I was afraid Drew would stop me. You do not know how determined he can be. I . . . I did not dare to tell him," stammered Drucilla, her eyes shimmering with tears.

"What exactly did you not dare to tell him?"

The words were calmly spoken and did not reflect the fatalistic sense of unwelcome knowledge that had assailed Miss Seymour on receiving Drucilla's confession. She scarcely heard the girl's whispered reply that she had not acquainted Mr. Massingham with the name of the old friend with whom she had departed so irregularly. It had not been at all necessary to receive verbal confirmation of her guess.

"I . . . I have some money with me, almost twenty guineas that I have saved. Surely I shall be able to buy some dresses with this."

"Yes, of course, my dear child, do not worry on that head," said Vicky soothingly, trying to smooth the line of her own forehead as the girl gazed at her hostess in anxiety. Clothes were the least of her worries at that point. There could be no doubt that upon reception of the clear insult conveyed by such a message, the very determined Mr. Massingham would be on their trail either personally or through the medium of the law. The only question was how long it would take him to ferret out her name and direction. She was not personally acquainted with the proprietor of the Candle and Unicorn, but it would be marvelous indeed if someone at the inn had not recognised the carriage. Amos was certainly known in Stamford. She could only hope that a fortune hunter would hesitate to involve representatives of the law in his doings, in which case they would be spared a scandal and would only have to cope with a nasty scene with the thwarted lover. That had always been on the agenda, of course, but she had counted on the solid background provided by the Oaks to keep the meeting civilised. Now she could not prevent a glance out into the dark void beyond the window, and her ears strained to detect the sounds of pursuit. Their own horses' hoofbeats and the far-off barking of a dog were the only noises discernible, apart from the occasional creaking of the carriage springs, and she sat back again, reassured for the moment.

Now that the initial panic had subsided somewhat, she was able to think more efficiently. Drucilla had revealed that the couple was travelling in a post chaise with only a pair of horses and that something had happened to the chaise, necessitating an unscheduled stop in Stamford. The reason she had been left alone at all was that her *fiancé* had been called from the dining room to see about the repairs. None of this argued a particularly full purse. The chances were that Mr. Massingham's resources had been strained to provide for a prepaid trip to Gretna Green and back. He might not be able to mount a search tonight if the repairs to the hired chaise should prove sufficiently time-consuming. In any case, no chaise and pair was going to catch Amos driving a specially built carriage behind a team of strong horses.

Miss Seymour's flashing smile lit the dim interior of the carriage as she embarked on a description of her home with the object of quietening the troubled spirits of her guest. After a few moments Miss Hedgeley stopped clasping and unclasping her gloved fingers and her voice took on more animation as she was drawn into a discussion of country living. Both ladies were engrossed in conversation and Lily was nodding spasmodically when the unmistakable sound of a gunshot rang through the air and the carriage came to a lurching halt at an angle that canted its passengers almost out of their seats.

Lily's squeak of alarm was lost in Miss Hedgeley's fearful ejaculation. "It's Drew, I know it is! He's followed me! What shall I do?"

Miss Seymour's lovely features set in lines of controlled fury as she proceded to remove a false cushion in the arm of the seat, from behind which she extracted a small pistol.

"If this is your Mr. Massingham, I shall give him a piece of my mind for daring to shoot at my coach," she clipped out, ignoring the exclamations of the others at sight of the weapon while she checked that it was loaded. "Where can I hide it?'' she muttered to herself after trying in vain to stuff it unobtrusively into a small pocket in her pelisse. "If it's a thief, he'll be sure to search our reticules.''

"*A thief!*'' squealed Lily, beginning to quake as curt commands sounded outside.

"Here, take my muff,'' urged Drucilla, proving once again that she could think coherently when quick action was demanded.

Vicky stripped off her gloves and accepted the red velvet muff as footsteps approached the carriage.

"Let us hope the thief, if it is a thief, has no sense of fashion, my dear, because this crimson colour against the cinnamon brown of my pelisse is in shockingly bad taste,'' she uttered *sotto voce* as the door was flung open.

Drucilla swallowed a giggle that turned into a gasp of alarm as a masked figure appeared in the doorway and demanded that they exit the vehicle without any shilly-shallying.

"A parcel o' women!'' he exclaimed in disgust as the passengers complied with this order, standing close together as if seeking mutual aid in the face of danger. And the man accosting them did look dangerous apart from the heavy pistol he now stuck into a wide leather belt around his coat that already held one gun, presumably the one that had been discharged earlier. He stood well over six feet tall and was massively built. The lower part of his face beneath the black mask was covered with several days' growth of beard, accenting the misshapen mouth that pulled down on one side toward a heavy jawline.

"I'll take that,'' he growled, relieving Miss Seymour of the reticule dangling from her left arm with a jerk that took no account of her soft skin, leaving a red mark from the bag's strings on her wrist.

"No rings, no bracelets?'' inquired the highwayman, opening the reticule and removing a small pile of gold coins, which he deposited in a capacious pocket in that strange dark coat he wore, before dropping the reticule to the ground.

Miss Seymour slipped her left hand into the muff and withdrew her right, equally bare of jewels, for his scrutiny.

She emitted a slight gasp as a rough hand jerked open the top of her pelisse and inspected the slim column of her throat rising from the round-necked gown she wore.

"No sparklers? A well-dressed lady like yourself?" he demanded, eyes glinting evilly behind the face covering.

"I don't travel with my jewelry," replied Vicky in cold tones that refused to be intimidated by that massive hairy fist close to her face or the hint of liquor fumes reaching her nose as he leaned nearer with the obvious intention of menacing her.

"I'll have those ear bobs," snarled the thief, removing his attention to Miss Hedgeley and grabbing her reticule in turn. "I know just the prime article as will appreciate those gewgaws."

Watching Drucilla's fumbling efforts to remove the earrings with both hands, Vicky knew a rush of thankfulness that she had been too occupied with the last-minute details of leave-taking this morning to bother with jewels. The little gun was reassuringly firm in her tightened grip inside the muff. She was starting to draw it out when the man whirled toward her again, having pocketed Drucilla's money and ignored the cowering maid entirely. She froze in place.

"You're a prime article yourself for a gentry mort," he commented, stepping much too close for Vicky's liking and running his eyes over her person in an assessing fashion that brought the colour rushing to her pale face, though she stood her ground instinctively and refused to lower her chin. "It's my notion that whoever owns a grand rig like that one would be glad to pay down handsome to recover a little beauty like you. How'd you like to come along wi' me, sweetheart?"

Prudence departed Vicky in a surge of mingled anger and fear as she stared at the grinning gap-toothed lout. "I would not dream of going a step in your company," she retorted foolishly.

"We'll see about that!" Before the startled girl could blink, the man had twisted her left arm behind her back and was forcing her toward a big grey horse standing motionless in the mist.

In the split second of astounded silence that followed this unexpected development, the sound of approaching hoofbeats rang loud and eerily; then Lily broke into a run, screaming distractedly, "*No, no*, you can't *take* her!"

"Unhand that lady or I'll put a bullet into you!" commanded a steely voice from behind the carriage.

Several things happened at once then. The highwayman spun around to face the newcomer, using his hostage as a shield; Lily launched her small person at his bulk, clawing frantically and screeching like a banshee that he mustn't take her mistress; and two shots echoed almost simultaneously, followed in turn by a chorus of feminine screams. For a second all movement seemed suspended; then as the horseman slid off his mount, tumbling to the ground in agonising slow motion, the highwayman knocked Lily down with the hand that held a smoking pistol, thrust Miss Seymour aside, and headed for the body of their would-be rescuer.

Lily was sobbing frantically on the ground; Drucilla, recognising the fallen horseman, shrieked, "*Drew! Oh, no!*" and toppled over in a faint.

Miss Seymour, righting her balance after a staggering step, withdrew her hand from the velvet muff and addressed herself to the thief's back as he bent over the fallen man: "Keep away from him and raise your hands or I'll put a bullet into you," unconsciously adopting Mr. Massingham's own threat, though her traitorous voice shook a trifle in the delivery.

Apparently the highwayman was unconvinced of her resolution, for he leaped to his feet and hurled himself at her.

Vicky steadied her hand, closed her eyes, and fired. On opening them she was appalled to see that the huge thief was still headed her way, though he now clutched his left shoulder with his right hand in mute evidence that her aim had not been entirely lacking. He was emitting a steady stream of oaths, obviously bent on retaliation, which she must avoid. Her brain, churning along nicely, reached this conclusion, but no other part of her seemed capable of movement as she stood immobile, still pointing the discharged weapon.

"Run, Miss Vicky. I'll get him!"

The sound of Amos' voice brought Vicky's head sharply around to the front of the chaise, where the old coachman, hatless, with a countenance distorted by pain and rage, was struggling to descend, with one useless arm in a red-stained sleeve hanging at his side. Fortunately for Vicky's personal safety, the highwayman's attention had also been diverted to his first victim, who was bearing down on him, whip in hand. He pulled up short, then with a snarl of inarticulate loathing directed at the girl with the gun, altered his course and vaulted into the saddle of the twitching horse, bad arm notwithstanding, and rode off into the woods from which presumably he had launched his attack.

Though much relieved, naturally, to have escaped the thief's vengeance, Vicky discovered in herself a cowardly wish that she too might quietly faint away. A quick but comprehensive glance revealed chaos all about her. Drucilla lay in a crumpled red heap near the chaise, which was lurching dangerously with the distracted motions of the frightened horses; Lily was rocking back and forth on the ground, holding one side of her face and weeping spasmodically; while Mr. Massingham remained where he had fallen, ominously still. Amos had run to the horses' heads, and she followed him, tossing a sharp command over her shoulder to the maid to see to Miss Hedgeley.

"It's a miracle the horses didn't bolt, what with one thing and another, all that shooting," Amos muttered as she joined him in soothing the nervous beasts. "I'm right mortified, Miss Vicky, to pass out like that when you needed me, but the horses pulled so against the arm, the pain sent me clean out o' my head till I heard the shots."

"Never mind, Amos, you got them safely stopped and you came to in time to save me from a nasty beating at the very least. Are you badly hurt?"

"The bullet went clean through my arm. It's not so bad."

"Oh, Amos!" Vicky cried in distress. "It's bad enough, and we must get it taken care of, but if you can leave the horses for now, I must see about Mr. Massingham, I'm afraid." Her voice trailed off and she was grateful for the coachman's presence as they bent over the unconscious man a few seconds later.

"Oh, my God! He's bleeding from the *head*! Oh, Amos, is he . . . ? He's not . . . ?"

"Nay, lass, he hasn't stuck his spoon in the wall, not yet leastaways," replied the coachman soothingly as he gently straightened the limbs of the wounded man. "See, the bullet went into his leg here, but he must have hit his head when he fell. Look, didn't I say it? Here's this rock all bloody beside him."

Vicky's relief that Mr. Massingham had not apparently sustained a gunshot wound to the head was tempered by a fast-dawning apprehension. Their situation was grave enough as matters stood. The man's pulse was fast and weak and he showed no signs of coming round, but when she voiced her fears on this head, Amos assured her gruffly that the lad was better off unconscious until they could get him to a surgeon.

For the first time since the coach had stopped, Vicky had leisure to examine their surroundings. The results were scarcely comforting. A heavy mist hung in the air, reducing visibility considerably. The lamps on the chaise created a halo effect for a few feet, and then all was indistinct. Ahead of them the road wound into some woods, which had apparently sheltered their attacker. She shivered slightly and looked back the way they had come. After a few feet the road seemed to dissolve into nothingness. Fields stretched out on the sides of the road, but no lights glimmered anywhere and there were no sounds in the night except Lily's soft exhortations to Miss Hedgdley to wake up as she chafed her hands, and the soft jingle of the horses' harness.

"Try the vinaigrette in my reticule, Lily. It's on the ground somewhere," Vicky said mechanically; and then: "Where *are* we, Amos?"

The coachman reponded to the hint of panic in his mistress' voice, addressing her as though she were a child again. "Now, Miss Vicky, don't fash yourself, it's not so bad as it could be. We passed an old inn of sorts two or three miles back, outside o' Little Menda. It ain't much of a village and the inn ain't what you're used to, but this lad can't stand much of a ride, I doubt. The only thing is . . .'' He hesitated, and Vicky looked at him apprehensively. "I could have a mite o' trouble driving a team with this arm, and—''

"Oh!" she exclaimed in relief. "If that's all that's worrying you, Amos, I intended to sit up on the box to help you in any case. Between us we'll handle 'em. I agree that it's imperative to get Mr. Massingham to a warm bed with all haste—and a doctor of course." She frowned and massaged her forehead with the fingers of one hand. "I only hope there is someone in the vicinity of this inn of yours."

"Now, Miss Vicky, it won't do to go all worritin' till we need to. One thing at a time, my old pa always said."

"Sufficient unto the day . . . or rather the moment," murmured Miss Seymour to herself. "You are right, of course, Amos. Ah, I see that Lily has succeeded in reviving Miss Hedgeley. Now we can set about getting Mr. Massingham into the chaise with the least possible disturbance."

This last was easier said than done, for the wounded man, though lean, was tall and well-muscled. His injuries were sufficiently serious to complicate the task of lifting a considerable deadweight, and one of the girls had to be in the carriage to receive him, since it would be advisable to support and cushion his head to spare him as much jostling as possible on the journey. Drucilla, with tears of pity in her eyes and words of self-reproach on her lips, begged to be allowed to perform this service, which left the slightly built Lily and a one-armed man to assist Miss Seymour in the formidable task of transferring Mr. Massingham to the carriage. After much straining and some unavoidable jerkiness that wrenched a moan from the unconscious man's lips, they succeeded in depositing him securely in Drucilla's lap. Miss Seymour had bound up the head wound, using their handkerchiefs as a makeshift bandage, but no real attempt could be made to stanch the blood from the thigh under the circumstances, and she bit her lip to keep from crying out as her hand came away bloodstained from arranging his legs as best she could in the confines of the chaise. She was already trembling with fatigue, and the nightmare trip was still to do.

"Don't you go a-swooning on me, Miss Vicky," admonished Amos, noting her white tense face as she climbed up onto the box in his wake and accepted the whip with a hand that shook despite her efforts at control.

A short, unamused laugh answered him. "Have no fear, Amos. There is neither time nor space enough to indulge in a ladylike fit of the vapours. But I confess the sight of your old inn will look as welcome as the pearly gates to me tonight!"

4

Despite her rash prediction, Miss Seymour's first glimpse of the ancient and somewhat dilapidated Green Feather did not give rise to favourable comparisons with the Gates of Heaven, though it was assuredly a blessed relief to reach any destination with chaise and passengers intact. It had not taken long to discover that driving was never intended to be a partnership activity. It was indeed fortunate that Vicky was not cursed with excessive sensibility, for Amos suffered from no reluctance to criticise her awkward handling of the whip when his professional instincts were affronted. However, she was able to console herself with the knowledge that without her assistance, unskilled though it undoubtedly was, they would not have stirred far from the spot where disaster had befallen them. Amos was unused to controlling a team with his right hand, and the addition of Vicky's strength at several points had made the difference between a steady, safe pace for the injured man and a possible accident.

Their arrival at the Green Feather could not be described as propitious. At an unoccupied moment sometime in the hazy future Vicky might recall with amusement the landlord's expression of ludicrous dismay at sight of the luxurious chaise being driven by a panting, sweating, bloodstained old giant and a slim, pale, and dishevelled young lady, but at present she was shaking with fatigue and dismay herself. The innkeeper was even less prepared for a revelation that one of his unexpected guests was badly injured and would require the immediate services of a doctor, but after the initial shock he whipped into action, sending the stable boy galloping off with a message for the nearest medical practitioner and himself supervising the removal of the wounded man to one of the two guest chambers the inn boasted. The landlord had hastily introduced himself as Septimus Tolliver over the inert form of Mr. Massingham as he took on the major burden from the stumbling Amos, now nearly at the end of his tether. Vicky expressed their gratitude in incoherent terms as she helped to support the victim's head on the short trip up a steep staircase. The room was Spartan but clean, she saw with thankfulness as she hurried ahead to open up the bed. The sight of Mr. Massingham's greyish complexion when she got her first good look at him by the light of a lamp hastily lighted from a candle carried upstairs by Drucilla was so alarming as to deaden her powers of observation from that point on. It was Mr. Tolliver who bellowed for his daughter to come kindle a fire in the grate and to bring a warming pan with her. Vicky had gotten so thoroughly chilled from her stint on the box that the frigid temperature of the bedchamber did not immediately register.

The next half-hour passed in a furor of activity, some of which would have been required upon the arrival of any ordinary traveller, but much of which was directed toward preparing the wounded men for examination by the doctor when he should arrive. Since no other traveller was at present enjoying the Green Feather's hospitality, it was a simple matter to designate the larger of the two rooms as the ladies' accommodation. After starting the fires, the landlord's daughter Sukey was dispatched to make up a cot for Lily. The landlord's wife occupied herself in the kitchen preparing hot drinks for all. One look at the strained young faces of her two companions had decided Miss Seymour to banish them forthwith to bed. Both protested, but as there was no material fashion in which either could assist at present, Vicky acknowledged their willingness with becoming gratitude and kept to herself a stronger sense of thanksgiving at being able to reduce her problems by two. With the willing Sukey in attendance to see to their comfort, she bade them a hasty good night, cutting short Drucilla's appeals to be allowed to take part in nursing Drew.

A cot had been set up in a corner of Mr. Massingham's room for Amos, whose endurance was strongly tried before the ordeal of removing all coverings from his wounded arm was over. Vicky had ruthlessly overridden his protests that he must first help to get the real patient undressed, and that it wasn't proper for her to be present at all. She pointed out with indisputable logic that the first essential was to get Mr. Massingham warm before causing him any further discomfort. The other issue she avoided by promising to call in Mr. Tolliver, after he had seen to the horses, to assist Amos in disrobing the victim and preparing him for the doctor's visit. Since she had been peeling away the layers of clothing from the coachman's arm during this discussion, he submitted perforce to having his wound cleaned by his mistress and dusted with basilicum powder unearthed from his cloak bag. The bleeding had nearly stopped and Vicky saw with relief that the bullet had exited through the back of the arm as Amos had claimed. She covered it loosely to await the doctor's inspection and turned with much less confidence to attend to the man whose harsh breathing had been playing a persistent accompaniment to her activities since she had entered the room. His pulse was somewhat stronger but she didn't like his colour, and above all she didn't like that difficult breathing. Observing his somewhat restless movements in the bed, Vicky found her teeth and fingers clenching as she wondered whether or not this was a hopeful sign after an hour of deep unconsciousness. Did it signify that he would be coming around? Was that wholly desirable with a bullet still in him?

Resolutely she banished unprofitable speculation arising from what she knew to be a woeful ignorance of all things medical, and faced the immediate task.

"Those boots must come off, Mr. Tolliver," she said to

the landlord on his return, assuming an air of calm control, "but he must not be disturbed more than is absolutely necessary. Perhaps we had best cut them off."

The innkeeper was utterly scandalised at such a blatant example of waste. "Lord, miss, the gen'lman won't thank you for that! Those boots weren't made by no country shoemaker—likely they're worth twenty or thirty guineas. We'll have them off in a brace o' shakes. Just you hold his leg steady like and I'll do the rest."

Miss Seymour refrained from voicing the tart rejoinder hovering on her lips, to the effect that saving Mr. Massingham's money was never likely to be an object with her. Having been put firmly in her place, she meekly did as she was told, though not without much anxious scrutiny of the patient's ashen visage during the operation. He did stir restlessly once or twice, but showed no other signs of pain as Mr. Tolliver pulled off two prime examples of Mr. Hoby's genius with leather. At this point Amos roused from the lethargy into which he was sinking to demand that his mistress leave the room while they got the victim undressed and into a nightshirt offered by the landlord.

"Very well, but I shall have to see the wound to clean it, you know."

"I'll do that, miss," volunteered Mr. Tolliver. "You can go below and wait for the sawbones while my missus gets you something hot to drink. You look nigh frozen still. Can't have you going down sick too."

Vicky looked deeply into the open, honest countenance of Mr. Tolliver and knew him for a kindly man. She capitulated with a weary smile and a murmur of thanks and proceeded to follow her host's sensible advice.

The tiny inn did not boast anything as grand as a private parlour. Miss Seymour peeked into the deserted taproom, where the fire had burned low in the last hour, before heading for the kitchen. This was a large, low-ceilinged chamber comfortably heated on this autumn evening by a huge fireplace. The room was obviously used for family living, as it contained several chairs, two of which were now occupied by a woman who must be Mrs. Tolliver and the girl, Sukey. The latter jumped to her feet and pushed another Windsor-style chair nearer to the fire for their guest.

"Here, miss, you'll soon warm up next to the fire. Can I get you some nice chocolate like I took the other ladies? It's still hot," she remarked, indicating a pan standing on a trivet amongst the coals.

Miss Seymour would have preferred coffee, but accepted the chocolate with a smile of thanks and sank wearily into the hard chair. At least its unyielding surface would ensure that she didn't nod off and miss the doctor's arrival. The landlady, a small thin individual wearing an enormous mobcap over her greying locks, stared at her intently from an upholstered wing chair. There was a pile of sewing in her aproned lap, but she had abandoned it on the entrance of her guest.

"I see you have a quantity of hot water ready," Miss Seymour remarked, nodding toward a huge kettle over the fire. "I am persuaded the doctor, when he gets here, will be glad of it." She essayed a smile that failed in its object of softening the deeply etched lines of the face staring back at her, and realised with a further descent of her spirits that the simple human kindness evident in father and daughter was entirely missing in the wife. Mrs. Tolliver resented their presence and took no pains to hide the fact.

The landlady's thin colourless lips moved minimally and she spoke in a hissing voice that seemed to have to force its way out between barriers. "Be the injured gentleman your husband?"

So that was it! Mrs. Tolliver's sharp nose scented scandal. Without an instant's pause Vicky took the expedient way out. "No, he is my cousin, the son of my mother's only sister, and almost like a brother to me," she embroidered glibly.

"But Miss, the *other* Miss, I mean, said the gen'lman was her betrothed!" blurted Sukey.

"He is that too," agreed Vicky in equable tones that revealed nothing of her newborn impulse to box Drucilla's ears for her loose tongue. "He was escorting us to my home when we were set upon by a highwayman. Both my coachman and Mr. Massingham were shot by the thief in the course of the robbery."

A wide-eyed Sukey shuddered and exclaimed in sympathetic horror, but her mother remained unmoved by the afflicting tale. Her snapping black eyes narrowed to slits. "Did he take all your money and valuables?"

Miss Seymour blinked at the question that hissed out like steam escaping from a valve. "Why, yes, he—"

"Then how do you figure to pay the doctor? Dr. Jamison isn't one to offer his services for nothing." Mrs. Tolliver's jaw took on a belligerent line, and Vicky saw it was her own charges the woman was concerned with. For an instant her mind went blank; then a picture of the highwayman bending over his victim, about to search his pockets, flashed into her head. It would be she who would relieve Mr. Massingham of his purse tonight, in a good cause, she decided, and hoped devoutly that it wasn't empty.

"The thief did not have time to rob Mr. . . . my cousin before he rode off," she explained with dignity. "We shall use his funds until a message can be gotten to my servants, who will dispatch whatever is necessary tomorrow."

"Why did he lope off without he took everything?" persisted Mrs. Tolliver, whose suspicions had not been entirely laid to rest by this reassurance.

"I shot him."

Vicky's terse statement reflected both her impatience with the conversation and a desire for silence to confirm the noises her alert ears had picked up that could mean an imminent arrival. Let it be the doctor, she prayed silently, aware all at once of how tensely she had been waiting for some indication of this anticipated event. The landlady's dropped jaw made no impression on her consciousness as she half-rose, her hands gripping the arms of the chair to hold herself suspended in place until the opening of the door into the taproom released her.

At first glance the man who stalked into the room was not particularly prepossessing. The doctor, immediately identifiable as such by the shabby bag he dropped onto the floor with a thud, was an irascible-looking man of middle height and middle years. He removed his hat, revealing an untidy shock of greying red hair, and fixed the landlady with a pair of bulbous but piercing blue eyes. "What's all this nonsense about a dying man in a ducal carriage to drag a man away from his own fire in the middle of the night?"

Having ascertained a few minutes earlier that it was not quite nine o'clock by the tiny watch on her dress that had escaped the highwayman's notice, Vicky decided to ignore that complaint as she spoke up quickly. "My name is Victoria Seymour and it was I who sent for you, Dr. Jamison. I don't understand the part about the ducal carriage and I earnestly trust that my cousin is not dying, but he has been shot by a highwayman in the left thigh, and I fear there is also a head injury. My coachman has been wounded too, but in his case the bullet went clean through his arm."

The doctor had now divested himself of gloves and overcoat, which he tossed carelessly over the back of a chair, not even noticing when the gloves followed the law of gravity and slid promptly to the floor. He concentrated that disconcerting stare on Miss Seymour for an instant, then his eyes left hers to travel around the room. Correctly interpreting this rather odd behaviour, Sukey retrieved his medical bag and placed it in his hands. She also deposited the gloves in a pocket in his greatcoat.

"There's a good girl," he murmured absently before turning to head for the stairs, still without having addressed a single word to Miss Seymour. After a startled pause, she followed him, determined not to allow herself to be treated as though she were invisible or incompetent. It would have been beneath her dignity to race him up the stairs, which was the only way she could reach the door first, but she was hard on his heels as he walked into the correct room without the formality of knocking. She had been expecting an inquiry as to the location of the patients, and now stood stock-still, seething with indignation at the thought that he might just as easily have invaded the room housing Drucilla and Lily. Rousing herself almost immediately, she entered the sick-room behind him.

"What kept you?" remarked the doctor, but since he didn't even favour her with a brief glance this time as he muttered a greeting to the landlord and Amos before advancing on the bed, she declined to answer the taunt, remaining quietly just inside the door, where she could not be considered in anyone's way. This effacement didn't last long, however. The doctor had scarcely bent over his patient before he demanded, "Bring those lights closer."

Mr. Tolliver, who was positioned on the opposite side of the bed, removed the lamp from the bedside table and held it over Mr. Massingham. Miss Seymour's eyes located the branch of candles on a stand near Amos' cot and she brought it to the doctor's side, going past him to the head of the bed.

"Don't drip any of that tallow on him," growled Dr. Jamison, not looking up. "Nasty-smelling stuff."

Miss Seymour accepted this unnecessary stricture in silence, her eyes following every movement of the doctor's hands as he checked the patient's pupils, then unwound the makeshift bandage and felt the lump at the back of his head. The silence in the room lengthened as he next proceeded to count the pulse.

"When did all this carnage occur?" he inquired, indicating that he now wished the light to be moved lower while he examined the gunshot wound.

"About seven," put in Amos from his dark corner.

The doctor grunted an acknowledgement and proceeded to pull back the bedcovers to expose the loosely covered thigh wound, with, obviously, no thought expended on the subject of propriety. He took his time about it, using those long strong fingers to probe the entire area, which was swollen rather badly by now.

"Missed the kneecap, at least, for one small blessing, but

the bullet will have to come out tonight. I'll want hot water, plenty of it, and some clean bowls. I'll use that table for my instruments''—nodding toward the bedside table—''and I'll want both of you to help.'' The doctor paused in his search through his bag and again subjected Miss Seymour to that electric blue gaze.

''I'll help you, sir.'' This from Amos, who had dragged himself off his cot and was approaching the center of the room.

''Not you, old man. Get back there. I'll attend to you while Septimus here sees to the water and bowls.'' The doctor's eyes never left Miss Seymour's and she met the challenge coolly, calling over to Amos that she would assist Dr. Jamison. She came up behind him with the candles when he made his examination of Amos' wound. ''You'll do,'' he asserted briskly, binding up the arm with a roll of bandage taken from his kit. ''Keep it covered, keep it clean, and don't use it for a few days. It's going to ache like the devil for a time, so have the lady make you a sling tomorrow.''

Vicky smiled at Amos, then fixed him with a warning eye before turning to the doctor to ask, ''What about my cousin, Dr. Jamison?''

''Can't say yet. He's concussed for certain, but he seems to have the constitution of an ox. He'll need it, too. That bullet's in deep.''

At that moment Mr. Tolliver returned carrying a large kettle of steaming water. He was trailed by Sukey with an assortment of bowls, and the operation commenced with the doctor rattling off a spate of instructions to his staff. Mr. Tolliver set the table on the other side of the bed and poured water into the bowls provided before taking up his stance once again with the lamp. Miss Seymour brought the candle stand over to the bed to set the candlestick on, since the doctor wanted her hands free.

''What is that solution?'' she inquired, watching him spill something into one of the bowls.

''Liquid soap,'' he answered shortly, dumping a number

of instruments into the same bowl. He paused in washing his hands and looked up at her again. "Do you have a strong stomach? I'll be too busy to pick you up off the floor."

Miss Seymour handed him one of the linen towels from the towel stand by the dresser. "You needn't worry about me, doctor," she replied in level tones backed more by pride and ignorance than confidence.

The next half-hour tried that pride to the limit and banished ignorance forever. She was kept busy swabbing blood and handing over instruments to the surgeon, her movements impeded by the constant necessity to keep herself out of the field of light, inadequate as it was. For the most part, Dr. Jamison worked in silence, apart from snapped orders, but when the carefully uncovered bullet resisted his initial efforts to extract it, his muttered oaths, because more intelligible, proved almost as horrifying as the thief's, even for a girl who had spent every allowable moment of her childhood in the vicinity of the stables. She recognised with reluctant charity that he was totally unaware of her existence as a female, so concentrated was his attention on the task at hand. He was perspiring freely and she nipped in to wipe his forehead with a towel when he raised an arm to use his sleeve.

"Thank you."

The short phrase of appreciation and a dawning sense that she was really proving of assistance in a vital and difficult task helped her to triumph over the persistent queasiness aroused by the sight of the open wound and the reluctance of the body to render up the foreign element that had invaded it. She had felt the tremor that had shaken Mr. Massingham's form at the unsuccessful probe. Fear and sympathy for his possible suffering joined nausea. Her hand holding the swab shook so badly that the doctor snapped at her with a brutal callousness that shocked protests from Mr. Tolliver and Amos.

"It's all right; I'm all right. Go ahead," she said, steady once again, unaware that her teeth were gripping her lower lip with excessive force until she tasted the sickish sweetness of blood. Her concentration on the field of operation nearly equalled the doctor's at that moment. He must get it out soon; already Mr. Massingham showed signs of thrashing about, and his breathing was harsher than ever.

"Hold that leg steady."

She dropped the swab and did as commanded, using all her strength to prevent movement as Dr. Jamison tried for a better purchase on the bullet. Fortunately this effort proved successful, because Vicky had never felt more physically depleted in her life. She continued to follow the doctor's orders while he cleaned and bandaged the wound, but her motions were slow and mechanical now.

"Here, miss, you sit down in this chair. I'll do the cleaning up," said Mr. Tolliver, setting down the lamp he had held so uncomplainingly during the entire operation. He brought the room's solitary chair, an armless example of carved dark wood from an earlier period, over to the fireplace and half-led Miss Seymour to it. "You look plumb tuckered, and small wonder at it, the way you pitched in and helped the doctor as if you was born to it, and all the time the poor gen'lman here was your own cousin. I call that right spunky, I do."

Miss Seymour scarcely made sense of the rambling discourse of the admiring landlord, but the doctor's gruff admission that she "hadn't proved entirely useless" was a magnificent concession indeed. She summoned up a weak smile for both as she half-collapsed onto the hard seat.

"What you want is some brandy, Miss Vicky. It'll set you up again." This from Amos.

"We could all benefit from that prescription," agreed the doctor, who was drying his instruments on the towel.

"If it's all the same to you, sir, I'd liefer down a glass of daffy."

"I can't guarantee the medicinal properties of gin," replied the doctor with a faint smile in Amos' direction, "but the narcotic effect should be equal." He nodded to the landlord, who had looked a question, and Mr. Tolliver departed to fill their requests.

"No brandy for me, thank you." Vicky concealed a yawn

behind her hand. "I just want to sleep. It's been a hideously long day; in fact, it's been a hideous day without qualification. *Ohh!*" She turned toward the surgeon, who had gone back to his patient's side. "I was forgetting poor Mr. . . . my poor cousin! He'll require someone to sit with him, of course. If Mrs. Tolliver would be so kind as to make me some coffee, I shall do very well." She eased her stiff body out of the chair and approached the bed. "How is he?"

The doctor was frowning down at the still face of his patient, colourless beneath a summer tan. "The pulse rate has slowed down, he's comfortable at the moment, but that leg is going to ache like hell presently." He made no apology for his language and Vicky expected none.

"Will he sleep through the night? *Is* he asleep at all, or is this state some kind of coma?" she asked anxiously.

"Time will tell."

There was no opportunity to question the doctor further, for Mr. Tolliver returned at that moment with a tray containing clanking glasses. Amos had his gin and water while the others sipped brandy, Miss Seymour under the doctor's compulsion.

Mr. Tolliver wouldn't hear of her sitting up all night with the patient, but when she reminded him that he had duties to perform in the morning, they compromised, dividing the watch into two shifts of four hours. Having obtained a promise that he would wake her at three A.M., Vicky ordered Amos to go directly to sleep, thanked the doctor for his services, paid him from a dismayingly small supply of coins in Mr. Massingham's purse, and bade them all a relieved good night.

As the door closed behind her, Mr. Tolliver raised his half-empty glass in tribute. "There goes a real lady."

"Aye, she's a good 'un clean through, a spirited filly and tough to break to bridle at times, but she's a thoroughbred." Amos was unstinting in his praise of his mistress as he settled himself for the night.

The doctor conceded that the lady was less squeamish than the majority of her sex and went on to give instructions to the innkeeper regarding his patients.

In the other room, Vicky saw by the light of the candle Mr. Tolliver had given her that Lily had laid out her night things, but she did no more than remove her dress and the pins that anchored her heavy hair on top of her head to relieve the dull ache she had been conscious of for the past hour before crawling into the big bed beside Drucilla and falling instantly asleep.

5

It seemed no more than a moment later that Miss Seymour became aware of someone speaking her name. The voice was unfamiliar, soft but insistent, and she struggled up from the depths to respond, focusing her eyes with difficulty on the dark figure outlined in the dim light coming from behind a half-opened door.

"Yes?" The word was no more than a mumbled sigh, and the figure shifted its weight from one foot to the other and said apologetically, "You asked me to call you in four hours, ma'am. It's just gone three."

"Oh, Mr. Tolliver! Thank you, I'll be there in one moment." Awareness swept over Miss Seymour like an incoming tide and she was swinging her legs out of bed almost before the landlord withdrew from the doorway. Fortunately he had left the door ajar so that she was able to scramble into her discarded travelling dress without bothering to kindle a light. The dress buttoned down the front, which was a distinct advantage also, but luck deserted her when she attempted to locate the pins she had removed from her hair before going to bed. Her searching fingers running over the top of the chest of drawers swept the small pile to the floor. An impatient exclamation was bitten off in mid-utterance as Lily stirred in her cot. Miss Seymour, on her hands and knees in front of the chest, raised her head from an unsuccessful hunt in the shadows. No further movement ensued from either sleeping

61

girl, but she got to her feet awkwardly, abandoning the search after recovering just two pins. She seized the hairbrush from the top of the chest and left the room, closing the door quietly behind her and blinking in the lamplight issuing from across the hall.

Mr. Tolliver was waiting for her beside the bed.

"How is he?" she whispered, noting with approval that the landlord had placed a screen so that the light would not shine directly on the patient.

"He's been asleep the whole time," replied Mr. Tolliver after a brief hesitation, "but to my mind it's not as deep as it was at first. He's moving about restless-like and I'm not sure but what he may be coming over feverish."

Miss Seymour heard him with a dismay she attempted to conceal. "Is there anything for him to drink if he should waken?"

"Just water." He nodded toward a cracked pitcher on the bedside table. "Perhaps I'd best stay here with him, miss. He might be more than you could deal with if he wakes up from all that thrashing about."

"No, Mr. Tolliver. You must have your rest. I'll manage nicely." Vicky's firm confident tones, assumed for the innkeeper's benefit, had the desired effect, and he went off to his bed after extracting a promise that she would call him if she required assistance.

More than once during the next several hours Vicky was on the point of seeking aid. For a short initial period Mr. Massingham remained asleep, though not quietly so. Miss Seymour was able to check that Amos was quite comfortable, snoring gently away in his corner, and she took a couple of logs from the small woodpile to the mouth of the fireplace to simplify that chore when it should become necessary to build up the fire which Mr. Tolliver had replenished before leaving. There was time to brush her sleep-ruffled hair smooth, though with only two pins she could do no more than confine its heavy length insecurely behind each ear. This accomplished, her eyes travelled around the room, taking inventory of its contents—a simple room, austere in its furnishings, but clean and, thanks to Mr. Tolliver's efforts, warm at present. There was only one window in the room, on the wall opposite the fireplace. She drifted over to it, moved aside the chintz curtain to peer out. The rain had stopped earlier and now the night sky was filled with stars, though a misty cloud, a mere veil of vapour, trailed across the moon. A sound from the room brought her attention sharply back to the man writhing about on the big bed. Hastily she dropped the curtain and went to him.

The injured man was no longer pale but a trifle flushed as he thrashed about. Miss Seymour pushed aside the screen that partially shielded the bed from the light and took up the lamp with some idea of checking the bandages on his leg to make sure the restless movements had not started the wound bleeding again. As she turned back toward the bed, two incredulous dark eyes met hers and a hoarse voice ejaculated, "An angel, by God!"

Having no idea of the picture she presented with the lamplight behind her head turning her flowing hair to molten gold, Miss Seymour was instantly persuaded that her patient was delirious, and she frowned heavily, gripping her bottom lip in her teeth to hold back a moan of dismay at this turn of events.

"No, not an angel, angels don't frown," continued the voice in a dreamy fashion. "Besides, if you were an angel, that would mean I was dead, and it doesn't hurt to be dead. I hurt all over; ergo, I cannot be dead." Having reached this reasoned conclusion, the man on the bed frowned himself and posed a reasonable question. "If you're not an angel, who are you? And where am I?" This last was added during an unsuccessful attempt to raise himself on his elbow, and was succeeded by a groan as he fell back on the pillow.

"For heaven's sake," begged Miss Seymour in alarm, "do not try to move. You have hurt your head and you must lie still."

Her hand, going out instinctively to restrain any further attempts at movement on his part, was seized in a grip that surprised her by its strength as her fingers were crushed mercilessly.

"I want to know who you are," the injured man demanded in a peremptory fashion, ignoring her wince of pain and retaining his cruel grip on her fingers.

"And so you shall," Miss Seymour replied coolly, "when you have released my hand." Two pairs of determined eyes clashed briefly, each mirroring its owner's strong will. "And not until," she added calmly, refusing to acknowledge by so much as a flicker of an eyelid the very real discomfort resulting from the increase in pressure he had applied to her hand in defiance of her ultimatum. She could tell by the beads of moisture appearing on his upper lip that he was taxing his strength, but some instinctive understanding of his character warned her that for his own sake she must not let him gain the upper hand. It was obvious that Mr. Massingham was disposed to be a very bad patient; therefore it was essential to establish her supremacy at the outset if he were to be prevented from doing himself an injury. She clamped down on her natural sympathy and stood quiescent, waiting in expressionless silence for him to relax the pressure on her fingers, which he did suddenly with a crack of humourless laughter.

"Well, at least I can be sure you are no ministering angel— angels are gentle beings, so I'm told." Then, reverting to his original question: "Who are you and how did I come to be here?"

Miss Seymour could not quite disguise her concern as she countered, "Do you not recall the circumstances of your injury?"

"No, I . . . *wait though*! I remember an ugly customer in a mask—a thief! He was trying to abduct a girl, the girl from the inn!" The dark eyes focused more intently on Miss Seymour's face. "Was it you?"

Relief that his senses did not appear to be disoriented after all flooded through Vicky. "Yes, it was I. He shot you in the leg and you fell off your horse and hit your head on a rock."

"Stupid thing to do," muttered Mr. Massingham in much weaker tones. "No wonder my head aches. So does my leg, and I am thirsty."

Miss Seymour poured out some water with hands that

shook slightly and slipped an arm under the injured man's shoulders to raise him to a position where he could drink from the glass. After a few sips a look of such weariness passed over his wan features that she was constrained to ease him back against the pillow, pausing just long enough to turn it so it would be cooler for him. She had noted with trepidation the heat of his body beneath the nightshirt and made a casual gesture of brushing back a lock of dark hair her excuse for feeling his forehead. The light touch confirmed her fears that he was already feverish, but he seemed so exhausted that she dared to entertain the hope that he might sleep it away. She was repositioning the screen to shield his face from the lamp's rays when his lids fluttered open again.

"Still don't know who you . . . are." Each word was an effort now.

Miss Seymour smiled a reassurance at the man she had, unbelievably, still not been introduced to, and said casually, "For the present I am your cousin Vicky."

Again those black brows drew together. "Don't have a cousin Vicky . . . silly name." Long lashes that would be coveted by any female stirred again, then settled onto lean cheeks as Mr. Massingham drifted into sleep once more.

Miss Seymour released a soft breath of relief as she stood unmoving for several minutes, watching the rhythmic rise and fall of her patient's chest. Even as she stole away to seat herself in a chair by the fireside, doubts assailed her as to the likelihood that this peaceful sleep would last during the rest of the night, doubts that shortly proved well-founded. Within fifteen minutes Mr. Massingham was thrashing about again, followed almost immediately by disjointed snatches of conversation. At first Miss Seymour was startled. She approached the bed thinking she was being addressed, but one look at his flushed face caused her composure to evaporate to vanishing point. The delirium she had dreaded earlier had developed.

The next three hours passed in a nightmare of fear and indecision, interspersed with bouts of frantic activity as Miss Seymour sought to restrain her patient's periodic attempts to rise from his sickbed and go into battle. From the few clear bits of dialogue amongst his ramblings she realised early on that Mr. Massingham had been in the military service. If the names and places mentioned in his feverish state were a true indication, he had seen a lot of action over several years. Vimeiro, Oporto, Talavera, Ciudad Rodrigo, Badajoz, Salamanca, Vitoria—the foreign names conjured up images of dust and blood and battle and privation. At one point he shouted, "Chase Soult *out!*" and rose from his pillow, evidently with the immediate intention of setting about this task. Miss Seymour found it necessary to exert considerable strength to prevent him from leaving his sickbed and would have gone for reinforcements then had not the fear that he would reinjure himself in her absence been of overriding concern. As a last resort she would have to wake Amos, but she resisted the impulse—the old man was sunk in a sleep of total exhaustion, helped along no doubt by the generous measure of gin and water downed before retiring. The soothing tones of her voice repeatedly droning she knew not what eventually exerted a calming influence on the ex-soldier, and his mutterings decreased in volume. Frequent bathing of his face and hands with a flannel wrung out in tepid water seemed to soothe him for a time also.

"That feels good," he murmured after one such application of the wet cloth, and Vicky's hopes rose that the delirium might have passed, but within minutes he was complaining again about riding all day on the dusty plains of Spain.

"So thirsty—where's that damn water bag?" He began rolling his head about, perhaps seeking the bag in question.

"Here it is." Vicky slipped an arm under his shoulders and presented a glass to his lips. He drank greedily, staring at her blankly for a moment before recognition dawned in fever-bright eyes.

"Oh, it's you, the angel—no, not an angel. Who did you say?"

"I'm your cousin Vicky," she replied matter-of-factly.

"I told you I don't have a cousin Vicky!" He was becoming agitated again and she spoke with great firmness.

"You have now. Go to sleep."

Surprisingly enough, he did just that for nearly thirty minutes, allowing his drooping nurse a much-needed respite. The respite was from physical activity only, however. Miss Seymour, sitting slumped in the chair by the fireplace, was engaging in some heightened mental activity concerned with the probable events of the immediate future as she reviewed the situation of their party. At five o'clock on a cold morning in October optimism was at a low ebb. No longer did she indulge the naive hope that Mr. Massingham would awaken from this sleep free of fever and on the mend. He was a very sick man, indeed a dangerously sick man, and she trembled at the responsibility that suddenly sat so heavily on her shoulders. It didn't bear thinking about to question Dr. Jamison's professional competence—he was the only medical adviser within easy reach, and there was certainly no question of moving the patient in his present condition. Like it or not, they were marooned in this primitive inn for an uncertain period of time, with practically no money, a hostile landlady, and little in the way of medical supplies; in fact, Mr. Massingham and Drucilla did not possess so much as a toothbrush between them, though the girl was welcome to share her hostess' clothing. Her glance flickered and settled on the man sleeping heavily on the cot in the corner. Amos could not drive with one arm and, at his age, would require at least one day of complete rest before subjecting his injured arm to the jolting of a horseback ride. She assumed they were about equally distant from the Oaks and from Stamford, where the elopers' baggage must still be located. Since Mr. Massingham had been unencumbered by even a small cloak bag, it must have been his intention to take Drucilla back there with him, probably to the Candle and Unicorn. The first priority tomorrow—today, rather—would be to cancel the hired chaise and retrieve the couple's belongings. Of equal importance was the necessity of alerting her own household to their plight before her servants sent up a hue and cry in the area and dispatched messages that would frighten Aunt Honoria in

London. She had been expected at the Oaks today—no, yesterday.

Miss Seymour gave a little shake of her head as she puzzled over who there might be to accomplish these urgent errands. Her one glimpse of the stable boy had revealed a lad of no more than eleven or twelve years, too young to be entrusted with the responsibility of obtaining the baggage at Stamford, especially if, as Miss Seymour suspected, there was a reckoning due. Her own servants, then. She must write detailed instructions for Cavanaugh. She was mentally embroiled in the wording of these instructions when her patient awakened and put an end to any activity unrelated to his immediate care.

By the time Mr. Tolliver tapped lightly on the door at seven-thirty, Miss Seymour had been forced to abandon any lingering hopes that she might be safely home before this new day was finished. Although Amos volunteered to assist her in nursing the injured man and Mr. Tolliver overrode her protests and insisted on remaining with him while his nurse sought the common room to replenish her strength with an ill-cooked but sustaining breakfast, such breaks were of necessity of short duration once it became apparent that Miss Seymour's was the only voice that could exercise the least calming influence on Mr. Massingham in his more agitated states.

At one point during the second night, when Miss Seymour was trying to snatch an hour or two of sleep, a timorous but willing Drucilla had been introduced into the sickroom by Mr. Tolliver, it being hoped that her status as the patient's *fiancée* would invest her presence with some of the soothing quality that Miss Seymour's had for him, but it hadn't answered. Mr. Massingham, far from being comforted by the sight of his betrothed's anxious face, had not seemed to recognise her, and had querulously demanded the instantaneous appearance of his "angel" at his bedside. Understandably mystified and not a little disturbed by this ominous request from one whose language up till then would not have led anyone to suppose him intimately acquainted with members of the heavenly host, Mr. Tolliver had committed the well-meaning error of trying to cozen the injured man by assuring him that Miss Hedgeley was indeed an angel specifically deputised to care for his comfort. The scene that ensued had caused Drucilla to dash from the room in floods of tears, her hands over her ears to block out the worst of Mr. Massingham's scathing rejections. Fortunately Miss Seymour's light sleep had been penetrated by the sounds of disharmony from across the hall, and she reappeared in the sickroom before her patient had worked himself into a state that might have set his recovery back. Since Dr. Jamison was adamant in declaring rest and quiet essential to his patient's recovery and was reluctant to administer the heavy doses of laudanum needed to achieve this artificially, the lion's share of the nursing for those first days thus fell to Miss Seymour's lot.

Vicky was far from being a tender plant, but she had very little prior experience of nursing, both parents having succumbed after short illnesses. As a child of twelve she had not been permitted near her mother, who had contracted influenza, and her father had died as the result of a fall on the hunting field without ever regaining consciousness. She felt woefully inadequate for the task which had been thrust upon her, but took courage from the doctor's gruff assertion that keeping the patient quiet enough to allow nature to heal his body was the only skill required of her. For some inexplicable reason hers was the only voice and touch that exercised a restraining influence on Mr. Massingham when in the grip of the fever that developed after the operation. The irony of this was not lost on her as she bathed the wounded man's brow repeatedly and firmly restrained his periodic attempts to leave his bed. She had not forgotten the almost disdainful indifference with which he had regarded her in the dining room of the Candle and Unicorn or the speed with which he had tracked her down later when she had interfered so drastically with his plans for Drucilla. That there was a reckoning due between them was not open to question—if Mr. Massingham recovered, and Vicky was fiercely determined that he should recover. She did not like the man; nothing that Drucilla had conveyed in her artless way either in admiration or dispraise of her suitor had served to imbue her hostess with a desire to know him better. Even barring the fact that he was a gazetted fortune hunter, she had no opinion of his type of man, fearless and efficient on the fields of war and sport unquestionably, but totally lacking in the other virtues that went to make up a man of character. She would wager that his wits were sharp enough, especially where his own advantage was concerned, but that his intelligence wouldn't encompass the deeper concerns of mankind. He would be quick-thinking, quick-acting, and shallow, a physically impressive shell of a man. To men of this stamp women existed merely to minister to their comfort and provide them with pleasure on demand—in between wars and sporting events, of course. And, Vicky conceded with a rueful twist of her lips as her eyes roved over the beautifully chiselled features of her sleeping patient, so potent was the attraction of these fine male specimens that the sillier members of her sex (who were legion) flocked to them in droves, willing and eager to pander to their conceit. It wasn't only in the bird kingdom that the fine feathers were a prime asset.

But, personalities aside, Mr. Massingham had in all likelihood saved her life, for she had no illusions about her probable fate at the hands of the rapacious highwayman, and in rescuing her had put his own life in danger. She felt totally responsible for his present plight and dedicated herself to preventing him from slipping over the edge. She slept in snatches when her patient slept, with the door open so that she might hear him when he woke. Amos and Mr. Tolliver relieved her at these times because after the fiasco of Drucilla's visit it was deemed advisable to spare the two young girls any exposure to Mr. Massingham's unrestrained tongue while he remained in a state of delirium. Lily waited on Drucilla and accompanied her on short walks in the immediate vicinity of the village to relieve the tedium and assure that they should not lose the benefits of fresh air and mild exercise while confined at the Green Feather. Drucilla had pleaded not to be sent on to the Oaks in Miss Seymour's carriage while Drew was in such danger, promising to behave with the greatest circumspection and tearfully repeating her willingness to perform any task set her to hasten his recovery. Unwilling to leave the sickroom for any length of time and feeling herself unequal to the chore of convincing her little friend to abandon her former *fiancé* without chancing hurt feelings, Vicky had allowed her to remain. Drucilla proved her good intentions by bearing the tedium and discomfort of their stay at the inn without complaint. She even contrived to produce a sustaining broth for the invalid, under Lily's direction, from chickens provided by the villagers.

The main stumbling block to the smooth transition of the inn household into a hospital *cum* guest house was Mrs. Tolliver. She was resentful of the crowding of her house and unwilling to put herself out in any way for her unwelcome guests. To Vicky it was inconceivable that the woman should always have gained her livelihood by catering to the needs of travellers, so unaccommodating did she prove. Vicky herself had little time to deal with Mrs. Tolliver, which was perhaps fortunate in her uncertain frame of mind, for she had a quick tongue in her head and poorly developed instincts for conciliatory behaviour. Cavanaugh, her majordomo at the Oaks, took in the situation at a glance when he arrived in person on the day following the accident. It was thanks to his diplomatic handling of the landlady and his skill at organising a household that a tenuous working arrangement was arrived at without setting Vicky and Mrs. Tolliver any deeper into adversary positions. Once convinced of the uselessness of trying to persuade his mistress to delegate her nursing duties to her own former nurse and come home, he turned his talents toward providing a support system for her efforts. Thus it was that the unappetising offerings of the Green Feather's kitchen were supplemented by deliveries of foodstuffs from the Oaks, and the invalid was able to refresh himself with quantities of lemonade when he awoke in a feverish thirst. Sweet-smelling sheets of finest linen now adorned his bed, and the lumpy pillows had been replaced by down pillows from his nurse's home.

It was on the forenoon of the third day of their enforced stay at the Green Feather that Mr. Massingham was finally pronounced out of danger by Dr. Jamison, who had been visiting his patient twice daily. Miss Seymour, who had not quite dared allow herself to believe that this time the quiet breathing of her patient really did signal the final victory over the fever that had impeded his recovery, experienced a giddy sensation of mingled relief and weakness that caused her knees to buckle. The doctor shoved her onto the room's only chair and cast a professionally assessing eye over her pale features and brimming eyes.

"Bed for you, my girl, right this minute, and when you wake up I want you out in the fresh air for at least an hour. Take a brisk walk or just stroll in the village, but take yourself out of this place for a time."

"Oh, but I cannot leave my cousin just yet; he won't sleep for very long, and—"

He cut into her protests with ruthless candour. "Unless you wish to be my next patient, someone else can sit with him from now on. If I don't see some colour in your cheeks when I come back this evening, I'll dose you with the foulest-tasting tonic in my dispensary."

Miss Seymour's lips curved in faint response to the rare twinkle in those piercing blue eyes. "I believe you would enjoy that," she retorted pertly, rising with effort from the chair. "Very well, doctor, your command is *my* command. I feel as though I could sleep for a week."

After a final glance at Mr. Massingham that reassured her that he was at last enjoying a natural sleep, his devoted nurse crossed the hall and lost no time in obeying the first part of the doctor's prescription.

6

Late afternoon found Miss Seymour striding along the tree-bordered road leading out of the village. She had slept for five undisturbed hours and awakened refreshed and ravenous to consume a late luncheon with more enjoyment than the quality of the food warranted. Though eager to be off on her walk, she had peeked in on her patient before collecting her pelisse and bonnet from the room she shared with Drucilla and Lily. Both girls were in attendance on Mr. Massingham, who was sleeping once again after having eaten solid food for the first time since the accident. Drucilla's face had sparkled with elation as she reported that Drew had not only recognised her but also allowed her to feed him, even going so far as to compliment her on the quality of the chicken broth she had prepared, before he dozed off again.

For a time Vicky banished all problems from her mind while she walked toward and through the tiny village, observing a few children at play and two women visiting in front of what appeared to be the only shop amongst the sprawl of cottages that made up the hamlet of Little Menda. She could not but be aware that her progress was observed with unconcealed interest by those inhabitants of the village in evidence at present, and she nodded pleasantly in response to the women's shyly bobbed curtsies as she passed them, and smiled at a child who chased an errant hoop across her path. All too soon the last cottage with its neat garden was behind her and she was walking along the road with nothing in particular to catch her eye or divert her mind. The crisp air felt marvelous on her cheeks and she inhaled gratefully of the woodland scents, but within minutes she was back to pondering the immediate situation of their small party. It was a wonderful relief to know the crisis was past, but it was time to give some thought to the next step. Every scrap of her resolution and all her mental energies up to now had been devoted to *willing* Mr. Massingham to survive the fever that had racked him. If one could believe Dr. Jamison, the injured man's convalescence would now proceed normally, but although the debilitating fever had run its course, it would be idle to pretend that a day or two would see him on his feet again.

Nor was the Green Feather an ideal spot for a convalescence. Miss Seymour's heart swelled with gratitude when she dwelt on the kindness and helpfulness of Mr. Tolliver and Sukey during the late emergency, but it was beyond question that they could not continue to impose on the innkeeper's good nature indefinitely, even though adequate financial compensation had not been a problem once Cavanaugh had arrived.

Obviously the next step was to decide on a place in which Mr. Massingham could complete his recovery, and, when the doctor gave his approval, to convey him to this location wherever it might be. Plainly stated, this did not sound an insuperable problem, but no immediate solution presented itself to her intelligence.

Miss Seymour's furrowed brow and inward concentration at that moment would have warned an observer that she was paying insufficient attention to her surroundings, particularly to the road under her feet, but there was no one in sight to give warning as she stepped on a good-sized pebble and gave her ankle a turn.

"Ouch! Idiot!"

The pain that gave rise to this exasperated exclamation brought her to a sense of her surroundings once more. The scenery hadn't altered much. The road still wended its way between stands of tall trees that occasionally thinned out enough to allow glimpses of meadowland off to either side. She had been ascending a gentle incline and continued on her way, hoping to find a more extensive prospect at the top of the hill. So far there had been no traffic, either wheeled or pedestrian, on the road. For the moment she was all alone in her small corner of the universe, which, on reflection, was a most agreeable sensation. For the past few tension-packed days and nights personal privacy had been an unknown quality. Immediately her thoughts returned to the reason for this situation, and the little line reappeared between her finely arched brows.

Were Mr. Massingham indeed her cousin, the obvious course would be to remove him to the Oaks as soon as it was medically feasible. Unfortunately, as she was a single woman without even Aunt Honoria's presence to lend her countenance, this solution was not to be considered, except, of course, that circumstances forced her to consider it. She had no precise knowledge of Mr. Massingham's circumstances, not even his address in London. Drucilla, when asked if there was some-one who should be notified of her ex-*fiancé*'s condition, had replied vaguely that he had a married sister whose name she could not immediately recall. Nor was she any more knowl-edgeable concerning his residence. She believed he had lodg-ings in St. James's Street, but naturally a young woman would not have dreamed of so much as driving down that exclusively masculine haunt. Further questioning had elicited the fact that Drew had a devoted groom whom he had left behind in London, but nothing of any use in the pressing consideration as to where it would be best for him to recuperate. In any case, London was a full day's journey away, and this was inadvisable, surely, in his weakened state.

Miss Seymour thoughtfully grawed at her bottom lip as she considered the pros and cons of removing Mr. Massingham to a cottage on her own estate with her old nurse in attendance. This solution avoided the disadvantages attendant on a lengthy journey as well as satisfying Drucilla that Drew was being well looked after. On the other hand, the last thing in the world Miss Seymour would elect would be to have the ex-soldier within easy access of his former *fiancée*. Nothing she had yet learned of his circumstances or his character tended to negate her first impression that he was a fortune hunter bent on hurrying into marriage an heiress too young and innocent to know her own mind. Not that it would do to try to inform Drucilla of this. The girl was naively convinced that her soldier burned with love for her, and she would resent any suggestion to the contrary. It was a deucedly awkward fix, whichever way one looked it, but perhaps now that he was rational again Mr. Massingham would himself have some plan in mind for the period of his convalescence that would remove him from Drucilla's vicinity. On this hopeful thought Miss Seymour attained the summit of the low gradient and paused to gaze about her in pleasure.

The prospect, though not vast, was sufficiently pleasing to make the climb worthwhile. Low hills, mostly tree-covered, rippled to the horizon on one side of the road. On the other side, flattish meadowlands gave way to a real forest. Here and there thick hedges separated the fields, but nowhere was there a sign of habitation, if one excepted a faint plume of pale grey mist that might have indicated a chimney beyond the next curve in the road. Looking at the watch pinned to her dress, Miss Seymour was surprised to discover that she had been walking for nearly an hour. A glance upward revealed that the sun was far advanced in its downward curve and the breeze seemed to have freshened somewhat also. If she wished to arrive back at the Green Feather before anyone became concerned with her lateness, she had best forgo the view around the next curve and set a brisk pace back the way she had come.

Unfortunately, in carrying out this sensible plan, Miss Seymour reckoned without the condition of the road becoming a consideration. She hadn't gone a hundred yards when she stepped once again on a large stone, and this time the wrenching she gave her foot had more serious consequences. The pain in her ankle was only momentary, but she stared down in dismayed disbelief at her kid half-boots and groaned aloud when her eyes confirmed the bad news. Lying in the road totally disassociated from its sole was the heel to her right shoe. She picked it up and turned it over in her hands, hoping to discover some magical way to reestablish contact, but to no avail. The road before and behind her was still empty, as it had been for the past hour. There was nothing to be done but to continue onward. This she did at a limping pace that became more and more uncomfortable as the minutes passed. She was toying with the idea of trying to break off the heel on the other shoe to even off her gait when the unmistakable sounds of a vehicle behind her caused her to pull up short at the side of the road and turn around hopefully.

Even a farm cart would have been a welcome sight, but it seemed her luck was in, for a smart curricle drawn by a pair of matched greys was already slowing down. Its driver brought it to a smooth halt that barely raised the dust on the road. As Miss Seymour's hopeful gaze met a pair of curious hazel eyes, the slight sense of caution that had held her rigid vanished. Even seated, the owner of the curricle was seen to be of an imposing size, tall and massively built, but the mild expression of his pleasant regular features was most reassuring.

"May I be of some assistance to you, ma'am?" he inquired, raising his hat politely.

"Yes, if you would be so good, sir. I am heading for the Green Feather Inn farther along this road and have had the misfortune to lose the heel of my boot. If it would not inconvenience you, I would be most grateful if you could convey me to the inn."

"Of course, ma'am, with the utmost pleasure." As he spoke, the driver had signed to his groom sitting beside him to get down, and the latter proceeded to assist Miss Seymour into the curricle. In another few seconds the man had gotten up behind, and the driver had given his horses the office to start.

Miss Seymour sat back with an exclamation of relief. "I am more thankful than I can say, sir, for the chance that brought you to this spot at this moment. Do you know, I have been walking on this road for over an hour and yours is the first vehicle to pass? I do trust it will not inconvenience you to deliver me to the Green Feather?''

The driver of the curricle looked into slightly anxious brown eyes and smiled reassuringly. ''Far from it, ma'am. I am myself headed for the Green Feather.''

''Oh, good.''

The dazzling smile with which Miss Seymour favoured her rescuer caused that gentleman to draw in his breath audibly. He stared into her glowing face for some seconds, as though mesmerised, then blinked and returned his attention to his driving. After a moment he said in a voice of creditable calm, ''If you will permit me to introduce myself, ma'am, I am Sir Hugh Lanscomb of Meadowlands.''

''How do you do? My name is Victoria Seymour.''

Sir Hugh turned to his passenger, a touch of curiosity in his eyes. ''I am slightly acquainted with a Mr. Richard Seymour.''

''That was my father,'' she said quickly in response to the hint of a question in his tones.

''Was?''

''Yes, he died two years ago.''

''Miss Seymour, I beg you will forgive my *maladroit* tongue. Please allow me to offer my belated condolences.'' Real contrition showed in the countenance he presented to her. As she made a gesture of acceptance, he continued, ''My only excuse is that my acquaintance with your parent was of the slightest and I have been away from the area for an extended period. In fact, I have only recently returned to my home after military service in America.'' He hesitated briefly before going on in a diffident fashion. ''I must confess that my prospective visit to the Green Feather is not just coincidence. I had cause to summon Dr. Jamison to my home yesterday. In the course of our conversation he happened to mention that he was treating a patient by the name of Andrew Massingham at the Green Feather. It is not a particularly common surname, and it occurred to me that this might possibly be the same man I served with in the Peninsula. Consequently, I am on my way to the inn to discover if I may assist in some way if the patient should turn out to be my old comrade in arms.''

At the beginning of this speech Vicky had turned eagerly to face the driver. Now she broke in to assert that Mr. Massingham had indeed served in the Peninsula under Wellington.

"And you would be the cousin who has been nursing him so devotedly?"

"Why . . . yes."

If Sir Hugh noticed the reluctance with which this assent was produced, he made no comment, but went on to say, "Then you will be able to tell me if this is the same man. My friend was from Sussex."

When she didn't reply immediately, he removed his attention once more from his horses and looked inquiringly at the woman sitting in embarrassed silence beside him. In her turn Vicky subjected the face of her companion to a protracted scrutiny. What she saw must have reassured her, for she said with only a trace of constraint, "Mr. Massingham is not really my cousin. I only put that story about to placate Mrs. Tolliver, who was looking for a reason to refuse us assistance. The truth is that Mr. Massingham's intervention saved me from being abducted by a highwayman who held up my coach a few nights ago. I said what was expedient to ease our path in the emergency."

"I . . . see. Then Mr. Massingham was unknown to you before this incident?"

Again Vicky hesitated, but she drew confidence from the nonjudgmental expression on Sir Hugh Lanscomb's fine-featured countenance. He appeared every inch the gentleman, and she yielded to an uncharacteristic impulse to confide in someone. She lifted troubled eyes to his and confessed the whole story.

Vicky was uncomfortably aware, as she lapsed into silence, that Sir Hugh's groom had probably heard every word she had uttered, and could only trust that his was a reticent nature. Normally she wouldn't have spoken before a servant, but there had been no time to consider. When she failed to identify the patient's home, Sir Hugh would have known that she had lied about her relationship to Mr. Massingham. In the circumstances, she had made a lightning decision to acquaint him with all the facts. As the silence between them stretched out, she began to wonder if she had made the right choice. Perhaps the smoky situation had given him such a disgust of the affair that all inclination to be of service had fled his mind. They were approaching the village street now, and she flicked a covert glance at his unrevealing profile as he checked the speed of his horses. The inn was no more than a half-mile distant now.

"It is rather an awkward situation, to be sure," he said finally with quiet understatement, "but it strikes me that our first consideration must be Major Massingham's recovery. In that respect, perhaps I can prove helpful. I came prepared to offer the hospitality of my home to him during his convalescence. Nothing you have told me would mitigate against this course. I am aware from Dr. Jamison that you have been in constant attendance on Major Massingham, ma'am, under trying conditions. You must be longing to return to your home."

Vicky permitted herself a small nod of agreement in response to Sir Hugh's questioning look, and he became businesslike, requesting a report on his comrade's progress. By the time they entered the inn, with Miss Seymour in her broken boot leaning on her escort's arm, they had arrived at an understanding.

Vicky ran upstairs to see if Mr. Massingham was able to receive his caller, stopping only long enough to put off her bonnet and pelisse and change to soft house shoes. Within a minute or two she presented herself at the door to the sick-room and was admitted by George, one of the footmen from the Oaks, dispatched by Cavanaugh to shave the invalid now that his fever had abated. In response to her murmured question, he revealed that Mr. Massingham had been awake for over half an hour and seemed much stronger than in the morning.

Vicky dismissed the footman to his dinner and stood for an instant just inside the door, unaccountably reluctant to approach the man watching her in silence from the bed.

"Do come in, Miss Seymour," he invited with smooth civility. "Granted, we have not been formally introduced, but I am told that in all probability I owe my life to your nursing talents. It would seem that circumstance should constitute a sufficient introduction even in the highest circles.''

Which circles I'll go bail you don't grace, thought Vicky, misliking his tone and instantly on the defensive. At least his lightly coated sarcasm sufficed to release her from that temporary paralysis.

"You need not regard that circumstance, however, Mr. Massingham," she replied with suspicious sweetness. "Since *in all probability* your timely intervention saved me from a fate worse than death at the hands of that brutish highwayman, I would say the honours are even.''

She had been gliding forward as she spoke, and now paused at the foot of his bed, looking, did she but know it, particularly lovely with sparkling eyes and colour deliciously heightened by her time outdoors. If Mr. Massingham was aware of this circumstance, he concealed it admirably, reacting by no more than a slight narrowing of dark eyes as she came closer. There was no trace in his lean countenance of the admiration that had been so evident in Sir Hugh's just moments earlier. Nor was the formal speech of gratitude for her stint of nursing which he next uttered delivered with a degree of warmth that would lend credence to his sincerity. Miss Seymour accepted it with a small bow and an equally meaningless polite disclaimer, after which she remained silent, waiting for his next move.

He certainly looked a different man today, and it was not entirely due to the removal of a four days' growth of beard. His eyes had lost that feverish glint and were normally alert, which meant about half again as active as the average person's. Even from a sickbed he seemed to radiate controlled energy. Only the laboured quality of his voice betrayed his debilitated condition. Miss Seymour continued to stand quietly at the foot of the bed, her natural stock of sympathy for an invalid rapidly dwindling in the face of Mr. Massingham's ill-concealed hostility.

"Well, ma'am," he said when the pause had lasted overlong, "what next?''

As he spoke, he was trying to heave himself into a sitting

position by using his elbows. Miss Seymour was at his side on the instant, assisting him and placing pillows to support his position more comfortably.

He thanked her briefly, adding with a strong sense of ill usage, "I cannot imagine why I should be so unfit. I'm as weak as a cat."

"You have been very ill with a fever for days, and of course you have lost a lot of blood," she explained in matter-of-fact tones. "The wound bled very freely before we got you here, and Dr. Jamison cupped you on the following day."

"*You let that leech drain my blood?*" Outrage was easily distinguishable on his features, and Miss Seymour sought a change of subject to avoid an argument.

"Are you acquainted with a man called Sir Hugh Lanscomb, Mr. Massingham?" she inquired hastily. "He is waiting below stairs, if you feel able to receive him."

He seemed to be struggling to readjust his thinking to encompass this new factor, saying at last, "I knew a Colonel Lanscomb once, but that was a long time ago."

"Well, he knew a Major Andrew Massingham in the Peninsula. Shall I send him up?"

"Yes, of course."

Miss Seymour was aware of his eyes boring into her back as she left the room at a pace she kept decorous with an effort of will. It would not do to show weakness before the enemy. Rather breathtaking, the speed with which her patient had reverted to his former position of adversary in her thinking.

In the public room she found Sir Hugh making himself agreeable to Drucilla, who, on seeing her hostess, exclaimed with delight that the newcomer was an old friend of her *fiancé*'s.

"Yes," said Miss Seymour, smiling at them both. "If you are *Colonel* Lanscomb, he does indeed remember you and will be delighted to receive you."

"My father was still living in those days," Sir Hugh replied by way of explanation before making his excuses to Drucilla as he prepared to accept Miss Seymour's escort to the sickroom.

Vicky opened the door after a tap to announce their arrival, then stood back to allow Sir Hugh to enter.

"I would not have credited it on any report other than the evidence of my own eyes," this gentleman jeered as he headed for the big bed with outstretched hand. "Major Drew Massingham, the scourge of Napoleon's forces, flattened by a common highwayman."

Vicky backed quickly out of the room so that she only half-heard her patient's ribald answer before the door closed. She was still smiling as she started down the stairs, but the intrusive memory of her recent acrimonious meeting with the man for whom she had concentrated all her energies for the past three days wiped the smile from her lips well before the bottom stair was beneath her foot. She chided herself for having experienced the slightest surprise or chagrin at her reception by Major Massingham once he was restored to the full possession of his senses. The situation was now exactly as it would have been had not the accident and a spell of nursing intervened. But for her interference he would be married to his heiress by now and would not have a hole in his leg. Naturally, she was not his favourite person at the moment. With a resolute shrug she banished the irritating Mr. Massingham from her thoughts and went into the coffee room to sit with Drucilla until supper.

7

Two events of interest occurred at the Green Feather the following morning. Dr. Jamison, on his regular visit, was so greatly pleased with his patient's progress that he agreed to his transfer to Meadowlands on the next day. He sent word to Sir Hugh, who replied that his travelling coach would be available for transport at any hour designated by Mr. Massingham and the doctor. On hearing this news from Sir Hugh's groom, Miss Seymour felt free to make arrangements with her own staff for her return to the Oaks as soon as her patient had removed from the inn.

The other occurrence was the delivery by the same groom of a note addressed to Miss Seymour, containing a politely worded invitation to the two ladies staying at the inn to take tea that afternoon at Meadowlands. Miss Seymour read this epistle, which was signed Harriet Lanscomb, with a little surprise but every inclination to accept. An outing of any sort would be a treat for poor Drucilla, who had borne the discomforts of the last few days without complaint. Until yesterday the child had not even been allowed to share in the nursing of her former *fiancé*, which task, though most worrisome in the beginning, at least had the benefit of keeping one from dwelling on the tedium of a sojourn in a tiny inn with few amenities.

For her part, Vicky would be happy to extend her personal thanks to Sir Hugh's mother (for so the lady identified herself) for her extension of hospitality to Mr. Massingham. She had to admit also to harbouring some curiosity as to Sir Hugh's background. It must be thought a trifle unusual that such a personable gentleman could have reached the age of four- or five-and-thirty without being married. The women of the area must be a very unenterprising lot, she thought with a gleam of mischief. She also admitted to herself that she was more than passingly desirous of seeking an opportunity to find out something about Mr. Massingham from Sir Hugh, who, before his departure the previous evening, had merely confirmed the acquaintance with a civil expression of pleasure on coming downstairs after a short visit with the invalid. Just how to phrase a query that essentially asks a man whether a friend might be a fortune hunter was a ticklish problem that would have to wait upon the opportunity. Miss Seymour dispatched by the waiting groom an acceptance of the invitation couched in civil terms that did not reveal her eagerness to pursue the acquaintance. She then divulged to Drucilla the treat in store for them and was gratified by the young girl's obvious pleasure. Drucilla headed upstairs to examine her limited wardrobe for a suitable costume in which to take tea with Lady Lanscomb, but before Vicky could do the same, Sukey entered the public room. The youngster dipped a clumsy curtsy and announced in carefully rehearsed phrases that Mr. Massingham presented his compliments to Miss Seymour and desired an audience with her at her earliest convenience.

Correctly interpreting this request as an imperious summons, Vicky smoothed out the incipient frown that appeared whenever she thought of Mr. Massingham and presented herself at the door to the sickroom. Her knock produced a command to enter, delivered with an impatience that travelled through the wooden portal. She wiped all expression from her face and approached the bed under his critical stare, noting in passing that several books and a bowl of fruit had been delivered from the Oaks to add to the patient's comfort. He was freshly shaved and there was some healthy colour in his cheeks today.

"Good morning, Mr. Massingham. You are looking much improved."

The man on the bed made a dismissive gesture with one

hand. "What is this nonsense about our being cousins, ma'am? The doctor has been singing the praises of 'your cousin, the nurse,' and the landlord's daughter referred to you as my cousin when she removed my breakfast tray."

"Whatever happened to 'good morning'? Illness has not improved your manners, Mr. Massingham." Vicky's silky tones sent a surge of dark red up under his cheekbones, and his lips compressed briefly.

"Good morning, ma'am. Thank you for your concern. I am feeling much better today. I trust you are enjoying your customary good health?"

Vicky ignored the sardonic inflection and replied suitably. Mr. Massingham drew an impatient breath and repeated his original question.

"The explanation is simple, sir. The assumed kinship was an expedient measure to discourage the scandal broth that Mrs. Tolliver scented on our arrival. You were going to require constant nursing and I was the only person available at the time. It has served its purpose; you may now repudiate the connection, though I beg you will wait until you are quit of this place."

"And my *angel*? That fool girl made some giggling reference to my 'angel.' Is that you too, ma'am?"

"I'm afraid so, but that is entirely your own fault!" The coolness she had maintained throughout the first explanation deserted her under a sustained regard from hostile dark eyes. Black brows escalated, inviting further comment, and Miss Seymour rushed on. "You became delirious within hours of the operation. You mistook me for an angel and refused to let anyone else minister to you. We feared that in your agitation you might do yourself some permanent injury, so you were allowed to have your own way, even though it meant I got very little sleep."

Several fleeting expressions—astonishment, disbelief, disgust—chased across Mr. Massingham's arrogant features. Sympathy for his nurse or regret for the trouble he had caused were conspicuous by their total absence.

"Well, I must accept your account of the matter, ma'am,

since evidently there were abundant witnesses to my . . . my aberration." He ignored the resentful stiffening of the slim figure facing him and went on in disgusted tones, "Marvelous the tricks one's mind can play on one, mistaking you for my good angel when all the time you have been playing just the opposite role in my life!"

"I beg your pardon!" she exclaimed in scathing accents, drawing herself up to her full height. "Allow me to tell you, Mr. Massingham, that I do not choose to play *any* role in your life! I shall be quite content to have our acquaintance, such as it is, cease this very minute!"

"Hah! It's a bit late for that, ma'am! What do you call abducting my *fiancée*, if it's not playing my bad angel?"

"I did no such thing, and well you know it! Drucilla came with me most willingly. She was desperate to escape from your clutches. If a charge of abduction is to be levelled by anyone, it will be by her uncle against *you*, sir!"

He dismissed this diatribe with a wave of one hand. "Gammon! No matter what she told you, the chit came away with me of her own free will. And if it had not been for your interference, ma'am, your officious *meddling*, none of this would have happened!" gesturing to his bandaged leg. "Do you realise, Miss Seymour, that had you started out one hour earlier or one hour later on your journey, I'd be a happily married man by now? You're worse than a bad angel, you're *Nemesis!*"

Vicky curled her lip scornfully and gave him look for look, her own golden-brown brows elevated. "Happily married? Wealthily, I grant you, but *happily*?"

"With a little piece of perfection like Drucilla for my bride, how could I be other than the happiest of men?" He assumed an air of bland surprise that was oddly incompatible with his saturnine features and brought a considering look to the light brown eyes studying him dispassionately.

"Perhaps," she conceded dryly, "you *could* be happy with a bride who stands in absolute dread of your foul temper and dictatorial ways—and who is young enough to be your daughter into the bargain."

Surprisingly, he laughed out at that. "Oh, come now, ma'am. I am only two-and-thirty. I cannot permit you to think me so precocious as to have been fathering children at the tender age of fifteen. No, no, I must decline the compliment."

Miss Seymour ground her even white teeth and snapped "Considering the unelevating tone of your conversation, Mr. Massingham, it is small wonder that a day cooped up in a travelling carriage with you should have caused Drucilla to have second thoughts about going through with a marriage that never meant more to her than an escape from difficult home conditions."

"Second thoughts she may have had, ma'am, but they were no more than the irritation of the nerves most brides experience before their weddings. Saving your interference, she would have speedily overcome them."

"You seem exceptionally well-versed on pre-wedding jitters, Mr. Massingham. One might wonder if this was not your first experience at eloping with an heiress."

"Don't hide your teeth out of any consideration for my feelings, I beg of you. Say what you mean."

"Very well." Miss Seymour immediately availed herself of this indulgence. "Since an honourable man would have presented himself to Drucilla's guardian to request permission to pay his addresses, I strongly suspect that you are a fortune hunter. Therefore it must be a source of satisfaction to me that I have succeeded in providing the poor child with an opportunity to extricate herself from what would have been a disastrous mistake."

"I suggest that your self-congratulations may be a bit premature." There was a hint of a white line about Mr. Massingham's compressed lips and more than a hint of venom in his voice. "It is not my intention to defend myself, since your tenuous relationship with my *fiancée* entitles you to no explanations, but I'll give you fair warning that I have every intention of proceeding with the marriage as soon as I am on my feet again."

Vicky shrugged this aside. "Naturally I have no real authority over Drucilla. If she were so misguided as to deceive herself that yours could be a happy union, there would be nothing I could do to stop her. That would be up to her uncle.'' Before her antagonist could reply to this implied threat, she brought the subject to a close. ''Come, sir, enough of this useless dagger drawing. You would do better to restore your strength by following Dr. Jamison's orders for your convalescence. I daresay you will be very happy to leave this place. At least you will have more comfortable surroundings in the home of your friend.''

For a moment Vicky's aloof expression had warmed to a slight smile, but there was no answering softening of Mr. Massingham's countenance as he made a curt acknowledgment of her sentiments. Nothing about her former patient's demeanour induced a disposition to linger in his company, and she took herself off to her room to dispatch a message to the Oaks containing instructions for her staff.

At three that afternoon Sir Hugh's carriage arrived to transport the ladies to his home. Each had taken pains with her appearance in honour of the occasion, and the results were delightful. Drucilla was attired in a frothy white muslin sprigged with tiny red flowers that made the most of her petite figure. Red ribbons at the high waist and puffed sleeves fluttered when she moved and matched the cherry-coloured hat that so became her dark curls and sparkling eyes. The day was too warm for a pelisse, so she had draped over her arms a red shawl lent to her by her hostess.

After some thought Vicky had chosen a stiff cotton in the exact shade of the amber lights in her eyes. The style was deceptively simple, made high to the throat with long tight sleeves, but the delicate lace that trimmed the bodice and sleeves was exquisite. Drucilla went into raptures after her first glimpse of her friend when she came back to the room for fresh gloves. Lily was just handing her mistress a hat.

''You look positively beautiful, Vicky. That unusual colour makes your hair seem an even brighter gold by contrast. How I wish I could wear mine in a smooth coil like yours,'' she said wistfully, "but it will curl so, there is no doing anything with it at all."

Vicky laughed. "Most of the females I know would give their eyeteeth for hair that curled naturally like yours. Think of all the hours you don't spend wrapping it in curl papers!"

"You don't have to curl yours either to get that smooth gleaming look. You must have simply yards of hair!"

"My father would not allow me to cut it," Vicky explained with an almost imperceptible quiver of her lips. "The style is not at all fashionable, though, my dear, just a means of keeping it out of the way so I can get a hat on, and if I should desire to dress it for a party, it takes hours to arrange. One of these days I am going to chop it all off." Vicky was setting a narrow-brimmed hat of brown straw at a daring angle atop her shining hair as she spoke.

Drucilla gasped. "Never! It would be a crime—a sacrilege—even to think of cutting it! How I wish I were an elegant blonde like you."

Vicky chuckled again as she anchored the hat with a dangerous-looking pin. "You have just proved that females are never satisfied with their lot. I have often longed to be transformed into an exciting dark-eyed beauty with raven curls like yours."

"Though brunettes may come into fashion occasionally, gentlemen generally gravitate to the blondes," the other girl insisted, shaking her curls mournfully.

But when, a few minutes later, they went in to parade their finery before Mr. Massingham, something Drucilla insisted to a reluctant Vicky that she had promised faithfully to do, it was evident that one gentleman at least preferred brunettes over blondes. Certainly his quick eye missed nothing in summing up the older girl's appearance, from the crown of her dashing hat to her soft kid shoes, but his attention was expeditiously transferred to the younger, whom he proceeded to shower with well-turned compliments.

"Flatterer!" Drucilla scoffed gaily, her dimples playing hide and seek as she looked down her pert little nose at him. "Why you should suppose me to be so corkbrained as to swallow all that butter is a thing that has me in a puzzle.''

"Saucy minx!" Mr. Massingham grinned at her affectionately and provoked a giggle.

This spontaneous smile, the first she had been privileged to witness since meeting him, produced quite another reaction in Vicky. It took years from his age and transformed him in a twinkling from a churlish Byronic hero to a pleasant-tempered man who might cause flutterings in any young girl's heart. It crossed her mind that his feeling for Drucilla might be deeper and more sincere than she had credited to him, and she experienced a momentary compunction for the part she had played in the abortive elopement. This regret was transitory, however, because whatever his feelings, a runaway marriage could only lead to social ostracism for his young bride. Still, she stood observing their interplay with sharpened senses, though only half-hearing the exchange of badinage as she attempted to distill the emotion behind it. She was alerted therefore to the look of triumph, quickly disguised, that he cast her way as Drucilla blew him an airy kiss before departing the room.

"Enjoy your visit at Meadowlands, Miss Seymour," he said pleasantly as she prepared to follow Drucilla.

"Thank you, I am persuaded I shall, Mr. Massingham."

"Hugh is a good chap, sober, reliable, a solid citizen. No one could disapprove of *him*."

"I feel sure you are quite correct, sir." Vicky looked back over her shoulder, her expression surpassing his in guilessness.

"And his manners are particularly pleasing, are they not?"

"They are indeed. Why, Drucilla was saying the very same to me just these few minutes past." With that young lady halfway down the stairs and out of hearing by now, Vicky felt safe to offer the bold lie and was rewarded by a swift gathering of the invalid's formidable brows.

"You look a trifle off colour, Mr. Massingham. We must have tried you. Try to rest while we are away," she urged with sweet solicitude as she closed the door gently behind her.

The drive to Meadowlands was short, taking no more than

twenty-five minutes, and was enlivened by chatty observations from Drucilla. There was one awkward moment when Vicky gently requested her young guest to refrain from making any reference to Mr. Massingham as her *fiancé*, or indeed to any prior acquaintance with that gentleman while in Sir Hugh's home. Innocent dark eyes were turned questioningly to her, but she nipped Drucilla's instinctive protests in the bud by explaining that, apart from keeping Drucilla herself totally unencumbered during her visit, silence on this subject would spare Mr. Massingham a degree of embarrassment amongst his hosts, "because it is not at all the thing, you know, my dear, to persuade a minor into an elopement."

"But Sir Hugh already knows," blurted out the girl.

"Yes, but I would wager my mother's pearls that he will agree with the wisdom of this course, and it would be advisable to have his mama regard us simply as two ladies who were rescued by Mr. Massingham. It is fortunate the Tollivers don't employ any outside servants who might gossip, for nothing ensures the spread of rumour faster than having the servants get wind of it!"

Though she could not quite like the necessity of denying Drew's importance to her, Drucilla saw the wisdom in keeping silent. Vicky made a mental note to acquaint Sir Hugh with this decision, assuming that he had not already revealed the true situation to his parent.

Their first glimpse of Meadowlands provoked unreserved admiration from the ladies. It wasn't a particularly imposing structure, being neither of great size nor impressive antiquity, but featured a graceful balanced facade in the style that had become popular during the reign of the first George. The house stood three stories high, of rosy brick, and was graced by large white-painted sash windows that gave it a cheerful open look. It was attractively surrounded by well-maintained green lawns and formal shrubbery with large shade trees at a small distance.

"Oh, it's lovely!" breathed Drucilla, her eyes taking in every detail of the scene before her.

"Yes, very neat and pretty," agreed Vicky.

THE LUCKLESS ELOPEMENT

The carriage had scarcely stopped in front of the central entrance portico when the door opened and their host strolled out to meet them. After cordial greetings were exchanged, he escorted them to the ground-floor drawing room, where two ladies awaited the callers. Looking at the elder, who had come forward to meet them, Vicky found her description "neat and pretty" as applicable to Lady Lanscomb as to her residence. Sir Hugh's mother was an attractive, well-preserved woman of neat appearance, whose smile contained just the correct degree of welcome for acquaintances of her son's. Her waistline may have thickened somewhat with the inexorable passage of time, but she was still a fine figure of a woman, small and trim, with only the slightest sprinkling of grey amongst the soft nut-brown tresses showing beneath a dainty lace cap. Her smooth skin displayed a fresh colour and she welcomed her guests in a soft pretty voice that was consistent with the image she projected of youthfulness retained far into middle age.

"And this is my mother's ward, Miss Elaine Fairchild."

Sir Hugh beckoned to the other person in the room, who came forward a trifle hesitantly to be presented. Vicky, who was used to consider herself fairly tall for a woman, was obliged to look sharply upward to meet the blue eyes of Miss Fairchild, who easily topped her own five and a half feet by another four or five inches. The girl, for she appeared to be no more than nineteen or twenty, was built along queenly lines also, but her statuesque figure was perfectly proportioned and she carried herself well. She had unremarkable though regular features in an oval face framed by lovely golden-brown hair. In any other company than that of the massive Sir Hugh she would be bound to stand out, and Vicky made a shrewd guess during the next half-hour that self-consciousness about her size might account in large measure for Miss Fairchild's extreme shyness. When spoken to directly, the girl answered intelligently, but she volunteered no opinions and uttered no unsolicited remarks. Lady Lanscomb treated her like a daughter and was unsparing in her attempts to draw her into the conversation. Miss Fairchild called her guardian Aunt Hattie and obviously returned her affection.

The situation with Sir Hugh was not quite so clear-cut, Vicky decided after a bit more observation. He seemed to regard his mother's ward in the light of a young sister, addressing her by her first name with the familiarity of an indulgent brother, but though she called him Hugh, Miss Fairchild did not match his ease of manner. Watching the two young girls engaged in somewhat stilted conversation, Vicky couldn't help contrasting Drucilla's chatty vivacity with Elaine's innate reserve. She was thinking that the older girl was doomed to suffer agonies of embarrassment when she made her come-out next spring (as Lady Lanscomb had announced) if she was this ill-at-ease with the gentleman she knew best, when Miss Fairchild turned her glance on Sir Hugh as he spoke to Drucilla.

In the next instant she was staring down again at the hands in her lap, but the look had lasted long enough for Vicky to read the hopeless yearning in large blue eyes and to understand the root of Miss Fairchild's constraint. Involuntarily her own eyes searched Sir Hugh's benign countenance for some sign that he was aware that his mother's ward was in love with him, but if he was conscious of the fact, he concealed it perfectly during the tea party. He continued to treat Miss Fairchild with a brotherliness that must have been torture to a sensitive girl who longed for his love.

Glancing toward his mother from time to time, Vicky became convinced that her hostess did not share her son's blindness, and she began to make some sense of little nuances that had struck her as odd earlier. The comprehensive scrutiny from hazel eyes like her son's when he had made the introductions no longer seemed a trifle out of character with Lady Lanscomb's overall softness. Vicky had not been at all disconcerted by the slightly probing nature of her hostess' questions, since in her experience the major concern of middle-aged ladies was generally the personal affairs of all those who entered their orbit, however temporarily. There had been one or two moments, though, when she had wondered if she detected the faintest hint of antagonism in Lady Lanscomb's attitude toward the visitors. The next moment she had chided herself for indulging an excess of sensibility.

No one could have charged Sir Hugh's mother with being remiss in any attentions to her son's new acquaintances; she performed her duties as hostess with graciousness and charm. Puzzling this out while she watched Lady Lanscomb refill Drucilla's cup and present it to her with a smile, Vicky could only conclude that, whether intentional or not, the impression had been left that their hostess had performed her duty conscientiously but entertained no personal desire to pursue the acquaintance.

Sir Hugh, on the other hand, had let it be seen that he had every intention of doing just that. Though his manners were too good to permit him to ignore the claims on his attention of the other ladies present, he had, in his quiet way, clearly conveyed his admiration and interest in herself. Miss Fairchild's downcast eyes and Lady Lanscomb's frozen smile might be indications that they too had discerned this preference.

At one point Vicky expressed the sense of her obligation to her hostess for her kindness in offering shelter to Mr. Massingham during his recuperation.

"Not that Miss Seymour wouldn't have seen to his every comfort at the Oaks, ma'am," Drucilla had interpolated loyally. "Her servants have been wonderful to him at the Green Feather, but it will be delightful for Dr . . . Mr. Massingham to enjoy a visit with an old friend."

"My dear Miss Hedgeley," her hostess replied with amused condecension, "there could be, of course, no question of Mr. Massingham's convalescing at Miss Seymour's home. As I am sure she would explain to you, her status as an unmarried woman would always preclude such an arrangement." She smiled kindly at the young girl, who had been thrown into acute confusion by this sweetly uttered set-down; then she tactfully changed the subject to draw attention away from Drucilla's flushed countenance. Vicky, who certainly had reached the same conclusion herself, firmly suppressed a sudden impulse to challenge her hostess' complacence by announcing that she would have housed the invalid had not Sir Hugh come forward when he did.

He came forward now, saying with his slow smile, "I am persuaded, Mama, that Miss Seymour would have found an unexceptionable way to supervise Major Massingham's convalescence had I not appeared on the scene. She is a young lady of great resourcefulness, and I am aware that she feels deeply indebted to him for his rescue efforts during the holdup."

This led to a lively recounting of the robbery for the benefit of the Meadowlands ladies by Drucilla, who confessed that she would never live down the shame of having fainted at the crucial moment.

"Well, I for one cannot take you at fault, my dear child," declared Lady Lanscomb with a shudder. "Such a terrifying experience would be sufficient to overset the nerves of any female of sensibility. I do not at all wonder at your reaction."

Perhaps she herself should beg pardon for having remained conscious, Vicky was thinking when Drucilla leaped to an animated defence of her friend's courage and presence of mind in standing up to the highwayman.

"That will do, my dear," Vicky intervened, and shifted slightly in her chair to face her hostess directly. "The simple truth is that I have never been so frightened in my life, ma'am, and in the end it was really my coachman who saved the day, not I."

"But you actually shot the thief, did you not, Miss Seymour?" asked Miss Fairchild in her first unprompted remark of the afternoon.

Vicky smiled at the quiet-faced girl. "Yes, Miss Fairchild, but I must confess it was rather desperation than courage that squeezed the trigger, and"—she pulled a rueful face—"the only result was to enrage the highwayman, who would surely have done me great injury had not Amos, my coachman, come to his senses in time to drive him off with his whip."

"I still hold that it required great resolution and courage to take a stand," Miss Fairchild said quietly.

Sir Hugh smiled warmly at his mother's ward. "I am persuaded we are all in agreement on that point, Elaine. Miss

Seymour is far too modest, but we must not embarrass her further.'' He rose to his feet and extended a hand to Vicky. ''I propose to change the subject by taking her into the study for a moment to show her a book that her father very kindly sent me a half-dozen years ago.''

''Why do you not ask Ferris to fetch the book, Hugh?'' Lady Lanscomb was quick to suggest. ''No doubt we should all enjoy seeing it.''

Her son chuckled at that. ''What? A book on horse breeding, Mama?'' he teased. ''You have always held that it was not a fit subject for a lady's drawing room. Miss Seymour happened to mention that she shares her father's interest in breeding thoroughbreds, so I hoped she would be pleased to see it.''

His mother's thin smile was a mere formality, but she made no further attempt to prevent the *tête-à-tête*, and Sir Hugh escorted his guest down the hall to a pleasant book-lined room facing the back gardens.

While her host searched for the book in question, Vicky looked around her, admiring the handsomely panelled walls between sections of shelves and the view of the shrubbery glimpsed from the long windows. She wandered over to the fireplace to study a portrait of a large man in hunting dress, with Sir Hugh's cast of countenance but iron-grey hair. ''Your father?'' she asked as he approached carrying a thin volume. ''You are very like him except for having your mother's eyes.''

He chuckled again. ''Mama is wont to say that if it were not for the fortuitous passing on of her hazel eyes, no one would ever believe she had produced such a hulking specimen as myself.''

''You are certainly a large man,'' Vicky agreed. ''Miss Fairchild, too, is taller than most females, though she is so attractive and beautifully proportioned, one is put forcibly in mind of the heroic statues of ancient times.''

''I wish Elaine could take such a sanguine view of the matter. The poor child is convinced that her size will quite destroy her chances of forming an eligible connection, which is nonsense, of course. I try to joke her about it and have promised to comb the town for suitors who can look me in the eye, but she persists in believing herself destined for spinsterhood.'' He shook his head, marvelling at the irrationality of females, while Vicky privately railed at the inability of some men to see what was under their noses.

"She will soon lose these fears, once she gets caught up in the gaiety of the Season,'' she predicted lightly.

"That is what I have assured her repeatedly. And it isn't as if she were portionless, after all. She is very well dowered.''

Vicky bit her lip to keep from asking if he had repeatedly assured Elaine of this advantage also. Really, men were abysmally obtuse! "May I see the book?'' she asked instead, with a glittering smile that concealed her impatience. She recognised it as a copy of one in her father's collection on the subject, and they spent a moment or two discussing the views put forth by the author.

"That is how I became acquainted with your father,'' Sir Hugh volunteered. "We happened to sit down together at a horse sale, and one thing led to another. He was so kind as to send me this after our meeting, but before our friendship could proceed further, my regiment was ordered to Spain, and I never saw him again. I regard it as a great pity.''

Vicky smiled at him through eyes suddenly gone misty. "My father was a marvelous companion; I still miss him dreadfully.'' She stared fixedly out of the window for a moment, striving to get her emotions under control, and only half-heard Sir Hugh's hasty remark that he had had another reason for bringing her to the study.

She raised her golden-brown eyes to his. "Yes?''

"After giving the matter some thought,'' Sir Hugh began in his serious way, "I decided to tell my mother and Elaine only the bare facts behind your presence at the Green Feather. As far as they are concerned, Major Massingham was a stranger whom chance led to the scene of the robbery. It seemed to me—and I hoped you would concur—that the simpler the tale, the better, under the circumstances.'' He looked a question and Vicky nodded slowly. "This way,

Drew can simply be my old friend, and there need be no embarrassment in future intercourse between the two households. For a moment in the drawing room I feared Miss Hedgeley might betray a prior acquaintance that would have led to awkward explanations.''

''I warned her not to,'' Vicky put in quickly, ''but Mr. Massingham has served notice on me that he still intends to pursue an elopement if he can secure Drucilla's consent, which he has little doubt of obtaining, though I do hope that by writing to her uncle I may have succeeded in putting a spoke in his wheel.''

Sir Hugh was looking grave. ''I must confess that I cannot regard an elopement with anything but the strongest disapprobation—the clandestine nature of the act itself, plus Miss Hedgeley's extreme youth, must cause their well-wishers and her family the severest misgivings—in short, I have determined to impress upon Major Massingham that while he is under my roof, Miss Hedgeley is to be regarded in exactly the same light as any other young woman of his acquaintance . . . yourself or Elaine, for example.''

Miss Seymour tempered the exultant nature of her satisfaction at this development into a careful expression of considered agreement with Sir Hugh's conclusions. Then, taking a shallow breath, she experimented with a look of fluttering appeal. ''Sir Hugh, may I be frank with you?''

''I hope that you will realise in time that I shall always welcome your confidence, Miss Seymour.''

''Thank you.'' She swept her long lashes up and down again in pretty gratitude, then appeared to hesitate before plunging. ''Sir Hugh, though it grieves me deeply to entertain suspicions about a friend of yours, and indeed one who has rendered me a signal service, I . . . that is, the nature of this elopement must necessarily give rise to some conjectures. I have no knowledge of Mr. Massingham's circumstances, but Miss Hedgeley seems to be a considerable heiress, and I cannot help wondering if . . . that is . . .'' She paused delicately, and Sir Hugh obligingly came to her rescue.

''You are quite naturally wondering if Drew's offer for

Miss Hedgeley's hand might have been motivated by a desire for worldly advantage. I should hate to think it, and indeed I should be surprised to find it so. It was common knowledge in the regiment that he is old Lord Mallard's heir—at least he is next in line for the title," he added with scrupulous attention to accuracy. "I realise this is not conclusive proof of his solvency or his disinterested affection. Nor do titles and fortunes invariably go together, though Lord Mallard is rumoured to be very wealthy. That is the extent of my knowledge at present."

"I do trust you are correct, Sir Hugh. My mind is much relieved." Vicky produced a soft smile designed to conceal her private reflection that, despite Sir Hugh's avowed disinclination to believe ill of his friend, a title in the offing was no guarantee of pure motives as the basis of Mr. Massingham's pursuit of Drucilla. She contented herself with having planted the warning, though if it had been really necessary she would think less of Sir Hugh's perspicacity in future.

Her mission accomplished, an attentive and relieved Vicky encouraged her host to expatiate on the contents of his library as they strolled back to the drawing room. There they found the two girls happily absorbed in conversation and the mistress of the establishment giving a fine performance as a mother *not* counting the minutes that her son has been absent in the company of a female who could wreck her plans for his future. Lady Lanscomb continued in this vein, expressing civil regret that the young ladies would not be able to stay to dine, and when they took their departure shortly afterward, almost outdoing her guests in the graciousness of her *adieux*.

8

Despite an emphatic denial from his guest, Sir Hugh could see by the pallor that belied his brave words that the short journey from the Green Feather had taxed Mr. Massingham's returning strength. Closing his ears to protests, he had the invalid installed in a bedchamber without delay. And there Mr. Massingham languished, well cosseted but unvisited by his host until the following morning. He had just consumed an enormous breakfast and was accepting a second cup of coffee from Ferris when Sir Hugh entered the large well-lighted chamber that looked over the carriage drive at the front of the house.

"Ah, that smells good. If there is another cup, Ferris, I'll join Mr. Massingham."

"Certainly, sir. I took the precaution of having another cup sent up," replied the butler without a flicker as he poured out the aromatic liquid from a silver pot. "Will there be anything else, sir?"

"No, that will be all, thank you, Ferris."

"Very good, sir." The butler signalled to a silent footman to remove the large breakfast tray, leaving just the coffeepot. After an encompassing glance around the room to see that nothing had been omitted, he followed the footman out, closing the door soundlessly behind him.

"What an admirable creature, anticipating your every wish!" exclaimed Mr. Massingham in mock awe. "You do yourself proud, Hugh."

Sir Hugh, unmoved by his guests's teasing, studied his face as he took a sip of the steaming brew. "You are looking decidedly better this morning. How does the leg feel?"

The other man grinned. "It feels fine until I drop something on it like that book a few minutes before breakfast arrived; then it hurts like the very devil. I shall try walking on it a bit later."

"Not until Dr. Jamison has signified his approval, you shan't."

Mr. Massingham's expression grew stormy, but the fire died out of his eyes as his host continued to sip his coffee, his hazel glance steady and calm as ever.

"When is that damned leech coming?" the patient demanded irritably.

"He said he'd call in around noon."

Mr. Massingham looked mollified and made an effort to remember his manners. "I haven't even thanked you properly, Hugh," he said a trifle awkwardly. "It's good of you to put up with me. I've thrown your whole household into an uproar."

"Nonsense. Did Ferris appear to you to be crumbling under the strain of your presence?"

"God, no!" Mr. Massingham laughed. "He strikes me as one who wouldn't start at the blast of the last trump. He'd finish whatever task he was performing before presenting himself for judgment."

This sally drew an appreciative smile from Sir Hugh.

"All the same, I'm mighty grateful to you for having me."

His host brushed aside this attempt at thanks. "Nonsense," he said again. "I plan to enjoy your company immensely as soon as you are on your feet, and Mama and Elaine will delight in cosseting you in the meantime."

"Elaine?" queried Mr. Massingham. "You didn't mention a wife the other evening. Is Elaine your sister?"

"Practically, I suppose. She is my mother's ward and a most agreeable girl."

"Ah! An heiress perhaps?" inquired Mr. Massingham with a knowing smile. "May I wish you success?"

A short silence succeeded this pleasantry; then Sir Hugh

sighed resignedly. "You never did know the first letter of the word tact, Drew. If that dark face and clacking tongue of yours hadn't made it a simple matter to pass you off as a Frenchie so he could slip you behind the lines on occasion, Wellington would have banished you to the farthest outpost of the campaign."

"He kept me at arm's length unless he wanted information. Said I was too brash by half," Drew admitted ruefully. "You did say she was like a sister to you. I was out of line there, though I meant nothing by it."

"No, but now that you have broached the subject, I think we might clear the air a bit. Miss Seymour tells me you intend to go on with this elopement if Miss Hedgeley acquiesces."

"So she told you about that, did she? She would."

"She could scarcely have avoided the issue under the circumstances," Sir Hugh pointed out in a reasonable spirit, "so you needn't look as ugly as bull beef. Miss Hedgeley is only seventeen, and she was in some distress when Miss Seymour found her. You could not expect anyone who possessed a conscience to abandon the child without making a push to rescue her."

"Good Lord, anyone would think I'd abducted the girl! Drucilla was mighty eager to elope with me, which she'll tell you herself if there is any truth in her. What was I supposed to do when she started putting on die-away airs in Stamford, eighty miles from London? Could I bring her back at that point, and no one the wiser, when she'd been gone all day and left a note behind detailing her intention to marry me?"

"You were in a bit of a cleft stick, to be sure," conceded Sir Hugh, "but we needn't consider that at this point. I gather Miss Seymour's credit is good enough to envelop Miss Hedgeley's absence in an aura of respectability if her uncle keeps his wits about him." He looked a question.

"I have heard of the family," replied Mr. Massingham grudgingly. "She is a niece of Lady Honoria Blakney, I believe. M'mother and Lady Honoria were bosom bows back in their schooldays."

"Then all's right and tight so far." Sir Hugh eyed his brooding companion and charged ahead abruptly. "Is your heart set on wedding this girl?"

"I've run away with her, haven't I?"

Sir High considered this reply for a moment, then said slowly, "Miss Seymour fears that your primary interest may be in Miss Hedgeley's fortune."

"That woman's a menace! Except for her interference, I'd be married by now. And I'd be a good husband to Drucilla, too!"

The other man made no comment on this evasion, but asked instead, "Why did you not obtain her guardian's consent to the match?"

The dark eyes of the man on the bed shifted away from his host's and his lips tightened. For a time it seemed he had no intention of answering, but after a charged silence he turned a deliberately blank gaze back to the patiently waiting Sir Hugh. "Her uncle don't approve of me or my rackety existence. He's a fanatical Methodist—rails against dancing, gambling, racing, everything, in fact, except attending lectures by dissident preachers. Thinks Drucilla should sit home and sew or visit the sick in her spare time. Won't let her have pretty clothes or go to parties—at least not Ton parties."

"Miss Hedgeley was quite fashionably attired on the two occasions on which I have been in her company."

"She bought some of those things on the sly and the rest before we left town. Kept me waiting and walking the horses for over an hour before we could set off. Very determined girl, Drucilla."

"However did you meet her? It doesn't sound as though you travelled in the same circles at all."

"That was pure chance. She and her aunt were in a hackney carriage that bolted when a dray cart broke loose and ran across the street. I was on horseback and managed to stop the hack before any damage was done. The ladies were grateful and the aunt gave me permission to call. Things were going along swimmingly until the uncle decided I wasn't a proper influence on a young girl. So we had to find ways to meet without his knowledge."

"Or you could have dropped the acquaintance, since Miss Hedgeley's guardian did not approve of the connection." Sir Hugh ignored Drew's thinned lips and flared nostrils. "What about Lord Mallard? From what you have told me of Drucilla's family, I cannot help wondering if he too might not regard such a marriage as a *mésalliance*."

"I would not be at all surprised."

Something in his friend's voice caused Sir Hugh's gaze to sharpen. Drew was facing the fireplace, but Hugh was seized with a sudden conviction that those dark eyes were staring at an internal picture, not perhaps a pretty picture, but one that was affording him a certain grim satisfaction.

"My esteemed great-uncle had done me the honour of selecting my bride." The man on the bed glanced back at his host, and the absolute stillness of expectancy encouraged him to continue. "Her lineage, as you may imagine, is impeccable. No, Drucilla won't win my uncle's heart with her black eyes and dimples. Her birth's unexceptionable on the paternal side, but just let him get wind of a pack of religious merchants!" He let out a rude crack of laughter and lapsed into silence.

Curiosity and good breeding warred in Sir Hugh's breast for a time when it looked as though Drew had finished with the subject. Eventually curiosity triumphed. "Was the girl an antidote?"

"Who? Oh, my uncle's choice! No, she's quite good-looking if you like 'em cool, blond, and heartless, which I emphatically do *not*! She's in the same style as the Seymour female."

"I scarcely think any *female* who nursed a patient around the clock for days could be accurately described as *heartless* by the beneficiary of that devotion, unless he himself had too little heart to recognise the quality," declared Sir Hugh, not bothering to conceal his contempt.

Mr. Massingham had the grace to look ashamed. "I shouldn't have said that," he admitted honestly. "The woman has only done what she thought was her duty, but you must see that she's thrown my life into chaos!"

"What were *you* doing to your life by contracting an

impulsive marriage that will be much disliked by both families?''

There was another tense pause; then Mr. Massingham quoted in a flippant tone that contained more than a trace of bitterness, "I am 'one whom the vile blows and buffets of the world have so incens'd that I am reckless what I do to spite the world!' ''

"If by 'the world' you mean your great-uncle," retorted Sir Hugh, reducing the high-flung quotation to prosaic terms, "how does your reckless marriage spite him?''

Drew looked at his friend with a kindling eye. "My uncle's choice of bride was not merely a suggestion, you understand; it was an order! And do not be thinking the affair was to be gracefully arranged with a noncommittal introduction performed by a mutual friend and the two parties being given an opportunity to become better acquainted under pleasant conditions like a house party. My uncle had no opinion of such niminy-piminy foolishness as that! To him a facade of good manners is sheer hypocrisy, as well as a waste of time, a commodity about which he is almost as clutch-fisted as with money. No, I was summoned to his side almost the moment I returned from Brussels and presented with a *fait accompli*. He believed it high time I married, he had selected a suitable girl for the honour, she was waiting in the pink saloon, and I was to lose no time in making her an offer.''

"Rather disconcerting," murmured Sir Hugh.

"To say the least! The only insult he omitted was in not having the girl present while he delivered the ultimatum.'' Drew raised a hand to forestall any comment. "And whatever you may believe about my lack of finesse, Hugh, I remembered that he was an old man and that he was out of touch with my generation. I even reminded myself that he was desperate to see me married with a son who would keep my cousin Harry out of the succession. I had had to keep him in the dark about joining the army," he explained in an aside. "He despised Harry's father wholeheartedly, so that my health is a great concern to him. I promised him that I would meet the girl with an open mind.

"Now, you might think he'd be pleased to find me so amenable, but not he! He merely threatened to cut me off with the proverbial shilling if I did not do as he commanded."

"And you could not bring yourself to comply?"

"Not after I saw whom he had chosen for me, not for two fortunes!"

"Dear me. And yet I believe you said the girl was not unattractive?"

"Oh, Melissa's pretty enough—at least I imagine a stranger would find her so—until he got to know her for the vain, cold, vindictive, and heartless creature she is and always has been."

"You were already acquainted with this unappealing lady?"

"All my life, or so it seems. The families were friends. She was always around during my childhood, and many's the punishment I've endured because of that lying vixen and her tricks. But that is neither here nor there, though the fact of her being still unwed at twenty-seven should tell you something. I told the old man as gently as I could that nothing on earth would induce me to marry her. I even offered to take her younger sister if it was the breeding that concerned him, but he flew into a rage. I wouldn't have been surprised to have seen him carried off then and there by an apoplexy. Roared all the traditional oaths, warned me never to darken his door again, cut off the allowance he had made me while I was in the army, and promised to change his will so that I'd never see a penny or an acre that wasn't part of the entail."

"While you were remembering his age and his desire to keep your cousin out of the succession, perhaps you should have recalled also that he held the purse strings," suggested Sir Hugh dryly.

"I have no intention of dancing to any tune of my great-uncle's piping."

Sir Hugh read stubbornness in the set of his friend's jaw, and resentment in his narrowed eyes. "And so, to show Lord Mallard that he had no power to command your obedience, you cut off your nose to spite your face by embarking on this marriage venture," he summarised, not mincing words.

"It wasn't like that," protested the man on the bed, moving his legs restlessly. "Drucilla's a delightful piece, and a man must live, after all. I might be able to retrench and manage on my income if I were still at Heather Hills, but the place is leased for the next fifteen months. After my mother died, the estate started to go downhill. I couldn't trust the bailiff when I was out of the country, so I had my lawyer lease it for me. I didn't know I'd be coming back to England so soon. Life is damned expensive in London. One has to spend the time doing something! I've run up some debts and—"

"How deep in dun territory are you?"

"Not too badly dipped, though without that allowance I'll never come about." He shrugged broad shoulders under the brocaded robe. "Some people live on their expectations for years, never more than one step ahead of the tipstaffs. I don't want that."

"Hence Miss Hedgeley?"

"Well, I admit I had not planned on becoming a tenant for life for a while yet, but it's a solution, and if I must be married, I'd as soon marry Drucilla as any of those whey-faced milk-and-water misses that parade through Almack's every year. She's good fun and good-tempered, though I did think she had rather more spirit. But," he added philosophically, "one can't have everything, and though I have no desire to sound like a coxcomb, she certainly did not need much persuading into that elopement."

"Perhaps she wished to spite *her* uncle also."

This suggestion, offered in a somewhat facetious spirit, was considered seriously by Mr. Massingham.

"That may be part of it, but the girl is attached to me, and I'm not going to let her down by crying off now. That *would* be the act of a cad. I'm well aware Miss Seymour thinks me no gentleman, but I wouldn't sink so low as to break that girl's heart!"

After two meetings with Miss Hedgeley, Sir Hugh's opinion was that her heart was made of sterner stuff than her betrothed imagined. He would have said she was simply testing her wings, so to speak, and had not as yet formed a lasting attachment. Before he had the opportunity to articulate this observation, however, a disturbance at the door heralded the arrival of Ferris with the information that Lady Lanscomb and Miss Fairchild would like to meet Mr. Massingham if he felt able to receive them.

At Drew's nod, Sir Hugh told Ferris to show the ladies up. He barely had time to warn his friend not to betray any prior acquaintance with Miss Hedgeley, a command that brought a lowering scowl to the latter's face, when Lady Lanscomb entered the room in a soft rustle of skirts. Elaine slipped in behind her, and the butler withdrew.

Sir Hugh performed the introductions, drawing up chairs for the ladies around the huge tester bed.

Mr. Massingham was staring thunderstruck at the older woman. "No, no, you are hoaxing me, ma'am," he protested, raising his hostess' extended hand to his lips. "I *might* be persuaded to accept you as Miss Fairchild's mama, but it is inconceivable that you could be the parent of this great gawk. It is pure anachronism!"

"Pshaw, you naughty man!" exclaimed Lady Lanscomb, all dimples and smiles. "Hugh told us that you were noted in the regiment as a fearful tease, but he failed to mention that you were also a flatterer!"

Mr. Massingham clutched his left breast in agony. "Your doubt of my veracity wounds me to the quick, my lady. Someone has been traducing my character."

"Fustian!" declared her ladyship, settling happily onto the chair nearest the bed. "It's my guess that for once rumour has been most accurate."

When Sir Hugh left the room in response to a message five minutes later, his lively parent and his outrageous guest were well-launched on a light-hearted flirtation under the appreciative eye of his mother's ward.

9

Humming softly, Miss Victoria Seymour let herself out a side entrance and headed toward the stables at a leisurely pace. Overhead, two or three cotton-puff clouds appeared stationary in a dazzlingly blue sky. The grass under her feet was soft and resilient, the air was warm with the barest hint of an autumn nip—a glorious day, perfect for exercising Shadow, perfect for any outdoor activity, perfect for simply existing. There was a spring in her step, and the gravel under her feet made a satisfactory crunching sound. Her booted feet executed a little skip as she flung her arms up into the air in an all-embracing gesture of delight, following which she cast a quick embarrassed look around, hoping none of the servants were observing their mistress' odd behaviour. She was still completely alone, and once more she experienced that strange little tingle of pleasure in solitude that had occurred when she walked on the road leading from the Green Feather.

Coming home had been the right thing to do. That deepening restlessness and *malaise* that had overtaken her in London must have been the result of the constant need to deal with an unending stream of people. There was no privacy in a city. One week at the Oaks and she felt like a new person, relaxed, confident, contented. Though social contacts were much fewer, her interest in the people around her was rekindled. Drucilla was delightful company, fitting happily into the quiet country life for the present. Her curiosity and interest in every aspect of country living gave Vicky a new outlook on the existence she had always known.

They had not been entirely without social contacts this past sennight. Lady Lanscomb and Miss Fairchild, escorted by Sir Hugh, had called a few days ago with cheerful tidings of Mr. Massingham's progress. The squire's lady, accompanied by her two daughters, had dropped in one afternoon to welcome their neighbour home. Without her aunt's presence it wouldn't be possible to do any extensive entertaining at the Oaks, but she and Drucilla would surely be able to accept invitations from the genteel families in the vicinity for evening parties. It might not be London society, but Drucilla would not find Leicestershire devoid of attractions.

Mr. Mortimer, Drucilla's uncle, had replied to her letter in civil though slightly grudging terms. He had expressed his gratitude for her intervention in the elopement attempt and agreed that his niece might remain in Miss Seymour's care for a time to lend credence to the story of a visit to an old friend. Fortunately Mrs. Mortimer had had the presence of mind to give a visit as the explanation for her niece's absence after she had discovered Drucilla's note, so the household had not been set in an uproar before the advent of Miss Seymour's letter, and they thus had every hope of avoiding gossip. Vicky had wondered on receiving Mr. Mortimer's cool reply if he had read the notice of her broken engagement in the papers. Though it seemed unlikely that a devoutly religious merchant would be interested in society news items, it would adequately account for his coolness. She was persuaded her life-style would appear scarcely more commendable than Mr. Massingham's in Mr. Mortimer's eyes. Drucilla, when shown her uncle's letter, had not even noted the absence of warmth in her pleasure at obtaining permission to remain with Vicky. She had written an explanation and apology for her hasty action in eloping and now danced away to write another note expressing her gratitude and requesting a larger portion of her wardrobe.

Once settled at the Oaks, Vicky had found time to send one additional letter, a detailed account meant for the delectation of her aunt of her adventures with runaway heiresses, fortune hunters, and highwaymen. So far she had not had any reaction from the outspoken Lady Honoria, but that was one missive she was watching for with mischievous anticipation. Picturing her aunt's chagrin at missing all the excitement brought a little smile to Vicky's lips now as she slipped into the stables to pick up a snaffle bridle for Shadow. She exchanged a few pleasantries with two of the stable lads and was caught when her voice reached the ears of Manley, her father's head trainer. He was convinced she would wish to check on the progress of a mare with a sprained tendon. Since it was always quicker in the long run to go along with the testy Irishman than argue with him, Vicky dutifully examined the mare's leg and agreed that the swelling had gone down considerably. She advised him to continue the cold treatment, which he would have done in any case, listened with concealed impatience to a list of supplies that were urgently required, and at last make her escape when one of the grooms came up to speak to Manley.

Safely outside once again, Vicky wasted no more time admiring the autumn scene. She had left Drucilla contentedly practicing on the pianoforte, but it would be uncivil to abandon a guest indefinitely to her own devices. No longer humming, but whistling a march tune, she speeded up her footsteps directed toward the field where Shadow grazed.

A sense of well-being softened the lines on the face of the man riding up an avenue of large trees. A perfect day for his first substantial outing, a good horse under him and no more than a tenderness in the wounded leg; all conditions contributed to this momentary contentment. He slowed to a walk, ambling along the avenue admiring the handsome oaks and the lush green fields on either side of him. Pleasant country, Leicestershire. His enforced stay had certainly offered compensations. Life at Meadowlands this past week had been relaxing and serene after the frenetic pace of the last few months and the tense period that had followed his abortive elopement. Physically he was nearly recovered, and mentally he had been soothed and warmed by the companionship of the family at Meadowlands. Lady Landscomb was a marvelous hostess, fully attuned to her guests' comfort without hovering over them or infringing on their privacy. Hugh was a good chap too, a trifle pedantic perhaps and overly conventional, but with a good-natured acceptance of others' differences. Miss Fairchild also contributed to the pleasant atmosphere. Although too big for his taste and much quieter than the females of his acquaintance, she was an agreeable companion and he liked her modesty and complete lack of affectation. Not a girl to expect a man to cater to her whims. Not very exciting, but would undoubtedly make some fellow an unexceptionable wife.

His hosts had conspired to keep him sedentary for several days, though his leg had rapidly grown stronger. He had not been permitted to accompany them when they had returned Miss Seymour's call.

He found himself very curious about the establishment he was approaching. It had been apparent from the luxurious travelling coach that his erstwhile nurse was not purse-pinched, and her clothes, though restrained in style compared with those of other ladies of his acquaintance, were of the finest fabrics and workmanship. Lady Lanscomb and Miss Fairchild had been much impressed by the size and air of settled elegance about the Oaks. Hugh had divulged that he was astonished at the scope of the horse-breeding operation still carried on by Miss Seymour since her father's demise, and astounded to realise the extent of her personal involvement in the business. Miss Victoria Seymour was apparently a woman of parts. This unusual background undoubtedly accounted for that arrogance and unfeminine decisiveness that was so unnatural in a young woman. Not that she was all that young, of course. Though she looked scarcely older than Drucilla and Miss Fairchild, there was a certain distinction and an air of assurance that set her apart. That might be attractive to some men; certainly Hugh appeared to be completely enchanted with the woman, but it was otherwise with himself. He

113

infinitely preferred females who stayed in their own orbit and left the decisions and the business enterprises to their menfolk. Drucilla was much more in his style, even if she was silly and frivolous at times. His own mother had been a capable woman, but she had never left one with the impression that she considered herself entirely capable of conducting her affairs without consultation or assistance from any man.

Small wonder Miss Seymour remained unmarried despite her undeniable beauty and tangible assets. What discerning man would care to take on the burden of a wife who clearly thought herself his superior, be she ever so beautiful and well-endowed? *He* would not. It was supremely ironic that he should have discovered a woman with looks, birth, and fortune who shared his chief interest in raising horses and yet remained totally ineligible in his eyes. If his doddering but dictatorial great-uncle could see past the tricky Melissa, he would consider Miss Seymour the ideal bride and himself a certifiable madman for not having a touch at the heiress.

Not that she would give him a second look, of course. From the very first clashing of eyes in that inn dining parlour, instant and mutual antagonism had flared up between Miss Seymour and himself, which, when one stopped to ponder the matter, was a fairly bizarre reaction between civilised persons of the opposite sex. He frowned suddenly, a swift gathering of black brows, and for a moment was oblivious of his surroundings while he pursued an elusive thought, but presently he concentrated on smoothing his expression. The matter was too unimportant to warrant pondering. Why was he wasting time thinking about that irritating female in any case, when it was Drucilla he had ridden out to see today? If he was to combat the insidious effect of Miss Seymour's disapproval, it was vital that he continue to see his *fiancée* as often as possible. Fortunately the two households appeared to be in the process of consolidating the new relationships formed so accidentally. As a guest at Meadowlands he would naturally be included in communal activities, but he had elected to take his attack to the enemy unaccompanied on this first visit, in case Miss Seymour's attitude caused undesirable speculation amongst the Meadowlands ladies. He had taken the precaution of not mentioning his destination when he had ridden out an hour ago.

Somewhere to his left, movement and colour brought Mr. Massingham to a new awareness of his position. While lost in thought he had not observed the thinning of the trees or the presence of another living soul, but now he realised there were two creatures in addition to himself enjoying this beautiful day. He reined in to watch a magnificent black horse cantering about in a large fenced-in field on the left of the avenue. The horse was being ridden bareback by a youth, and the communion between the two brought a smile of empathy to Mr. Massingham's lips as he automatically headed his horse toward the near fence to get a better view.

The cantering pair made a splendid splash of colour in the green field under intense blue sky. The observer could not see a spot of any other colour on the black horse. No blaze or stockings interrupted the pure ebony of his glistening coat. His rider provided abundant contrast in fawn breeches and white shirt under a sleeveless brown vest. The youth also wore a flat cap of some kind in a startling clear red crushed down over his hair. The colours became a blur as, under the appreciative eye of the newcomer, the black stretched smoothly into a gallop at an unseen command from the rider crouched low over his neck. Around the entire perimeter of the field the two flashed in perfect harmony.

Mr. Massingham gave a soft whistle. "My God, what a turn of speed! If that animal belongs to Miss Seymour, she's got herself a winner!"

Horse and rider were slowing down now. The black trotted past the nearest spot to Mr. Massingham's position and the latter could sense the residual elation in animal and jockey as they headed for a spreading tree at the corner of the field.

"Well done, lad!" shouted their admirer impulsively.

Mr. Massingham surprised even himself by his exuberant compliment, but the effect on the unknowing pair was electric. The black had almost come to a stop, and the rider was

easing back from his position on his neck when the lust
shout rang out on the still air. Before Mr. Massingham'
horrified gaze the startled horse planted his forefeet and
kicked out with his back legs. His rider, caught between
positions, changed direction and went flying over his head
landing with a thump that whitened Mr. Massingham's cheeks.
He was off his own mount and over the fence in an instant,
ignoring the twinges of protest in his weak leg as he sped
toward the still figure on the ground. He thought, he *hoped*, it
was only a case of having the wind knocked out; it didn't
seem as though the lad had hit his head in landing. There
could be broken ribs, though; the boy was slightly built. A
stream of medical possibilities including the necessity for
finding splints for broken bones was jumbling through Mr.
Massingham's head as he reached the fallen boy at the same
time the black horse reached down and nuzzled the ear of his
rider.

"Stop that, you brute, you might hurt him!" growled Mr.
Massingham, pushing the velvety nose aside unceremoni-
ously as he knelt beside the prostrate form and reached for a
wrist.

The delicacy of this wrist and the almond-shaped nails on
the white hand below it almost rocked Mr. Massingham off
his heels. His incredulous gaze flew past the black's head,
which was still nuzzling the figure on the ground. The horse
had dislodged the red cap that had tilted over its wearer's
right eye after the fall. Golden hair spilled from under the cap
over the brown shoulders and the green grass.

Disbelief, heart-stopping fear, and black rage struggled for
mastery in Mr. Massingham's breast for a second of acute paralysis until the necessity to act attained the ascendancy. He
concentrated on counting the pulse in the limp wrist still in
his hand. Relief coursed through his body at finding it nearly
normal. He carefully replaced her hand at her side and started
to examine her limbs for possible broken bones. All this was
accomplished with patient unwinking precision, and until he
had satisfied himself on this score, he kept his eyes on his
probing fingers. He ascertained that shoulders and collar-

bones were also intact before reluctantly turning his eyes to the colourless features of the girl on the ground. A muscle twitched in his cheek and his teeth were clamped tightly together. Just for a heartbeat her stillness revitalised the fear that was driving him, but her breasts beneath the silk shirt were stirring slightly and regularly. He brushed a tendril of hair from her lips, noting as he did so that the waxy pallor was being replaced by a faint returning colour in her cheeks. Long brown lashes, golden at the tips, stirred, then lifted slowly. Golden-brown eyes stared dazedly into intense grey-black ones, closed again in murmured protest. *"Oh, no!"*

"Oh, yes, Miss Seymour. You are still amongst the living despite that foolhardy stunt."

"If I am still amongst the living," the victim replied in a voice that was rapidly gaining strength, "it is no thanks to you! I suppose it *was* you who shouted and spooked Shadow?" When her eyes opened this time, the haziness had disappeared, to be replaced by animosity.

He glared back at her. "I admit my yell was ill-timed, but what were you doing trying to ride that brute bareback? Of all the perilous, ill-advised, bacon-brained, *unfeminine*—"

"Nonsense!" she interrupted this catalogue briskly. "Shadow and I understand each other perfectly, and if you don't mind, I'd prefer to hear the lecture standing on my feet."

As she struggled to rise, the angry face just above hers came even closer for a second. Despite the best will in the world to offer battle, her weakened condition prompted an involuntary retreat from the danger therein. Long lashes sank and she could not control a faint tremour in her lips. She turned her head aside to hide her weakness and set herself the enormous task of getting to her feet again. This effort, however, was denied her as two strong hands grasped her shoulders and stayed her progress while their owner hoarsely demanded, "Does it hurt to breathe? There is a possibility you may have damaged your ribs in that fall."

Vicky managed a negative shake of her head, though she was actually none too sure that everything inside her was functioning correctly. There was a very odd sensation in the pit of her stomach for one thing, and her breathing was peculiarly ragged, though not precisely painful.

A moment later, when she had been set gently on her feet, she could add dizziness to her list of symptoms. She closed her eyes to shut out the disturbing vision of the oak trees whirling against the sky and would have buckled at the knees had the band of iron across her shoulders been removed. Thankfully, it was not, though Mr. Massingham did shift his other hand from her shoulder to her chin, which he lifted. She felt strangely defenceless under his intent scrutiny of her wan countenance but was too taken up with fighting the giddiness to raise objections.

"Are you all right, no pain anywhere?"

"I'm fine, thank you."

In proof of this brave statement, Miss Seymour gathered all her resources and stepped back from her rescuer's arms. She opened her eyes cautiously. To her infinite relief the world had stopped spinning and her legs were bearing her weight again. She raised her chin, which felt chilled now that his hand had been removed, and attempted a smile.

"Thank you. I am feeling more normal every minute." She reached a hand up to pat the neck of the black, which had not moved off throughout the entire rescue operation. "Poor Shadow is trying to apologise for his behaviour just now. In general he is a perfect gentleman, you know. You startled him."

"Yes. I apologise. He's a beauty, and built for speed. Nice small head and sloping shoulders, plenty of heart room behind that deep chest, I'd say." Mr. Massingham gentled Shadow and walked all around the motionless colt. "Not short of bone, and good rounded quarters; good, clean, well-defined knees; in fact, beautiful conformation altogether."

This knowledgeable praise of her favourite brought a glow of pleasure to Miss Seymour's lovely face. For once she was totally in charity with Mr. Massingham. "He's a magnificent animal and has a generous disposition, too."

"How old is he?"

"He's two."

"A young two, surely?" said Mr. Massingham, seizing the colt's bridle and looking at his teeth.

"Yes, he was foaled in June. My father was alive then and he predicted from the start that we had bred a champion. His dam is descended from the Godolphin Arabian."

"Do you intend to enter him on the circuit next year?"

"I hope to, if he continues shaping well."

"You shouldn't be riding him, especially without a saddle. Let him get used to a jockey who can race him for you."

"I intend to train him my way," said Miss Seymour, her tone revealing her objection to this gratuitous piece of advice.

Mr. Massingham shrugged. "You could ruin a good horse that way, but there's no denying he's yours to ruin."

Miss Seymour gasped at the insult conveyed. She did not trust herself to answer, but her eyes shot arrows of rage at the uncaring man before she turned her back on him and picked up a piece of sacking she had brought with her. When she started rubbing down the colt, she found the cloth taken from her hands.

"You shouldn't be doing this after the shaking-up you have had," he said roughly, proceeding to do the work himself.

Miss Seymour hunched a shoulder and allowed him to perform the task for her. There was no further conversation while Mr. Massingham attended to the horse, and Miss Seymour, suddenly overwhelmed by a dismayed realisation of the dishevelled picture she must present, tried to straighten her appearance. She brushed loose grass and dirt from her breeches and retucked her shirt into the waistband, frowning at the grass stains on the elbows. Her hair had come loose from its neat coil, and a cursory search of the ground failed to turn up any of the pins.

Mr. Massingham had been concentrating on Shadow during this cleaning-up process, but when she seized the red cap and started to bundle up her long hair under it, he intervened. "Must you make more of a figure of yourself than you already have in that ridiculous costume? Leave it alone."

"I thought I made rather a handsome youth," retorted Miss Seymour defiantly, continuing her efforts to stuff the golden mass under the cap.

"Well, you don't. You wouldn't fool a blind man."

"I fooled you. You called me lad."

"From behind and from a distance only." The roving glance Mr. Massingham sent slowly over her long-legged and slim-hipped figure in clinging knit breeches was insultingly comprehensive and lingered on her breasts, heaving with ill-contained fury. Colour flared into her cheeks and she dropped the cap from fumbling fingers.

They bent together to retrieve it and cracked heads.

"*Ouch!* Now look what you've done!"

Tears that were more fury than pain sprang to Vicky's eyes, and Mr. Massingham's hands shot out to steady her as once more he assisted her to her feet.

"Again I apologise, Miss Seymour. Please allow me to remove the grass from your hair," he proposed in a neutral tone.

"Pray do not trouble yourself, sir. It does not signify." Vicky was very much on her dignity as she turned aside to head for the fence.

"Perhaps it doesn't signify to you, but when we appear at your door I'd just as lief not have your state of disarray laid at *my* door. People *will* talk, you know."

"Oh, you are *odious*!" snapped Vicky, even more flustered than before. She stopped short and began frantically combing her fingers through the blond tresses to loosen any bits of grass that clung.

"I begin to think I am," he agreed softly, watching her efforts for a time with a softened expression she didn't see. "Allow me, Miss Seymour."

Before Vicky knew what he was about, Mr. Massingham had moved behind her. He lifted the shining mass away from her shoulders, then gathered it together in one hand. With the other he meticulously picked out any remaining blades of grass or straw.

At his first touch she had attempted to pull away from him,

but the inevitable yank on her scalp as he held on kept her motionless, though fuming, for the few minutes it took to rid her hair of all foreign matter. When the task was finished, he ran a smoothing hand down the silken length to restore order to the degree possible without a brush. His other hand reached to repeat the gesture, then clenched in midair and returned to his side. His teeth were clenched too as he stepped back, but she didn't see that either.

"You'll pass muster now," he promised tonelessly.

"Thank you." Vicky cast him a fleeting glance before walking purposefully toward the next fence. Mr. Massingham went back to retrieve his horse, and presently came up with her at the edge of the next field, where she had opened the gate. He was carrying Shadow's bridle.

"You may leave him here to graze if you like," she offered. "I have been gone longer than I intended. Drucilla will be wondering what has become of me. I left her playing the pianoforte, but it is nearly teatime. What brings you to the Oaks, Mr. Massingham?"

"I came to visit my *fiancée*."

"If you are referring to Drucilla, it would be more accurate to describe her as your former *fiancée*. I believe she has come to the realisation that one shouldn't choose one's life partner hastily."

"Hastily or not, it will come to the same thing in the end."

Vicky opened her mouth to refute this, but before she could utter a syllable, her attention was diverted to the avenue, where the sound of horses and the rattle of wheels on gravel proclaimed the approach of a vehicle. They had been walking across the fields toward the back of the house and the stables. She paused and put up a hand to shield her eyes as she peered through the trees trying to identify the carriage that was about to turn to the right to go around to the main entrance.

"More company for tea," predicted Mr. Massingham lightly.

"I cannot appear before guests like this," Vicky said, indicating her masculine attire with a frown. "I shall have to slip in the back way and change. You, sir, may present yourself at the front door as if just arriving, while I . . . Good heavens, it *can't* be!'' she exclaimed, breaking into a run as the chaise pulled by four horses turned onto the carriage drive that circled around to the front.

''Who can't it be?'' asked Mr. Massingham, loping along beside his hostess.

''My aunt!''

10

"Your aunt? Do you refer to Lady Honoria Blakney?" asked Mr. Massingham, suiting his steps to Vicky's as she cut across a corner of an area of shrubbery to head for a gate in the brick wall.

"Yes, of course. Why, how do *you* know my aunt's name?" she demanded, pulling up short and facing Mr. Massingham squarely.

"She and my mother were school friends."

"You *know* my aunt?" Vicky was astounded.

"I was used to, but I haven't seen her since I was a schoolboy myself. It must be all of fifteen years," mused Mr. Massingham.

"Why did you never mention the fact before?"

He looked faintly surprised at the suspicious expression on Miss Seymour's face, but answered readily, "The subject never came up."

Vicky showed a disposition to question this simplistic response, but the man gestured to the wooden door. "Through here?"

She nodded absently and led the way through the gate onto a flagstone terrace that bordered the carriage drive. Her thoughts were in a whirl, but there was no time to examine them, for her aunt's travelling chaise, with its trim newly painted bright yellow, had already pulled up to the entrance as a second carriage loaded with baggage entered the drive. Cavanaugh was opening the chaise door as a breathless Vicky arrived in front of the entrance with Mr. Massingham in tow. She had just time to note the oddity of a saddle horse tied to the back of the coach when a familiar figure descended stiffly from it, assisted by Cavanaugh.

"Aunt! How glad I am to see you, but why did you not let me know that you were coming?"

Vicky launched herself at her relative, embracing her exuberantly until the older woman complained, "That's enough, child, you've knocked my new hat askew."

"And what are you about, wearing such a quiz of a hat in the first place?" teased her niece gaily. "I leave you for no more than a fortnight and you appear . . ." She broke off to stare openmouthed at the man who had followed her aunt onto the drive. "*Gregory*! What are *you* doing here?"

"Victoria, you will give Ellerby a very odd notion of Leicestershire hospitality if you continue to goggle at him in that ridiculous manner," Lady Honoria said warningly. "He's here because I invited him, of course. I was very grateful for his escort on the journey."

"Yes, of . . . of course. How do you do, Gregory?" stammered Vicky, giving the embarrassed man her hand. "Please forgive my lapse of manners, but this is all so unexpected." Her eye fell on Mr. Massingham standing quietly at her side, regarding this newest arrival with interest. "Allow me to present Mr. Massingham to you both," she said quickly, feeling as witless as a Bedlamite under the combined onslaught of surprises. "Lady Honoria Blakney, Lord Ellerby, sir."

The men bowed politely, but before they could open their mouths, Lady Honoria exclaimed, "Massingham? *Andrew* Massingham?" The older woman peered closely at the man beside her niece in lively astonishment.

"The very same, Lady Honoria," he admitted, kissing her hand with a warmth that Vicky had never seen him display before. "It has been a very long time, ma'am, since I have had the pleasure."

A suspicious moisture shimmered in Lady Honoria's eyes.

"Andrew, I am persuaded I would have recognised the smile anywhere. You have changed, of course. You were only a boy when last we met, but you still have your mother's smile." Her expression grew sad. "I was terribly sorry to hear of Marie's death, Andrew, and glad I had seen her just two months before."

"Your letter was most welcome, my lady."

"Yes, well, we were very old and dear friends." She sighed and seemed to become aware of the others watching this tableau in silence. "Well," she said again, briskly this time, "how came you to be acquainted with my niece, Andrew?" Lady Honoria's eyes travelled to the bemused girl, and her gaze sharpened as she took in the masculine garb and the hair streaming over Vicky's shoulders. "Victoria! What have you been getting up to in that absurd costume?"

Vicky had been all too aware of Gregory's growing astonishment as he had assimilated her strange appearance. "I've been exercising Shadow," she explained hastily, avoiding Mr. Massingham's wickedly appreciative eye, "and I must change this instant. Come inside, everyone. Cavanaugh will show you to your room, Gregory, and we'll all meet shortly for tea."

She ushered the company indoors, striving to present a serene facade while longing desperately for some privacy in which to gather her scattered wits in preparation for a tea party which promised to be the ultimate in embarrassing confrontations. She could see that her aunt was determined to buttonhole her first and didn't know whether to be grateful or not when Mrs. Simmons, the housekeeper, appeared in the hall the moment they crossed the threshold and bustled over to welcome Lady Honoria. Mrs. Simmons was a voluble and purposeful woman. She took Lady Honoria under her wing and swept her upstairs while Cavanaugh escorted Lord Ellerby to a guest chamber. Thank heaven that Mrs. Simmons prided herself on being ready for guests at a moment's or even no notice!

With two of her problems temporarily accounted for, Vicky looked around and beckoned a footman forward to show Mr.

Massingham into the main drawing room, but not before that gentleman whispered with odious satisfaction, "You brought it on yourself, you know, by parading around in that revolting outfit."

Which was the outside of enough! A sorely tried Vicky flashed her unwelcome guest one look of loathing before flouncing off upstairs.

A half-hour later an outwardly composed but inwardly palpitating young woman made her reluctant way to the drawing room to preside over an assemblage of oddly assorted persons, not one of whom she could greet with honest pleasure at the moment. Her appearance at least was now above criticism. Thanks to Lily's nimble fingers, her hair was once more gathered smoothly back from her face and arranged in a neat coil at the nape of her neck. She was attired (or armoured) for the occasion in one of her newest gowns from London, a drifting and floating affair of finest mauve muslin rather daringly low-cut for daytime wear but undeniably feminine. Her head had begun to ache and there were bruises coming up in several places as a result of her recent toss, but none of this would be visible to the company.

Her brain had been scrambling in circles ever since the carriage had disgorged Lady Honoria and Gregory, or perhaps it might be more accurate to admit that she had already been confused by a variety of inexplicable sensations arising out of her afternoon dealings with Mr. Massingham before this newest complication occurred. Ordinarily she would have been delighted to welcome her favourite relative, but what demon had possessed her aunt to drag along her niece's rejected *fiancée*? Of all the awkward situations! And if the awkwardness of consorting with a former suitor on a daily basis in one's own home weren't conducive to sufficient embarrassment, there was the additional factor of an old and seemingly valued acquaintance between her aunt and the fortune hunter Vicky was determined to drive off.

How had she never heard of such a connection before? Lady Honoria had referred to Mr. Massingham's late mother as Marie, but the only Marie that she had ever mentioned to her niece had had a French surname. Vicky's brows wrinkled in concentration as she left the staircase and headed for the drawing room. *St. Croix*, that was it! Her aunt had been at school with a Marie St. Croix. Not that it signified if the two Maries were one and the same, of course. The real problem was how to explain Mr. Massingham's presence to the newcomers.

Vicky reached the drawing-room door and the conclusion that she must simply play everything by ear at the same time. She had already turned the handle when her name was softly called from behind. The door swung inward a couple of inches as she released the handle to turn around. Lord Ellerby, smiling somewhat diffidently, was approaching.

"I hope you found your room comfortable, Gregory?" she inquired with what she hoped was a natural smile of her own.

"Oh, yes, everything is perfect. Vicky, my dear, I fear my appearance has been an . . . unwelcome surprise to you. I did not know . . . that is, Lady Honoria did not tell me that you were unaware that she had invited me here. I must apologise."

"No, no, it is I who should do that," replied Vicky warmly, distressed by his obvious distress. "Of course you are always welcome, Gregory. It is simply that I was so surprised. I was not expecting *anyone*."

"If it is awkward for you, I shall go," he said quietly.

The devil fly away with Aunt Honoria! her undutiful niece fumed silently. This man was too fine to play games with. Her aunt must have led him to hope that she might be regretting her decision.

"No, please stay, Gregory. But you should know at once that this doesn't mean that I have changed my mind about marrying you."

"I haven't abandoned all hope yet," he said with a stubborn jut to his chin.

She shook her head and pushed open the door. Her first step inside brought her up against Mr. Massingham almost literally, and she jumped back like a scalded cat.

"I beg your pardon, Miss Seymour. I had intended to shut the door, which seemed to have opened by itself."

Vicky felt herself stiffening in suspicion. She distrusted the facile explanation. How much had he overheard? She and Gregory had been speaking softly, but that bold dark face was too bland to be believed.

She opened her lips, but whatever she might have said was lost in the simultaneous arrival of Drucilla from the music room and Lady Honoria from the stairs. Vicky hadn't spared her young guest a thought in the last hour, but she chuckled now at the girl's round-eyed surprise at the number of strange persons clogging the entrance to the drawing room.

"Do come inside, everyone. Poor Drucilla is at a loss, not having been informed of our visitors."

She shepherded her small flock into the bright, comfortable reception room and saw them seated after general introductions were made. Vicky may have forgotten about her house guest for a time, but all her faculties were suddenly concentrated on her as the young girl acknowledged Lady Honoria's greeting with a pretty curtsy before turning to extend her hand to Lord Ellerby.

Thinking back over the succeeding chain of events, it became obvious to Vicky that they had been privileged to witness the oft-written-about but rarely seen phenomenon that had inspired countless poets down through the ages, namely, love at first sight. At the time, she merely wondered, with a twinge of impatience, what had gotten into the girl. The gregarious Drucilla, whom her hostess had quite accurately labelled an instinctive coquette on the evidence of her previous behaviour in the company of gentlemen, was suddenly rendered tongue-tied. After one startled, wide-eyed look at Lord Ellerby's smiling face, her eyes fell, her colour fluctuated alarmingly, and she seemed to have lost the use of her motor functions.

Lord Ellerby's conventional smile faltered and he looked to his hostess for help. Ignoring the sudden scowl on Mr. Massingham's face, Vicky requested him to place a chair for Drucilla. She surreptitiously pushed the girl onto it while inquiring brightly of her aunt and Lord Ellerby for details of their journey. Once launched, this trial balloon took them through the arrival of the tea tray, by which time Drucilla had come out of her reverie to the extent that she was able to answer direct questions in a soft little voice. The fact that she avoided looking directly at Lord Ellerby over the next half-hour possibly went unnoticed by anyone but Vicky, who was beginning to get the glimmer of a suspicion as to the cause of her vivacious guest's present unnatural shyness.

Under cover of general conversation she tried to study Gregory with fresh eyes. It didn't take a prodigious imagination to see that he might easily be mistaken for a fairy-tale prince by an impressionable seventeen-year-old. His blond good looks and air of breeding would always make him an appealing figure even before one could discover the lively intelligence and good-tempered kindness that were an integral part of his nature. He was a thorough gentleman, too, and invariably treated the fair sex with a respect that bordered on reverence.

Her thoughtful glance lighted on Mr. Massingham's saturnine features as he lounged in a negligent posture. There could scarcely be a greater contrast in the attitude of the two men toward females. Perhaps a closer association with the charming Lord Ellerby might serve to point up Mr. Massingham's dearth of husbandly qualities without a word being spoken in his dispraise by Drucilla's hostess. In fact, closer acquaintance with Gregory might very well have—

"Victoria, where are you off to? I have spoken to you twice," complained Lady Honoria, breaking in on her niece's mental scheming.

"I'm so sorry, Aunt, I was woolgathering, I fear. What did you say?"

Vicky smiled brilliantly into shrewd old eyes that narrowed in response.

"I still haven't learned how you became acquainted with Andrew. Such a strange coincidence," mused her aunt in all innocence.

All conversation seemed to have ceased for the moment. Across from her, Drucilla replaced her cup on the tea table with a little crash. She was blushing furiously and staring at her hands clenched in her lap. Mr. Massingham, the fiend, was sitting at his ease, wearing the expectant expression of one about to enjoy a good story, and Gregory was politely attentive.

Vicky fixed her aunt with a warning look and said tonelessly, "Mr. Massingham chanced to come upon us just after a highwayman had held up my chaise. He helped to thwart an attempt to abduct me, and got shot for his pains."

It was apparent from Lord Ellerby's horrified exclamation that he had been told nothing about the holdup, but before Vicky could relax, Lady Honoria had given a start and leaned forward. "Then *Andrew* must be the *fortune*—"

"Yes, I am the *fortunate* fellow whose privilege it was to render your niece and Miss Hedgeley a small service."

Vicky's eyes had closed for an agonised moment when Mr. Massingham had interrupted Lady Honoria's impulsive exclamation. When no explosion occurred, she opened them cautiously. Drucilla was breathing more easily; her hands had released each other so she could reach for her nearly full cup once more. Lord Ellerby was bombarding Mr. Massingham with questions about the robbery. She slanted a glance at her aunt and was not surprised to see that lady biting her lip and looking pensive. She was somewhat puzzled but infinitely grateful to discover that Aunt Honoria had not poured the whole tale into Gregory's ears after receiving her letter.

Gregory too had evidently found this noteworthy. Bewilderment showed in his fine eyes as they located Lady Honoria. "Am I correct in assuming that you knew of this holdup, ma'am?"

"Why, yes. Vicky wrote me an account of it, but she didn't mention Mr. Massingham by name. *That* was a surprise."

For a second Vicky's glance met that of Mr. Massingham, brimful of amusement, and resentment surged through her veins. That maddening care-for-naught was actually enjoying this excruciating conversation!

Lord Ellerby, impervious to any byplay, was faintly shocked. "And you did not think to mention the incident to me, ma'am, during the two days we travelled together? Why, Vicky might have been killed . . . or *worse!*''

"What is worse than being killed?" Vicky asked flippantly, refraining this time from looking at her antagonist, who might have been tempted to enumerate some fates worse than death. "Don't fuss, Gregory. The incident must have slipped from my aunt's mind."

"*Slipped from her mind?* Something that might have resulted in the death of one who is like a daughter to her? I don't think I understand you."

It seemed Gregory was determined to be difficult, and Vicky's glance pleaded for assistance from Lady Honoria, who said lamely, "Well, it didn't slip my mind precisely, but I did not believe Vicky would care to have the affair bruited all over town, so I didn't mention it."

"I see. I regret that anything in my conduct might have led you to believe that I would *bruit* such a story about town," Lord Ellerby replied stiffly.

"I didn't mean you necessarily, Gregory, so you needn't get upon your high ropes," snapped Lady Honoria, who was beginning to feel as besieged as a modern Pandora who couldn't get the lid on again.

Lord Ellerby was clearly unmollified, but he closed his lips firmly.

"Miss Seymour herself made very little of the incident," offered Mr. Massingham in soothing accents. "I was unconscious at the time, but Amos tells me she was as cool as could be when she shot the thief. You should be proud of her courage, ma'am."

This complimentary speech, ostensibly addressed to Lady Honoria, was well-received by Lord Ellerby. "I must have known that you would keep your head, of course, my dear Vicky," he said with a warm smile.

Vicky summoned up a weak effort to meet his.

Throughout this discussion of the robbery, Drucilla had sat silent, her eyes following each speaker in turn. Vicky had noted that her brightness dimmed temporarily after Lord Ellerby had made his concern for herself so unmistakably plain. Now the brightness was back as she turned to Mr. Massingham and engaged his attention with questions about the welfare of the family at Meadowlands. If the memories of Vicky's own girlhood were an accurate indicator, her young friend was now going to demonstrate her complete noninterest in Lord Ellerby for the benefit of anyone who cared to observe. Obviously the plan half-germinated in Vicky's mind in the last half-hour was not going to find perfect soil conditions for sprouting without some intensive spadework on her part.

Lady Honoria was intrigued by the description of the Meadowlands residents and made Mr. Massingham the bearer of an invitation to them to dine at the Oaks a couple of days hence.

The uncomfortable tea party broke up when Mr. Massingham, who had an hour's ride to face, took his leave. By this time Vicky was as interested in having a *tête-à-tête* with her aunt as Lady Honoria had been immediately after her arrival. Fortunately all present signified their intention of retiring to their respective rooms to rest before dressing for dinner. Within five minutes of going their separate ways, she was knocking on her aunt's door.

The door was opened to her by Trotton, who had travelled in the baggage coach with Lord Ellerby's valet. She was busily unpacking her ladyship's trunks when Vicky arrived. She replied to the latter's welcoming speech with an assessing look and the blunt remark that it wouldn't surprise her in the least if her mistress had done nothing but drag her hair back anyhow ever since leaving London. Undaunted by this criticism, Vicky grinned and confessed to that particular misdemeanour. She was informed that she might expect things to change from this moment forward. It was agreed that Trotton should come in an hour to arrange Miss Seymour's hair, but in the meantime she was to close the door to Lady Honoria's sitting room so the two ladies might have a private cose before dressing.

"Why did you not advise me of your arrival or even mention that you were coming?" demanded Vicky, wasting no time in coming to the point once her aunt was seated in a wing chair covered in a crewelwork design. "And whatever possessed you to bring Gregory here?"

"Sit down yourself. You have too much the appearance of an avenging angel hovering over me that way," replied Lady Honoria, who never cared to be put on the defensive. "I didn't even know I was coming until yesterday—you know I hadn't planned to leave town immediately: That's why we were two days on the road. We got a late start."

Vicky waved a hand toward the door leading to the bedchamber. "That's a lot of baggage for a woman who decided to take a trip on the spur of the moment."

"Well, I was of two minds about whether or not to come until yesterday, if you must split hairs. And I have brought no more than the barest necessities." Indignation rang in Lady Honoria's tones.

Knowing it to be her aunt's invariable practice to bring every belonging that wasn't nailed down and could even remotely be considered necessary to her comfort, Vicky abandoned this line of argument.

"And what made you drag Gregory along? What did you hope to accomplish by this ploy, beyond my mortification and raising false hopes in Gregory's breast?"

Lady Honoria's eyes slid away from her niece's unyielding face. She sounded much less assured as she admitted that she had invited Lord Ellerby after rumours had reached her ears that he had been distinguishing Lady Mary Ashley with his attentions this past week.

Vicky was appalled. "All the more reason to leave him in peace."

"I thought a spell of boredom in the country would bring you to your senses, so when I received your letter full of adventures and new acquaintances, it seemed vital to have Ellerby on the scene too before these new people drove him out of your mind altogether. Though after meeting that pretty little ninnyhammer you have staying with you, I'm not so confident I did the right thing. Unless I miss my guess, she is vastly taken with him. If you continue to give him the cold shoulder, you'll drive him right into her arms!

What man wouldn't prefer a warm, willing female to a human iceberg?''

"And you haven't even seen her dimples at work yet!" Vicky laughed. "Drucilla is a natural honeypot." She became serious as her aunt snorted in ladylike disgust. "Of course it is far too early to tell, but there might be a match there. I should think they'd suit very well. Gregory needs a girl who will adore him, and Drucilla should welcome his gentleness and innate chivalry after consorting with Andrew Massingham these past weeks."

Lady Honoria threw up her hands in disgust. "I give up! You are impossible! Men of Ellerby's calibre are not so thick on the ground that you can afford to pass them over to all your unmarried friends. You are not getting any younger, my child."

When her niece merely twinkled naughtily, Lady Honoria gave a helpless shrug and honed in on another subject. "And speaking of Andrew Massingham, why did you never mention the name of your unsuccessful eloper? I very nearly made a terrible *gaffe* this afternoon."

"Why did *you* never mention knowing the man?" retorted Vicky. "Besides, I thought I did identify the man Drucilla was eloping with."

"You did *not*," said her aunt definitely, correcting this impression. "In your account of the affair you merely referred to him as 'the fortune hunter' or as 'Drucilla's soldier.' ''

"If I'd had the least suspicion that you were acquainted with him or guessed you would come charging up here to play Cupid, I would certainly have identified him, but you may rest easy on the other score. Mr. Massingham nipped in very neatly to cover your *bêtise*. He's quick-witted enough, I'll give him that."

"I cannot believe that Andrew is a fortune hunter. He was a handful as a boy, but there wasn't an ounce of malice in him, and besides, he is Lord Mallard's heir. He has no need to marry money, nor would he be permitted to form a connection with the niece of a *bourgeois*, no matter how large her fortune. From my limited exposure to Lord Mallard—for which blessing, by the way, I am eternally grateful—I'd say he's as stiff-rumped as they come, very high in the instep.''

"I don't believe he asked anyone's permission," commented Vicky dryly. "If you don't accept him as a fortune hunter, then it must be love. Did Mr. Massingham's behaviour today strike you as being that of a man in the throes of a grand passion?"

"How can I tell? Only a moonling would wear his heart on his sleeve for the world to see, and Andrew is not that, I thank God!"

"Do you think he is in love with Drucilla?" persisted Vicky. "Do you believe a man of his type would make a good husband for that child?"

"I haven't seen enough of Andrew as an adult to guess whether or not he is in love, but this I *will* say: *when* he loves a woman, he will be a *very* good husband."

"There I must differ with you. Men of his sort regard women as playthings to be kept in reserve for light moments and shunted aside when important matters intrude. They spend the greater part of their lives in the company of like-minded males."

"That is true only until they form a deep attachment. Andrew's father was just such a one as you describe until he met Marie. They shared everything afterwards."

Vicky looked sceptical. "I am sorry to disagree with you, Aunt, but I do not believe Mr. Massingham is capable of forming a deep attachment. Certainly he has not done so for Drucilla, though he assures me he is determined to wed her. Well, I am equally determined he shall not. She and Gregory might suit very well, though I shall have to take a hand after what happened this afternoon. Obviously she thinks he is mine."

"Now who is playing Cupid?" asked Lady Honoria, torn between amusement and annoyance, the gleam in her eye at variance with her tightened mouth. "I must say that life in Leicestershire promises to be much more amusing than I had anticipated. Why are you rubbing your forehead like that?

Come to mention it, you are looking a trifle pale also. I hope you are not sickening for anything, my dear.''

"No, I have the headache a trifle, that's all. Your Mr. Massingham spooked Shadow this afternoon and I took a toss. Nothing to signify,'' she added as Lady Honoria's countenance reflected sudden alarm, "but I am going to have a number of bruises in unmentionable places by tomorrow."

"Have a hot bath and go directly to bed with a tray," recommended her aunt. "I shall make your excuses at dinner."

"Nonsense. I am perfectly capable of eating my dinner sitting at table. I should be dressing by now, however, and Trotton insists on doing my hair." She pulled a rueful grimace and rose from the setee with a little difficulty. Dropping a kiss on her relative's cheek, she said simply, "I'm glad you're here."

As Vicky went out of the room, Lady Honoria stared after her, aware that she had been given much food for thought since her arrival in the country.

11

That first evening with a swollen household went more smoothly than might have been predicted, given Vicky's battered physical condition, Drucilla's suspected emotional upheaval, Lord Ellerby's natural disappointment at his reception at the Oaks, and the fatigue that an elderly lady might be expected to experience after two days of travelling. Drucilla was admittedly a bit subdued early in the evening, but as the newcomers had never witnessed her in high spirits, there was no notice taken by anyone save her hostess, who viewed the situation with a tolerance born of understanding. The other three members of the house party had lived long enough in society to be more adept at disguising their feelings. Lord Ellerby, who had received a much better upbringing than Lord Byron, would not have dreamed of sulking in a corner or being rude to perfectly inoffensive persons because he had been crossed in love. No hostess of his acquaintance had ever had cause to complain that he ignored his dinner partners or failed to uphold his end of the conversation.

As far as Lady Honoria was concerned, the only time she ever admitted to fatigue was when she was being heartily bored by the company, and that was clearly not the case in Leicestershire. Those shrewd blue eyes might be somewhat faded in colour, but they missed nothing of the human dramas being enacted in her vicinity. From what Vicky had observed of her aunt's astringent wit at dinner, coming into the country had revitalised that lady. She had been thinking the same of herself just a few hours earlier, but now she felt rather like a farmer who prayed for a rainfall to germinate his seeds and received a downpour that threatened to wash the seed away. There was no denying that life was suddenly fraught with interest, but she could not take an entirely sanguine view of the immediate future.

This much she acknowledged to herself before rejoining the others for the evening. Perhaps it was fortunate for her peace of mind that there was no time to dwell on the possibilities for disaster inherent in the diverse cast of characters now assembled on the stage that was the circumscribed life at the Oaks. Trotton saw to it that her mistress' attention was concentrated on what her dresser considered the primary concern of this or any day, her appearance. In her zeal to remedy the cumulative effect of a fortnight of neglect, the dresser was prepared to spare no expenditure of time or energy necessary to create a hairstyle worthy of a ball at Carlton House. Great was her chagrin when Vicky declared with great firmness that she would be quite content with the simple style achieved by Lily scarcely two hours earlier.

"Am I to understand, Miss Seymour, that you would prefer to dispense with my services entirely?"

Vicky eyed the spare figure of her abigail drawn up in wounded dignity, her normally unyielding features even more graven, and knew that she had erred disastrously. It required all the tact at her command plus a cowardly recourse to a plea that her poor head couldn't stand any hair brushing tonight to smooth Trotton's ruffled feathers. She tutted disapprovingly at Vicky's censored version of her afternoon mishap but sprang into action in ordering a bath to be made ready immediately.

The hot bath had been marvelously soothing to her aching body. It had taken repeated prodding on the part of the abigail to coax her out of the tub after a mindless interval of pure sensation. The next few minutes were spent in a mad scramble to complete her toilette and get to the saloon before her guests. It would not do to add to Gregory's uneasy suspicion of having intruded. Had she been able to conceal her initial dismay at sight of him today, there would be no problem. This shock, following quickly on her spill and its sequel of another antagonistic encounter with Mr. Massingham, must have unnerved her to a degree where she had betrayed her years of exposure to all kinds of social situations, but the blame was hers alone. Therefore it was up to her to make atonement. And what better atonement than to make Gregory a present of an adoring bride?

Trotton, recognising the look of pure mischief on her mistress' face, halted involuntarily before resuming her route to the dressing room with the discarded towels. Her own inexpressive countenance concealed a burgeoning curiosity. She had guessed from her ladyship's abrupt decision to return to Leicestershire after declaring herself situated in London that Miss Vicky was getting up to something in the country. The mystery had deepened with the inclusion of Lord Ellerby. She had always known there was something smoky about that broken engagement. Not even a celebrated toast of the town like Miss Victoria Seymour would calmly throw over a catch like Ellerby unless there was a bigger prize in the offing, though she had certainly kept the identity of this prize dark. In the servants' room there had not been the slightest breath of anyone new dangling after her. Whoever it was had obviously not come up to scratch. Having burnt her bridges behind her, Miss Vicky had departed in a huff, but her aunt had evidently been working on her behalf, for here was Ellerby again, ripe for the plucking, if she was any judge. Still, that look on Miss Vicky's face just now was more than satisfaction at getting Ellerby back. She was up to something when all was said. It would be enlightening perhaps to discover what the talk in the Hall made of this unknown miss she had visiting her. Lady Honoria had merely let drop that piece of unadorned information when the abigail had gone in to unpack for her. Cavanaugh had not even bothered to mention the presence of a guest when he had greeted her and Grooby, Lord Ellerby's valet, on their arrival this afternoon.

Nor had he had anything to say about that Mr. Massingham who had been with Miss Vicky—and her looking more like a hoyden than a lady of quality—when she had appeared on the coachway. Her ladyship hadn't been aware of *his* presence, that had been evident, though she seemed to know him.

Trotton's impassive facade and deliberate motions as she put a clean handkerchief in the reticule she presently handed to her mistress belied the simmering cauldron of conjecture that was her brain at the moment. She was as eager to see her mistress descend to dinner as the latter was to avoid being late. There would be plenty to be learned from the conversation in the Hall when the upper servants had their meal.

If Vicky went in to dinner that night in happy ignorance of the amount of speculation about her activities rife among the servants, it was because she was still adjusting to the change in circumstances herself. The conversation at table would not have furnished the footman who assisted Cavanaugh with any titillating tidbits to pass on to the staff. Lady Honoria and Lord Ellerby filled Vicky in on the social happenings since her departure from town, and she, with an occasional assist from Drucilla, related the details of how they had been spending their days in the country. From time to time Lady Honoria posed questions about certain of the local residents which only her niece could answer. During these intervals Drucilla shyly revealed her reactions to country life at the prompting of Lord Ellerby.

After dinner the ladies retired to the drawing room, where they were soon joined by his lordship. Vicky was softly playing on the pianoforte and he urged her to continue as he settled himself comfortably in one corner of the plush sofa. She smiled her acquiescence, then returned her attention to the keyboard. She selected a sonata by the new German composer Ludwig van Beethoven, which was a particular favourite of Lady Honoria's.

"Thank you, my love," said that lady when the last note died away. "That was lovely. You have a marvelous sure touch. It is always a pleasure to listen when you play, which is more than can be said about most 'accomplished' young lady musicians.''

"Since playing the piano is my sole feminine accomplishment, it is fortunate that I do it passably well." Her niece laughed, rippling her fingers over the keys.

"I must respectfully differ with you there, Vicky," put in Lord Ellerby, smiling intimately at her. "There isn't another young woman in London who can claim the half of your accomplishments."

A gurgle of amusement escaped from Vicky's lips. "I thank you, Gregory, and wouldn't dream of embarrassing a guest by challenging you to name another accomplishment. Honesty will compel you to admit that singing certainly isn't among my talents. Luckily for us, Drucilla has a lovely voice. Will you give us the pleasure of hearing you sing, my dear?"

"Oh, please, my voice is nothing at all out of the common," pleaded the young girl, reluctant to be thrust forward, "and I was so enjoying your playing. Won't you continue?"

Lord Ellerby turned the full force of his charming smile on the shrinking girl and added his voice to that of his hostess in requesting a song or two.

"Your modesty does you credit, my child, but I promise you we are not severe critics," said Lady Honoria briskly, "merely people who enjoy a little music in the evening."

"In that case, ma'am, I shall be glad to sing for you." Drucilla's shyness was routed by a greater fear of seeming ungracious in the eyes of this somewhat formidable lady, who was regarding her not unkindly but with every expectation of being obeyed.

"Shall I play for you, or would you prefer to accompany yourself?" asked Vicky, preparing to rise from the instrument.

"Oh, no! I'd rather not have to worry about my fingers too. Please play for me."

Drucilla was a trifle awkward initially, but once she was launched into a melody, the pleasure of producing music overcame her diffidence. Her sweet soprano, though not strong, had been well-trained and she possessed abundant musical sense and timing. Encouraged by an appreciative audience, she relaxed and forgot herself completely by the second song.

Vicky, admiring the picture her *protégée* made in a becoming coffee-coloured muslin gown that had been altered to fit her by Nurse just the other day, was persuaded there could scarcely be a man breathing who would be immune to the appeal of the girl's entrancing prettiness and sparkle. A glance from under her lashes at the only gentleman present, however, revealed that his eyes at that moment were fixed not on the singer but the pianist, with an unmistakable warmth in their expression. Her trained fingers continued to produce the correct accompaniment, but her thoughts branched off again, plodding over familiar ground with the monotony of oxen plowing a field. What was wrong with her? *Why* could she not be thrilled and grateful for such devotion from a man she both like and respected? What more did she expect from life?

The end of the musical selection brought this fruitless self-questioning to a halt. Vicky was encouraged to read genuine pleasure and admiration on Gregory's face as he praised Drucilla's performance. It was evident by the young girl's downcast eyes and fluttering lashes that she too had discerned his sincerity but was still too timid in his presence to return the sort of raillery she engaged in so naturally with Mr. Massingham. This unaccustomed shyness, Vicky decided, would do the girl no disservice in Gregory's eyes. He was extending himself already to set her more at her ease, so that when Vicky suggested they try their hand at a duet he exerted every effort to persuade Drucilla to embark on the musical experiment, after warning her his voice was not really worthy to be associated with one of such fine quality. Naturally, no very young lady would desire to leave the impression that she considered her talents above those of her companions. Drucilla speedily agreed to engage in a duet with Lord Ellerby.

The improvised concert delighted the ears of their audience despite the lack of rehearsal. The gentleman's easy light tenor blended beautifully with the soprano voice, to the enjoyment of all. Flushed with pleasure at the response of Lady Honoria and Vicky, Drucilla was emboldened to initiate a search through the music stored in the rosewood cabinet against the wall for additional songs she and Lord Ellerby might attempt for another evening.

Vicky took the opportunity thus afforded to move to a seat beside her aunt. "I think the evening has gone rather well, do not you?"

"That depends on whose advantage you are consulting," returned Lady Honoria, eyeing without favour the dark and fair heads absorbed in a sheet of music they had unearthed from the cabinet. "I should say it has gone well from Miss Hedgeley's point of view."

Vicky grinned at the acerbic tones but demanded, "Don't you agree they make a handsome couple, with Gregory's fairness such a perfect foil for Drucilla's dark beauty?"

"They are a good-looking pair, certainly," conceded Lady Honoria, "but so are you and Gregory, and there are those who prefer a matched pair."

"We were not matched in the more important sense of the word, Aunt."

Hearing the earnest quality in the quiet reply, Lady Honoria searched her niece's serene visage for a moment with a probing blue gaze. "Is your mind set on this absurd match?" she asked abruptly.

"Not, of course, if they should prove unsuited on longer acquaintance, but somehow my instincts tell me that I am onto a winner in this instance."

A resigned sigh signalled her aunt's acceptance of this answer to the question she had *not* asked. A second later she removed her attention to Drucilla, who was inquiring if anyone was familiar with a song by Bonancini that looked interesting. When Lady Honoria pronounced it to be a very old favourite of her late husband's that she hadn't heard in years, Drucilla's sparkling face took on an added glow. "Then I shall learn it for you, if you would like it, ma'am?"

Lady Honoria studied the enchanting face looking up at her

expectantly and felt her resistance crumbling. "Thank you, Drucilla, I should like that very much indeed."

Lord Ellerby's approving look at the young girl was not lost upon his hostess, who took it as a sign that some little headway had been made this first evening.

Although bruised and sore in too many places to enumerate by the time she crawled thankfully between the sheets of her bed, Vicky's last thoughts before succumbing to the spell of Morpheus were not of her aching limbs. It would not do to give way to overconfidence so early in the game, but it might not be beyond what was reasonable to indulge a little cautious optimism that Gregory's arrival would prove the very thing needed to wean Drucilla away from her lukewarm attachment to Mr. Massingham. And if at the same time Gregory could be beguiled into transferring his affections to a much more suitable female—well, there was no harm in killing two birds with one stone, surely. And so Miss Seymour drifted off to sleep smugly pleased with her masterly strategy, regrettably having forgotten so soon her own sage warning against just such presumption.

Vicky's scheme to promote a rapport between her two guests received a temporary setback the next morning when she asked Lord Ellerby if there was anything he particularly desired to do that day. The three younger members of the household were having breakfast in the small sunny room formed by one of the three protruding bays on the east front. Lady Honoria, who steadfastly declined to face the morning sun until after eleven o'clock, always breakfasted in her own rooms. The younger element, seated around a small oval table in the bay, far from objecting to the light and warmth admitted by ranks of long narrow windows on three sides, were lingering over second cups of coffee and soaking up the October sunshine. Vicky, still a bit stiff from her tumble, had to rouse herself from a pleasant lethargy induced by the sunshine to play the role of conscientious hostess.

Lord Ellerby smiled lazily at her and declared himself entirely at her disposal.

"Lobbing the ball back into my court, Gregory?"

His lordship's smile widened to a grin at this challenge, but he made no effort to defend himself as he selected another apple muffin from a silver basket.

"Well, then, perhaps you would care to ride over the estate on such a lovely day?"

"That sounds delightful if Miss Hedgeley will not find it tedious to repeat what must have been a recent outing for her too." Lord Ellerby smiled a question at the silent girl across from him.

"Oh, no. That is to say, I do not ride, but you must not regard that. I shall amuse myself quite happily in the music room."

"You never ride, Miss Hedgeley?"

Drucilla blushed rosily as the blue eyes of the gentleman widened in surprise. "I can't ride; I have never learned," said the young girl half-defiantly. "Besides, I prefer walking."

Here Vicky intervened. "Perhaps you will succeed where I have failed, Gregory, in convincing this foolish child that she will not be placing life and limb in jeopardy by agreeing to accept some elementary tuition. I have promised her the gentlest horse in the stables, but all she will say is that she is too stupid to learn, which is a great piece of nonsense."

"Of course it is. Learning to ride demands no special talents, Miss Hedgeley," Lord Ellerby assured the unbelieving girl in a kindly manner. "And once you have acquired some competency, you will find so many more possibilities open to you than walking allows, at least in the country."

"Vicky drove me around the estate in the gig," said Drucilla, yielding not an inch.

"I drove you around the perimeter, where there were paths," corrected her hostess. "You have not been in the home wood or down by the stream, which is lovely this time of year. I have offered to teach her, indeed I have begged to be permitted to teach her to ride."

This last was addressed to Lord Ellerby, who promptly offered his services in the cause, smiling at Drucilla with a charm that was nearly impossible to resist.

"I am *afraid* of horses!" The shamed admission was jolted out of the pretty brunette as she was manoeuvred into a corner by the combined onslaught of the two people she would most like to please. "I have always feared them. They are so very large and . . . *twitchy*! One never knows what they will do next," she blurted defensively, driven to further explanation by the shocked silence that greeted her confession.

"My dear, pray forgive me for seeming to press you," said Vicky contritely. "This puts a very different complexion on the matter. *Not*," she added in firm tones as some of the tension drained out of her young friend, "to learning to ride, of course. *That* remains an eminently desirable accomplishment, but first we shall have to rid you of these perfectly idiotish fears."

"They're not idiotish!" flared Drucilla, goaded into retort. "You cannot deny that horses are huge *and* unpredictable, always throwing up their heads and backing away as if fearing one meant them harm, when in actuality they are the most cosseted creatures on earth."

"Certainly they are large," conceded Vicky in soothing accents, exchanging an amused glance with Lord Ellerby, "and if the equine disposition were akin to that of the tiger, their size could well engender fear, but it is not so—the opposite, indeed. Am I not correct, Gregory?"

Thus appealed to, Lord Ellerby assured the disbelieving girl that in his experience horses had been, with few exceptions, very well-disposed toward mankind in general.

Drucilla preserved an unconvinced silence, which her hostess prudently decided to ignore, saying briskly to Lord Ellerby, "It seems to me to be of the first importance that Drucilla should become a little more accustomed to being around horses before her riding lessons actually begin. Do come with us to the stables this morning, my dear, and meet several of my favourites while the grooms saddle horses for Gregory and me."

Again she preferred not to recognise the reluctance on her guest's face, ruthlessly bearing Drucilla upstairs to her own rooms to keep her company while she changed to her habit, activated by a shrewd suspicion that if she took her eyes off her the girl would contrive to vanish in the meantime.

On the whole the results of the morning's events were highly satisfactory. Drucilla had surrendered to *force majeure*, accompanying her hostess and Lord Ellerby to the stable block. If it was not exactly what she would have chosen had her wishes been consulted, at least her manners and sense of obligation were such that she exerted herself to show willingness. If she was unable to counterfeit any appreciable enthusiasm for the enormous equine specimens she was called upon to examine at rather closer quarters than she would elect, she did manage to express sincere aesthetic appreciation for the magnificent Othello, who had sired Shadow and whom Lord Ellerby would be riding while his own mount rested after two days of travelling. The big black, though well-mannered, was of a slightly nervous temperament. He stood still for one brief pat on his handsome nose but eyed Drucilla in a manner that caused her to shrink back immediately, though she tried to conceal this with a laughing remark that he made her feel her breeding was inadequate to rub shoulders with him.

Lord Ellerby had chuckled at this nonsense, but Vicky said quite seriously, "That is very perceptive of you, Drucilla. Othello is a bit top-lofty, to be sure. You must meet Sheba, who despite her royal name has a very humble nature and is always grateful for any small attentions."

Drucilla had followed her friend inside, where the nearly recovered mare was still confined. Sheba, with her soft brown eyes and smaller stature, was certainly more to her taste than Othello. She crooned in sympathy over the mare's injury and laughed aloud as the velvet nose nuzzled in the vicinity of the pocket that contained a carrot thoughtfully provided by her hostess. When Sheba bared her teeth to reach for the carrot, the incipient friendship had suffered only the merest flicker of a reversal. At sight of those large efficient dentures, Drucilla snatched her hand back, earning a reproachful whicker from the mare. Once Vicky had demonstrated the proper open-handed technique for offering treats to horses, her guest had speedily redeemed herself, and girl and horse parted friends. Since Manley decreed that Sheba might begin gentle exercise the following day, it was settled that she should be Drucilla's first mount, and the initial riding lesson was scheduled by Vicky and Lord Ellerby for the next morning. By some oversight Drucilla's opinion on the matter was not consulted.

Lord Ellerby's tour of the grounds with his hostess was a pleasant interlude, though by the time they returned to the house there was a slight but perceptible dimming of the high spirits with which Vicky's former *fiancé* had greeted the rare opportunity to have the object of his affections all to himself. He had admired the beauty spots in the area with becoming enthusiasm, asked pertinent questions about the game to be found in the woods, and responded with well-bred civility to an introduction to one of the tenants who farmed Seymour land, encountered while riding back for lunch. Vicky could not be certain that she was not being overly sensitive to nuances that may have existed only in her own mind, but she could not help wondering if Gregory had been a trifle taken aback by the sheer size of the estate. He could not have been unaware that she was widely regarded as a matrimonial prize in London, but there would not have been any reliable sources of an accurate estimate of her fortune. The Seymour family had sadly dwindled in numbers of late, and though well-connected, had not been prominent in the social scene in London during her father's lifetime. He and her mother had preferred to remain in the country year round. Lady Honoria, daughter of an earl and the recent widow of a baronet, had overseen the social career of her dead sister's child. To all polite questions or indiscreet inquiries as to the girl's expectations, she had consistently returned the same vague answer, that her niece was well-dowered. Over the years the estimate of Vicky's fortune had steadily risen, and she had warded off her share of fortune hunters since her long-ago come-out.

Gregory, himself the possessor of a very pretty estate in Bedfordshire, had no need to make an advantageous marriage.

His patent lack of interest in her eligibility had formed no small part of his attraction for Vicky. Now she wondered if she detected a hint of restraint in his manner as she reeled off figures and information on the crops raised by her tenant farmers. Certainly there had been an intensity in his gaze as he listened that was very different from his customary admiring expression, and she could not attribute this to any intrinsic interest in the subject under discussion. It wasn't until they had stopped to watch the antics of three colts frolicking about their proud mothers in a sunny field that another explanation for Gregory's slight reserve offered itself for her consideration.

For the last few moments she had been rattling away on her favourite subject, the racehorses that were bred and trained on the estate, and there was no doubt that Gregory's interest was caught. It had been his suggestion that they stop and admire the colts at closer range. The curious youngsters obliged by crowding around to investigate their company, nudging each other out of position along the rails. Their admirers disagreed mildly over which looked the most promising, Gregory pronouncing in favour of a large roan with abundant high spirits, while Vicky held to it that a dainty grey mare gave more promise by virtue of her sloping shoulders and lovely smooth action.

"The roan was bred for strength and speed, but I fear he has inherited his sire's straight shoulders and he might be a trifle short of bone in back. He has an ungainly stride at this point but might make a good hunter with training. Good wide quarters, as you can see, nicely rounded. He should jump well."

"He could surprise everyone. Not all champions are in the same style."

"True enough," admitted Vicky, gathering up her reins in preparation for departure. "Wait until you see Shadow, though. There is not time now if we are not to be disgracefully late for lunch, but I venture to predict you will find him the most perfect creature, a horse in a thousand," she enthused, "if not a million, and with a champion's heart, I vow."

As he turned Othello's head away from the fence, Lord Ellerby's eyes kindled with appreciation of the glowing girl at his side, whose beauty was always enhanced by enthusiasm. As she went on to detail her progress in training Shadow, however, the admiration was replaced by consternation.

"You can't mean . . .? Is *that* what you were doing yesterday dressed . . .?" He stopped and got command of his voice, which had sounded shocked, before starting again in more moderated tones. "Surely you do not intend to do the actual training of this horse yourself?"

Vicky's golden-brown brows elevated. "Why, yes, of course I mean exactly that at this stage. Before I enter him on the circuit, naturally I shall see that he becomes accustomed to the jockey who will ride him for me." Her level glance met Lord Ellerby's incredulous gaze calmly, but there was a hint of defiance in the set of her rounded chin, and the soft lips were rather compressed at that moment.

"It is not for me to criticise you," began Lord Ellerby in hesitant tones, "but is that altogether wise? Apart from the potential danger to yourself, surely you will agree that for a woman to don male attire and engage in an activity that has always been the sole province of men is to present a very singular appearance and to court the kind of notoriety that I am persuaded you would deplore."

Long lashes concealed the impatient gleam in Vicky's eyes. Here was the second man in twenty-four hours to take it upon himself to censure her conduct, though from vastly different motives. The Massingham man was concerned only for the fate of a good horse in a woman's inherently unskilled hands, but Gregory, to do him credit, had her best interests at heart, or rather, what he as a member of the superior male persuasion considered to be her best interests. Appreciation of his motivation softened her response.

"I do not propose to ride Shadow in a race meet, Gregory, and what I choose to do on my own estate can scarcely be thought to injure my reputation abroad. In general I try to conform to the nonsensical restrictions imposed upon females, though it frequently goes against the grain to submit meekly to conventions that should have vanished like the dinosaurs long ago. In this case I feel I am more than competent to undertake this particular task, and raising horses is my business, after all.''

Lord Ellerby looked as though he would like to enter a caveat, but he closed his lips firmly.

Vicky, about to exert her best efforts to smooth over the situation, suddenly pulled up short as she remembered that it would advance Drucilla's interests faster if Gregory should remain out of charity with herself for a while. In this cause she added a little fuel to the fire by boasting gaily but inaccurately, ''Besides, there isn't a horse on the estate that I cannot handle.''

That should help convince him that the girl he had worshipped was in reality a hurly-burly female with no delicacy of principle but possessed of a conceit of herself as competent to enter a masculine sphere of activity. She urged her horse into a gallop, throwing a challenge to race over her shoulder to her escort. Of necessity, Lord Ellerby had to keep pace with his hostess or find himself abandoned in strange territory. After a bit the exhilarating effect of galloping *ventre à terre* with a strong, beautifully paced mount under him pushed his troubled thoughts into the background. The two riders approached the stable block neck and neck, for Vicky had gotten a good jump on the stronger horse and Gregory had to exert all his skill to beat her at the finish.

Miss Seymour congratulated the victor for his prowess, he disclaimed and complimented his mount, and the two headed for the house in laughing camaraderie. But a tiny hole had been enlarged in the wall of chivalrous myopia and self-deception that prevented Lord Ellerby from seeing his beloved as she really was. His perception of her as the perfect ornament to a ballroom or drawing room had allowed her neither imperfections nor any of the more homely virtues. She had felt stifled and resentful under the loving tyranny of his expectations. Gregory's discomfort with this new conception of his beloved seemed to support her intuitive belief that it was not herself he loved, but some perfect creation inside his head. It also helped to dispel some of the guilt she was experiencing at overdrawing the picture of a perversely independent creature determined to usurp masculine prerogatives. Harsh situations often demanded harsh solutions.

12

The rest of the day passed uneventfully. Lady Honoria joined the young people for lunch and then requested the services of the coachman to convey her on one or two visits to pensioners whose welfare had been on her mind of late. Lord Ellerby installed himself in the library to write letters, while the young ladies brought their sewing onto the sunny terrace so they might enjoy the benefits of a day that was more like midsummer than early November. What there was of conversation was intermittent in pattern and trifling of nature, both girls being rather more absorbed by the work in their hands or the thoughts in their heads. Over the past week or so the kind of close association enforced by dwelling under the same roof had forged a workable harmony based on feelings of friendliness and goodwill. That they had not attained a state of perfect intimacy was due less to the relatively short duration of their acquaintance than to differences in their personalities and respective stations in life. On Drucilla's side there was the inhibiting factor of her extreme youth and the great admiration, almost amounting to hero worship, in which she held her hostess; and on Vicky's, an intrinsic reserve that generally kept her from offering her innermost self to others, as well as a recognition of the lack of shared experiences between herself and a girl raised in a restrictive, uncongenial town atmosphere. Nevertheless, they were contented and comfortable in each other's company and did not feel constrained to avoid silence at all cost.

Vicky glanced up to see her guest gazing with pleasure upon a colourful border of chrysanthemums, her hands idle in her lap.

"This is such a heavenly spot, Vicky," she murmured, catching the older girl's eye on her. "Everywhere one gazes, there is a pleasing prospect."

"And not even man is vile," agreed Vicky smilingly as she lowered to her lap the slipper she was embroidering. "We have been uncommonly fortunate in being able to enjoy a spell of unusually fine weather so late in the season. I believe it will last another day or two so that we may make a good beginning on your riding instruction. By the way, Nurse reports that she has altered that old habit of mine if you will like to try it on after tea, my dear."

She returned her eyes to her work, affecting not to see the shadow that flitted over Drucilla's countenance at mention of the dreaded riding lessons. The girl had committed herself to learning the rudiments of riding, but she was plainly unhappy at the prospect. Vicky's lips parted impulsively to assure her guest that she need not feel coerced into participating in any activity which she would rather avoid, but she closed them again before any such sentiment could escape. It might be difficult to reconcile such coercion with her duties to a guest, but it would be for Drucilla's eventual good, after all. She would be bound to feel the lack of the accomplishment sooner or later, especially if she should marry a man who did not reside all the year in town. It must add to her self-confidence too if she could overcome her fears in this area, fears she herself recognised as irrational. She had summoned pride to her side in agreeing to try, and Vicky chose to believe her pride and resolution strong enough to carry her through the initial ordeal. And apart from this idealistic consideration, riding lessons were a heaven-sent excuse to throw Gregory and Drucilla together without the inhibiting effect of her own presence. Most assuredly she did not plan to participate in any instructional sessions beyond the first.

The subject of horseback riding was avoided for the rest of the day. The various members of the household met together for tea and dinner and found abundant food for discussion in other areas. It being discovered that Drucilla's strict upbringing had precluded instruction in any card games whatsoever, music once again became the main employment after dinner, but this was no sacrifice on anyone's part. Lady Honoria, to be sure, was immoderately fond of a game of whist, but her fondness did not extend so far as to embrace the experience of initiating a newcomer into the mysteries of cardplaying. True to her word, Drucilla had learned the Bonancini song, which was universally well-received and even brought a hint of moisture to her ladyship's eyes. Tonight the young girl needed no urging to partner Lord Ellerby in a few duets. Their performance benefited from the greater feeling of ease that was present after an additional few hours spent in each other's company. When Vicky casually expressed the opinion that if the time might be found for another practice session before the dinner party on the morrow, their guests could not fail to be impressed by the professional quality of their collaboration, both performers were quick to agree that they could spare a mutually convenient hour or two in the pursuit of excellence. In twenty-four hours Drucilla had come such a distance in accommodating herself to Lord Ellerby's disturbing presence that her colour fluctuated scarcely at all, though she was profoundly grateful that no one could possibly be aware of her galloping pulse rate.

The equestrienne neophyte presented herself at breakfast the following morning appropriately and most attractively garbed in the refashioned habit of brown gabardine, topped by a dashing brown velvet hat set at a perky angle on her riotous black ringlets. Her pulses were still racing but the healthy colour had deserted her cheeks from the moment of rising. She had no control over such involuntary physical manifestations but summoned to her aid all that a determined pride could do to present a composed appearance. It wasn't quite sufficient, however, to permit the muscles of her throat to relax to the degree that would allow more than a morsel or two of food past the lump that had taken up residence there, and that only when the others' eyes were upon her.

Vicky, well aware of her friend's discomfort and secretly cheering her fortitude, kept up an animated flow of conversation on every topic under the sun save the one that most concerned the nearly silent Drucilla. Like most men, Lord Ellerby remained oblivious of any atmosphere and partook of a sustaining repast.

At last the meal was over and the little party repaired to the side entrance, where three horses awaited them in the care of a couple of grooms, who were soon dismissed, it having been privately agreed between Vicky and Lord Ellerby that Drucilla would fare better with no witnesses to her initial efforts. The girl had been all docility since her capitulation to her companions' entreaties, but at sight of the saddled Sheba, her step faltered and she ejaculated faintly, "She looks much larger than I remember."

"Actually Sheba is quite a small horse," Vicky assured her in soothing accents. "You may give her one of the sugar lumps now if you wish."

Not loath to try what bribery might do to incline the horse in her favour, Drucilla solemnly presented the sugar to the expectant chestnut and was somewhat reassured of her mount's kindly intentions by soft brown eyes that followed her movements.

Lord Ellerby lifted the girl onto the mare's back and shortened the stirrup a bit while Vicky helped Drucilla to arrange the folds of the riding dress comfortably. It had been decided to allow the novice some time to accustom herself to the motion of the horse before giving the reins into her control. Once in the saddle, Vicky took charge of them until Lord Ellerby was mounted and could relieve her.

They set off at a walking pace, leading Sheba between the other two horses. It was some few moments before Drucilla was able to keep her eyes open, since an inadvertent downward glance from such an unaccustomed eminence would snap them shut again, but after a time the unvarying rhythm of Sheba's gait calmed her most immediate fears and she was emboldened to look about her with real interest. They were making for the home wood as an easy ride with little variation in grade. Vicky ventured a comment on the passing scene and was rewarded by the first natural movement Drucilla had made since being placed in jeopardy. She turned her head and shoulders toward the speaker. When no disaster resulted from such imprudence, the rigidity with which she held herself underwent a visible improvement. A look of shared triumph passed between her instructors, and the little party continued on, admiring the colourful foliage as they entered the wood.

Had the riding lesson terminated after half an hour or so, all parties to it must have rated it an unequivocal success. By that time Drucilla was handling the reins herself, experiencing the satisfacion of having Sheba respond to her directions as they forked left or right on intersecting paths. They were already wending their leisurely way back toward the house when another element was introduced by the intrusion of the unforeseen. Drucilla was in the middle of a lively description of her uncle's selection of reading matter fit for the improvement of a young lady's intellect when a hare darted across the path. Sheba was a beautifully mannered horse, but at this she did display surprise and displeasure to the extent of tossing her head and sidling away a step or two. The excursion had been so smooth and uneventful to that point that Drucilla had actually forgotten its purpose. Her mind was far from her precarious position atop a huge animal, and having little idea of control, she lost the reins and her balance in her surprise. She might well have righted herself unaided, for Sheba had stopped on Vicky's command, but Lord Ellerby was off Othello in a flash and his strong arm was around the trembling girl. He lifted her down and kept a supporting grasp on her while Vicky gathered up the chestnut's reins again.

"Are you all right, my dear?"

"Oh, yes, so foolish of me . . . it was my own fault entirely for not attending." Drucilla was a trifle pale but her voice was almost under control as she reassured her friend. She stepped away from Lord Ellerby's hold, being careful to avoid his concerned gaze.

"Well, no harm done," Vicky replied with a cheerful air that evidently struck the gentleman as excessive, for he said quickly:

"Perhaps the lesson has run a bit too long. Shall I take Miss Hedgeley up on Othello with me for the return?"

He was already reaching for the reins of the waiting black when his hostess' voice, even more offensively cheerful than before, stopped him in his tracks. "Heavens, *no*, Gregory! You know it is always advisable after a spill for a rider to get right back on. Of course Drucilla didn't actually fall, but the principle still applies."

Lord Ellerby's handsome face wore an expression of gravity as he looked steadily at his goddess and replied with a suggestion of gentle reproof. "I think you cannot have considered, Vicky, that this is Miss Hedgeley's *first* lesson. It would surely be most *in*advisable to extend it beyond an optimum time. We have been somewhat remiss, I'm afraid, in not discovering that she has become a trifle fatigued."

"Oh, yes, to be sure. I have so little sensibility myself that I don't always allow for it in others. Forgive me, my dear. The lesson was overlong and Lord Ellerby shall now take you up with him."

Vicky had striven for just the right note of unconcern to rob her words of their conciliating spirit, and she read success in the continued gravity of his lordship's expression and the sudden firming of his lips as he repressed speech with difficulty.

Before he could act, however, opposition came from an unexpected quarter.

"I thank Lord Ellerby for his kind offer, but I am not in the least fatigued and have every intention of riding home on Sheba," declared Drucilla, approaching her mount with decision in the lines of her body and uplifted chin.

Vicky, silently applauding her young friend's courage, preserved her facade of insensibility while Lord Ellerby repeated his protestations and Drucilla stood firm in her decision to return on Sheba's back. His lordship's conscientious concern for the novice rider's welfare was not again called into action during the uneventful return trip. Drucilla withstood the ordeal well and would have been crushed to learn that her heroic attempt to conceal her fear was entirely transparent to her instructors.

The ride home was enlivened by a stream of mindless chatter from Vicky, which, luckily, called for little response from the young girl, who was concentrating on maintaining her dignity in a trying situation, and the silent gentleman, who was busily reassessing the essential nature of the woman he had desired so desperately to make his wife. Fortunately the riders all went their separate ways to change, for each had much with which to occupy his mind, and Vicky, especially, required some time to recover from the fatiguing effects of producing that marathon monologue.

When the members of the household reassembled for lunch, everyone's private concerns were safely tucked out of view and general civility prevailed. A passing reference to the expected dinner party on Vicky's part produced the hoped-for fixing of a rehearsal session for that afternoon by Lord Ellerby and Drucilla, which had the double advantage of throwing her prospective lovers together and freeing her own time for a visit to Shadow. She had been too stiff after yesterday's extensive tour of the grounds with Gregory to exercise her favourite, but her muscles had unbent sufficiently today to make her impatient to be off to the field.

Satisfaction and tiredness were equally blended when Vicky returned to her rooms several hours later. She allowed Trotton to persuade her to rest in lieu of drinking tea in company, and was actually asleep by the time the dresser returned from delivering her mistress' excuses. It was Trotton, pointedly oblivious of the subsequent look of dislike directed her way, who shook her awake two hours later to begin the ritual of dressing for the evening. Vicky sprang up at the disturbing touch, looked woozily around her, and slumped back against the pillows. Now, when it was too late, she remembered why she was seldom tempted to indulge in what her aunt referred to as a restorative nap. The plain truth was that sleeping in the afternoon did *not* restore one's energy; on the contrary, one arose more exhausted than before, cross and fuzzy-minded, with a bitter resolution never to fall into that particular snare again. She swung her legs off the bed and shook her head to clear it of the taunting memory of just such a resolution formed the last time she had indulged this weakness. Trotton had her bath ready and she submitted with unwonted docility to all the dresser's directions over the next hour.

When the foggy rooms in her brain cleared enough for thoughts to move in, she found herself anticipating the dinner party with genuine interest. Their guests were all attractive and personable, and Sir Hugh, at least, possessed a pleasant address and a well-informed mind that must make him a welcome addition to any gathering. Miss Fairchild's shyness was a surface disadvantage, certainly, but unless she was vastly mistaken, the girl's manner concealed a lively intellect and a good understanding. She would never shine in company, indeed brilliance was probably a quality she would be frightened to covet, but Miss Fairchild would never be left with nothing to contribute to a rational conversation through paucity of mental resources. It would be her hostess' task perhaps to see to it that Elaine was not permitted to retire into the background tonight.

Her thoughts passed on to Lady Lanscomb. That the latter had been a reigning belle in her day, at least in provincial circles, was a theory that did not admit debate. Sir Hugh's attractive mother enjoyed the company of gentlemen, but with the possible exception of herself (and that was understandable), she seemed well enough disposed toward her own sex. Vicky spared a quick hope that her cosmopolitan relative would not put up Lady Lanscomb's back by careless name-dropping. Lady Honoria was never above her company or above being pleased, but she travelled in the first circles socially and had a wide acquaintance among the more prominent thinkers of the day. If the slightest hint of patronage should be suspected by Lady Lanscomb, the inevitable strained relations between the elder ladies could well strew obstacles in the path of Vicky's plans for the younger. Well, if necessary, she could just drop a hint to her aunt that Lady Lanscomb must be spared any feelings of inferiority in the event it was in her nature to take offence. She only hoped her aunt would not devine her plans for Elaine; she had not taken to her niece's other matchmaking scheme.

There was one other expected guest, whom she could do without tonight, or any night for that matter. Mr. Massingham's presence she chose not to dwell on; it was a necessary evil to be endured, it added nothing to her enjoyment or contentment. In the process of not dwelling on Mr. Massingham, an idea struck her with unexpected force, causing her to sit up straighter on the dressing-table bench. Since the silent and dedicated Trotton was brushing her hair at the time, the results of this sudden movement were momentarily painful enough to jerk her attention back to the present. By the time Trotton had scolded and Vicky had apologised in an absent manner, she had identified the potential problem and was mentally taking corrective measures.

In forty-eight hours her main object had shifted from merely ensuring that the sundered engagement between Drucilla and Mr. Massingham not be taken up again to actively promoting a match between Gregory and Drucilla. She could say with honesty that some little progress toward this object had been achieved, but it was undeniably desirable, nay, mandatory at this stage, to conceal her scheme from Mr. Massingham. Most decidedly did she desire that he should not redouble his efforts to woo a wealthy bride while these efforts might still be effective. His public attentions to Drucilla must be discreet, because Sir Hugh had required a pledge that he should not reveal the past connection between them, but she would not put it out of his power to get the girl alone by some means or other. It was sheer stupidity to underestimate an opponent, and she had never questioned Mr. Massingham's resourcefulness. A small frown creased Vicky's forehead as she recalled that too much had been said of the prospective duet between Gregory and Drucilla to draw back now. Lady Honoria would be bound to request the pleasure of hearing them, and the performers themselves would wonder about the omission should she hint her aunt away from the subject. The fact of the riding lessons could be concealed, however. She must forestall any announcements on this subject. Perhaps she could catch Drucilla before the girl went downstairs.

"What time is it, Trotton?"

"Nearly six-thirty."

"So late?" They had compromised between country and town hours because the Meadowlands party was coming such a distance. "Are we nearly ready?"

"Yes, miss. As soon as I place this *aigrette* in your hair, you'll be able to dress. I have everything laid out."

"*Feathers?* Good heavens, Trotton, this isn't a full-dress ball, merely a country dinner party, and a small one at that!" Vicky's eyes flashed to the mirror while she uttered the protest.

The reflection confronting her could not be other than aesthetically pleasing if to look one's best was a condition to be desired, but Vicky eyed the complicated hairstyle rather dubiously, swivelling sideways to glimpse the twisted swaths at the back and the topcurls cascading over her ears. Trotton's angular figure, stiffly drawn up, caught her eye, which climbed to encounter a mulish expression on the dresser's sallow face.

"Is there something amiss, Miss Seymour?" she asked in sibilant tones.

"Well, it's too late to worry about it now," returned Vicky with ill-timed frankness; then, seeing the alarming rigidity of the abigail's stance, amended hastily, "No, no, it's most attractive, Trotton, but no feathers, please. In fact, no ornaments at all. Anything else would spoil the effect. It's been quite some time since my hair was arranged to such advantage. It's just that it seems a shame to waste such an elaborate style on a small family party, that's all."

And that is positively all the conciliating I am prepared to do tonight, she vowed silently, closing her mouth and jumping up from the bench. She presented her back to the disapproving dresser as she headed for the bed, where her gown was laid out. There was no time to pursue the topic, but she did acknowledge some passing curiosity as to what lay behind Trotton's action. It wasn't diminished when she recognised the gown being slipped over her head. This was a bronze-green affair of delicate silk, undeniably attractive but shockingly expensive, and more suited to a London salon than a country drawing room. When she moved, every line and curve of her body was emphasised by the diaphanous fabric. "Provocative" was the only word for it. She couldn't appear in company with Lady Lanscomb wearing something so expressly guaranteed to excite censure from a respectable matron already predisposed to take her in dislike.

"Not this dress, Trotton," she protested. "It's inappropriate."

She would have said more, but the abigail was behind her fastening up the buttons. "You wore it to Lady Melbourne's *soirée* last month and received several compliments, so you told me."

"*Trotton!*"

"You are going to be late, Miss Seymour."

Vicky glanced at the clock on the mantelpiece. "Oh, Lord, so I am." She bit her lip in momentary indecision, then said, "Fetch my Spanish shawl, Trotton—the black one."

When the dresser began to protest against this desecration, her mistress continued snappishly, "There is a great purple bruise below my shoulder in back. I just saw it in the mirror. If you had not selected such a low-cut gown, I would not be needing a shawl. Quickly, please, I am already shockingly late."

She made a business of fastening topaz earrings, and the indecision was now Trotton's. After a second or two the abigail stalked over to a high lacquered chest and took a black lace shawl from one of its drawers. Still radiating disapproval, she draped it over her mistress' arms and across her back. Her eyes flickered once, then dropped, but Vicky, watching in the dressing-table mirror, had seen the reluctant admiration at the effect created by the lacy texture against the silk.

She gurgled with laughter at the abigail's dilemma. "Admit it, Trotton. You know the result is really quite elegant, even if it wasn't your idea. And," she added with satisfaction, "it cancels the effect of this immodest gown—*nearly* cancels it, that is," as the glass reflected a suggestion of hipline and

rounded *derrière* as she moved toward the door, fastening
bracelet to match the earrings as she went.

"It looks very nice, Miss Seymour."

That stiff concession, Vicky well knew, was all the admis
sion Trotton would ever make that her own taste might be
fault. She twinkled saucily at the maid, told her not to wa
up for her, and went gaily out of the room.

Vicky would have been greatly amused to discover that he
faithful abigail was reflecting sourly that there was no helpin
some people at all. The way she saw it, Miss Seymour was i
great danger of counting her chickens before they hatched i
what they were saying in the Room about Lord Ellerby an
that Miss Hedgeley spending hours together supposedly prac
ticing singing was true. She might think he was too much he
slave to look at another woman, but there was many a sli
'twixt cup and lip, and Miss Hedgeley was a mighty pretty
girl. The word in the Room was that she was also an heiress
You couldn't prove it by her luggage, which was meager, bu
it was said that her trunk would arrive any day from London
And here was Miss Vicky scarcely bothering with her hai
and running around in men's clothes half the time, which was
a scandal in itself. And when her dresser had spent hours
devising an exquisite hairstyle and rigged her out in a gown
no young miss not even out yet could hope to compete with,
what had been the result? Had she been grateful for the
trouble and effort, or pleased to have the best made of
herself? *Not she!* No, Miss High and Mighty had merely
complained about her hair and proceeded to ruin the effect of
the gown. But that was Miss Vicky all over. Headstrong was
what she was and always had been, what with Mr. Seymour,
rest his soul, encouraging her to go her length in everything
without curb. It was to be hoped that she did not come to
regret this night's work, but Trotton wagged her head dole-
fully as she bustled about tidying up the bedchamber. It
wasn't too late for Ellerby to cry off, not by a long chalk it
wasn't, and Mrs. Simmons had seen a period of turmoil in
the tea leaves this afternoon.

Blithely unaware of the sorrowful future in store for her if she did not mend her ways, Vicky headed down the corridor, having already forgotten her appearance, and prepared to enjoy her evening. Mindful of her mission, she tapped on Drucilla's door, to be informed by the maid that the girl had gone down earlier. As she hurried toward the staircase, she was accosted by the housekeeper, who spent the better part of five minutes detailing a complaint concerning the laundress. She was not released until she had twice assured that lady that she might use her own discretion in handling the affair. Her ears had caught the sounds of arrival in the lower hall. She went dashing down the stairs, but slowed to a more decorous pace when it became evident that she would not be able to reach the hall before her guests entered.

Conscious of her own lateness and several pairs of eyes on her, Vicky felt her customary self-possession desert her briefly. Her colour was rather high and she stammered an apology to Lady Lanscomb that included the others. Sir Hugh was staring at her in patent admiration. Intercepting Mr. Massingham's comprehensive assessment that seemed to annul the purpose of the shawl, she hitched it higher on her arms in a defensive gesture and directed a frosty glare at him before offering her hand to Sir Hugh.

By the time Cavanaugh and the footman had helped the Meadowlands party to divest themselves of their outer clothing, Vicky had herself well in hand again. She had already received an account of the journey in reply to her polite inquiry to Lady Lanscomb and had complimented the ladies on their appearance. Now she waved the butler off and herself escorted her guests to the main drawing room. Mr. Massingham went ahead to open the door while Vicky stood aside to usher in the new arrivals. As the others filed past, a low voice meant for her ears alone murmured sardonically, "Seeing you in such high force relieves my mind of all worry that you might have suffered repercussions from your fall."

Vicky favoured him with a brief glance. "I thank you, sir, for your concern, but it is quite unnecessary, as you can see. I suffered no ill effects at all."

With that deplorable sense of poor timing common to

inanimate objects, the black shawl slipped from Vicky's shoulders just as she obeyed Mr. Massingham's gesture to precede him into the room. The next instant she stiffened involuntarily as warm fingers rearranged the folds of lace across her back.

"Thank you," she muttered between clenched teeth, casting him a swift look from under her lashes.

Mr. Massingham's eyes were fixed on a point over her shoulder as he bowed in polite acknowledgment, but his jaw had taken on a certain rigidity. She could not deceive herself that the bruise had escaped his notice. Fortunately the necessity to perform general introductions put a quick end to the moment of awkwardness.

The elder ladies took each other's measure in the intervals between uttering gracious speeches indicative of their great pleasure in the acquaintance. Lady Lanscomb had the felicity of perceiving herself in a higher state of preservation than the grey-haired, aquiline-featured Lady Honoria, and the latter was quite satisfied with the recognition, after a few minutes of conversation, that her counterpart was a frivolous creature with more hair than wit. Naturally, these discoveries increased the pleasure they might be expected to derive from an initial meeting.

Conversation was general until Cavanaugh announced dinner. As Vicky had foreseen, Miss Fairchild spoke only when directly addressed, but her few contributions were pertinent and she appeared to be enjoying herself in a quiet way. Seeing that she continued to take an active part in the evening should be a relatively simple matter now that any qualms over the reactions of the two elder ladies seemed superfluous. With only three gentlemen, the table could not be balanced, of course, nor was it possible to come up with an entirely satisfactory seating arrangement, but so small a party might discard the rules and converse across the table at times. Vicky and her aunt sat at opposite ends tonight, Lady Honoria having firmly proclaimed her position to be that of permanent privileged guest when she came to reside with her niece after the death of her brother-in-law. She had no intention of playing hostess anywhere except in her own home. Vicky had placed Lady Lanscomb between her son and Lord Ellerby on one side of the table and Mr. Massingham between the younger girls on the other. This had the advantage of conceding the older woman two gentlemen as dinner partners as well as keeping Elaine at her hostess' side, where she might unobtrusively see that the girl stayed in the thick of things. It also placed Drucilla too near Mr. Massingham for comfort, but Lady Honoria on the girl's right hand would see to it that he didn't monopolise her attention. On the way into the dining room, Vicky found time to advise Drucilla in an undervoice to keep her riding lessons secret until she could surprise the others with a demonstration of her skill. Although she looked surprised at the mention of the lessons out of the blue, the girl had readily agreed.

Only Mr. Massingham was even aware of the hurried exchange. Vicky found his speculative gaze on them when she glanced away. The odious creature saw entirely too much! She passed him with head high, a chilling look in her own eyes, which was a mistake, she knew at once, as those dark grey orbs narrowed thoughtfully. Her countenance reflected none of her irritation as she took her place at the head of the table and prepared to do the honours of her home.

At least the dinner might be regarded as an unqualified success, she assured herself later without conceit. It wasn't fashionable to employ a woman as cook in a large establishment, but she'd challenge the haughtiest French chef to fault Mrs. Baker's cooking and presentation for a company dinner. She had never dined at any board presided over by a male chef who could equal Mrs. Baker's way of roasting venison deep-basted and flavoured with tarragon and other seasonings, nor had she ever come across pheasants that were as succulent as those Mrs. Baker cooked in clay. Both specialities had appeared tonight among the two courses and several removes and had been enthusiastically received by the guests. Lady Lanscomb, whose eyebrows had climbed on perceiving Miss Seymour presiding over the table, praised a number of the dishes effusively and paid her the compliment of requesting the cook's recipe for a savory vegetable *mélange* smothered in a delectable wine sauce. The others showed their appreciation by doing hearty justice to all the cook's efforts.

If the level of the conversation and wit displayed at table had not attained the heights recorded by the late Dr. Johnson and his intimates, it had at least transcended personalities on occasion to roam about the realm of ideas. By the time she led the female exodus into the drawing room, Vicky considered that she had cause for self-congratulation, and that pleasant feeling lasted for the few minutes it took her to realise that the two elder ladies were circling each other warily.

Partially to give her aunt an opportunity to converse with Sir Hugh, whom she hadn't met before tonight, and partially to keep Lady Lanscomb's jealousy unaroused on Elaine's behalf, Vicky had seated Sir Hugh on Lady Honoria's right hand and as far away from herself as possible. She had thought this a brilliant stroke at the time, but obviously it hadn't prevented Lady Honoria from getting the glimmer of an idea with regard to her niece and this newest acquaintance if Vicky were correctly interpreting the drift of her questions and comments to Lady Lanscomb. This lady in her turn was intent upon discovering what, if anything, was between her hostess and Lord Ellerby. It was time to do some quick revising of her plans for the evening's entertainment unless she wished to chance open hostilities before the tea tray was brought in. Both ladies were addicted to whist, so without a qualm she sacrificed Sir Hugh and herself to the goal of keeping them too much occupied for idle conversation. This left Mr. Massingham and Lord Ellerby to entertain the girls. It would do nothing to forward Elaine's cause, she conceded with a shrug, but Rome hadn't been built in a day.

The gentlemen cooperated nicely by curtailing their port-drinking session to rejoin the ladies in short order. Her proposal to make up a table for whist if anyone should care for cards produced an identical gleam in the eyes of the elder ladies and a flatteringly quick offer from Sir Hugh to make a fourth.

"That leaves you young people to amuse yourselves with round games or music, as Drucilla does not play cards."

Her bright smiling look casually roved their faces, then passed swiftly over that of Mr. Massingham, which had taken on a startled, somewhat affronted look at being classed with the youngsters. She preserved her countenance with difficulty and paused expectantly in her role of anxious hostess.

"Do you not care for cards, Miss Hedgeley?"

Drucilla looked a little wistfully at Miss Fairchild. "I was never permitted to learn how to play cards, but you must not mind me. I shall enjoy watching if you should choose to play."

"But we could teach you; nothing could be simpler!" declared Miss Fairchild generously.

Vicky could have hugged her. The gentlemen were now neatly trapped, the older ladies would be able to channel their aggression into an acceptable activity, and as an additional bonus, the duet singing had been avoided for the present.

Any pangs of conscience she might have suffered for such a high-handed disposal of her guests' time were thoroughly quietened by the subsequent sounds of merriment and unmistakable enjoyment emanating from the table at the other end of the room. These noises became almost raucous as Drucilla's quick wit and ability to concentrate were severely tested by her teachers, who evidently thought she might as well learn a half-dozen popular games at one sitting.

All was strictly business and the conversation was kept to a minimum at the whist table, but it would not be too extravagant to claim that the enjoyment was no less despite the lack of vocal expression. In cutting for partners the two widows had wound up pitted against each other, which just suited their inclinations. Sir Hugh, partnering Lady Honoria, and Vicky, struggling to hold up her end as his mother's partner, were continually pressed to display every ounce of skill they possessed in the hard-fought contest that ensued. To sweeten his sacrifice, the gentleman had the exquisite and unalloyed pleasure of gazing upon his opponent's lovely profile and engaging her attention in snippets whenever circumstances permitted. The object of his admiration, on the other hand, was unable to derive any other satisfaction than that which accompanied the knowledge that the evening was saved. The cumulative effect of Sir Hugh's unsought admiration and his mother's silent resentment of it on those occasions when her attention strayed from the cards was such as to keep Vicky suspended in a state of acute discomfort that she must perpetually exert herself to disguise.

The eventual arrival of the tea tray secured her release and she rose with alacrity, leaving the others to add up the totals while she directed Cavanaugh in the disposition of the refreshments. As everyone drifted back toward the center of the room, Mr. Massingham's sapient eye ran over her rather limp form stationed behind the teapot.

"You appear to be in some need of a restorative, Miss Seymour. Did you find yourself at a stand amongst such accomplished players?"

The hint of satisfaction in his tone had a bracing effect on Vicky, but this was negated in the next moment by Lady Lanscomb, who, mellowed by a close win, conceded magnanimously, "Miss Seymour does not play at all badly. I have always held that whist is a game for the mature. No matter their natural aptitude for cards, the very young haven't the head for whist. Elaine, for example, shows great promise, but it will be many years before she will play as well as Miss Seymour."

Having dexterously succeeded in paying a compliment and settling a score at one and the same time, Lady Lanscomb navigated her way into a corner of the plush sofa and directed a sweet smile at her hostess.

"It was a pleasure playing with someone of your calibre, ma'am," Vicky said smoothly before the attendant pause could stretch beyond what was comfortable. "How do you take your tea?" She gave the task of preparing it her careful attention and presented the cup for delivery to Mr. Massingham, who appeared as dumbfounded as a child who has just been bitten by his pet dog. At another time she would have applauded something that could disconcert the abominable Mr. Massingham, but now there was a hint of warning in her bright voice as she declared that she would continue to make use of his services to present the next cup to her aunt.

"And then you may be dismissed with thanks, sir, for I know my aunt is most anxious to have some speech with you after so many years. I shall enlist Lord Ellerby's assistance for the rest."

Mr. Massingham came out of his trance, took the cup, and carried out his hostess' instructions while the soft murmur of conversation resumed. He stayed beside Lady Honoria a little apart from the others for the remainder of the visit. Nothing untoward occurred to mar the last half-hour of a very successful evening as everyone contributed to a pleasant, easy conversation. Possibly the only person whose regrets at the eventual parting were insincere was Vicky, who felt as drained as though she had worked in the fields all day. A mild elation at having pulled off a difficult feat enabled her to get through the "talking-over-the-party" session indulged in by the residents without betraying her longing for privacy and bed, but she was more than grateful when her aunt declared herself ready to retire.

Once prepared for bed, however, she discovered that her eyes refused to close. Whether due to her afternoon nap or the overstimulation of walking a social tightrope for hours, the result was that various scenes from the evening just past kept intruding into her memory when she tried to compose herself for sleep. On the whole she had been pleased with the outcome of the dinner party, but pictures of Lady Lanscomb watching her like a cat at a mousehole and bristling with ill-concealed resentment whenever her son paid her any attention caused her no little concern. If her ladyship persisted in her inimical surveillance, it could not fail to become evident to others also. The least mischievous result would be a general embarrassment. She didn't like to speculate on the wounding effect on Miss Fairchild, to whom Vicky had taken a sincere liking. It would be surprising indeed if the incipient friendship survived. Elaine had her share of pride; her behaviour would be everything that was correct, but the tentative warm advances toward a mutual understanding would cease. Yes, Sir Hugh's mother was becoming a problem, she thought, accompanying her troubled reflections with rhythmic poundings of her pillow as she rearranged herself amongst the bedclothes. If Mr. Massingham, whom she had not credited with unusual sensitivity, had recognised the malevolence beneath the sweetness, then relations between the two houses would soon be jeopardised. Strangely enough, though, it wasn't this disturbing possibility but the image of Mr. Massingham's thunderstruck countenance that occupied her last waking moments before she drifted off to sleep with a little smile curving her lips.

13

"Mr. Massingham."

As Cavanaugh's resonant voice reached the woman in the crimson wing-back chair, she lowered her newspaper and gazed with slightly widened eyes at the man coming toward her.

"How do you do, Mr. Massingham? Won't you sit down?"

"Good afternoon, Miss Seymour." He released the hand she had extended and settled into a companion chair. "You look surprised to see me, but not, I trust, unpleasantly surprised?"

She didn't trust the gleam in those wicked black eyes, but murmured suitably and waited.

"I came to call on Lady Honoria, but Cavanaugh informs me her ladyship is resting at the moment."

"Yes, but she will be coming down shortly to tea if you would care to wait."

"Thank you."

In the pause that followed, it occurred to Miss Seymour that she and Mr. Massingham had never yet conducted a purely social conversation. She wondered if he would begin with the weather.

"What were you reading?" He indicated the paper she was now folding.

"An account of the recent peace talks in Brussels. What do you think of this so-called Holy Alliance the Allies signed in September, Mr. Massingham?"

"I don't see the need of it as far as an instrument for containing French aggression is concerned. The Quadruple Alliance of 1813 is being renewed and is more to the point."

"Then you would agree with Castlereagh in not signing?"

"I don't see that it makes much difference." He shrugged. "Alexander in an evangelical mood. England will have plenty to do in getting her economy back on a peacetime basis, and so will Russia and all the Allies. I suppose there's no harm in it."

After a second or two, Miss Seymour suggested, "It's now your turn to initiate a topic of conversation."

He stared at her. "What is this, Miss Seymour? You've never been shy with me before."

This sally earned him a cool little smile. "And I am not shy with you now, Mr. Massingham. I was merely observing the rules of civility in trying to conduct a conversation with you."

He gave a bark of laughter at this and replied with an ironic inflection, "The rules of civility haven't troubled you significantly in our previous conversations, as I recall."

"But I am your hostess today, Mr. Massingham," she reminded him sweetly. "Very well. I shall now ask after the health of the family at Meadowlands. I trust the drive home last night was uneventful and the ladies are not too fatigued today?"

"The drive went smoothly and the ladies are in prime twig today, or should I say they are in excellent health and spirits?"

"That would perhaps be a more socially acceptable description," she agreed gravely.

"Speaking of Lady Lanscomb," he began, then hesitated, a rather odd expression in the dark eyes.

When an encouraging look produced no more than a pulling in of the corners of his mouth, Vicky exclaimed archly, "Why, Mr. Massingham, can it be that *you* are shy? And I never guessed it!"

"Touché!"

He had smiled in just that delightful fashion once before—at Drucilla in the Green Feather—and it had caused Vicky to question briefly her reading of his character, but that had been nothing to the way it affected her when directed solely at herself. She could feel her pulses flutter and there was a ridiculous breathless quality to her voice for an instant as she prompted hurriedly, "You were saying? . . . about Lady Lanscomb?"

The smile was gone and her pulse settled down to normal.

"Her ladyship is a charming woman and a wonderfully considerate hostess."

He paused and sent a challenging look at Vicky, who replied mildly, "She is indeed."

"Then why did she . . .?" He stopped again. This time she did not offer to fill the pause, but merely waited with a questioning expression that snapped his black brows together.

"Don't playact with me!" he grated impatiently. "Miss Victoria Seymour, always the perfect hostess."

"Thank you, I do try to be."

When his glare intensified, she abandoned her spurious affability. "Would you prefer that I emulate *your* manner?" she inquired dryly.

"I would *prefer* an honest answer!"

"But you haven't as yet asked a question," she pointed out with unanswerable logic.

For an instant he looked a bit nonplussed, then recollected himself and said with a sheepish air and a softened voice, "Lady Lanscomb was quite intentionally insul . . ." He bit off the word and substituted, "*uncivil* to you last night."

"I think you are refining too much on an awkward slip of the tongue," said Vicky easily. "She was merely trying to make a point about whist players."

"She was *trying* to give the impression that you are so much older than Drucilla and Miss Fairchild as to be relegated to another category entirely."

"And so I *am* much older than Drucilla and Miss Fairchild."

"Nonsense! You cannot be a day over four- or five-and-twenty, and look eighteen," he added, running an expert eye over her glowing complexion and the lithe, slim figure becomingly clad in a raspberry-coloured cotton gown.

175

She stared at him in amusement, a faint smile curving the beautiful mouth.

"I cannot help wondering why Lady Lanscomb should have taken you in dislike."

"Do you not think you are being a trifle absurd, Mr. Massingham?" she asked coolly. "There is no reason to believe Lady Lanscomb has done so, though I am much obliged to you for your concern—and a bit surprised by it."

Mr. Massingham's expression had been a study in bewilderment and impatience. At this provocative addendum he ran a restless hand through his hair and grinned disarmingly. "Well, yes, I imagine you might be, but it isn't *concern* precisely, rather a rooted dislike of injustice."

This outrageous remark served to reverse any softening in Vicky's attitude brought on by his earlier statements, and her reply was offhand. "It seems to me that dislike is a matter of personal inclination rather than justice or injustice, but since I remain unconvinced that Lady Lanscomb has taken an unreasoning dislike to me in the first place, any discussion of the subject would be pointless, do you not agree?"

Nothing about Mr. Massingham's dissatisfied expression bespoke agreement on any point whatever, but Lady Honoria's entrance at that moment put an end to any further discussion. Until Drucilla and Lord Ellerby drifted in to join the others for tea, Mr. Massingham concentrated his facile charm (Vicky's description) on Lady Honoria, and thereafter switched to Drucilla, whom he engaged in a lighthearted conversation that all but excluded the others and attracted a speculative glance from Lord Ellerby from time to time. With eight years on the social scene at her back, not to mention her father's love of a challenge, Vicky contrived to appear totally at her ease and oblivious of any intended snub. She had the ultimate satisfaction of earning a jaundiced glare from Mr. Massingham on his departure after tea. She smiled brilliantly at him and bade him a safe journey in dulcet accents.

He had given her something to think about, however, and her thoughts were not so calm as her demeanour; in fact, they were mildly chaotic. Until their last exchange before her aunt had interrupted them, Vicky had been receiving an impression, a *tentative* impression, that Mr. Massingham was concerned for her. In light of his final explanation about the justice of the matter, she might perhaps dismiss her perception as a fanciful notion, except that there had been an uncharacteristic element of uncertainty, if not self-compulsion, in his manner that had puzzled her exceedingly. However, when one considered that Mr. Massingham didn't like her, regarded her (accurately) as an obstacle to his plans for Drucilla, one could most likely account for his manner. It must be galling to have to defend a foe. For some reason this explanation afforded her no satisfaction either, but the original incident and its aftermath were too trifling to waste thought on.

Except that she was forced to think about it later when she found herself alone with her aunt for the first time since the dinner party. Drucilla and Lord Ellerby had both gone to their rooms to change when Lady Honoria said abruptly, "The next time that irritating Lanscomb female thinks to make you the object of her poisonous tongue, I shall give her a piece of my mind, no matter how public the occasion."

Vicky, who had found her thoughts reverting to the whole incident, started and looked up, instantly made uneasy by the martial glitter in her relative's eye.

"What can you possibly mean, ma'am?" she asked with a fair assumption of innocent surprise.

"That's trying it much too rare and thick, my child," was the tart rejoinder, and Vicky marvelled anew at her ladyship's collection of cant phrases.

"I think you are refining too much on a mere slip of the tongue," she replied with a sense of *déjà vu*.

"Very well, you do not wish to discuss it. My lips are sealed, but don't try to gammon me! I wasn't born yesterday!" snapped Lady Honoria.

"Yes, ma'am . . . I mean, *no*, ma'am."

Lady Honoria shot her a suspicious look, then continued, "Besides, only a cloth-head like that perennial belle would imagine that she could promote a match between her son and her ward merely by disparaging the competition. But my lips are sealed,'' she repeated, rising and shaking out her skirts with a bland smile for her niece before sweeping majestically out of the room.

Vicky, watching the impressive exit with rueful admiration, decided her wisest course was to ignore the episode completely. After all, Drucilla's visit must eventually come to an end; therefore, her romance must be Vicky's primary concern. There was no immediate urgency to act on Elaine's behalf. She had enough on her plate at the moment. In fact, it would suit her book if some little time might be allowed to elapse without any intercourse between the two households.

Vicky's wish was granted, for the family at the Oaks was not honoured by visitors from Meadowlands during the next few days. They pursued their own activities, individually or collectively, in perfect accord. Vicky's gamekeeper took Lord Ellerby out with a gun one morning for birds, and the riding lessons continued apace. Music remained the chief communal activity indoors, though all were called upon at times to pander to Drucilla's newborn passion for card games. Vicky rode daily with Lord Ellerby and managed to slip out to see Shadow most days.

She was riding him one afternoon, racing round and round the huge field, less for training purposes than because the participants in the joyful activity found the sensation of speed mutually gratifying. It was another in the series of unusually balmy days they had been experiencing this fall, and Vicky was glad of the slight breeze to cool her heated cheeks as she and Shadow came to a reluctant halt at last. She was about to rub him down before allowing him to drink when a familiar voice said, ''I'll do that,'' and the cloth was taken from her unresisting fingers.

''Must you always appear so unexpectedly, Mr. Massingham, popping up everywhere like a jack-in-the-box?'' she asked crossly, annoyed with the sudden quickening of her heartbeat (from shock, of course) and fearful that he might attribute her heightened colour to some cause other than heat and exercise.

He grinned, unabashed. ''Of a nervous temperament, are

you, Miss Seymour? You surprise me. Or are you simply endeavouring to put the upstart in his place?''

Refusing to rise to the bait, she shifted her glance from the amused mockery in those bold black eyes and looked back toward the fence. ''Where is your horse?''

''In the stables. We approached the front door today like polite afternoon callers.''

''We?'' Vicky looked down at her breeched and booted person in some dismay before casting a startled glance around the field.

''Yes, Hugh and I. Relax, Miss Seymour, Hugh is inside reading the papers. You are safe from observation at the moment, although if you will persist in wearing that revolting costume, you'd be well served if I had Lady Lanscomb and Miss Fairchild with me.'' He turned back to Shadow, who, impatient for his drink, was beginning to sidle away from the restraining hands. ''Whoa, boy, all in good time,'' his handler soothed, applying himself to the task with brisk efficiency.

Vicky bit her lip. She was *not* going to be put in the position of defending her actions to this aggravating creature, she resolved, and promptly broke her resolution. ''You will allow, sir, that my 'revolting costume,' as you are pleased to call it, is the most practical outfit to the purpose. Raising horses is my business, you know.'' At least she had succeeded in keeping her tone level.

''Yes, I know. Why?''

''Why? Why what?''

His glance this time was serious as he paused in the act of rubbing Shadow's hind legs. ''Why are you *personally* involved in the business of raising horses? There is no need, surely?''

''One must do *something* with one's life,'' she retorted impatiently. ''Or are you one of those persons who believe all females should do nothing save sit in a corner and embroider altar cloths?''

''No, of course not. You could marry,'' he suggested, voice and features expressionless. ''Why else is Ellerby here except to persuade you to resume your engagement?''

"How did you . . .? *Aunt Honoria!*" Vicky's face was flushed with annoyance as she bit off the words, but Mr. Massingham denied that Lady Honoria was the source of his knowledge.

"I read it in the *Gazette* before I left London," he explained.

"But you didn't know me, you . . . you couldn't have known who I was," she stammered, utterly confounded.

"I met your parents once when I was a schoolboy. Besides, I have an excellent memory." This last was said with a modest pride that intensified Vicky's chagrin. The man was *insufferable*, he was . . . She didn't know what he was! In impotent fury, hands clenched at her sides, she watched him finish his grooming chore, then slap the colt on the flank as he released him to his watering trough near the tree.

He returned his attention to the silent, rigid girl and advised kindly, "Don't work yourself into a pelter. You probably know more about me than I like also."

A lambent look from the corner of her eye was her only reaction as she turned and strode purposefully in the direction of the house. Mr. Massingham fell into step beside her, and they crossed the first field in silence.

"Do you disapprove of the married state, Miss Seymour?" he inquired conversationally when it began to seem as if the entire trek to the house would be accomplished in hostile silence on the lady's part.

"Of course I don't disapprove of marriage—for some," she snapped, keeping her eyes directed straight ahead.

"But not for yourself?"

"I didn't say that!"

"Ah? Then you do intend to resume your engagement?"

Her head finally swung around in his direction, and he was treated to a brief exposition of flashing golden-brown eyes. "That, Mr. Massingham, is none of your concern!" she flared, abandoning any pretence of civility and resuming her brisk pace.

"Of course it isn't," he agreed, suiting his step to hers. "*Do* you?"

Almost betrayed into an untimely giggle by his effrontery,

she was so incensed at her weakness that she flung the truth at him. "No, I do not!"

"That's good. You wouldn't suit at all."

She stopped dead and faced him with her chin at a challenging angle and her eyes narrowed. "Considering that you are scarcely acquainted with me and have only twice clapped eyes on Lord Ellerby—"

"Three times," he corrected.

"Three times, then," she conceded through gritted teeth. "It hardly signifies. Under the circumstances, I find your remarks highly impertinent."

"If the circumstances were as you describe them, I would allow you to be correct, but you mistake, Miss Seymour. I am *very* well acquainted with you indeed, and, having observed Lord Ellerby's behaviour toward you on three occasions, it is quite clear to me that you two shouldn't suit. He's disposed to worship you, the poor fool. You can wind him around your finger, and that, you know, would be fatal to a marriage."

Vicky took a deep breath and counted to ten before answering repressively, "This discussion, if such it can be designated, is at an end, Mr. Massingham."

"Very well," he replied equably. After another silence he observed chattily, "Cavanaugh informed Hugh and me that though none of the family was in at present, all were expected shortly, so we remained, hoping for an invitation to tea."

Silence greeted this remark.

"Shall we be invited for tea?" he persisted.

"Yes, of course," she responded mechanically, then, lest he suppose that she was in any way discomposed by what he had said earlier, achieved a normal tone with effort. "My aunt and Miss Hedgeley have gone out driving this afternoon, and I believe Lord Ellerby had formed the intention of trying his luck at fishing."

"Ah, we are back to Miss Seymour, the perfect hostess."

Vicky ignored this provocation, being fiercely determined that nothing he might say should be permitted to inspire further retaliation on her part. She suspected that for some obscure reason Mr. Massingham delighted in brangling with her, and was resolved not to contribute further to his perverse enjoyment.

"Who is that over there?"

She followed his glance to where a farm vehicle was emerging from the woods onto the carriage drive.

"Probably one of the tenant farmers. They have permission to do some cutting in the home wood for a fuel supply for the winter. Yes," she added indifferently as the cart lumbered across the distant road, "that is Jeb Laycock, I believe. They look like his horses."

"He has that wagon dangerously loaded. I trust he doesn't intend to drive it across those uneven fields. Those logs could shift."

It seemed that driving across the fields was exactly what the farmer did intend, for he had alighted and opened the first gate almost by the time Mr. Massingham spoke.

"You there, Laycock!" shouted the latter, beginning to run toward the drive. "Don't drive into that field!"

The ex-soldier was fifty feet away before Vicky realised what was in his mind. She stood rooted in uncertainty for a second or two before heading in Mr. Massingham's wake at a brisk pace that quickened as she saw the unevenly loaded wagon lurching across the meadow. Jeb hadn't heard the warning over the noise of the cart. She hadn't gone more than a few steps farther when she began to run, realising from the jerky motion of the cart how very unsafe it was. It seemed no more than an instant later that the event Mr. Massingham had foreseen came to pass. The cart started to cant to the right, straightened itself momentarily, then overturned before Vicky could release the breath of fear caught in her throat.

Mr. Massingham was already at the scene by the time Vicky climbed the fence.

"Go for help!" he called before disappearing under logs and wagon.

She scarcely heard him, her mind being taken up with absorbing the details of the accident. She had seen Jeb hurtle through the air. Perhaps he had fallen clear of wagon and debris. As she came closer, the position of Mr. Massingham told her Jeb had not been so fortunate. The cart had gone over on its side; Mr. Massingham was braced against its midsection, trying to keep the weight off the fallen driver while the fear-maddened animals pulled against their traces. The first priority was to stop them from pulling the wagon all the way over and dumping the remaining logs on the two men.

"I'll free the horses," she called, averting her head from the scene as she ran past.

"No! Keep away! They'll *kick* you! Go get help!"

She was beginning to soothe the horses with hands and voice even as she answered, "There's no time! He could be crushed to death!"

She went at the buckles like a madwoman, closing her ears against Jeb's groans and the oaths issuing from Mr. Massingham. Her fingers were stiff, it seemed to take forever, but at least the horses were calmer. There, that was one freed at last! She could feel the cart behind her shifting postion, and sheer panic threatened to overwhelm her. If it tipped farther, he could be killed! *Don't think about that!* Concentrate on her task. *Why* wouldn't her fingers work faster? After an eternity she succeeded in getting the second horse unharnessed, and she steeled herself to turn around.

She transferred her gaze to the man on the ground after one swift look at Mr. Massingham's livid face. She couldn't worry about that expression of black rage now. Jeb was lying prone, buried up to his hips in logs. The side panel of the wagon seemed to be across his legs also, and it was this that Mr. Massingham was bracing as he moved as many of the logs as he could reach off the farmer.

"*Now* will you go for help!" Sweat was pouring off Mr. Massingham's face from the strain of bearing the great weight.

"No! It would take too long. His legs might be crushed in the meantime. He has five children."

Even as she babbled, Vicky started to dislodge some of the smaller logs, stepping gingerly in and around the shifting mass, incongruously aware of a rush of gratitude for her breeches.

"Get the ones still in the cart. Be careful, Angel. Try not to upset the balance."

Easier said than done, as Vicky discovered shortly. Some of the logs were too heavy for her to lift, but by methodically moving the smaller ones she succeeded in lightening the load so that their combined strength was enough to right the cart. They had worked in grim silence for the most part, although Vicky whispered directions and cautions to herself from time to time, and once Mr. Massingham had said encouragingly, "Not many more to go. I can almost move it now. Can you manage, Angel?"

She had redoubled her efforts, and a few seconds later had the enormous satisfaction of seeing the wagon lifted off the farmer's legs. For an instant the panting rescuers stared at each other in wordless communion that surpassed in intimacy anything Vicky had ever experienced with another human being. A strange excitement raced along her blood, and her heart sang. Then reality in the form of the injured man intruded. He groaned, and both rescuers sprang toward him.

"How is he?" Vicky was nearly breathless as they knelt over the prone figure.

"I haven't been able to tell," replied Mr. Massingham grimly as he started flinging the remaining logs off the victim's body. "It will be miraculous indeed if his legs aren't crushed," he muttered in lowered tones as Vicky was murmuring soothing words to the semiconscious man, whose hand she was holding tightly.

But it seemed miracles were in season after all. When the last of the debris had been cleared off Jeb Laycock's legs in fear-filled silence, Mr. Massingham looked up from his careful examination and said wonderingly, "The left leg is definitely broken, but it feels like a straightforward fracture. As far as I can tell with his clothing on, the right leg is not injured at all. The logs must have fallen in such a way as to form a . . . a temporary *structure* is the the only way I can describe it, that actually prevented his legs from being crushed."

Tears of reaction and thankfulness were pouring silently down Vicky's cheeks. Her slim form in the torn and soiled white shirt sagged visibly in relief.

"Don't faint on me now!" cried Mr. Massingham in mock alarm.

This elicited a tremulous smile and a determined straightening of his fellow rescuer's shoulders.

"Your cruel aspersions wound me deeply, sir," she retorted with a brave attempt at insouciance as she struggled, more stiffly than she liked to have witnessed, to her feet. "*Now* I shall go for help, which is what you have desired me to do all along."

Mr. Massingham eyed his gallant companion with unusual solicitude. "You are exhausted!" he exclaimed. "I'll go for assistance if you will stay with Mr. Laycock."

"Perhaps if you were to catch one of the horses for me," she suggested, casting a weary look around the field.

A piercing whistle made her jump skittishly. Mr. Massingham had already set off in pursuit of one of the wagon horses peacefully cropping grass. He was back in under a minute, leading a heavily ribbed grey.

"There's no danger that this noble beast will throw you," he remarked dryly. "The problem will be in getting him to go at all."

Vicky chuckled as she approached the horse. "I believe you are a snob, Mr. Massingham. Old Granddad here has nobly earned his keep for many years."

"This collection of bad points is unworthy of his rider," he insisted, placing firm hands on Vicky's waist and lifting her easily onto the grey's back. "Be sure the grooms, or whoever you send back, bring something to use as splints, and cloth or string to tie them on with."

"I will."

His hands were still at her waist. As he removed them somewhat lingeringly, serious dark eyes gleamed up into hers with a light in their depths she had never expected to see.

"Don't come back here yourself. You have my word that everything will be done for him as you would wish. Go home and rest."

"Very well," she acquiesced meekly, then added, not so

meekly, "I must go ahead to Jeb's house to warn his wife first, though."

"*No!* You are near collapse. Send someone else to warn Mrs. Laycock. That is an *order*, Miss Seymour!"

Her chin elevated in automatic defiance at the fierceness of his protest. "You forget, Mr. Massingham, that *I* am not one of your military subordinates. *You* do not issue orders on *my* property!"

Instead of taking umbrage at her haughty tone, Mr. Massingham laughed in genuine amusement. "How gratifying to find you have just confirmed my judgment. Ellerby is definitely not the man for you. He would never know how to control you in a thousand years."

As her lips parted to take up this new challenge, he placed a finger on them. "Now is not the time to resume hostilities, my dear girl. You are tired and dirty, and I suspect your hands are full of splinters that need prompt attention."

So he *had* noticed the wince she had tried to conceal when she had grasped the old grey's mane. She hesitated, the independent side of her nature unwilling to capitulate.

"*Please,* Vicky, do as I say this one time. You look completely done up."

She was spared the ignominy of voluntary capitulation by the forceful smack Mr. Massingham administered on the rump of the patient horse at that moment.

Rider and steed moved off with a motion that, while far from beautiful, was at least purposeful. As she leaned down to open the gate leading to the carriage drive, Vicky glanced back for the first time. Mr. Massingham was on his knees beside the injured man, his back firmly turned to her.

14

Mr. Massingham had been quite correct in his assessment of Vicky's present state as "done up." If asked the cause, he would have replied that her condition was the result of the gruelling physical ordeal she had just experienced, and in this assessment he would have been essentially mistaken. Vicky could have told him, but she'd have died first, that the primary cause of her depleted state was emotional, not physical, and was directly attributable to himself.

The recent emergency had called forth great physical effort on her part in an automatic unthinking reaction to her tenant farmer's plight. When the immediate danger had passed, however, enabling her thinking processes to reactivate, she had been struck, with a force equal to that pile of logs, by the unwelcome knowledge that the sick sense of panic that had swept over her while she was struggling to free the horses had been entirely due to a fear that *Mr. Massingham* might be crushed. The implications of this revelation had left her weak and shaken.

Her first reaction to such a calamity had been a spirited denial of the situation. The look that had passed between them had merely been an expression of the mutual satisfaction any two persons in like circumstances might be expected to experience. It was totally impersonal. The sensation of faintness that had overcome her at the touch of his hands on her waist had been a delayed reaction to such unusual and sustained labour. The trembling that had seized her when he had cajoled her obedience with a smile and soft words was mere physical weakness, *not* a longing to be held and comforted. Oh, yes, there was a reasonable explanation for all these manifestations.

But she had not been able to explain away the desolation that had swept over her when she had glanced back from the gate and seen all his attention focused on the injured Jeb. Somehow that vision had unleashed a flood of memories that came rushing in on her in a tide she was powerless to resist. She had suffered just such a sense of desolation when Edward had gone to war and again when news came of his death. After so many years she had forgotten the feeling. She didn't wish to recall it ever again, and especially she didn't wish to associate it with Andrew Massingham. He was the last person in the world she would choose to love. She didn't even *like* him above half.

Vicky hadn't realised she was repeatedly pounding her fist into her thigh until contact with one of the splinters jerked a cry of pain from her and brought the grey's head around in mild surprise. She was almost in sight of the stables, having mechanically guided her mount despite her dazed emotional condition. There were things to be attended to immediately; her own problem must wait. She kicked the grey smartly and increased the speed of his shamble for a bit. Further exertions were spared her, for one of the grooms, spotting his mistress approaching on a mount unworthy of the name, came running to meet her. Within five minutes a rescue party had been organised and supplies gathered to take out to the scene of the accident. Vicky saw them off, then ordered a horse to be saddled.

"And who would the horse be meant for, Miss Vicky, if I may be so bold?"

Vicky jumped. "You startled me, coming up behind me like that, Manley. It's for me, of course. I must ride over to Jeb's cottage to warn his wife about what has happened."

"Well, now, seeing as it's going to take me the best part of half an hour to get those splinters out of your hands and the lads will likely have him back afore then, you'd best send one o' the stable hands to ride over with the news.''

"She'll take it better from me, Manley. I promise I'll have my maid take care of my hands as soon as I have seen Nora.''

"That you won't, Miss Vicky. That city woman will wring her hands and pussyfoot around and end up causing you more trouble than the splinters themselves. You know I'm the nearest to a doctor on the place, and I'll make a quick clean job of it.''

"Then I'll come back after I've seen Nora.''

"Your pa would have had my hide if I let you ride off like that. Now, give over argufying, Miss Vicky, and go on back to my room while I send one of the lads off to Laycock's.''

And such was Vicky's exhaustion at the moment that she did refrain from further argument. A scant half-hour later she was entering her own rooms to change. As promised, Manley had made a clean job of her hands. They were sore but free of splinters. She only wished she could say the same for her heart. That formerly well-armoured organ had been pierced in a surprise attack that had left her gasping. Almost the last thing she would elect to do at the moment was face any other human being while her thoughts were in such turmoil, but if she did not appear for tea, questions would be raised, and that was an even less palatable option. Sir Hugh was downstairs now, and Mr. Massingham himself would drift in before long.

She rang for Trotton and wandered listlessly over to the long mirror in her sunny green-and-yellow boudoir. The pale and heavy-eyed reflection that stared back at her was sufficiently disconcerting to produce a tiny spurt of self-disgust. What she needed was an infusion of courage, but, barring that, she was going to do her level best to transform this woebegone creature in the glass. If she didn't want her wounds probed, then it was up to her to disguise those wounds.

Consequently, when Trotton arrived on the scene, she found her mistress in an unusually demanding frame of mind.

Nothing would do but she must wear her daffodil-yellow muslin with the French tucks and frothy lace.

"But, miss, that dress is for summer!" exclaimed the abigail, scandalised by such a solecism. "This is November!"

"Never mind, Trotton, it is the happiest colour, like liquid sunshine, and I have a great desire to wear it one final time. Winter will be upon us before we know it."

For once she wasn't perfectly content to simply renew the smoothly coiled hairstyle she adopted for daytime wear, but asked Trotton if she could perhaps make a double coil.

"And do we not have some ribbon that matches the yellow gown, Trotton? Could you wind it around the edges just to confine the coils? But hurry, mind, I'm terribly late."

Mystified but never unwilling to exercise her prized talents, Trotton set to work with dispatch. Ten minutes later she was slipping the muslin confection over a hairstyle that she did not consider completely contemptible, considering the inadequate time span allotted her. As she did up the buttons, half her attention was on her mistress' odd behaviour. She had expressed satisfaction with the results of the dresser's manipulations but she was frowning into the mirror and now she was pinching her cheeks to produce some colour.

"Would you like me to apply a touch of rouge, Miss Seymour?"

Vicky started slightly. "No . . . no, thank you, Trotton, I must go down now. Are all the buttons fastened? Thank you very much."

She was out of the door before she finished, hurrying down the hall, but her footsteps lagged as she descended the last few stairs and it was necessary to gather her courage together. At the door to the drawing room her chin went up and her shoulders went back perceptibly. The man following the quiet-footed butler from the back of the house thought she looked extremely fatigued.

A moment or two later, when Cavanaugh announced him, his surprise was the greater to find a sparkling-faced Vicky accepting a cup of tea from her aunt while she gaily apologised to the assembled company for her lateness. He arrived in time to hear her declare that she had been detained on a matter of estate business. Mr. Massingham's black brows escalated comically, but he merely returned Lady Honoria's greeting with the warm smile he seemed to reserve for her.

It was Drucilla who exclaimed at the torn and stained condition of his pale tan pantaloons, which no ministrations of Cavanaugh's had served to restore. Vicky had already noticed the darkening bruise on his chin, no doubt caused by contact with a log, and the glance of revulsion he cast at the teapot. While her aunt expressed concern over the former, she remedied the latter situation by rising and pouring him a glass of Madeira, which he accepted with an absent murmur of thanks, his attention being claimed just then by all the other occupants of the room demanding to know what had occurred. His brief factual account of the accident was not permitted to stand unremarked, nor was Vicky's part in the affair to remain dark, though her eyes sent a warning signal to Mr. Massingham, a signal that went unheeded as he proceeded to describe her participation in the most laudatory terms that rendered the earlier cheek-pinching quite superfluous. Her flustered squirming was intensified when Drucilla said admiringly, "And just look at you in that delectable gown, looking as though you had never lifted a finger all day except to ring the bell for a servant to bring you another sweetmeat from the dish."

The others laughed and Vicky buried her scratched hands in the folds of her gown, a gesture not lost on Mr. Massingham, who said only that he envied her her maid and could only wish he had been in a position to correct his own appearance before joining them all.

"Never mind about your clothes," soothed Lady Honoria. "It was a fortunate thing for Jeb Laycock that you were both at hand when the accident occurred. It could have had much more serious consequences than a broken leg."

"Who finally set the leg?" Vicky inquired of Mr. Massingham.

"I was most happy to resign my claim to the honour in favour of one of your trainers answering to the salubrious title of 'Twister,' who claimed more experience than I in setting bones."

"Yes, he is quite clever at it with animals, and humans too," Vicky said seriously, and looked a bit surprised when the others laughed at her unconscious order of preference. "So the only casualties were Jeb's leg and your boots, which are sadly scratched. I fear they are ill-fated. They escaped ruin after the holdup, only to be spoiled in another accident."

"I have every confidence my groom will be able to conceal all but the worst of the marks," Mr. Massingham said easily, "but what is this about the holdup? I don't recall any injury to my boots at all on that occasion."

"I had formed the intention of cutting them off you to spare your wounded leg further injury, but Mr. Tolliver wouldn't let me."

"God bless Mr. Tolliver!" exclaimed Mr. Massingham fervently.

Vicky, observing that all the gentlemen present wore identical expressions of horror at the contemplated sacrilege, produced a trill of airy laughter. "I vow you men are all alike in valuing your precious boots above humans."

All three were quick to deny this accusation as pure calumny.

"The real difference is that we men become attached to our clothes and, unlike females, are not forever looking for an excuse to change them," Lord Ellerby explained patiently.

The others nodded in solemn agreement.

"And we females reserve our affection for humans. So *that* is the real difference between the sexes! Thank you for explaining it so clearly," twinkled Vicky.

She took charge of the conversation then, steering it to light topics and keeping it entertaining by the power of her sparkle and wit. It was a scintillating performance that induced a mood of hilarity in the company, though she did wonder once or twice when discovering her aunt's eye fixed on her in a calculating manner if she might be in danger of overplaying her role of social butterfly. Though she contrived to pass over Mr. Massingham for the most part, on those few occasions when their glances clashed, she was left in no doubt that he too remained uncaptivated by her performance. There was a brooding quality about the look he bent on her, containing more than a hint of displeasure.

Sulky as a bear with a sore head, she thought with perverse satisfaction, taking in his negligent posture as he lounged in the chair. He had no manners at all. Both Sir Hugh and Lord Ellerby cast him quite into the shade.

The elder of these two paragons, whose manoeuvres to get his hostess' undivided attention had not been so subtle as to go unperceived, finally succeeded in establishing himself next to her on the blue sofa by the device of bringing her another cup.

"Allow me to tell you that it was a magnificent thing you did for your tenant this afternoon," Sir Hugh began in a voice meant for her ears alone.

"Nonsense," replied Vicky rather shortly. "Anyone who could lift more than a pennyweight could have done what I did. A seven-year-old child would have been of equal use in that situation."

"Now it is my turn to cry nonsense, though your modesty does you great credit and is just what one would expect from someone of your generous nature, always so ready to assist those in difficulties." His smile was warm with admiration, but it caused a chill of apprehension to feather down his hostess' spine. Not this too, on top of everything else she had borne this afternoon!

After eight years on the social scene it was almost second nature to parry fulsome compliments, but such was her flustered state that all her skill deserted Vicky at this moment. "I fear you are trying to flatter me, sir," she protested weakly.

"Acquit me, I beg of you, of any charge of insincerity." Sir Hugh's hazel eyes echoed the plea. "I am quite serious."

Vicky was casting around in her unresponsive mind for something to discourage him. "And I, sir, am almost never serious. My nature is almost entirely frivolous, so be warned," she said with desperate flippancy, feeling utterly besieged. It was too much to bear in one day. She must escape!

Sir Hugh was smiling indulgently. "Now you are joking

me to pay me back for embarrassing your modesty with my praises. Very well, I shall be silent on that subject.''

"You do not pay me the compliment of believing me, sir.''

"How can I, when your conduct belies your words? Is it frivolous to nurse a wounded man through fever? Is it frivolous to run a thriving business?''

Vicky achieved a tinkling laugh despite her jangling nerves. "As to the first, I daresay I can rise to an emergency as well as the next person, but your second example is invalid because I only dabble in the business for the short periods that I am in residence at the Oaks.'' She shuddered theatrically. "I could never bear to spend any considerable stretch exclusively in the country. I should go perfectly mad from boredom, isn't that so, Aunt?''

"What's that, my love?'' Lady Honoria looked up from her corner, where she was chatting quietly with Mr. Massingham.

"I am calling on you to support my word, Aunt. I have been explaining to Sir Hugh that I would expire of boredom if I had to reside in the country for more than a month or two at a time.''

While she was speaking, Vicky pinned her relative with an imperative stare that caused that lady to blink once or twice before she answered smoothly, "Er, yes, so you say, my dear.''

After this corroboration Lady Honoria's glance reverted immediately to Mr. Massingham, but she suspected she had lost something of the gentleman's attention. He listened courteously to the anecdote she was relating and produced the appropriate reactions, but his hooded gaze seemed to be drawn to her niece's profile as steel to a magnet, and she sensed that he was straining to hear the latter's conversation.

This proved less personal than what had gone before, since Vicky had determinedly brought Drucilla and Lord Ellerby into a discussion of musical tastes. Sir Hugh had become noticeably less voluble and even had to beg pardon once for inattention. He watched his hostess in some bewilderment while the conversation degenerated into a three-sided debate on modern composers.

Vicky's nerves were nearly at screaming pitch when their callers finally took their leave, but she felt she had acquitted herself well under trying circumstances. She hoped she had given Sir Hugh something to think about this afternoon. In this case, necessity had resulted in inspiration, for it had suddenly become crystal clear to her that that solid country gentleman would never seek a bride from amongst the town belles. His was not a passionate nature; his emotions were moderate and would be governed by rational judgment. She doubted her attraction for him would long survive the painful intelligence she had just conveyed respecting her preferred life-style and place of abode.

Even more important, she was persuaded, after her performance at tea, that no one could possibly suspect that her feelings for Mr. Massingham had undergone a startling reversal that had left her bemused and shaken.

Therefore, it was a distinctly unpleasant surprise to find her aunt awaiting her in her boudoir when she finally thought to achieve some privacy. The smile she summoned to her lips was contradicted by the wariness in her golden-brown eyes as she leaned against the door for support and regarded her relative with concealed trepidation.

"Surely you are not surprised to see me here," said Lady Honoria as Vicky made no effort to initiate a conversation. "Curiosity was ever my besetting sin. You must have expected that I would wish to know why I was called upon to attest to a monumental falsehood just now."

Relief surged through Vicky and brought her away from the door. Her secret was still safe.

"And very cleverly did you do it, ma'am"—she chuckled—"without putting your ultimate salvation at risk."

"At my age I've learned one point more than the devil," her aunt acknowledged with exaggerated modesty. "When did your sudden antipathy for country living develop?" Her glance sharpened, and Vicky hesitated fractionally before admitting:

"When it occurred to me that Sir Hugh would never want
wife who preferred to live in town."

"I might have known; in fact, I did know. You are deter
mined to die a spinster to spite me." Lady Honoria ros
from the cane-backed chair and rustled over to the door
"And who is this latest eligible reject destined for? Mis
Fairchild?"

Vicky nodded, smiling faintly at her aunt's resigne
expression. She hugged that poor lady impulsively in passing
"She loves him, Aunt, and if he were not blind and stupi
like the majority of his sex, he'd see that she would suit hin
admirably."

Lady Honoria made no comment on the tinge of impatience
almost verging on bitterness, in her niece's voice, saying
merely, "Men are not the only ones guilty of mismanaging
this love business. In my day arranging marriages was the
parents' responsibility and it was better done thusly than by
consulting the wishes of foolish youngsters who don't have
the wit to see that love has nothing to do with marriage."

"Nonsense, you know you adored Uncle Hector!"

"Exactly!" pounced her aunt with a triumphant smile.
"But if my parents had allowed me to have my way, I'd have
wed a man milliner with no expectations who wrote bad
poetry in praise of my nonexistent beauty. And I believed
every word of it, too! I thought Hector was staid and
unromantic."

Vicky could see that her aunt was away in a land of
memories. "You were one of the lucky ones, dearest," she
said softly.

Lady Honoria came swiftly back to the present. "Nothing
ventured, nothing gained."

"That's all very well in gambling or sports, but I'd prefer
better odds before venturing into matrimony. The risks are
greater."

"Chicken heart!" mocked her aunt.

"You have said it. At least too chickenhearted to accept
Sir Hugh." She leaned closer to her relative, whose hand was
now on the doorknob, and lowered her voice to a stagy

whisper. "You see, I am persuaded he is staid and un-romantic."

Lady Honoria chuckled richly and her pale blue eyes held a faint reflection of the mischief dancing in the warm golden-brown ones confronting her. "You know, I believe you are right," she whispered back before switching to her normal voice. "You are certainly going the right way about it to frighten him off. That exhibition today of high-powered charm and fascination would scare away any man of sense. I was fagged to death just witnessing it!"

She was out the door on the words, so missed the bleakness that settled over Vicky's countenance as she recalled the real reason for her feverish gaiety at tea. She wandered farther into the room, picking up a jade ornament from a small rosewood table and turning it absently in her hands. If marriage with the pleasant, even-tempered Sir Hugh was a gamble, what would one call a union with the volatile and bossy Andrew Massingham?

Her hands stilled abruptly at the horrified realisation of whither her thoughts were wending. The man was a *fortune hunter*, for heaven's sake! Nothing more needed to be said, but even if he were the soul of integrity, he disliked her actively despite a mutual attraction that she was too experienced to fail to recognise and too honest to deny. It was the fatal attraction of a snake and a mongoose. No good could come of it, and she would stamp it out from this moment forward.

She replaced the jade figurine on its table with a decided crash and headed for her bedchamber with resolution written in every line of her bearing.

15

During the next week or so Vicky discovered that framing a sensible resolution and carrying it out were two separate and unrelated activities. Only a simpleton would acknowledge a *tendre* for a fortune hunter, but each time she saw Andrew Massingham it was necessary to reaffirm her resolution to drive his image out of her heart. She had decided after careful analysis that it must be a case of infatuation, an unreasoning disorder of the senses that had never been known to be fatal. This must be counted a comfort, of course.

While it lasted, though, the pangs of infatuation resembled those of unrequited love closely enough to make a sufferer from the malady acutely miserable, she admitted with an unconscious twist of her mobile lips, as, from her excellent vantage point at the pianoforte, she covertly watched Mr. Massingham putting himself out to entertain Drucilla. She must have been self-deceived when she thought she recognised attraction on his part during their rescue of Jeb Laycock. Certainly there had been no repetition of that moment of shared intimacy and no indication on Mr. Massingham's part that he even recalled such a moment. Long lashes swept down to conceal the hurt in her eyes as her fingers moved into a soft rendition of "Jesu, Joy of Man's Desiring."

Perhaps the change in tempo caught Mr. Massingham's attention, for he flicked an impersonal glance in her direction before turning back to Drucilla with a flash of white teeth.

Pride and training kept her back straight, her expression composed, and her fingers moving knowledgeably over the keyboard. Before the accident in the field, Mr. Massingham had seemed to possess the omniscience of a mischievous genie where Vicky was concerned—a perpetual, uninvited witness to all her embarrassing moments. She had been constantly steeling herself against whatever he might say to exacerbate the momentary situation. Now he had nothing to say to her beyond polite commonplaces delivered with impeccable courtesy when the occasion demanded. His interest was reserved primarily for Drucilla, though not so noticeably as to incur a charge of incivility. There was abundant charm and good nature for everyone save his hostess, and always time for private converse with Lady Honoria.

This neglect on his part should have ensured the success of her determination to expunge him from her heart, but Vicky felt the removal of his attention keenly. After several days of denial she had stopped trying to convince herself otherwise. A period of ruthless self-evaluation resulted in the discovery that she had enjoyed her undeclared verbal warfare with Andrew Massingham. Since meeting him she had felt more intensely alive than at any period of recent memory. This admission altered nothing, of course, except to compound the difficulty of her self-imposed task. At times she had to bite her tongue and exercise the strictest control to prevent herself from issuing challenges to provoke his attention, even his hostile attention.

Appalled at her own lack of moral fibre and chafing under self-imposed restrictions, Vicky had become restless after a few days. As always, she sought relief in activity, spending ever longer hours supervising the training of the horses. This left Drucilla on her own more than was desirable, but Lord Ellerby was always most willing to accommodate his fellow guest in whatever activity might take her fancy. The steadily growing intimacy between the two was the one bright spot these days. Lord Ellerby's manners were too elegant to ever neglect his duty to his hostess, but Vicky was not deceived by his attentiveness into thinking she had any longer the lion's share of his affections. His quiet surveillance of Andrew Massingham's attempts at flirting with Drucilla and the unobtrusive measures he took to counteract these were quite intelligible to his former *fiancée*.

He had stepped in now to draw Drucilla into a discussion on riding. Vicky finished her selection and sat unmoving at the pianoforte, her gaze roving idly over the company. If Mr. Massingham wished to engage his hostess in conversation, there could not be a more propitious opportunity. After a moment or two, when he did not so much as glance her way, Vicky left her perch to sit beside her aunt, whom he was now addressing. Lady Honoria looked up with a welcoming smile and Mr. Massingham repeated his observation for Vicky's benefit, but though he politely included her in his remarks, she could not persuade herself that any of his efforts were primarily intended for her attention.

When Mr. Massingham took his leave of her aunt, he raised that lady's hand to his lips in an affectionate salute.

"Ah, that is blatant partiality," declared Vicky gaily, obeying a defiant impulse and extending her own hand.

With no perceptible pause Mr. Massingham touched the offered fingers briefly with his lips as he replied smoothly, but with a muscle twitching in his cheek, "I trust I would never be guilty of treating you differently than your aunt, Miss Seymour."

Vicky kept a smile pinned to her lips but she mentally acknowledged defeat in that encounter. Her pride rose up in rebellion. Never again would she afford him an opportunity of giving her a polite set-down, she vowed stormily.

A day or so later Vicky was trudging toward the house, having just left the stables, where she had been applying hot fomentations to the fetlock of a promising colt that had been kicked. She had wanted to stay to talk over some of the schedules with Manley, but it was nearly teatime and she did not like to neglect Drucilla two days running. She had noticed Mr. Massingham's horse in the stable on her way out and had veered through the kitchen garden to avoid the possibility of coming up with him on the way in. She was garbed in her favourite breeches and boots, with a fairly discreditable shirt, thanks to an accident in mixing a bran poultice. Her hair was hanging carelessly down her back, tied at the nape with a piece of string she had found after having had her neat coil dislodged earlier by thrusting muzzles while she worked among the playful colts.

There remained some late blooms in the rose garden, and the scent of one bush enticed Vicky to pause and fill her nostrils with the delicious odour. It would soon be over, this beautiful autumn. The air was still summer warm at midday, but the declining sun meant chilly afternoons. On impulse she broke off the pink rose and twirled it in front of her nose. Tomorrow it would be past its peak. How sad that lovely things like roses had such a brief existence.

As she stood there frowningly contemplating the blossom in her hand, a sound, soft but alien to a garden, penetrated her abstraction. Her head came up in a listening attitude and her eyes scanned the boxwood hedges to her left. If something were moving beyond them, she might catch a glimpse through the occasional gap, but a few seconds' strained attention produced no change in the green wall and no repetition of the noise. Vicky was preparing to move on, the rose pressed to her nose, when she heard it again, and this time she identified the sound as a stifled sob. Swiftly she moved toward the first break in the hedge, where she entered the ornamental shrubbery, heading instinctively for the wrought-iron seat on the far side of the fountain. Her almost silent entrance went unheeded by the huddled figure on the bench.

"Drucilla, my dear child, what is wrong?"

The young girl sprang to her feet at the first sound of her friend's voice, averting her face while she tried to wipe the tears from her cheeks with the backs of her palms.

"Nothing is wr-wrong. I . . . I was startled, that's all. I did not hear you approach."

Vicky regarded her friend's brimming eyes and trembling mouth for a second before walking forward and seating herself on the bench, smiling up at the girl, who avoided her gaze.

"How could you hear me over the sound of weeping? Come, my dear, tell me what has happened and how I may help you." She patted the seat beside her invitingly, and after a moment of indecision, Drucilla sat reluctantly. She didn't speak, but sat there gnawing her bottom lip and trying to get her ragged breathing under control while Vicky waited.

"Have you received bad news from home?" she probed when another minute went by in silence punctuated by an occasional hiccupping sob.

"No, no, nothing like th-that." Another pause. "But . . . but I think I had best go home quite soon now. That is, I am exceedingly grateful to you for inviting me to stay and all you have done for me, teaching me to ride and pl-play cards—I have never enjoyed anything half so much in my life, but now . . ." Her voice became wholly suspended by tears at this point, and Vicky wrapped a comforting arm about shaking shoulders and waited patiently. When Drucilla had mastered this fresh bout of sobbing and grown calmer again, she removed her arm and handed the girl a handkerchief.

"I b-beg your pardon for behaving like a watering pot," Drucilla said with a gallant attempt at a smile as she mopped her eyes. "You must think me a perfect ninny for crying for no . . . no reason."

There was a tiny vertical line between her brows as Vicky regarded her guest with concern. "I do not think you are crying for no reason, my dear, but I do not as yet know what has upset you so. Has anyone at the Oaks done anything to make you unhappy?"

"Oh no! Everyone is most kind. You mustn't think . . . Lady Honoria, Lord El-Ellerby . . ."

For a second Drucilla's lip trembled again, and Vicky said hastily in an attempt to coax a smile from her, "Come, we are making progress. We now know that neither Aunt Honoria nor Gregory is responsible for your tears. Did *I* do something?"

"Of . . . of course not. You weren't even here."

This telling phrase drew Vicky's brows together, and a picture of a familiar horse in her stable flashed into her mind.

"Did Andrew Massingham have anything to do with this upset?" she demanded abruptly.

Betraying colour stole into Drucilla's cheeks as she met the smouldering gaze of her hostess.

"Yes, but he didn't mean to . . . *Vicky, no!*" she screeched as the older girl jumped to her feet, her intention of confronting Mr. Massingham written plainly on her indignant face. "He . . . he only asked me to marry him," Drucilla blurted, grabbing her friend's arm.

She soon realised restraint was unnecessary and took her hand from the arm that had gone rigid beneath her touch. Vicky's lovely features were cold and lifeless as she said quietly, "Did he try to . . . force your acceptance?"

"No! Oh, I am explaining this very badly! Let us sit down again."

This time it was the younger girl who led the way to the bench. They sat and Drucilla addressed that mute, questioning face quite composedly. "Drew's conduct was everything that was correct. He is a gentleman, Vicky." This was said with a gentle dignity that evoked a faint smile from the other girl. "He said he was prepared to continue with the elopement immediately if my sentiments were the same as in London."

Golden-tipped lashes sank involuntarily, then lifted in silent query.

"I . . . I was obliged to tell him that my sentiments *had* undergone a change, that I no longer felt we were suited to each other."

Light brown eyes searched dark ones. Vicky had to clear her throat of an annoying obstruction before she could produce a sound. "Was he very disappointed? Is that why you were crying—because you had made Drew unhappy?"

"As to that, it's my belief that he was relieved, though he tried to conceal it," replied Drucilla with a flash of something that might have been pique as she tossed her dark curls.

At that moment Vicky was engaged in that same activity of attempting to conceal relief. Her heartbeat, which had halted for an instant, resumed its normal pace, and some of the tension with which she had been holding herself drained out of her. She pushed her reactions to the background. Time enough later to examine her own feelings.

"Then what were you crying for, Drucilla?" she asked, greatly puzzled.

Vicky almost regretted the question as tears once more crowded into the brunette's eyes, but Drucilla blinked them away.

"I . . . must be crying because I'll never be married now that I've refused Drew."

"Now, *that* is a farradiddle if ever I heard one!" declared her friend merrily. "I'd venture to predict that there is a very eligible gentleman in the immediate vicinity who would be more than willing to prevent this disaster."

The teasing smile fleeting across Vicky's lips as she uttered this prediction was succeeded by an openmouthed stare of amazement as Drucilla rounded on her almost fiercely.

"How could you think I would be so disloyal after everything you have done for me? I . . . Oh!" Her fingers flew to her mouth as the sense of what she had revealed dawned on her, and she rose abruptly. "I didn't mean to imply . . . My wretched, wretched tongue! Oh, can you not see that I can't stay here any longer? I *must* go back to London!"

Drucilla was twisting her hands together in her agitation, her face, already blotchy from weeping, a picture of misery. Vicky, on her feet also, was hard pressed to preserve her countenance as she tossed aside the rose she had been crushing and possessed herself of those tense gripping fingers, squeezing them lightly.

"There, there, calm down, my dear, before you make yourself vapourish. This is a case of the dismals indeed, and all for nothing." She was guiding the younger girl back to the iron seat as she spoke soothingly, and now she pushed her gently onto it, retaining her hold on the cold little hands as she sat down beside her distraught house guest.

Giving delicacy the go-by in favour of frankness, Vicky plunged to the heart of the matter. "Please, I beg of you, rid yourself of any nonsensical notions that I have the least claim on Lord Ellerby's affections.'' She smiled directly into pansy-brown eyes that were looking half-drowned within their tangled frame of wet lashes. Drucilla sat absolutely still, not daring to breathe as she searched her friend's features with painful intensity.

"But he . . . he is in *love* with you!'' This protest was uttered in tragic accents.

"I think in your heart you know differently. Gregory and I were betrothed until I realised we were not really suited. I ended our engagement just as you have done yours.'' Vicky gave her friend a straight look and continued, choosing her words carefully, "It is my belief that Gregory was in the *habit* of thinking himself in love with me. He came here believing that, but it has become quite apparent to me that he has overcome his previous infatuation in these last weeks. I shall leave it to you to seek an explanation,'' she finished gaily, getting to her feet after bestowing a final pat on Drucilla's hands, now motionless and relaxed in her lap.

"Well, I must hurry out of these working clothes if I am not to be late for tea. You might wish to bathe your eyes before you meet Drew or Gregory.''

"Yes, of course. I must look a perfect fright!'' Drucilla bounded up, tears forgotten, and prepared to accompany Vicky to the house. "We won't be seeing Drew, though,'' she mentioned as they passed out of the shrubbery. "He decided not to stay for tea.''

"Oh?'' Vicky kept face and voice noncommittal.

"Yes, he called solely to renew his offer to me before leaving.''

"*Leaving?* Leaving for *where*?''

"Well, London, I expect. He said it was time he wound up his visit with the Lanscombs.'' Drucilla glanced at her hostess' pale, frowning face and clarified her last statement. "He is not leaving today, of course. He would not go away without taking formal leave of us here. He just mentioned that he would soon be bringing his visit to a close.''

The two girls reached the side entrance from the flagged terrace as Drucilla finished speaking. Vicky invented an appointment with the housekeeper to secure her escape. She required time to recover from this latest shock.

After a few minutes of solitude in the library she had succeeded in rationalising Drew's imminent departure as just the impetus needed to help her banish him from her thoughts. He and Sir Hugh, sometimes accompanied by Miss Fairchild, had fallen into the habit of calling at teatime most afternoons. The frequency of his visits was responsible for this false notion that she had known him very well for a long time—this and the fact that they had met under circumstances that had thrown them together in more intimate contact than might ever occur with many persons one had known conventionally from childhood. They may have skipped all the initial stages of acquaintance, but what did she really know of Andrew Massingham's mind and heart beyond her own limited observations? Pitifully little. She could say with some confidence that impatience was the keystone of his personality. Himself quick-thinking and quick to act, he did not suffer fools or plodders gracefully. He was careless of accepted conventions regulating social behaviour, rejecting formality and trading on that flashing smile to smooth his path and atone for his multiple misdeeds. He displayed an inherent tendency to tease his female acquaintances, and she strongly suspected he possessed a rather reprehensible sense of humour. She was coming around to her aunt's view that there was no malice in his character, but what did she know of a more positive nature? She had no idea of his sentiments on serious subjects. No, once he removed his disturbing presence from the area, she would soon subdue her unruly inclinations in this direction.

Having convinced herself that Mr. Massingham's leaving was a blessing in disguise, Vicky departed her sanctuary and hurried upstairs to change. The first opportunity to demonstrate her contentment with her lot came at tea. This chore was rendered much simpler by Drucilla, whose spirits were in alt after her chat with Vicky in the garden. As diligently as Vicky was trying to conceal her soreness of heart was Drucilla endeavouring to restrain her vaulting optimism, but her contagious effervescence affected the others and enlivened the daily ritual.

Vicky was unprepared therefore to undergo a session of gentle interrogation when Lady Honoria requested her niece's presence in her boudoir to give an opinion on the merits of a sage-green walking dress that represented a departure from her ladyship's custom of wearing only neutral colours. When the effect of the dress held against its owner's form had been duly admired and her qualms about its suitability dismissed, Lady Honoria motioned Vicky to a chair and seated herself on an elaborately carved chaise longue.

"You haven't been yourself for the last fortnight or so, my love," she began without preamble. "Oh, you have been quite convincing in your perpetual performance as a girl without a care in the world, but I know better. What is troubling you lately?"

Swift alarm had leaped into Vicky's eyes at her relative's first words, but she was smiling coolly by the end.

"I apologise, Aunt, if I have seemed a trifle *distraite* recently. Actually, I have been greatly enjoying having Drucilla and Gregory here but have been so busy with the horses that I have felt guilty about neglecting them at times."

Lady Honoria was shaking her head before her niece completed her glib explanation. "That's not the truth, at least not the whole truth. To me, you appear less *distraite* than dispirited. Have you had second thoughts about throwing Drucilla at Ellerby's head? If so, I fear you are too late to undo your work in that direction—he's clearly *épris* with her."

"Of course I'm not sorry! That *affaire* is proceeding just as I had hoped." There was an infinitesimal pause before Vicky added carelessly, "For a while lately I feared that she might succumb to Andrew Massingham's dubious charms, but she told me today that she had definitely refused him."

Lady Honoria inspected her niece's unrevealing features, her own expression thoughtful. "I was persuaded she would refuse him and am most relieved. She is far too young for Andrew and not at all the sort of girl to make him a good wife. She will do very well for Ellerby."

"I thought in your opinion Gregory deserved the very best—in other words, your favourite niece."

"I cannot abide sarcasm in a female," said Lady Honoria mildly. "Gregory Ellerby is a delightful young man and a very eligible *parti*, but I acknowledge that he wouldn't do for you—he's too conventional. He will cherish Drucilla and take great care of her. That will be enough for her, but it wouldn't do for you."

"Well, at least you now realise that Andrew Massingham wouldn't make Drucilla a good husband."

"I never thought he would. Andrew is like his father. He will demand more from his wife than a pretty widget like Drucilla is capable of giving. He was in honour bound to repeat his offer, of course, and I don't mind telling you that I was on tenterhooks lest she might accept him, thinking Ellerby irrevocably pledged to you. It cost me something to remain on the sidelines, but I promised myself that I wouldn't meddle."

"You sound as if all your concern were for Andrew Massingham, who is no better than a fortune hunter when all is said," accused Vicky.

"Are you still harping on that theme?" asked Lady Honoria disgustedly. "I would have credited you with greater perception. Andrew came home from years of fighting abroad in dismal conditions to find his mother dead and his estate leased. His great-uncle greeted him with the news that he would be required to marry a girl he had disliked all his life if he wished to retain the allowance he had grown used to as the heir. What would you expect him to do—submit meekly to this blatant attempt to dictate his life? He did what nine out of ten young men would have done in such circumstances—he rebelled. He tried to forget that his life no longer had a clear purpose by indulging in gambling and sporting activities with a set of similarly circumstanced young men. He dallied with the West End comets, overspent, and found himself under the hatches in short order. Since this isn't his essential nature, he welcomed the appearance of Drucilla Hedgeley in his life. She is devastatingly pretty, good-natured, respectable, and exceedingly well-dowered. Given the circumstances, it was inevitable that he should have convinced himself that he had found the right girl. He is most fortunate that she has allowed him to escape the snare he built for himself."

Silence followed this impassioned speech. Vicky had become very thoughtful, and Lady Honoria's silence was the expectant kind. At last Vicky remarked evenly, "Drucilla told me that Drew plans to leave for London almost immediately."

"I was afraid of this." Tears stood in the old woman's eyes, but she blinked them resolutely away.

Vicky looked at her in wonder. "You have grown amazingly fond of him in such a short time."

"Andrew is the son I never had, just as you are the daughter I always wished for."

"I am surprised that you haven't tried your hand at matchmaking between us." The words were out before Vicky could prevent them.

Lady Honoria snorted. "I trust I know when to hold my fire. You and Andrew both want to dominate. You two would lead a cat-and-dog existence."

"No doubt you are correct, ma'am." Vicky's voice had flattened and she rose from her chair, making a production of shaking out her skirts. She was unaware therefore of the intensity of her relative's regard as she added brightly, "In any event, he will be leaving the area shortly."

"Yes, there is very little time left."

"Time? Time for *what*?"

"Don't bristle at me, my girl, and don't pretend ignorance, either. If there is any truth in you, you will admit that your low spirits stem from the discovery that you are head over heels in love with Andrew Massingham and you don't know what to do about it."

Vicky's gaze had dropped before the challenge in Lady Honoria's, and she dropped back onto her chair, unable to trust her limbs to assist in a dignified exit. Never one to surrender abjectly, however, she countered pugnaciously, "A moment ago you said we should lead a cat-and-dog existence."

"So you should, until you both want the other's happiness more than supremacy."

Too agitated in spirit to remain still in body, Vicky jumped up again. "Why are we talking about a possible marriage when nothing could be further from Drew's mind? He isn't interested in me at all—in fact, he dislikes me!"

"Nonsense, he's as besotted as you are."

The calm certainty with which Lady Honoria produced this bombshell caused large golden-brown eyes to widen as Vicky stared at her aunt. not quite daring to admit hope into her heart.

Lady Honoria rose and eliminated the distance between herself and the tense and troubled girl she had loved for so many years. She put a hand under Vicky's chin and said softly, "Andrew loves you, Vicky, but he will not ask you to marry him. He is well aware that you consider him a fortune hunter. Neither honour nor pride will permit him to approach you while his uncle lives."

Vicky's lips were trembling and her eyes were shimmering with unshed tears as she whispered despairingly, "What can I do, then?"

"Do? Why, go out and get him, of course!"

16

Lady Honoria's advice, though definite in concept, was short on implementation, Vicky discovered as she pondered her aunt's words over the next day or two. Very little time sufficed to prove it utterly impossible of accomplishment. Assuming—and it was an assumption unsupported by evidence other than her aunt's intuition—that Andrew did love her and would wish to marry her under other circumstances, the knowledge did nothing to alter the case. He would not offer for her, she could not propose marriage to him, and he would soon take himself out of her life. Even if she were to remove to London, there would be little likelihood of meeting him socially. Unless she could compromise him, the case was hopeless.

To her everlasting shame, Vicky did devote some time to intensive consideration of such a solution. It was not the presence of principles that would mitigate against it, but the lack of ingenuity that rendered the idea untenable. How could one compromise a man who took great care never to be left alone with one? It was a prodigious struggle just to support her spirits while anticipating the inevitable announcement that would end her all-too-brief association with the only man in eight years who had succeeded in arousing a response in her heart and her senses.

The blow fell two days after Drucilla's revelations in the garden. The entire contingent from Meadowlands had come calling, including Lady Lanscomb, whose manner toward Vicky had grown noticeably more cordial as her son's interest waned. Mr. Massingham made the announcement of his imminent departure as they all sat around the tea table in the blue saloon, a smallish room that opened onto the cutting garden.

Vicky had steeled herself against this news. She joined the others in expressing conventional regret at being deprived of his entertaining company. Her spirit winced and hope withered behind a disciplined composure that might have been mistaken for indifference. Her glance could not meet that of Mr. Massingham for more than a passing second, but that was no problem, for he was looking everywhere but at her, just as he had been doing for over a fortnight now. She was unable to rouse herself from a state of frozen despair to contribute anything to forward her cause at this last meeting.

Lady Honoria, taking in the scene from her position in the corner of the blue brocaded sofa, spoke up casually. "I hope you will consider delaying your departure until after the trip to Mendlesham to see the Norman church, Andrew. The girls have been hoping to arrange an excursion while the good weather holds, and it would be more pleasant for them to have three gentlemen in the party to make the numbers even."

Vicky took no part in the lively discussion that followed, but she flung her aunt a glance of passionate gratitude as the other two girls urged Mr. Massingham to join the party. Within five minutes a jaunt that had previously been mentioned only in passing became a firm appointment as all the young people decided this would be an appropriate ending to Mr. Massingham's visit in Leicestershire.

In her bedchamber that night Vicky alternated between elation at the reprieve and a disheartening conviction that one more meeting, or several, would have no effect on the outcome of her one-sided love affair. At one point, when optimism was on the ascendance, it appeared relatively simple to arrange that she and Andrew should find themselves alone at some time during their inspection of the church and its grounds. She recalled that there was a neighbouring manor house a short distance from the church that boasted a private cemetery in lovely grounds. Surely with so many attractions offering, she could manage some time to be private with Andrew. At this juncture her plotting ceased. She had no slightest notion of what she could say to a man who might or might not be in love with her, how to ascertain his sentiments other than by direct question, which was clearly ineligible. This conclusion sent her spirits into eclipse once more.

On the day of the outing, Vicky was in exactly the same state, her emotions seesawing from optimism to black despair. It had rained overnight and the weather had turned colder, but a weak sun was striving to burn away the cloud cover. Vicky had taken great pains with her appearance, selecting a light gabardine pelisse with smart shoulder capes and black braided buttons and trim. The rich burgundy shade flattered her bright hair and lent some needed colour to her complexion. A small neat hat of the same fabric was similarly trimmed in black braid and created a perfect frame for her smoothly swathed hairstyle. Black kid gloves and half-boots completed her attire. She looked beautiful, elegant, and serene. The beauty and elegance were authentic, but the serenity was counterfeit, for Vicky was a mass of raw nerves inside.

The gentlemen elected to ride to Mendlesham, while the ladies, in deference to Drucilla's lack of long-distance riding, decided to take the carriage, especially since Miss Fairchild had already had an hour's ride from Meadowlands before the party set forth. The village of Mendlesham was reached after a pleasant drive of just under two hours. It was warm enough to let the windows down so the ladies could exchange a few remarks from time to time with whichever of the gentlemen happened to be closest to the carriage.

All Saints Church was at one end of the picturesque village in a beautiful setting. The younger girls exclaimed at the size and antiquity of the surrounding trees and promptly vowed to make another visit in the spring, when they should be in full glory. The church itself, built of native stone, stood strong and massive, with the typical square tower. This one was topped by an octagonal conical roof with beautifully defined window openings within steep triangular pediments.

The small party alighted and strolled about outside for a time, admiring the rich decoration on the tower.

"It's marvelously ornamented, isn't it?" Vicky remarked to Sir Hugh at her side as they gazed at the rhythmic arcading on the sides of the tower above the corbel-table. The central arches framed the double windows, while the flanking ones were blank behind their graceful double columns.

"Amazing detail. I've never understood how they managed such workmanship under the conditions existing in those times. How old is it?"

"About 1140, I believe—the central structure, at least."

"The Normans made absolutely certain the vanquished Saxons and Celts knew who was in charge," said Mr. Massingham dryly in reply to Sir Hugh's musings. "Their churches are as solid and threatening as their military structures."

"It's lovely, though," Miss Fairchild put in quickly. "The ages have mellowed it perhaps, and I must confess that I have always had a partiality for those Romanesque rounded arches."

"Then you will appreciate the interior," said Vicky, leading the way to the entrance porch on the south side, while Lord Ellerby went to fetch the sexton to let them in.

All Saints wasn't especially imposing in size, having always been just a parish church, but the craftsmanship was of the finest, and perfectly preserved, thanks to the successive earls of Mendleship, who controlled the living of the parish. It was a simple three-celled church with a rounded apse and a gloriously decorated chancel arch featuring varieties of chevron and beakhead designs. Carved figures of the apostles growing one out of the other up the shafts of the arch gave great vitality to the simple interior.

"My word, look at that enormous baptismal font," said Drucilla as the sexton led them to the west end of the church.

"That is the original font and our pride and joy here at All Saints," he declared fondly, explaining that the graceful carved design of interlaced arches around the bowl was one of the loveliest of Norman motifs, but that the way the artisan had accommodated his square font to the octagonal pillared base by slicing away at the corners was what made the font unique.

"Why is it so enormous?" asked Drucilla curiously.

The sexton reminded his audience that immersion was the custom in those days.

"Poor babies," said Drucilla with a shudder, eyeing the stone receptacle without favour, despite its attractive carving.

"A mighty cold bath," Mr. Massingham agreed, grinning at her.

When the sexton finished pointing out the main features of the church, he suggested that they might like to ascend to the bell tower. The gentlemen acquiesced in this plan, but the ladies decided to wander back outdoors instead.

As the girls strolled through the lych-gate into the cemetery, Vicky uttered conventional inanities while she wondered despairingly why she had ever thought it might be a simple matter to get Mr. Massingham alone. She had actually considered climbing with the men to the bell tower and pretending to sprain her ankle on the steps, but the way her luck was running lately, it would have been one of the other men who came to her rescue and carried her down. No doubt Mr. Massingham would declare that the best way to get over a sprain was to use the injured member twice as much. She kicked at a pebble pettishly and was forced to ask Miss Fairchild to repeat the question she had asked.

"You mentioned a private cemetery in the vicinity that has lovely grounds, did you not? Is it too far from here to walk?"

"Heavens, no," said Vicky, coming back to the present. "A matter of five or six minutes through the copse over there. Would you like to see it?"

"Oh, yes, do let's go there!" exclaimed Drucilla, always eager for a new experience.

Elaine was slightly doubtful. "Should we perhaps wait for the men?"

Suddenly Vicky was seized by an inspiration. That sprained-ankle ploy might serve yet if she acted quickly enough. Pretending to consider Elaine's question, she responded thoughtfully, "The men are likely to be trapped by that loquacious sexton for quite some time yet. I believe we might as well head for the manor by ourselves. I'll just let the coachman know where we are headed so he can steer them after us when they come back down.'' She turned on her heel and took a hasty step back the way they had come before crashing down onto one knee with an exclamation of pain.

"What happened, Vicky?"

"Are you hurt, Miss Seymour?"

The young girls were beside Vicky in an instant, assisting her to her feet. She leaned against Elaine and said somewhat breathlessly, "No, I'm not really hurt at all, just gave my stupid ankle a twist. It will be fine in a moment or two, but I am persuaded I ought not try to tramp through the trees quite yet. You girls go ahead without me."

Both girls protested that they wouldn't think of leaving their friend to make her own way back to the carriage with an injured foot, but Vicky was adamant. She declared herself quite content to sit on the wooden seat under the huge chestnut tree in the churchyard for a while and urged the two girls to go ahead with their plans if they did not wish to make her feel she had spoiled their outing.

It took some little argument yet, but they went at last, reluctantly, leaving Vicky weaving her toils on the seat beneath the tree. The first part of her scheme had gone according to design, but there was no guarantee that matters would continue to fall out as she wished when the men returned.

As it happened, the outcome hung in the balance briefly while Vicky held her breath and tried to look regretful. She had explained the girls' absence and her own incapacity before offering to remain where she was until everyone should return from the manor.

Sir Hugh glanced at the sky in some concern. "The weather seems to be changing rapidly—we are in for a storm, and not very many minutes hence, unless I miss my guess."

"There is an umbrella in the carriage," said the practical Vicky. "Do not worry about me. You three had best go after the girls before the rain starts. I'll go back to the carriage and wait for you there."

Sir Hugh headed for the carriage almost at a run, and Vicky bravely began to follow him at a hesitant hobble.

"Someone must stay to help Miss Seymour," said Lord Ellerby abruptly. "Stop, Vicky, you must not try to walk unaided. I'll help you back."

"No, I'll stay with her. You and Lanscomb go for the others."

Vicky's eyes, which had closed in defeat when Gregory proposed to remain with her, flew open and briefly met the dark, unsmiling glance of Mr. Massingham. She had the sense to remain silent until first Gregory and then Sir Hugh, carrying the umbrella, passed them, heading for the path the girls had followed earlier. Mr. Massingham then offered his arm and they started slowly back toward the lych-gate, with Vicky leaning lightly on this support. She hadn't dared to look at him again, and now that she had achieved her object, her brain refused to function, leaving her incapable of formulating one single sentence.

Had it depended on her conversational ingenuity, the entire trip might have been accomplished in silence, but after a long moment Mr. Massingham said evenly, "I apologise for inflicting my presence on you, but I knew Drucilla would infinitely prefer Ellerby as a rescuer."

"Do you mind very much?" Vicky's voice was low and hesitant and her expressive face was full of compassion as she turned to him.

They had stopped walking by tacit consent. Mr. Massingham stared past her and shrugged his shoulders. "I am much too old for her. Ellerby will make her a better husband."

Vicky's eyes sank. "I . . . I'm sorry," she managed awkwardly.

"Spare me the platitudes, Miss Seymour. We both know you intended to prevent my marriage to Drucilla from the beginning."

"Yes, but not if you were in *love* with her! I would never have done that!" Vicky was appalled, and Mr. Massingham grimaced and bowed exaggeratedly.

"Again I apologise, Miss Seymour. You recognised a fortune

hunter at a glance. My compliments on your perspicacity."
He flashed her a mocking smile and offered his arm again.

Vicky stared at him in mute dismay. This meeting was not
progressing along the lines she had envisioned. She must make
him understand that she no longer thought of him in those
terms! "I . . . I beg you will not believe . . . What was that?"

"Just a flash of lightning. It wasn't close." Mr. Massingham
glanced down at the white-faced girl beside him, and his own
eyes widened in surprise. "Is something wrong, Miss
Seymour?"

A deafening crash swallowed up Mr. Massingham's question,
but Vicky was not attending in any case. She had started
violently at the noise, then froze in terror, her fingers digging
into her companion's arm with a grip that astonished him by
its strength. He prised her fingers loose and took her hand.

"Come, let us hurry back to the carriage before we get
drenched. The rain is beginning already." To his surprise,
she resisted his efforts to pull her after him.

"Sit in a carriage during a thunderstorm? *Never!*"

"Well, then, we'll head for the church. The entrance porch
should be unlocked at least."

The rain now began in earnest and increased in intensity as
they ran with linked hands through the church grounds. Lightning slashed through the sky, seemingly on all sides simultaneously, and the thunder reverberated around them before
Mr. Massingham flung open the entrance door and half-pushed,
half-dragged Vicky inside.

"Whew, that storm blew up as fast as they used to in
Spain!" he exclaimed as he shut the door in the teeth of a
sudden gust of wind. "Did you get very wet?" He was
shaking the water from his hat as he spoke, and he glanced
around at his silent companion. Quick concern leaped into his
eyes at the sight of the bedraggled girl pressed against the
wall of the porch. Her once elegant hat was a sodden lump on
wet hair, and water dripped down her face, but it was the
sight of the redoubtable Miss Victoria Seymour half-crouching
with her hands clapped over her ears and her eyes squeezed
shut that gave him pause.

"Miss Seymour, you are quite safe now," he said bracingly. "Come, sit on this bench against the wall and take off your wet hat. You will feel much better." His voice trailed away as he realised that his words, if they penetrated her terror at all, were having no effect on the taut figure against the wall. So far she had not uttered a sound, but as two deafening claps of thunder in rapid succession rattled the windows, a small moan escaped her lips and she pressed closer against the wall. As he put his hands on her shoulders and eased her down onto the bench, she reacted not at all, merely turning her head against the high sides of the settle as another crash of thunder sounded.

Mr. Massingham had often seen soldiers frozen by fear in battle situations, but nothing had ever affected him like the sight of Vicky cowering in the corner of that inhospitable settle. For another moment he stood there helplessly, feeling her renewed terror at each succeeding sound of the raging storm, before exclaiming in torment, "I can't stand this!"

He flung himself down beside her and gathered the huddled figure into his arms. "It's all right, Vicky. Don't be afraid, Angel, it will be over in a few minutes." As her trembling gradually subsided and she relaxed against his chest, he continued to murmur a stream of soothing nonsense. Perhaps Vicky heard none of it—he didn't even know what he said as he rocked her gently in his arms—but he felt his voice was of some benefit to her during those awful moments at the storm's zenith. He held her gently, but every nerve was aware of just the point when her fear subsided and she snuggled closer to him in gratitude (or contentment?). For an instant, restraint weakened and his arms tightened involuntarily about her until she breathed a regretful little sigh and pulled back, sitting upright within the circle of his reluctantly loosened arms.

"I . . . I beg your pardon," she whispered shamedly. "I can imagine what you must think of me, but I have always been t-terrified of electrical storms. When I was a little girl I was used to hide under my mother's bed during a storm." She gave a pathetic little laugh. "It would seem I haven't progressed very far in all these years."

"Don't, Angel, it's all right." Unthinkingly Mr. Massingham leaned forward and pressed his lips to hers to dam the apologetic torrent.

Vicky became utterly still. The intermittent sounds of the fast-moving storm faded from her consciousness. She was aware of nothing save warm lips on her mouth. Suddenly his arms tightened like a vise and those lips began to move persuasively over hers. Excitement and joy raced through her veins and she gave herself over to the exquisite agony of being kissed until she was gasping for breath. She had just decided that breathing could be dispensed with when Drew pulled away from her with an abruptness that rocked her on the hard settle as he leaped to his feet and put all the distance the small porch afforded between them.

"My God, I never meant to do that!" he exclaimed, breathing raggedly and running a hand through his hair in a distracted gesture. "Vicky . . . Miss Seymour . . . What can I say except that I apologise most sincerely?"

Vicky had regained control of her own breathing by now. The wet hat had been dislodged during that passionate embrace and her smooth hairstyle was somewhat disarranged and damp, but her manner was totally composed, except that her eyes glowed with love as she smiled at the aghast man facing her across the dim interior. "I am persuaded that a man who has kissed a girl in such a fashion should be permitted the use of her given name," she said irrelevantly.

"That's beside the point! This shouldn't have happened! We can't . . . You and I . . . Vicky, it's impossible, and well you know it!"

"That's better." She smiled as she rose from the settle and glided over to the man watching her warily. Her expression was thoughtful as she said with assumed censure, "There is a name for men who play with the affections of unsuspecting maidens when they have no real intentions in their direction."

"And there is a name for seductresses masquerading as unsuspecting maidens," promptly countered Mr. Massingham. He spoiled the effect of this *riposte*, however, by succumbing to the invitation in her eyes as he took her in his arms and possessed himself of her willing mouth once more.

Passion flared between them again, and Vicky was shaking slightly when Drew put her away from him at last. "I have been longing to do that ever since you looked up at me with those beautiful amber eyes after Shadow threw you," he said soberly, devouring her features with hungry eyes. "I didn't know whether to beat you or kiss you then, and it suddenly dawned on me that since I was never likely to be in a position to kiss you, it would be much safer to follow the other alternative, figuratively speaking."

"So that was why you were so objectionable at every opportunity!" cried Vicky. "I thought you simply resented my trying to prevent your marriage to Drucilla."

"I had just realised what a fool I'd been, but I couldn't cry off if she still wanted to marry me. I had dug my own grave voluntarily."

"Fortune hunter!"

Vicky made the accusation smilingly, but Drew was serious. "It wasn't quite that bad, but I offered for Drucilla without having formed a sincere attachment. I deserved everything that happened to me. And I'm in no position to offer for you now. I'm in debt, my house is leased, and it will be another year before I am in any position to support a wife. It will be damnably hard to wait, but—"

"I don't want to wait a *month*, let alone a year!" protested Vicky passionately. "I thought I would never know this feeling, and I hoped that you felt the same way . . ." She turned away, blinking tears out of her eyes, and her despair was the undoing of Drew's honourable resolutions.

"People will say I'm a fortune hunter," he objected weakly.

"Or they will say I compromised you in a church. Both are equally true or false, and are of no slightest significance."

"I have no home to offer you for a year or more."

"I have a lovely home here, and a house in London. You may take your pick."

"My nature is very domineering. I'll demand instant obedience from my wife."

"You won't get it, but I will love you forever," said Vicky, moving into his arms again.

When a loud thunderclap echoed through the porch, both surfaced reluctantly from another enchanted interval.

"That's very likely the dying gasp of the storm," Mr. Massingham said reassuringly to his beloved.

"What storm?" Vicky's voice was dreamy as she concentrated on tracing the line of his eyebrows and cheekbones down to the cleft in his strong chin.

Mr. Massingham chuckled. "At all events, we seem to have discovered the cure for your fear of electrical storms, my darling."

"The storm! Oh, my goodness, the others! I had forgotten them completely!" Vicky's expression was a blend of guilt and contrition as she peered through the small window at the fast-dispersing clouds.

"Is there anyplace they could have taken shelter?"

"Well, there is a little Grecian-style temple on the grounds, but it is open on two sides," said Vicky doubtfully.

"Then that is where we shall probably discover them, if you are not afraid of wetting your shoes through."

"The way I feel at this moment, I wouldn't even notice if I were wading through a stream," confessed Vicky.

Drew was holding open the door for her. "I feel as though I could walk on water myself right now," he confided with the flashing smile that always caught at Vicky's breath. It did now, and she stared at him for a moment, mesmerised with happiness. There was a world of meaning in his glance as he held out his hand to her. Unhesitatingly she placed her hand into his, and they walked together into the storm-washed landscape.